THE DARK
HILLS DIVIDE

THE LAND OF ELYON BOOK I

THE DARK HILLS DIVIDE

PATRICK CARMAN

SCHOLASTIC INC.

NEW YORK   TORONTO   LONDON   AUCKLAND   SYDNEY
MEXICO CITY   NEW DELHI   HONG KONG   BUENOS AIRES

This book was originally published in hardcover by Orchard Books in 2005.

ISBN-13: 978-0-439-86545-6
ISBN-10: 0-439-86545-X

12 11 10 9 8 7 6 5 4 3   7 8 9 10 11 12/0

Printed in the U.S.A.   40

This edition first printing, October 2007

For Karen

ACKNOWLEDGMENTS

I would like to acknowledge the following individuals and organizations for their contributions to this work:

Jeremy Gonzalez, Jeffrey Townsend, and Squire Broel. Without them this book would still be in a box in my closet.

The fine folks at Book & Game Company in Walla Walla, Washington; Third Place Books in Seattle, Washington; and Barnes & Noble in Kennewick, Washington. Your passion for the work was the spark that got things moving.

Brad Weinman for his epic cover illustration that caught the attention of so many.

Kathy Gonzalez and Matt McKern, a couple of hardworking, talented people without whom this book would not have seen the light of day.

Peter Rubie, a cool cat and a great agent. Thank you for your tireless work in bringing this book to market.

David Levithan. If you're lucky enough to find an editor with as much heart and talent as David, you have done well.

Gene Smith for finding, reading, and championing the book.

And Craig Walker, for whom I hold the deepest respect and admiration.

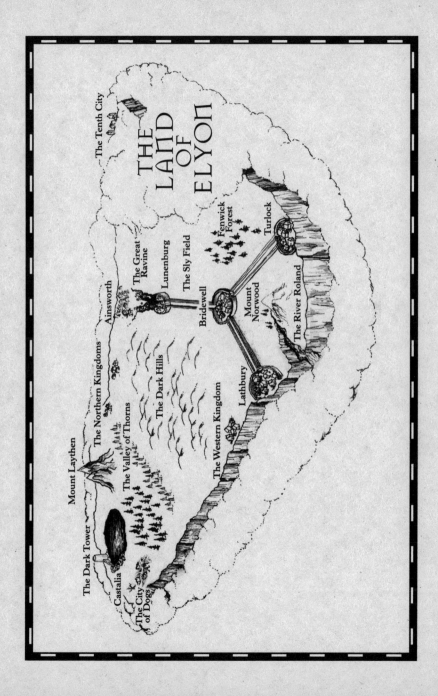

THE
LAND
OF ELYON

The Tenth City

Mount Laythen

The Dark Tower

The Northern Kingdoms

The Valley of Thorns

Castalia

The City of Dogs

Ainsworth

The Great Ravine

Lunenburg

The Sly Field

The Dark Hills

Fenwick Forest

Turlock

Bridewell

The Western Kingdom

Lathbury

Mount Norwood

The River Roland

At every locality where ocean meets land, there are the cliffs of dark, jagged rocks. If you look over the edge, there lies a mist a few feet below; so thick, you can't see the water. As far as the eye can see, nothing but white, puffy mist, as if we hang in the clouds and to step off the edge would leave us falling for days. If not for the violent sound of the waves against the rocks somewhere far below, one might suppose our lands were an island in the sky.

> *Beyond the Valley of Thorns,*
> ALEXA DALEY

Before I built a wall I'd ask to know
What I was walling in or walling out,
And to whom I was like to give offense.
Something there is that doesn't love a wall,
That wants it down.

> "Mending Wall,"
> ROBERT FROST

PART I

CHAPTER I

WARVOLD

"Stop that chattering or we'll have to go back and sit by the fire," said my companion. He removed his large, thick cape and draped it over my shoulders. I had to hold it up to keep it from dragging on the street, but it felt good, and my last few shivers quietly subsided.

The sun had set, and the lamps glowed above the streets with sharp yellow spears, one every twenty feet on both sides along our way. Illuminated by the soft light, the cobblestone paths made for a dreamy stroll. As we rounded each new corner we were greeted by another twisting row of lamps, houses, and small storefronts. Some of the doors were painted bright blue or purple, but the houses themselves, crammed tightly together, were all whitewashed stone.

We walked together, not saying a word. The town was quiet except for the occasional distant hoot of a perching night owl atop the wall as it searched for rats and other vermin. Down at the end of a darkened footpath we arrived at a locked iron gate. He produced a golden key from his pocket and drew it to a small oval container hanging from a chain around his neck — a locket I had seen many times. I watched as he opened the container and removed another key. He was our leader, the man who had ventured farther than the rest of us into the mysteries of the outside world. It made sense that he would be the keeper of a hidden key. He was the keeper of so much of our history and so many of our deepest secrets. I watched as he inserted the key into a lock on the gate and swung it open on its rusty hinges.

He disappeared into the darkness, calling me to follow quietly. I groped for his hand, which he took in his, and we walked farther, his cape now dragging behind me. He stopped, took my hand out of his, opened it full, and pulled it forward until I felt the smooth surface of rock still warm from the day's cooking. Reaching as high as I could, I felt a seam and then more rock.

"It's the wall," he said. "I thought you might enjoy touching it." Except for his breathing, I heard nothing. After a while, he continued. "I spent my youth building this wall to keep dangerous things away. I sometimes wonder now if I've kept them inside."

"Why would you say that?" I could make out his features as my eyes adjusted to the darkness. He was deep in thought, staring at the wall as he moved his delicate fingers across the seam. Lines ran all along his weathered face, and the hair from his head and beard tangled together into a fluffy, white mass.

"I tell you what, Alexa — why don't we sit a spell and I'll tell you a tale. We need to stay low or old Kotcher will get his dogs to come looking for a nibble."

He had a reputation for conjuring up frightening tales

4

about giant spiders crawling over the wall to eat children, so naturally I was concerned. "What sort of story are you going to tell?" I asked.

"Actually, it's more of a fable. I heard it a long time ago, during my travels, before all this." He swept his hand in front of him, a far-off look in his eye. "Most people don't know how much I traveled when I was young. I walked for miles and miles in every direction for months on end, all alone.

"But Renny and then Nicolas came along, and I grew more and more protective. I had terrible fears of being away from them, so I stayed closer to home. Before long I was building these walls to protect my family and everyone else."

Both of us were sitting now, and he looked me in the eye as he continued. "You remember one thing, Alexa. If you make something your life's work, make sure it's something you can feel good about when you're an old relic like me." He paused, either for effect or because he had forgotten what he was going to say next — I wasn't sure which. Then he resumed.

"When I was on one of my far-off journeys, I heard this fable. I liked it so much I memorized it." And then he told it to me, and it went like this:

> *It was six men of Indostan*
> *To learning much inclined,*
> *Who went to see the Elephant,*

Though all of them were blind,
That each by observation
Might satisfy his mind.

The First approached the Elephant,
And happening to fall
Against his broad and sturdy side,
At once began to bawl:
"God bless me! But the Elephant
Is very like a wall!"

The Second, feeling of the tusk,
Cried, "Ho! What have we here?
So very round and smooth and sharp?
To me 'tis mighty clear
This wonder of an Elephant
Is very like a spear!"

The Third approached the animal,
And happening to take
The squirming trunk within his hands,
Thus boldly up and spake:
"I see," said he, "the Elephant
Is very like a snake!"

The Fourth reached out an eager hand,
And felt about the knee.
"What most this wondrous beast is like

Is mighty plain," said he;
"'Tis clear enough the Elephant
Is very like a tree."

The Fifth who chanced to touch the ear,
Said: "Even the blindest man
Can tell what this resembles most;
Deny the fact who can,
This marvel of an Elephant
Is very like a fan!"

The Sixth no sooner had begun
About the beast to grope,
Then, seizing on the swinging tail
That fell within his scope,
"I see," said he, "the Elephant
Is very like a rope!"

And so these men of Indostan
Disputed loud and long,
Each in his own opinion
Exceeding stiff and strong,
Though each was partly in the right
And all were in the wrong.

"Not bad for an absentminded old man," he said.

"Stop being so gloomy. I think you've got a fine memory."

"A lot of secrets are held inside these walls; a lot more are roaming around outside," he said ominously. "I think the two are about to meet."

He mumbled something else about "them being right all along," but he was quieter now, muttering to himself.

We continued to sit and listened to the soft evening wind blow in. Something about his words — something about the night — crept under my skin and made me shiver even harder than before. Something felt very wrong. Something much bigger than me.

"I'm getting cold, can we go now?" I asked.

He gave me no reply, and as I glanced up at him on that clear, cold night, it was obvious at once that Warvold was dead.

CHAPTER 2
THE ROAD TO BRIDEWELL

I was twelve years old, short for my age, with skinny arms and knobby knees. My father often joked that he could run my forearm through his wedding ring (sadly, this was only a slight exaggeration). I had sandy-colored hair, which I kept in a braid nearly all the time.

A few hours before Warvold's death, I was traveling with my father from our hometown of Lathbury to Bridewell. Being a girl of twelve and lacking adventure, our annual trip there was the most anticipated time of the year for me. It had been a quiet day on the road, though hot beyond belief for so early in the summer.

In Bridewell there was a building that at one time had been a prison. A work camp, really, where the vagrants and convicts from our towns used to be kept. During the day, the prisoners would go outside the wall, doing the hard labor their sentences required.

When I say wall, I do not mean the prison wall, although that wall did exist. The wall I am speaking of is the one that surrounded all of Bridewell, which encircled not only the village and the old prison, but stretched out along each side of the roads leading to the three cities of

Lathbury, Turlock, and Lunenburg. Our kingdom was a wagon wheel made of stone. Bridewell sat at its hub, with the other three towns on the end of the three spokes. On the afternoon before Warvold's death, we were traveling on the Lathbury spoke on our way to Bridewell.

The walls loomed above us on both sides of the road, holding in the heat like a long, skinny oven. I was hot and bored.

"Father?"

"Yes, Alexa?"

"Tell me the story of when they built the walls."

"Haven't you grown tired of that old legend yet?"

Of course, I knew very well he enjoyed telling it. My father had a great love of storytelling, and this was one of his favorites. I didn't have to wait long for him to begin.

"Thomas Warvold was an orphan. On the day of his thirteenth birthday he wandered off from his hometown, all of his belongings stored in a single knapsack. For years no one knew or cared where he'd gone. A seemingly worthless child with no parents and no future to speak of; it's doubtful anyone even noticed he had departed. But he was a spirited boy, smart and full of adventure. Much later, after he became famous, there were those who speculated he was an aimless wanderer for twenty years or more, gathering treasures from far-off places in The Land of Elyon. Others suggested he lived in the wilds of the enchanted forests and mountains beyond these very walls. In any case, it would seem that he grew to be a forceful leader, for eventually he persuaded others to join him in a place most everyone believed was haunted, dark, and dangerous."

The sound of horse claps echoed off the towering walls as we advanced on Bridewell, and my father paused to scratch the golden stubble on his chin. He was a big man with red hair, long and twisted and tangled. In the winter he wore a beard, but the summers proved too much for him and he took solace in the cool relief of a shaven face.

"As Warvold began to thrive and prosper, more people became convinced that the area was indeed safe to live in, and so they came. The valley where Warvold first settled, which is now called Lunenburg, eventually filled up to capacity and provided no room for growth. High mountains rose on either side. On one end of the tight valley was the already established town of Ainsworth. On the other lay the uncharted dangers and scary legends of the wilderness. When yet more families moved into the town, Warvold decided it was time to expand.

"The north held giant mountains, the east a thick forest; the west was covered in what came to be known as The Dark Hills. The people of Lunenburg were afraid to venture out past the valley and into the wild.

"It was then that Thomas Warvold had a most wonderful idea."

My father stopped talking as a cart passed ours, kicking up dust with its two horses.

11

"Dear me, so sorry, Mr. Daley. I didn't realize —" the driver stammered as he went by. He was upset about carelessly overtaking the mayor of Lathbury and his daughter.

His carriage was almost past ours when my father whipped our two horses and yelled out, "Hya! Hya!" We quickly came neck and neck with the other cart, leaving about three feet between us, and three feet at either side of the wall. My father gave the rival driver a wicked look and proclaimed, "I've not lost a race on the road to Bridewell in five years!"

I was almost thrown from my seat by the thrust of the powerful horses as the race plunged into action. Our opponent, frothing with excitement at racing someone as important as my father, stayed with us for quite a long time. Dust filled the air and the furious sound of hooves and wheels churned down the road.

The walls flew alongside us, stretching into the sky for what seemed like miles. In reality, they were forty-two feet tall and made of three-foot-square stone blocks.

I thought about the wall extending all the way to Lathbury and to Turlock, which were butted up and walled in against The Lonely Sea, where fierce, mist-covered waves break against the soaring cliffs. The River Roland also ran through our land, so named for the only man known to have crossed it (a man whom no one had seen or heard from since). The river was a wide and powerful mass of fast-moving water, fed by mountains in yet-uncharted lands.

Lost in my thoughts, I had taken my attention away from the race. When my father pulled hard on the reins to slow the horses, my slight frame nearly flew forward off the cart.

"What a pleasant diversion," my father proclaimed as the challenger trotted his horses up beside us, covered from head to toe in a thick coat of dirt. "A shame about the dust."

"Quite all right, sir, quite all right. My horses are not what they used to be, but they gave it all they had," the man said. He was doing his best to shake himself off while we continued down the road.

"What brings you to Bridewell on this wretchedly hot day?" my father questioned.

"Actually, I'm off to Turlock, delivering the weekly mail from Lathbury."

"Have you a name?"

"Silas Hardy, at your service." He had finished dusting himself off and smiled back at us with bright, white teeth against a darkly tanned face.

"Well, Silas, how about you escort us the rest of the way to Bridewell? I wouldn't want to leave you behind with those unreliable animals dragging you into town. Besides, I'm just telling my daughter about the wall and how it was built. An enjoyable story you might as well sit in on."

Silas looked up at the walls on both sides and the hot sun above, beads of sweat running down his temples.

"I've heard it many times, sir, but I'm hot and bored

13

and my horses are too tired to outrun you. Let's hear it again." He wiped the sweat from his temple and rested his elbows on his knees, holding the reins loosely in his large, meaty hands.

Father resumed the story. "As I was saying before our new friend Silas joined us, Warvold had a problem. More people were immigrating to Lunenburg: pioneers, miners, merchants, and families. Many came to the valley looking for a better life, and the poor little town quickly became overcrowded.

"Then one day Warvold had an idea. A *tremendous* idea. He would build a walled road out into the unknown, and at the end of it he would build a new town. As long as the wall was in front of the people, the enchanted dangers that lurked about could be kept away." And then with a comical dark look, Father added, "Only, who would build the wall? Surely the people of Lunenburg were too afraid to stand outside, or near the edge, which is what would be required to build such a thing.

"No, Warvold needed other people to do the work. And so he met with the leaders of Ainsworth, the large city from which he had originated.

"Ainsworth had a prison that was overcrowded with the most terrible brutes and thieves in the city. In that place, if you were a convicted man, you were brought before two justices, branded with a *C* for criminal, and sent to the prison to perform hard labor."

A red-tailed hawk flew low overhead, and another sat

14

upon the top of the crusted wall to my right. This was a common sight, as hawks were always about the walls, and more appeared as we drew nearer to the city gate.

"Warvold made a deal with the leaders of Ainsworth," my father continued. "He was building a prison in Lunenburg, had been for some time, and he was willing to take three hundred of the foulest criminals Ainsworth had to offer. There was but one condition: After ten years, Warvold could return the convicts to Ainsworth, no questions asked.

"The leaders of Ainsworth thought this was a wonderful idea. Their own prison held only four hundred men, and was full to capacity. Giving the convicts to Warvold allowed them time to plan a new, larger prison. And besides, hard labor had been part of every convict's sentence.

"The deal was done, and within a year the Lunenburg prison was complete and the convicts delivered as promised. Warvold was not one to take chances, so he devised a plan of his own to make sure the convicts never escaped unnoticed. The branded C on every convict was always easy to see, making clear to everyone in Lunenburg who was a criminal and who was not.

"The rest is as I've told you a hundred times, Alexa," said my father. "Warvold put the criminals to work, and in three years they built the wall to what is now Bridewell. By that time, more people flooded into the valley. When the walled road was completed, Lunenburg popped like a cork from a bottle of sour wine. People streamed out of it to settle Bridewell, and many even helped build the two miles of wall that now surround the city. As quick as the wall around Bridewell was complete, two more walled roads were started by the convicts under Warvold's lead. Over the next several years the walled roads to Turlock and Lathbury were finished, thus completing our kingdom.

"Warvold brought the convicts back to Ainsworth as he promised. Many years ago, he returned all except a handful that had died of disease or injury." With that, my father was finished.

And we were at the gate to Bridewell.

CHAPTER 3

BRIDEWELL

Bridewell was at the center of everything in our small universe. It had three gates, just like the one we entered that afternoon — one gate for each walled road. Each gate was made of solid oak and iron, and was raised and lowered by chains with thick metal links the size of a horse's head. Towers flanked each gate so guards could observe everyone entering and leaving the encircled town.

"Raise the Lathbury gate!" yelled the guard atop the lookout to our left. "Mr. Daley has arrived."

The gate creaked ominously before us, stalled, and then burst back to life. It roared open, the chains grating against the stone wall, and the town crept into view as the sun hit the earth in front of us. I crouched down to see under the rising gate, and then I rose up along with the giant groaning door as the inside of Bridewell came into full view.

It was just as I had remembered it: full of tightly packed houses and buildings crisscrossed by narrow streets. Not a single house was constructed more than two stories high, so none was tall enough to look out over the wall. The houses and the streets were simple, well kept, and crafted with extraordinary care. The homes were a mix of stone and wood: stone for the walls, aged hardwood for the doors and windowsills, and wood shingles for the roofs. The roads and walkways were cobblestone, worn to a rustic brown but free of garbage and debris.

In the distance I saw the one building that was a full three stories, which peeked just over the west side of the barrier between the town and The Dark Hills outside. This was the old prison building, a place where I had slept, eaten my meals, and looked for secrets in the many rooms and passageways.

Once the convicts had been returned to Ainsworth, there was no longer a need for a prison in Bridewell. It had been converted, renamed Renny Lodge, and was currently home to a library, two courts, and several classrooms for art masters and apprentices of various trades. A portion of the large building was also devoted to the annual meeting we had come to attend. Fancy rooms for boarding, a large kitchen and dining area, a meeting room for official business, and a smoking room with a large fireplace (though hot during the day, it was cold at night in Bridewell, and a late fire was common even in summer months). The basement contained a musty old cellblock, hardly ever used except as a holding area for prisoners transported from town to town.

We were a simple, passive society and we generally kept to ourselves. The summers, though, were a time of trade for our craftspeople. In addition to the usual doctors, blacksmiths, storekeepers, and such, each of our towns housed facilities for bookmaking and repairing. We were known in Ainsworth as the finest and most reliable creators of ornate covers and sturdy spines; and it was said far and wide that we were a people skilled at the task of restoring the most treasured books and manuscripts.

In the heat of summer, Bridewell was deserted. Most of its inhabitants were in Lunenburg collecting damaged books for repair, taking on new projects, delivering finished volumes, and otherwise attending to the trade business of our society. Visitors from outside our kingdom would enter Lunenburg through a small, heavily guarded gate to collect finished goods. Often they brought along more books for repair and written manuscripts for setting into type and developing into finished books. With so many of our inhabitants traveling and working elsewhere, summer in Bridewell was calm: few people, an occasional quiet breeze, a place clean and tidy and ideal for exploring.

We approached the ponderous square mass of Renny Lodge and lurched to a stop. I was immediately down on the hard stone drive, glad to be free of the bumpy ride. A servant emerged and took my father's bags. I kept my own, and we walked the few steps up to the entryway. I hopped on each, counting as I went — *one, two, three* — and entered the stone building.

Renny Lodge was divided into several sections. The entryway was a large open space with a hallway leading to first-floor classrooms, courtrooms, and apprentice chambers. Red velvet drapes were pulled back from the windows, and a dust-filled streak of sunlight poured onto the wood staircase leading to the second floor. Another set of stairs, hidden in the shadows, led down to the cellblock.

"Oh, dear me, it *is* hot today. I imagine it only gets hotter as we get higher. Up we go!" said my father. He was bounding up the stairs ahead of me, two steps at a time. I scurried after him, pulling myself up by the banister, just catching his shirttail as we arrived at the top.

Father was prone to grand entrances, and he burst into the smoking room with both arms raised, clamoring for a hug from anyone who would offer one to a weary traveler.

"Well, if it isn't my favorite little lady!" came a voice, completely ignoring my father and whisking me into his arms. It was Ganesh, the mayor of Turlock, an amusing and lively man with a dry wit and a grandfatherly love for almost everyone he encountered. If Warvold was the brains of Bridewell, then Ganesh was its heart.

"It's so dry around here the trees are bribing the dogs," he said, his full black beard tickling my bare shoulder.

The smoking room was easily the most comfortable place in Renny Lodge. Lots of large windows adorned with velvet drapes — this time purple — filled the room with cheery light, and beautiful furniture was placed comfortably on ornate throw rugs. An imposing rock fireplace, surrounded by inviting couches and chairs, took up one wall. On another wall were double doors leading into the official meeting room.

I glanced over Ganesh's shoulder and saw Warvold, his weary old body crumpled in a heap on a plush red chair. He smiled at me and winked, then reached his arm out toward me. Ganesh set me back on the wood floor, looked my father up and down, and said, "James Daley! Still as full of wind as a corn-eating horse?"

Ganesh and my father talked while I walked over to Warvold and took his dry and bony hand in mine. He drew me near his weathered face, his eyes still the bright green of a young man, and he whispered in my ear, "Later, when the sun is low and things have gone quiet, meet me in the dining room and we will take a walk down the streets of Bridewell."

With the greetings complete and work to be done, it was time for me to go off to set up my room. On my way up the creaking oak stairs, my one bag in hand, I looked back at the massive smoking room — stone walls, dust dancing in the air, the echo of important men becoming reacquainted. I felt much too young to care about the politics of running our towns, and I sensed a strange sensation as my father glanced my way. His look told me I was not welcome in these discussions because it was not safe for me to know what they would speak of. Lurking in dark corners and listening would be met with unpleasant results.

For as long as I could remember, we always stayed in the same rooms, and no one else ever came with us or was a guest while we were visiting. Warvold had but one child, a son, who managed the affairs of Lunenburg in his absence. My mother did the same in Lathbury, which was why the annual trips to Bridewell were for me and my father alone. Warvold's wife had passed away only two years after the wall was completed, and he had not remarried (her name was Renny, thus the naming of the lodge). Ganesh remained restless and enjoyed the freedom of solitary life, and so always arrived alone and seemed perfectly content to do so.

Along the third-floor hallway, the smell was musty and dry, a smell I acquainted with adventure and freedom. A few steps beyond the stairwell were the doors to my favorite place in Renny Lodge: the library. There were many wonderful books in Bridewell Common, and most of them were kept at Renny Lodge, guarded by my best friend in Bridewell, an old codger named Grayson. The library was closed at this hour, so I turned in the opposite direction and walked to my room near the other end of the hall. I could hear distant voices traveling up the stairs, rising into a meaningless garble.

My room looked out over a sea of bright green ivy climbing up and over the wall. I gazed out along the edge where the rock became entwined with distant colors. I would be in Bridewell for the next thirty days with almost no supervision. While my father was busy running the kingdom, I would be busy exploring. And maybe, just maybe, this summer I would find what I had been looking for every other summer that I had come here:

A way outside the wall.

CHAPTER 4

PERVIS KOTCHER

From my room, and as far as I knew my room *only*, a person could catch a glimpse of the world outside of Bridewell. If I stood on the sill of my window, which was about three feet off the floor, I could look out from the top edge of the opening. From this vantage point I could see over the wall and into the distance. As soon as I arrived in my room I perched myself on the sill and looked out as far as I could in every direction.

I hopped down and went to my bag, unfastened the strap, and flipped open the leather cover. My father had scolded me for not packing more warm clothes, but the truth was, I needed the extra room in my bag for other things.

Once all my clothing was put away, I went to work untying the lace in the center of what appeared to be the bottom of the bag. I had sewn in two extra leather flaps, which met in the middle and were tightly tied together. This created the illusion of a bottom and covered the lower third of the space in my bag. Now I flopped the covers back, uncovering a curious collection of objects.

Hard candy from home, a pouch of coins, and a book; a wallet with small metal tools purchased from a traveling merchant in Lathbury; a compass, stationery with pen

24

and ink, my letter seal, candles and wood matches, an old watch. I rifled through my collection and found the item I was searching for: a small, ornate spyglass, an item that I had borrowed without asking from one of the drawers in my mother's bedroom.

I slid the cylindrical overlapping sections open and ran my hand over the smooth, decorated surface. Paisley patterns of orange and purple flowed watery along its face, with smart brass rings at the end of each section. I clawed my way back onto the sill and peered through the spyglass. I could see rolling hills in the distance, mostly treeless and covered with thick brush in different shades of green.

To the right, just in view, was the Turlock gate and its twin guard towers. This was where the one person in Bridewell who despised me spent a good bit of his time, a wretched little man who was convinced that everything outside the wall was evil and dangerous. For reasons I never understood, Warvold loved him, and had even made him captain of the guards. I had to concede that his tenacity for patrolling the streets and walls of Bridewell was legendary, but his suspicious demeanor weighed heavily against him. He seemed to naturally sense my interest in the world outside, and on every visit I had made in the past, he shadowed me relentlessly. Mean, nasty, and always watching me — to my thinking, that summed up Pervis Kotcher.

My eye caught a tick of movement, and I was

distracted from my thoughts of Pervis. Outside the north-east wall, the valley floor quickly turned to rolling hills, each one growing steadily higher and higher until it disappeared in the mist. The brush was thick and gnarly, colored in greens, browns, and reds. The farther the hills, the more the brush created a tapestry of color, ever darker. In the distance, they took on a somber, uninviting appearance.

I saw the movement again, about a hundred yards from the edge of the wall in a patch of red. Could it be a large animal roaming The Dark Hills or an evil beast stirring in the dense thicket? I drew the spyglass to my eye, squinting into the lens as I panned back and forth. Except for a rustle from the prevailing wind, the brush was still. Maybe all I had seen was a bush shaken by the breeze.

I continued inspecting the area, but eventually my neck burned and my back grew sore enough that I took a break. I collapsed my spyglass and turned to jump down off the sill, and there he was, standing in front of me.

"Well, well, well. Alexa Daley."

I yelped, lost my balance, and came tumbling out of the sill. It was Pervis Kotcher.

"What am I to do with you, Alexa?" he said, a condescending grin smeared across his thin lips. I rubbed my knee with one hand and placed the spyglass in my pocket with the other. I hoped he hadn't seen me using it. I rose and looked at him, feeling even smaller than my four-and-a-half-foot frame.

Pervis was barely a foot taller than I was. He wore his black hair at shoulder length and he had deep-set dark eyes. One can become lost in the depths of certain dark eyes, especially those of the handsome or pretty. But Pervis had eyes that reminded me more of rats and other creatures of the night, and I was forever turning away when I encountered them staring back at me.

He held his finger to his mouth, tapping on his thin lips as he stared at me. He had added a wimpy mustache during my absence.

"I see you're back and as careless as ever." He paced around my room until he neared my open bag. "It's been a nice summer so far in Bridewell, hardly a reason to work if you're a man of the uniform these days — just one lazy day after another. But of course, now that you're back I'll have plenty to keep me busy, won't I?" He hovered over my bag, ready to reach inside and dig through its contents.

"I think the mustache makes you look shorter," I said, knowing I was taking a risk in a room alone with him. He jerked his hand back from my bag and pointed it at me.

"Let's get one thing clear right now," he said. "If I see you on the sill again, I'll have a chat with your father." He paused, glared at me, and placed his hand upon the black stick hanging at his side. "I'm watching you, Alexa Daley. So much as go *near* the wall and you'll find my club against your knees — do we understand each other?"

I nodded.

"Oh, and one more thing — I'll take that spyglass in your pocket," said Pervis. "I wouldn't want any crazy ideas getting into your head."

"I don't know what you're talking about."

Pervis raised his voice. "Give me the spyglass *now,* or I'll march you downstairs and make you give it to me in front of your father, Ganesh, and Warvold."

If my father found out I'd been spying outside the wall, let alone with a telescope I'd stolen from my mother, he would seriously restrict my freedom for the duration of the trip. I pulled it out of my pocket, had a last good look at it, and tossed it to Pervis.

"You're a nobody, Alexa. A worm. And, just between you and me, so is your father." He started back for my bag with a surly grin on his face. He was about to put his hand in when footsteps approached my room. Pervis quickly concealed my spyglass in his jacket and ran his hands through his stringy hair.

Into the doorway strode Warvold, looking curiously at Pervis. "Kotcher, what are you doing here?" he asked, standing his ground between my room and the hallway.

"Just catching up on old times with Alexa. We haven't seen each other for some time, you know," replied Pervis.

Warvold stared at him accusingly, then moved out of the doorway.

"Back to work with you, protecting the city from evil

hordes and all that. Alexa and I have a date for which you have already made us late."

Pervis glanced my way. I could tell he was thinking about revealing the spyglass, but he didn't.

"Very well, sir. As you wish," he said. Then he bowed and slithered out the door.

Warvold escorted me out of my room, down the stairs, and into the night. The walk ended in his death, as I've explained, and it left me all alone, far away from the lodge, too scared to move.

After he died, I huddled up against the wall, searching for what little warmth remained locked away in the giant stones. My eyes fell upon the locket around Warvold's lifeless neck, and then to his closed fist clutching the locket key, which got me to thinking about things one really should not be thinking about at such a time. If ever there were a person who would know how to get outside the wall, it would have been Warvold. I didn't know what other things the key might unlock, but I had a suspicion that possessing it might get me one step closer to sitting with my back against the other side of the wall.

My desire for the gate key gave me an ounce of courage, just enough to touch the cold, bony wrist of a dead man in the dark.

Without his coat on, old Warvold's wrist was thin and bare, cold and clammy, covered with a dry dust of desert skin. Wrapping my hand around the wrist, I lifted his heavy and lifeless arm. At that moment all the shock I had been feeling left me, and I realized for the first time that my old friend Warvold was really gone. I'd never talk to him again, or hold his hand in mine, or listen to one of his frightening stories. I expected to feel dread when I touched his spiritless skin; instead I was sad and lonely. I sat in the dark, held Warvold's comforting hand, and cried bitterly.

It took me a long time to gain my composure, but finally I began to lift Warvold's hand up so I could pry the key out of his clenched fist. About halfway up I lost my grip and dropped his arm into the dirt with a thud. I carefully turned his arm over and set it in his lap, then peeled his fingers open, revealing the golden key. I drew the key up and unlatched the locket, then put the key back in Warvold's hand and closed his dead fingers around it. Inside the locket I found two more keys.

I held the locket with one hand and removed the keys. One was large and gold, the other small and silver. After thinking it over I returned the large one, the one that had opened the gate, thinking it best that something reside inside the locket to avoid suspicion when my father or Ganesh eventually checked it.

I rose to my feet, surprisingly sore from sitting in the cold for so long. After a final glance back at Warvold, I began walking in the direction of Renny Lodge. In a single walk I had lost so much . . . but I had found something as well.

CHAPTER 5

THE LIBRARY

Upon my return to Renny Lodge with the news of Warvold's death, I met Ganesh in the smoking room enjoying a pipe by the fire. He held me tight, warming both my body and my downcast spirit, and we sat quietly for several minutes with hardly a word spoken between us. When Father arrived he was immediately more practical about the matter.

"Where is the body? Are you all right, Alexa? We should think about what ought to be done next." But even Father, with his pragmatic approach to things, eventually flopped down next to me on the couch, his head in his hands.

It fell now on Ganesh and my father to get things right, to become the elder statesmen and take care of us all. As they sat in the flickering glow of the fireplace that night, the sense of responsibility they both faced weighed on them, forever sealing off a simpler past.

People began streaming back into Bridewell the next day. Within a few hours, hundreds of people had arrived, and once word spread to all the towns, a steady flow of citizens rushed in from all directions. By the morning of the funeral, three days after Warvold's death, Bridewell was bursting at the seams. The town was only a few square miles in size, and the guards had let in as many people as it would hold. The rest were lined up in caravans on the roads from Lathbury, Turlock, and Lunenburg. My father had been in one of the guard towers overlooking the Lunenburg gate, and he told me the line of carts and horses went back for miles.

It was decided that a processional would be the only way to accommodate the large crowds. Throughout the day of the funeral, the guards opened one of the gates and let a dozen carts in on one side and out on the other, then closed the gate and opened the next one a few minutes later. The circular procession lasted until darkness fell on Bridewell.

At the funeral, my father and Ganesh both spoke about Warvold and his many achievements. Listening, I was taken aback again by all that he had been: adventurer, architectural genius, devoted leader.

Pervis was as pesky as ever, poking his nose in at every turn, accusing anyone he could of wrongdoing, asking pointed questions. The crowds were also a problem, and poor little Bridewell took quite a beating during the days after Warvold's death.

Then, mercifully, things quieted down. Emotions settled and people thinned out. The town would soon be empty again. My father and Ganesh got down to the business of planning and welcomed Nicolas, Warvold's son, into their circle. Nicolas had the characteristic Warvold drive and ambition, but a generation removed; he was mellow and willing to listen and learn. It was clear that the three of them would work well together, and I thought I might see little of my father for the next few weeks as they met and discussed important issues.

It was time to refocus on the business at hand, which for me meant finding a way outside of the wall. Now more than ever, I burned to feel the freedom of the forest and the mountains, and I had a new key that I hoped would help me get there.

At three o'clock on the day after the funeral, with Bridewell reduced to a low hum of remaining visitors and residents, I crept up to the library to visit Grayson and get away from what was left of the crowds. In all the commotion since my arrival I had not once enjoyed the zigzag aisles of books or heard the intimate creaking along the wooden floors as I browsed lazily for new reading material. Opening the door to the library, I smelled the delightful familiar odor of old books, and I felt the peaceful quiet the place always emitted.

The library was a maze of high shelves piled ominously toward the ceiling with old volumes. Warvold had been a scholarly traveler, and the library was assembled from books he collected on his many trips. Later, as Warvold's trips became infrequent, he insisted that dignitaries from all of the towns in The Land of Elyon requesting a meeting bring a beloved book. The more fascinating or well-crafted a volume, the better a reception for the caller. As such, the library became widely known as the most expansive and envied in all of Elyon.

Thousands of books on all sorts of subjects lined the passageways. The labyrinth of shelves led off in several directions, some ending at stone walls, others at wood benches, still more winding around in circles or meeting up with other rows. But one trail of bookshelves led to what I considered to be the most perfect reading spot in all the world. Around one corner and then another, at the end of a long row, was a nook. In this nook was a small window that overlooked the ivy-covered Dark Hills wall. Set back in the corner was a cushy old beat-up rag of a chair and a wood box for a footstool. Tranquil, private, cozy . . . it was heaven on earth.

I often sat in the chair idly reading entire days away, alternately napping and flipping through volume after volume. Many were actually quite boring, legal works and treaties. But others were histories of the cities and towns and regions of our land. The best of the books contained made-up stories and legends, and some spoke of exotic animals found in fanciful jungles and marshland. I constantly searched for information about what might be outside the walls in the forest, the mountains, and The Dark Hills. But in all my searching I found almost nothing. The few scant references to the mysterious nature of the magic that prowled around in faraway places sounded like the tales I'd overheard people tell about our own wild area. But there was never much to go on, and never anything about matters close to home, or about what sorts of creatures might slink around outside our walls.

My napping was encouraged by Sam and Pepper, the two library cats who liked to take turns sitting on my lap in the afternoon sun, purring and begging for scratches under their necks. They wore peculiar but beautiful collars, jeweled leather all the way around, each dangling a small handcrafted medallion. The cats had belonged to the late Renny Warvold, and they had lived in the library for as long as I could remember. They were quite old — I think maybe fifteen or sixteen — and they slept most of the time.

Grayson came in five days a week and organized the shelves. He was also a master at repairing old books, and he spent most of his time in a small office in the library, where he worked on misbehaving spines and torn pages. I loved Grayson even more than I loved the old books. He was kind, gentle, and maybe the best listener I'd ever met.

I walked along the rows of books and poked my head around the corner into Grayson's office. He was hunkered down over a large manuscript that had been removed from its housing, and he was busy devising a new cover to replace the tattered remains of the old leather facing. When he saw me poke my head inside, he grinned from ear to ear and stood up to greet me with open arms. His big belly arched my back as we hugged, and I sobbed a little, still tender from all of the recent events. Eventually I managed to gain my composure and look into his deep brown eyes.

"You've gotten more reclusive since my last visit," I said, using my sleeve to dry my face. "How could you miss the largest funeral this place has ever seen?"

Grayson shuffled his feet back and forth nervously. "I know, I know, I should have attended. I hate crowds, though, *hate* 'em. I sat up here and pulled out Warvold's favorite books, shined 'em up, unfolded the dog ears, fixed a few ruffled edges." He moved back around to the other side of his desk, running his fingers through his thick, gray mustache. When he was seated he picked up a small, tattered book. "See this one? This was Warvold's all-time favorite, the one he really loved." He held it out to me, and I took it in my hands.

It was medium sized, black, leather bound, and in poor condition. The cover read *Myths and Legends in the Land of Elyon.* Grayson continued. "Warvold loved this stuff. Crazy made-up stories and fables from every corner of the land. He would wander in here after a long day of meeting with your father and Ganesh and sit a spell with that book. He'd sit right there, across from me. I would work on books, and he would read. It was nice, calm. Then he'd put the book back on the shelf and meander out the door, off to bed or to smoke a pipe by the fireplace."

36

I flipped through the worn pages: small text, some writing in the margins here and there. "It's sort of beat up," I said. "Are you neglecting your duties?"

He smiled. "No, ma'am. The old man never would let me work on that one. He seemed to like it well worn. I guess leaving that shabby old thing alone is my way of honoring him. Believe me, I'd love to make it perfect again — new cover, fix up the pages, clean it all up. But I get the feeling wherever he is, he would rather I left it tattered and torn."

"Can I borrow it for a little afternoon reading?" I said, running my fingers along its cover.

"Sure you can, but take these ones, too." He turned to his desk and picked up a stack of books. "These are on topics you were searching for last year: bears, forests, history of surrounding regions, that sort of thing. Not much, really, but I've been holding them up here for a while now, so either put them back or get to reading them."

It was so nice to be in the company of a weathered friend, someone who knew I just needed to sit in my favorite chair and fall asleep reading. Knowing Grayson was in the library with me lent a special peace to the feelings I had about this place. We talked little, but we understood the language of our movements and the need for quiet companionship. I took my books with a wink and made my way down a twisting row of towering books.

Rounding the corner to my chair, I saw a peculiar sight: Sam and Pepper sitting on the sill of the small window, and a hawk perched right there with them. When I came into view, the hawk beat its wings furiously, banging them against the stone wall before escaping into the open air. I jumped back, threw my books in all directions, and let out a loud shriek. Warvold's favorite book came apart at the stitching, and its pages scattered on the floor around me. I stacked the other books on the floorboards next to my chair while I scolded the cats. Both were already on the chair, rolled over on their sides, waiting for me to pet them.

I spent the next ten minutes picking up pages and sorting them out, trying to put the book back into one piece. It was in reasonably good shape when I was done, but it would need some repair work if it was to stay together. Warvold's one and only favorite book had been in my possession for only a few minutes, and already I'd managed to destroy it.

Exasperated, I pushed the cats aside and flopped down in the chair. They crawled up on my lap, and shortly thereafter I fell into a deep sleep.

CHAPTER 6

MORE TROUBLE WİTH MY SPYGLASS

I awoke slowly in the late afternoon heat, sweaty and sticky after what must have been an hour's nap. I felt around for the cats but they were gone, which was odd, because when I slept in the library they always stayed with me. After I rubbed the sleep out of my eyes and opened them, I saw why they had moved on.

"I was wondering when you might wake up." It was Pervis Kotcher. He was close enough that I could smell his breath, rank from a recent cup of strong coffee. He moved to the window, drew my mother's beautiful spyglass to his eye, and mockingly looked about the wall.

"What do you want?" I asked. Even in my sleepy state I was surprisingly irritated.

"I was just doing my rounds and I thought I might spy something with my new spyglass," he said. "The thing is, it isn't a very good one. I've half a mind to throw it out." He collapsed the spyglass and placed it in the pocket of his uniform, then turned toward me, an evil squint on his nauseating face.

"I saw you and Warvold when you went out by the wall. I lost sight of you from my tower, but you were out there a long time. Then I saw you slink past the gate, no big rush, just tottering back to Renny Lodge."

He had a hand on each arm of my chair, locking me into my seat, leaning his face close to mine. I was uncomfortable and scared, and I wished badly that he would go away.

"Now, Alexa," he said, a foul wave of his breath washing over my face, "what am I to think? Gone for over an hour with Warvold in a place you shouldn't be, carelessly skipping back to the lodge, and right after that we find him dead."

Then Pervis added something strange: "Has anyone contacted you from outside the wall?"

"Who's outside?"

"Don't lie to me, Alexa!" he yelled, visibly upset.

"What's all the fuss back there?" It was Grayson coming up the aisle, the floorboards creaking as he approached.

"Nothing. Nothing at all," said Pervis. "Go back to your books."

Grayson stayed right where he was, but I knew bravery was not one of his strongest characteristics.

"I said go back to your books," said Pervis, one hand on his guard stick. Grayson shuffled backward, turned, and walked away. Pervis looked back at me with a prideful sneer. He let the uncomfortable still moment hang in the air as the sound of Grayson's footsteps retreated farther and farther away. He paced back to the window and leaned forward into the sill with his hands clasped behind his back, looking for a long moment at the green and gray of the wall.

"You know, Alexa, now that Warvold is gone, I can do whatever I want. Your father and Ganesh can't control me. No one can," he said.

"How can you talk like that?" I gasped.

"I open my mouth and words come out — what could be easier?"

His thoughtless reply upset me. "My father and Ganesh are in charge now, *not* you —"

"I answer to *no one,* least of all your worthless father!" Pervis shot back, loud and unthinking. Right then, Grayson rounded the corner with Ganesh in tow.

Pervis went a deep red, stammered, and backed up against the window.

Ganesh had one of the cats in hand, scratching its head playfully. "I love these cats — don't you, Kotcher? So calm and gentle." Confrontation was not in Grayson's vocabulary, and he was well on his way back to his office by the time Ganesh set the cat down. "Off you go now. Catch some mice."

Ganesh looked squarely down at Pervis, towering over his short, wiry frame. Pervis tried to speak, but Ganesh put his hand up and motioned him to stop. "I want to make sure I have all the facts straight. I'd hate to misrepresent you, now that I understand the magnitude of your power."

Pervis turned redder, his lips thinned, and a scowl flashed across his face.

"I think what I heard was 'I answer to Ganesh and Nicolas, but most of all, I answer to Mr. Daley.' Is that correct, or did I leave something out?" said Ganesh. I couldn't help grinning, and Pervis shot me a wicked glance.

"It was either that," Ganesh continued, "or maybe it was that other thing I thought you might have said, which will drop your rank to private in charge of cleaning horse stalls and peeling potatoes. Which do you remember?"

Pervis was ready to give in, ready to concede defeat. He was a hothead, but he was also smart. He looked at me, then at Ganesh, then he reached into his pocket and pulled out the spyglass. He smiled.

"I apologize," he said. "Alexa has given me some trouble in the past and she's up to something now, that much I know. I got a little carried away. Of course you three are in charge, absolutely. I won't let it happen again, sir."

He gestured to the spyglass and went on, "Anyway, this toy belongs to Alexa. I found it lying around the smoking room." Then, pointing at me, speaking like a parent to a small child, he continued. "You really should take better care of your things, Alexa. Next time I find it I'll throw it away." And with that, he held the spyglass out to me. I was so excited to have it back I reached out to grab it. Pervis pulled it back, turned its face to the side, and slammed it into the wall with all his might, smashing all of the glass in the cylinder.

"No!" I cried.

"Now, Ganesh, you know a spyglass is strictly forbidden in Bridewell, unless of course you're a member of the guard, like me. Poor Alexa here will have to do without it, I'm afraid. Sorry, but rules are rules, and they must be followed." Pervis turned back to me. "Here you go, dear. You can have it now."

I took the broken spyglass in my hand. Ganesh looked like he was ready to throw Pervis through the window, but what could he do? I shouldn't have brought the thing to Bridewell in the first place.

Ganesh told Pervis to get out, and he was happy to do just that, but not before he made sure I got his I-told-you-not-to-mess-with-me look. I found out later that he stopped to talk with Grayson on the way out. He told him how snitches have their beds loaded with vermin at night — just the kind of veiled threat Pervis enjoyed using.

I pocketed the broken spyglass and steadied my breath. It was turning out to be a bad week indeed. Ganesh held out his hand and I took it. Warm, big, safe. He lifted me out of the chair and up into a hug, then he spoke with his wonderful, deep voice. "I'll get Kotcher off your back so you can explore Bridewell a little more freely. I know how you love to go sneaking around, and

I'm all for it as long as nobody gets hurt." I writhed loose and tumbled down into the chair, feeling much better. We both smiled.

"The problem we have with Kotcher is that he's been around a long time," Ganesh told me. "And he is very good at protecting Bridewell. His guards are always in top form, he works tirelessly, and his reports are excellent. He's just paranoid about the outside, and you seem to bring out the worst in him, which is bad indeed." He paused and looked at me with his piercing blue eyes. "To be honest, Alexa, I'm not sure how safe I'd feel if he wasn't around. Sometimes you have to take the good with the bad to get what you need. It's something your dad and I are still figuring out."

Little did I know that it was something I would soon have to figure out for myself as well.

CHAPTER 7

JOCASTAS

Following my afternoon nap I was feeling energized. I joined my father, Ganesh, and Nicolas for dinner off the smoking room in the main dining area. It was good to spend time with them, especially my father, who was looking a little worn out.

"I'd ask you to pass the bread, but you look so beat I'm not sure you could get it all the way over here," I said.

"You should join the jesters class in session downstairs. I hear they're looking for a good teacher," said my father. He did look tired, and even his comeback came off weak as he tried to bring some mental energy to the conversation.

"That's all right, Daley, you keep trying. Determination is one of your best qualities," said Ganesh.

"A distant third to my charm and good looks," added my father.

We talked and ate for over an hour, enjoying the easy quality of our evening meal. It was the most free-spirited gathering of the day, and we all looked forward to it. Nicolas was captivating, and he fit right in with all of us. He shared funny stories about Warvold and we all laughed, and he knew when to let someone else have a chance to talk after he'd been going for a while. Warvold had been late to fatherhood and Nicolas was a youthful twenty-five. He was a good-looking fellow, tall with trimmed dark hair and no beard or mustache.

"Did I tell you I promoted our new friend Silas Hardy?" asked my father.

"Who?" I replied.

"That nice deliveryman we raced on the way to Bridewell. I've made him our private courier, which means he carries letters for me whenever I want and burns all of the ones Ganesh tries to send out. Hardy and I are committed to saving poor Ganesh from embarrassing himself."

"Daley, you've got tongue enough for ten rows of teeth," said Ganesh.

"And you're so ugly your mother had to slap herself when you were born," said my father. This went on for some time, the details of which are not worthy of repeating here.

I wanted to get the conversation back over to Nicolas, so after a while I interrupted with a question. "Nicolas, can you tell me about your mother, Renny? I know almost nothing about her and I'd like to learn more."

Ganesh and my father settled down and reloaded their plates while Nicolas drank his wine and gathered his thoughts.

"Let's see . . . my mother was tall and slender and pretty, with dark hair and good teeth. I always remember her good teeth, I'm not sure why. Funny how our memories work, isn't it? Holding on to the strangest details about a person." He paused to take another sip of wine, and Ganesh kindly refilled the glass.

Nicolas gestured his thanks and went on. "She was terribly interested in precious stones and jewels. My father had quite a collection of rare gems from his travels. Some he traded for, others he won gambling. I'm told he was quite a hotshot at cards and dice, and I suspect he crisscrossed the globe taking advantage of rich, young rulers wherever he went.

"Renny began making her own bracelets and rings, just trinkets really, but she was good at it. I think most considered her a craftswoman of a high order. Later she became interested in tiny detailed etchings on sapphires and rubies called Jocastas, and the art remained her passion until she died." Nicolas pulled a necklace from beneath his shirt with a large stone attached.

He held it out so we could look at it clearly. "You can't see the real detail, because it's covered by a pattern that hides the real essence of the piece. On the surface you see an elaborate etching, but if you had a powerful magnifying glass, you'd also see that the Jocasta within is a rendering of our family seal: a crown of thorns." Nicolas showed the stone to each of us up close, and then turned it to look himself, straining to see the details below the surface.

"I was in such a rush to get here I left my glass in Lunenburg. Otherwise I would show it to you. I don't know how many she did — maybe thirty. The locket my father wore has a similar-looking pattern, only the Jocasta is two tiny hearts with an arrow through them, symbolic of the bond between my mother and father."

I found the idea of the Jocasta fascinating and wondered aloud if Nicolas knew if she had done any more that were still in existence.

"They took an awful long time to make, sometimes months for just one, so there weren't many to begin with. For all I know she made only a few instead of a few dozen. She gave them as gifts to close relatives and friends. My aunt has one, and there are a few in with the family jewels, but that's all I know of.

"In any case, without a powerful magnifying glass, you wouldn't know a Jocasta gem if it was sitting in your hand." Nicolas drank again from his wine. I recalled good wine as something Warvold enjoyed. It was clear his son was fond of it as well. "When I return home I'll bring my glass so we can look at this one, or I suppose we could send Silas off to get it, since there are only letters from Ganesh to deliver this week."

The three of them were quickly back at it again. I wondered how long it would take for my father and Ganesh to begin calling Nicolas by his last name, or if they ever would. It seemed that with them, you were a Daley, a Ganesh, a Warvold, or a Kotcher. Being called by your last name indicated you were an important adult to these men. I doubted they would ever call me anything but Alexa.

As they continued into the evening, wine flowing as freely as well-timed insults, I slinked out and went to my bedroom. I had seen my mother during the funeral, but she had stayed for only a day. My mother, much as Grayson and me, hated crowds, and this was the biggest crowd in the smallest space she or I had ever encountered. The walls had made it seem as though we were millions of ants locked in a glass jar, stepping over and crawling under one another.

I had to send her a letter — a letter I really did not look forward to writing but longed to be finished with. I dressed for bed and tidied up my room, flitting about in an effort to avoid my desk. I even reclined on my bed and started reading Warvold's book, which I had snuck out of the library, hoping I might tire out and fall asleep. But my guilt overwhelmed me. Sitting at my desk with pen in hand, I thus began:

Dear Mother,

I do hope your trip home was not too long. I suspect you encountered more dust than either of us knew could be kicked up by carts from here to Lathbury. I'm sure you endured a long day of travel, but it feels good to know you are home safe and sound.

Things have settled down here, almost back to normal. I enjoyed dinner with Father and Ganesh and Nicolas this evening. Everyone seems taken with Nicolas and I think he will do just fine. Father is tired, working too hard again — but we are getting along well, and we find our spare moments to wander off together often enough for the both of us.

I must tell you something now that I hope you will not punish me too greatly for upon my return home, though I will deserve nothing less than a sound thrashing with a willow. I wanted desperately to see farther outside the wall on my visit than I have been able to in the past, so I took your spyglass from your drawer and brought it with me. It gets worse. Pervis Kotcher saw me using it, and he took it from me. Later, he returned it, but not before smashing the glass out.

I am sorry, Mother. I promise to work day and night until I earn enough to repair this precious item that belongs to you. I know I was wrong to take it without asking. Can you forgive me?

I'm off to bed now, lots to do tomorrow. Grayson says hi.

My love,
Alexa

I folded the letter, addressed it to my mother, then dripped wax on it from my candle, and applied my seal. I would give it to Silas at breakfast.

I went back to my bed and began flipping through Warvold's old book. I felt sleepy almost immediately and placed the book under my pillow, afraid that Pervis would be lurking around my room in the middle of the night, looking through my things. Which reminded me, what did he mean when he had asked if someone had contacted me from outside the wall? It was an odd thing to say, and I rolled it over in my mind for several minutes until I drifted off to sleep.

CHAPTER 8

THE FIRST JOCASTA

The next day Bridewell became empty again with the last of the visitors streaming out of the gates toward home. As I walked around, I saw Pervis and his men raising and lowering different gates, checking identifications, searching carts, and generally controlling the flow of people out of Bridewell. I had to admit, he ran a tight ship, and his men seemed more than agreeable to follow his lead.

During my morning stroll around town, I noticed Silas waiting his turn at the Lathbury gate, and I ran to his cart to greet him. I had given him my letter at breakfast, and he had been more than happy to get on the road and deliver it personally to my mother's front gate. "Your father has a package for her as well. She will be so pleased to hear from you both," he had said. If only he knew how unhappy my mother was sure to be after reading my letter!

I arrived at the side of his cart and looked up at him. "It looks as though you have a bit of a wait getting out of town. Six carts in front of yours and the sun is already baking the leather off your boots."

"I'm a traveling man, Alexa — always have been. Being on my cart with Maiden and Jaz pulling me around is fine by me, no matter the weather," said Silas.

"Try not to get those old sawhorses into any races on the way home. They might go belly-up this time and leave you stranded," I said.

"Stop making fun of my horses!" yelled Silas. He was right; it was a careless attempt at being witty. A bad habit I had picked up from my father.

"Sorry, Silas." I moved in front of Maiden and Jaz and patted their noses softly. "And sorry to you, too. You are grand steeds, head and shoulders above all the other horses in the Bridewell barn." This put a smile on Silas's face, and he gave me a wink. I liked Silas; he was my kind of mail carrier.

The gate opened and carts lurched forward. I jumped out of the way so the horses could advance, and they stumbled forward a few steps, now five carts away from being set free on the road to Lathbury. Silas had some waiting left to do, and I decided to head back to the library before my reading spot became so hot I would sooner fry an egg on my chair than sit on it.

Upon arrival, I went to see Grayson, but he was strangely absent. His office was in its normal state: half-repaired books piled up all over, various tools strewn about, a sweater half hanging, half falling off a chair. He had been in, that much was for sure, since it was he who opened the library every morning. He must have stepped into the kitchen for something to eat.

I shrugged my shoulders and walked in the direction of my chair, stopping on the way to retrieve a volume of stories and a favorite book of poetry. I also had Warvold's book with me, which I planned to spend the better part of the morning browsing through.

Safely tucked into my chair, I had a brief moment of anxiety as I realized the possibility of another encounter with Pervis. This time Grayson was not in the library to save me. Just as I was nursing this unpleasant thought, Sam jumped up on my lap, followed a second later by Pepper. They purred and dug their heads into my chest, looking for all the scratching they could get. I kept rubbing Pepper's belly, only to have him turn and force his head under my hand.

"Since when did you cast off belly rubs?" I said out loud. He just kept on pushing his head into my chest, and then Sam started in with the same routine. I grabbed them both by the nape and lifted them up to my face. I stared them in the eye and they each gave a single *meow*. Then my gaze focused down to the jeweled collars and the medallions hanging from them.

For a moment I went cold, paralyzed, as I'd been when I'd realized Warvold was dead. *Meow, meow!* the cats screamed. I had forgotten I was still holding them both up by the backs of their necks.

I set them both down and apologized as I tried to gain my composure. The cats sat at attention and I took their collars in my hands. The medallions were each about an inch square; one was green and one red. They were adorned with beautiful alternating patterns. Since the cats had belonged to Renny, it was certainly possible that the medallions contained Jocastas. I was beside myself with anticipation about what they might reveal, and I knew exactly where I could find what I needed to unlock the mystery of the gems.

I leaped up, quickly placing the cats on the chair and pointing my finger at them. "Don't go anywhere, you two," I said. "I'll be right back." I ran down the zigzag aisles of books toward the front of the library.

When I arrived at the door to Grayson's office, I was overjoyed to find that he had yet to return from what I could only assume was a raid on the kitchen. I crept into his office and slid open the drawers to his desk. Grayson was more of a slob than I had imagined. The first two drawers were completely jammed with wads of paper, spines from old books, and various tools in ill repair. One drawer after another turned up the same collection of junk. The last drawer I looked in contained a half-eaten sandwich ripe from at least a week of neglect. It smelled worse than PKB (Pervis Kotcher Breath).

I slumped back in Grayson's chair and scanned the shelves, also loaded with old books and other junk. At the end of one shelf was a wood box with a latch. The box had been untouched for some time, and the lid was covered with dust. Upon opening it, I found a number of old tools, and the one thing I had been looking for: a printer's glass ring. It was just the thing for viewing a Jocasta. Powerful and precise, the printer's ring was used to magnify broken type and aid in the meticulous filling in of old letters on a printed page. Grayson had long since given up the practice in favor of making the books look good on the outside. "Good riddance to fixing type," he had told me several summers ago. "Nobody cares, and it's making me old."

I closed the box and was just about to place it back on the shelf when I heard the library door open. Footsteps approached as I fumbled with the box, and I almost dropped it to the floor with a bang before safely replacing it where I had found it. I pocketed the printer's glass ring just as Grayson appeared in the doorway.

He grinned, rubbing his belly. A red, sticky-looking substance crowned his gray mustache. "I tell you, Alexa, that kitchen makes the best fresh strawberry jam anywhere. Mmmm, mmmm, I could eat it on baked rolls all day long." From the looks of Grayson's belly, he had been partaking of the Renny Lodge culinary delights on a frequent basis.

"You better cut back on the kitchen raids, Grayson. Your walk is turning into a waddle," I said.

"Don't make fun of old people, it's in bad taste." We both smiled as he entered the office.

"What are you doing in here, anyway?" he continued. "If you're looking for something to eat, check that bottom right drawer. Fresh vittles from the chef."

Under normal circumstances he would have had me

fooled, but since I already knew the drawer contained a most rancid surprise, I passed on his offer and bid my farewell.

"Please be there, cats, please be there, cats," I repeated as I walked back to my chair. I turned the corner and saw them sitting at attention, waiting for my return just as I had left them, licking their paws absently.

My hands shook as I removed the tool from my pocket and positioned myself on my knees in front of the cats. Taking Sam's medallion in hand, I placed the printer's glass against its face, and squinted into the device. At first it seemed like nothing more than a jumble of dots and intricate lines. Then, I focused the glass ring by turning it on its dial with a *tic, tic, tic*. The tiny dots and lines came together to form a wave of pathways, but there was no clear beginning or end, and no indication of what their purpose was — just a scattered collection of winding trails. Could it be the streets of Bridewell, or maybe the pathways along the wall? There was a miniature sparkling mountain at the end of one dotted pathway, but that was the only clear suggestion of a place I could find. Renny really had been talented; this was an amazing piece of hidden artwork.

I raced back to Grayson's office to borrow an ink pen and some paper, returned, and meticulously duplicated the map on a full sheet. My lower back burned with pain from stooping over, and my eyes watered from the intense scrutiny of the Jocasta. I could now understand why Grayson had given up the process of fixing broken type.

Finally happy with my depiction of the etching in the Jocasta, I placed it on the sill so the ink could dry. I stood with a creak, my back screaming as I reached for the ceiling to stretch out my crumpled body. I was finished investigating Sam's medallion, so I got back down on my knees and hunched in front of Pepper. As I went to place the gem in my hand, Pepper violently screeched and lashed out with a bared claw, ripping a cruel scratch across the back of my hand. Wincing in pain, I scrambled back, lost my grip on the printer's glass, and hurled it as I jerked my hand away.

I heard it hit, and the pain in my hand was nothing compared with the crashing disappointment of hearing the lens pop against the stone wall. Even worse, I heard Grayson running down the aisles of books in my direction, hollering my name over and over in a worried tone. I had only enough time to grab the printer's glass and see that the lens was covered with a spidery crack. I struggled to my feet and pocketed the second item I had stolen in the span of only a few days that had ended up broken.

"What's going on back here?" asked Grayson as he rounded the corner. "I haven't heard either of these cats screech like that in years." Then he saw my hand. "Oh, my, that's a deep one. What did you do, pull his whiskers out?"

I didn't know what to say, so I just stood there, blood oozing down my arm. Then I realized I'd left the map I'd drawn sitting on the windowsill, and I moved between it and Grayson to block it from view. "I guess he was just in a bad mood today," I said.

"Let me take a look, make sure you're not going to bleed to death." Grayson took my hand and moved into the light at the windowsill. I stammered a little but couldn't find the right words to stop him. "Calm down," said Grayson, and then he was examining my hand in the warm light, turning it and dabbing it with his handkerchief.

"I think you'll be all right," he said. "It's actually not so bad, only *looks* terrible. Best thing for it is to leave it out in the open so it can scab over. In a few days, you will hardly notice it except for the itching."

Then he let my hand go, gave me a long, solemn look, and said, "I have a hankering for some more strawberry jam on biscuits. How about you join me for a stroll down to the kitchen?"

With a faint smile I nodded, and we began to walk toward the front of the library. At least we were away from my drawing. I just hoped nobody would find it while I was gone.

We walked the aisles of books, stopping here and there to fix up a shelf, a habit both Grayson and I had acquired from spending so much time wandering in the library.

"By the way," said Grayson, "that's a mighty nice map of the library you did. Very impressive."

"What did you say?" I asked, trying to keep calm.

"Your drawing on the windowsill back there. It must have taken you quite a while to figure out how this place winds around. I think you got close — at least it looked good from what little I saw."

My hands were trembling now.

"Are you all right, Alexa? Maybe we should pay a visit to a real doctor and make sure that hand is okay. You're shaking like a leaf."

I looked up at Grayson with a big smile. "No, I'm just so excited to try those biscuits and strawberry jam I can hardly wait." I began pulling Grayson down the row of books toward the kitchen. I had to distract him, and heading in the direction of food was definitely the best way to do it.

CHAPTER 9

ALONE IN BRIDEWELL

I wasn't ready to go searching around the library when I returned later with Grayson, so I retrieved the map and ran to my room. I stayed alone for a while and thought about what I would do next, then I went to the kitchen for dinner. When I returned to my room I sat on my windowsill, folded my arms around my knees, and gazed into the misty orange glow of the sunset. The evening breeze was a welcome change from the smoldering heat of the day. I had Warvold's silver key in one hand, my drawing of the etching in the Jocasta fluttering back and forth in the other. An hour later the orange sunset had turned to black night and I lurched out of the windowsill, crossed the room, and sat down on my bed.

I had a fitful night of sleep fraught with dreams of Pervis Kotcher's head bobbing grotesquely atop a cat's body, chasing me from room to room around the lodge. In the morning I awoke, dressed, and went to the kitchen. It was already hot, and the light breeze had completely disappeared. The sun would stoke Bridewell like a furnace all morning and bring it to a staggering boil by midday. I wondered how it might feel beneath the tall trees outside the wall on the cool forest floor.

Breakfast was buzzing more than usual. Grayson showed up for more strawberry preserves, this time on pancakes. Ganesh, my father, and Nicolas were in a debate over land use and expansion between Lunenburg and Ainsworth. Silas had returned from Lathbury earlier in the morning and was busy putting the finishing touches on a plate filled with toast, biscuits, and hotcakes, all covered with thick red jam, no doubt on advice from Grayson.

I poked Silas in the ribs from behind and greeted him. "Back so soon? I thought you would be gone at least another day."

Both he and Grayson turned in my direction. "You know those old horses of mine, they would rather ride in the dark than in the heat of the day," said Silas, and then he looked at me with a squinted eye. "If you tell them I said that, I'll glue your shoes together."

"I see you've discovered the fresh strawberry jam," I said. "Grayson is guzzling it by the gallon. I think he's a bear dressed up like a man, getting an early start on hibernation."

Grayson, a familiar red bead circling his thick mustache, raised one eyebrow at me and put an entire pancake slathered with jam into his mouth in one bite. It was disgusting.

"Any word from my mother?" I said, hoping the answer was no.

"I waited as long as I could, but she was out when I arrived. I did leave your letter and a note that I would return in a few days if she had anything for you or your father. I'm sure she will send it along."

Relieved, I drifted over to the buffet and filled a plate with food. Then I sat down next to my father. Nicolas was talking, and he was right in the middle of making a point.

". . . I tell you, if you don't pay attention to Ainsworth, they will one day rule Bridewell. We must expand Lunenburg northwest toward them before they sprawl too far. I know they seem friendly now, but I don't trust them, and neither did my father."

I received a warm good morning from Father, Ganesh, and Nicolas, and then they continued on, Father with his hand on my shoulder. It felt good to have his arm around me.

This kind of conversation was called fishing. Whenever Father and Ganesh were looking for opinions from everyday folks about issues of the day, they would float the topic out like fish bait and see which point of view caused the hook to be swallowed whole. Obviously, they had initiated Nicolas into this tactic as well, since he had thrown out the first line.

"I could not disagree more," said Ganesh, my father giving me a hidden wink. "If we build toward them they'll see it as hostile and we'll be pulled into a confrontation.

Now, I agree that we've got to expand — these last few days in Bridewell have clearly shown that. Within a few years Bridewell and the towns against the sea will be at maximum capacity, and then what will we do? We have over ten miles between us and Ainsworth, which I think is a good healthy distance. We can't expand off the cliffs from Lathbury or Turlock, so those are dead ends. Bridewell is stuck in the middle with no place to grow. I think our best option is to start building two- and three-story buildings. Grow up instead of out. We could grow to twice our size if we just abolished the single-level rule."

"That's an extremely bad idea." It was Pervis, who had quietly arrived at the dining room entryway unnoticed. He was leaning against the wall, hands crossed over his chest.

"Why aren't you out protecting us all from the bogeyman?" said my father. It gave me the creeps when he said it, but everyone else seemed to think it was funny.

"Laugh all you want, but I'm telling you, building higher is a dangerous idea. It exposes us to the outside and makes us vulnerable," said Pervis. "And once people start spending all their free time looking for strange things outside the wall, you'll have an even bigger problem. Get common folks curious, and you might as well set Bridewell on a barrel of gunpowder."

He was at the buffet now, loading up on eggs. I didn't like where he was taking the conversation.

"Take Alexa, for instance," Pervis continued. "We

give her the only room in Bridewell that has a window with a teensy view over the wall. She's only a child, and we assume a child is timid and afraid. What interest would a child have in the outside? But even sweet little Alexa here figured out that if she stands in the sill she can get a little taste of what's out there. And *then* what does she do?"

Here it came — I knew I was as good as grounded for the rest of my life.

"She brings a spyglass to Bridewell and parks herself up in that sill looking for who knows what. A *spyglass*. Those things have been banned in Bridewell for as long as I can remember. Or did you all have a change of heart and forget to tell old Pervis about it?"

I wished I'd skipped breakfast and gone straight to the library. I expected Father to recoil, to take his arm from around my tiny shoulder. He would have had every right. Instead he gripped my scrawny arm tightly in his big hand and pulled me closer. He reached over with his fork and stole some eggs off my plate, chewing them with deliberate slowness. The room was silent.

"Mr. Kotcher," said my father. "How much longer do you think Ganesh and I will be around?"

I'd seen my father like this before. His tone had changed ever so slightly, but it signified to everyone in the room that his claws were out.

"I really don't have the faintest idea, sir," said Pervis, staring him down.

Father rose and stood behind me with one hand on each of my shoulders, his firm grip unwavering.

"Take a close look at this girl. She's becoming a young lady, and in a few summers, she'll be a young woman. The day is coming soon when she will be part of the ruling council. She will have her opinions heard; she will be listened to. Unless Ganesh gets with it and has some children soon, Alexa will be running this place with Nicolas before long. She won't need me to come to her defense, and it will be her choice what rank you enjoy, or whether you remain here at all. You would do well to consider these things before opening up your mouth in a crowded room again."

My father sat back down and resumed eating from his plate. "Will there be anything else, Mr. Kotcher?" he asked.

I think Pervis and I both understood for the first time in our lives that one day I would have authority over him. He wasted no time in trying to defend himself. "But *that girl* is a troublemaker. Mark my words, Daley, she'll put us in a dangerous situation and bring us all down. I don't know how or when, but she *will* endanger us." He scanned the room for support, but everyone was either looking down at his food or glaring back at him.

"I will not bother her again," Pervis continued. "But not because I care about the absurdity of a future with her in charge. If I'm not here to run the guards, this place will be *totally* vulnerable. I've taken an oath to protect

66

Bridewell, and putting my tail between my legs to suit your ego and your spoiled child is fine by me. So long as Bridewell is safe, that's all I care about." He turned on his heels and stormed out of the room.

Grayson was halfway to the library before Pervis was even out of the dining area. The rest of the group started talking again and milling around.

"Would you all mind if Alexa and I excused ourselves?" Father said, walking with me out of the room, down the stairs, and out the door. We walked for a long time, and neither of us said a thing.

Eventually the silence took its toll on me, and I gave in with a shower of words.

"I've already written to Mother and told her I took the spyglass, but she hasn't responded. I know I shouldn't have taken it. I'm sorry, I'm so sorry. I just wanted a glimpse of what might be out there."

"Calm down, Alexa," Father said. He took my hand, and we walked to the center of town and sat on a bench.

"Warvold is gone, Alexa. I don't think anyone realizes how significant that is. Ganesh, Nicolas, and I, we're good leaders, but we're not Warvold. He built this place, and he had his own secret reasons for doing it. He knew a lot more about many things than he told us."

Father scanned the courtyard again before continuing. "We're already feeling pressure from Ainsworth to do things we don't want to do. They're testing our resolve now that Warvold is gone. And it's no secret that Pervis is getting further out of control at a time when we need his leadership." Father leaned forward with his elbows on his knees and began picking at his fingernails.

"Warvold talked about you all the time, about your obvious interest in the outside and how smart you were for your age. He saw a lot of the adventurer he once was in you, and he mentioned more than once how unfortunate it was that you were locked inside the walls he built. He understood why you liked to sneak around by yourself."

He paused and turned to look at me. "Did he tell you anything that night when he died?" It was an accusing question, and it startled me.

"No, nothing important," I said. "He acted very strange, though. He reminisced about the past and told me a silly fable about blind men, but that was all."

My father watched me carefully as I spoke, trying to see if I was telling the truth or not. He didn't ask about the key, and I didn't tell. It was too precious to give up without being asked about it directly. He sighed deeply, went back to picking his nails, and continued.

"People are worried down in Turlock, and they want me and Ganesh to make a visit. We're leaving this morning, and we'll be gone for two days. I know it's sudden, but these are troubled times and we're trying to keep things under control. I'll give Pervis a leave in Lunenburg while we're gone so you won't kill each other." He paused again and looked at me, his eyes warning me not to be a nuisance while he was gone. "I've spoken to Grayson, and he will look after you. Can I count on you to stay out of trouble, at least until I get back?"

I chose my reply carefully. "I've already had enough trouble for one visit to Bridewell."

My answer seemed to satisfy him. We stood and hugged briefly, then he started to walk away from me toward Renny Lodge. A moment later he was gone, and I stood alone at the center of town, the walls of Bridewell towering all around me.

Somehow I felt more like a prisoner than I had before.

CHAPTER 10

CABEZA DE VACA

It was nine in the morning when I left my room for the second time that day. I wore a leather pouch around my neck. In it, I placed the map, the key, and my pocketknife. My mother had brought me a sweater during the funeral, which I tied around my waist. I took nothing else with me, thinking even if I was lucky I would be gone for only a few hours.

When I arrived in the library I removed the map and began searching for a starting place. It was much more difficult than I thought it would be to decipher the locations. The map showed only the winding paths, no sign of doors, walls, or windows. From my low vantage point I could not see what the pattern looked like. It was clear only that the mountain on the map was along one of the four edges of the large room. It struck me as odd that Grayson would understand the map at first glance as he had, but then he had been in the library day in and day out for years and years, and had walked each aisle thousands of times. I visited only a few days a year, and I was thoroughly confused.

Every time I started down a twisting aisle of books that seemed to look like one on the map, it turned out to be a different path altogether. It was almost as if the map were changing as I was looking at it. I turned it every which way, started from different walls and entryways, but all my effort led me around in circles.

After an hour I wandered into Grayson's office to see if he would make a midmorning run to the kitchen with me. He was hunkered down over a beautiful green-and-yellow book, using gold-leaf paint to fill in some missing spots on the cover. My stomach rumbled, and he looked up from his work.

"I was just thinking the same thing," he said, and we meandered down the hall together, making small talk. We were mostly quiet as we sat in the kitchen drinking cold milk and eating strawberry jam on buns, and then I removed the map and set it on the table.

"See if you can guess where my favorite chair is on this map," I said, hoping for some insight that would help me find my way.

I turned the map toward Grayson, and he looked at it thoughtfully. He seemed to be having as much trouble as I was at first, then his brows went up. In his haste, he used a jammy index finger to poke where he thought my chair would be. It left a sticky red spot on an otherwise clean map, and he apologized, but I didn't mind. Grayson had just put a giant red dot by the mountain. Now that I saw it, everything shifted into place on the map. I realized where Grayson's office and the doors into the library were, along with the windows and the rolling pathways of books. It all made sense.

I could tell Grayson was likely to eat a lot more food and take his time getting back to work, so it was the perfect opportunity to duck out. "Thanks for the company, Grayson," I said. "I'll catch up with you later." As I stood to go, I added, "I'm going to be busy with something for the next few days, so if you don't see me there's nothing to worry about."

Grayson nodded and I walked out of the kitchen, which was about what I had expected. In all the years I had been coming to Bridewell, my father had never thought to investigate what sort of chaperone Grayson was. In times past when my father left for one or two days, he would always ask Grayson to take care of me, and Grayson was always happy to do it. Only Grayson never adjusted his behavior after the request. I'd see him in the library . . . or maybe I wouldn't. If I didn't cross his path for an entire day and night, Grayson thought nothing of it. After all, how far could I go?

I ran back to the library and zigzagged my way through the maze of aisles. Rounding a sharp corner, I bumped my shoulder on a bookcase and nearly sent rows of books crashing to the floor. I steadied the teetering shelf and continued on, my run toned down to a brisk walk. Before I knew it, I was standing in front of my favorite old chair. A hawk sat outside the windowsill and did not stir as I came into view. Then both cats were on the chair, watching me intently. It was weird how all three remained still and alert, following my every move.

I started by feeling along the wall and the sill, and then on the shelves near the chair, which were covered with books. I felt every nook and dimple carefully and pulled out a lot of old books I'd looked at before. I began to think that maybe a certain one might trigger a secret passage or reveal a hidden treasure. Before long, I had taken almost all the books out and placed them in teetering piles around me. This exercise produced a lot of dust but nothing of any interest, although the cats did enjoy chasing each other around and darting between stacks.

I put all the books back one at a time, and ten minutes later I flopped down in the chair, tired and frustrated. I looked over my shoulder and realized that the chair was pushed up against the only wall I had not checked, a wall that was shared with a staircase on the other side. I got up and pulled on the chair, a heavy beast that clearly had not been moved for a long time. It took all my strength to slowly budge it out into the open space.

With the chair out of the way, I could see an otherwise covered section of the wood wall, with its paneled dark brown accents. Just below the middle trim, dead center where the back of the chair had been, was a small green figure of a mountain. I ran my fingers over the image and felt a dimple at its center, though I could see no change in appearance. I took the silver key out of my pocket and held it in my shaking hand. I looked over my shoulder and saw the cats perched on the top edge of the chair watching me.

"You two are awfully curious today," I said. Looking over them I saw the hawk on the sill. "So is your feathered friend there at the window. Do you all know something I don't?" I said it half expecting an answer, but I received only a blank stare from all three, along with a wimpy *meow* from Sam.

I felt again for the dimple, put the key to it, and watched as it slid into the wall. Then I turned the key and heard a light *click*. I removed the key and placed it back in my leather pouch, quickly looking around to make sure nobody was watching. I pushed against the wall with one hand, and a panel, about two feet by two feet, slid open on creaking hinges. A soft whip of cool, earthy air escaped, running over my face like a faint whisper.

With the light pouring in from the library, I could see a ladder going down into the dark. An old oil lamp, complete with a small box of wooden matches, hung from a rusty nail on the third step of the ladder. I could see only the first six rungs going down and the first few feet of planks covering the walls. After that, the hole was swallowed by a deathly still blackness.

The cool air continued to work its way slowly out of the small doorway as if a frozen, sleeping giant was breathing steadily through the hole. It smelled like the dusty road to Bridewell just after a heavy rain had given it a good soaking. I turned to the bookshelf on my right and browsed through the items at eye level. I chose the smallest book I could find, a little red-covered volume with white lettering on the spine. *Adventures at the Border of the Tenth City* by someone with a strange name I'd never heard before. I opened the book, read the first page, and was immediately captivated by the audacious subject matter.

Cabeza de Vaca was an explorer who left his home in the Northern Kingdom during the seventh reign of Grindall.

After surviving a hurricane near Mount Laythen, he turned back and headed toward The Great Ravine, where he was trapped for a week in a cave by a relentless pack of wolves. When at last the wolves conceded, a hungry and tired Cabeza continued his journey into The Sly Field.

Cabeza lived on what he could find and traveled among the oddities of The Sly Field (of which there are many), searching for a way through the mist and into the mythical Tenth City. But each time he tried to enter the mist, it so covered everything around him he could scarcely see his own hand in front of his face. And so each time he wandered about for days in the shroud of that place, and always he came out near the same spot he'd gone in.

Eventually he gave up his quest for The Tenth City and went instead to Mount Norwood, where he wrote of his travels. This book is an account of

Cabeza de Vaca's adventures in The Great
Ravine, The Sly Field, and the mists that lie
ahead of The Tenth City.

According to chapter titles for the book, it would go on to talk about de Vaca's role in the government of the Northern Kingdoms, his later travels, and eventual death.

I closed the book and held it in my hand. "You didn't do too badly for yourself," I said. It was common for me to talk to authors this way; somehow it made them more real.

"Your travels are about to include one flight to the bottom of a creepy black pit." I held the book out over the opening and let go, sending Cabeza de Vaca freefalling into darkness.

It took a lot longer than I had hoped it would for the book to hit bottom. Not being a scientist, I lacked the ability to calculate the time, speed, and distance, but my best guess put the bottom of the hole in the neighborhood of thirty terrifying feet. It was hard to imagine what I would encounter at the bottom. Maybe there actually *was* a sleeping giant waiting for a tasty young lady to warm his belly.

I turned and looked back at the library. The hawk remained, but the cats were nowhere to be seen. I stood up and tried to scare the bird off, flashing my arms out and banging my feet on the floor. But the hawk sat silent and still, eyes fixated on my every move.

I crouched down, reached into the darkness, and took the lamp from the nail. The glass that protected the wick was jammed and I had to force it off. I wet the wick with oil from the basin, then broke two matches before successfully striking the third. My lighting problem solved, I turned back to the passageway.

The eerie dark breeze remained. It made my lamp flicker and sent faint shadows across the walls. I hung my feet over the edge and swung them out onto the ladder. Then I slithered through the hole and caught hold of the top rung with my left hand. I took the lamp in my other hand and hung it by the old rusty nail. There was only one thing left to do — seal myself in so no one would know where I'd gone. I reached back into the library and grabbed the leg of the chair, then I moved it in little spurts as I lunged back again and again on the ladder. With the chair in place, I swung the secret door shut from the inside and it clicked into position. The locking mechanism was simple to use from the inside, but I clicked it in and out several times to be sure. I took the lamp and hung it down as low as I could, rehanging it on the fifth rung. I stepped down the ladder and repeated this process until I was standing on a dirt floor, twenty-eight rungs underground.

Looking up was much like looking down had been, the light evaporating into a starless black sky after only a few feet. There were walls on three sides and a tunnel heading west under the library, in the direction of the mountains. The book I had dropped lay on the ground. Cabeza de Vaca had landed badly, and it appeared I now had two items in my possession that would require Grayson's attention. I was destroying books at an alarming pace.

One last look up, and then I started walking westward under the city. The walls were made of wood planks with earth peeking through the cracks; the floor was packed dirt. I passed old footprints, which sent my heart racing and even made me briefly turn back for home. I told myself over and over again that I was the only one in the tunnel, and eventually I began walking toward the mountains again. The tunnel did not change in height or width as I walked on, but my trek went uphill at an unexpectedly steep grade. After thirty minutes — about the time it takes to walk from one side of Bridewell to the other at a steady pace — the tunnel began to turn slightly to the right, then it straightened out and I walked at least as far again.

After a while I reached the end — a wall jutting straight up in front of me, another ladder hanging down, a familiar hollow blackness dripping on me from above. I was afraid to climb, and I imagined the sharp teeth of the giant closing on me if I went up into his gaping mouth. I was sweaty and tired, and I sat down in the dirt at the base of the ladder to rest before going up.

"Hey, Cabeza, how are you doing?" I said to the book in my hand. I wiped my brow against my shirt and looked back down the tunnel toward home. "Were there times you got scared and thought you might not make it? I bet there were. I bet you had those kinds of thoughts all the time.

"I think I'll have to leave you here now, since you really provide no use for the rest of my journey, which will probably end on the tongue of a giant at the top of this ladder. You wait here for me, and if I make it back, I promise I'll read all about you." I had to give him points for listening; he was an obedient adventurer, if not a very talkative one.

I stood up, faced the ladder, and began my climb. Twenty-eight rungs later, I bumped my head on boards at the top, and pushed with all my might to budge them out of the way. With no warning at all, the whole top flew up in the air, blinding me with an intense light that made me close my stinging eyes. Bits of dirt fell down onto my face and head. I nearly lost my grip and almost fell back into the hole. The lamp dangled precariously off the top rung and went out.

It was quiet except for noises I had heard only from a distance before — a breeze dancing through the trees, birds singing, bushes rustling all around me. I was terrified to emerge from my crouch on the ladder and look over the edge where the top had been blown off. Again, I contemplated turning back and running down the tunnel. I decided I would take a peek, and if it was scary, I would hustle down the ladder as fast as my feet could carry me.

I slowly moved up and peered over the edge. To my great surprise, the hawk was sitting on a large stone a few feet away, looking just as it had when I'd left the library.

"Well now, you are a small one, aren't you?" I turned quickly in the direction of the voice behind me. Balancing open the trapdoor was the smallest man I had ever seen. He could not have stood more than two feet tall. "They were right about that much, you're a little bugger, definitely small enough," the man said. The trapdoor wobbled back and forth with the push of a light breeze and the overcorrecting pull from the man. If it came crashing down, it would smack my head and send me falling like a rock to the dirt floor.

"I'll be needing you to come on out of there right quick," the small man continued. "I can't hold this door up much longer." He gave a nod to the hawk, and it was gone in a flash of feathers and screeching. "Darius will be pleased I've found you. With some luck, we'll be in the forest by midmorning tomorrow as he had hoped." I was out of the hole and on my feet, confused and not sure what I should do next.

The small man pushed the door down, and it slammed hard against the ground. It was covered with moss and had a long thin rope made of braided tree bark attached to the top edge.

"We can't stay out here in the open. Must be moving along. We have a ways to go, and hard climbing it is," said the little man, leaving me behind as he walked at a brisk pace away from me, into the mountains. He glanced back with a scolding look on his face. "Well, come on, Alexa!"

"Wait! Who are you? How did you know my name? Come back!" But the small man just kept on walking, and so I followed, racing to catch up.

He yelled to me, continuing on, not looking back, "My name is Yipes. I live in the mountains, and I am here to take you to your appointed destination."

We were in a closed triangle now, with the wall from Bridewell to Lathbury on one side, the wall from Bridewell to Turlock on another, and the wide Lonely Sea on the last. Mount Norwood stood prominently before me, filling much of the space between the walls and the sea.

I looked back over my shoulder and saw the walls getting smaller and smaller in the distance. I was surprised at how insignificant they looked, cowering at the foot of the mountains. Beyond the walls, The Dark Hills rolled on and on, into ominous and forbidding valleys unseen from Bridewell itself. I turned to the mountains and began walking again. The higher I went, the higher they seemed to go, ever farther and brighter in the sunlight, ever expanding to places I could never fully discover. I stopped and turned to look upon Bridewell again, and I saw it as I had never seen it before. It sat squarely between darkness and light, its roads a three-headed snake, bound at the center with a hideous head, dividing vast lands. It had a certain balance, a symmetry — as if each land were pushing against the walls, trying to bring them down, to dominate and to rule. As I began walking again, following the little man, I felt a profound sense of exhilaration and fear.

CHAPTER 11
THE GLOWING POOL

Yipes was a fast walker for such a small man, and keeping pace with him was hard work. My feet were blistering and my shoulders and cheeks were burned and tender to the touch. Sweat dripped down my nose and stung my eyes. I kept looking back as we climbed higher into the mountains, the walls diminishing into lifeless, stringy worms in the distance.

Yipes was not the talkative sort, or at least he was quiet during our trek. At first I asked him questions, but his lack of response and my exhaustion eventually wore me down, and we worked our way up the mountain in the heat of the day in relative silence. Now and then we would pass under a grouping of trees where the shade felt cool and leaves rustled high in branches beyond my view.

Watching Yipes scamper in front of me like a rabbit, it struck me that I was following a small, strange man into the wild. I might never return to my home, never see my parents or friends again, and never wander the rows of books in the Bridewell library. Even so, the reality of being outside the wall and the rush of the adventure were feelings that somehow comforted me. I felt as if I was doing what I was meant to do, and I knew no regret.

I don't know how long I was lost in my thoughts, but suddenly I nearly stumbled right over Yipes, who had stopped and turned in my direction. If not for his cry of "Whoa, young lady!" I might have put my knee right into his plump little nose. I crouched down to get a better look at him and take advantage of a rare chance to confront my guide face-to-face. He had dark eyes, a dainty mustache, and slight lips before a row of yellowy teeth. His skin was dark and leathery, toasty brown as though he'd been taking heat from the sun in large doses for quite some time. He wore a tan-colored hat over flowing brown hair, leather shorts, a simple top, and leather sandals.

"Thank you for stopping. I thought you might go on all day. You're quite the climber, aren't you?" I said.

Chin high, chest out, Yipes answered me with a comic high voice, "I'm not allowed to talk to you just now, sorry, so sorry. I wish I could. Strict orders from Darius." And then, looking all around him and leaning close to my face, he said, "Thank you for the compliment." He seemed completely harmless, casually standing in the middle of the path, a slight grin on his face.

"Can you tell me where we're going or who Darius is? We've been climbing for an awfully long time and I have no idea where you're taking me," I said.

He was back at attention now, stiff and serious. "Sorry, strictest orders. I must take you to the appointed destination as quickly as possible. Important meeting to-morrow, very important mee —" He stopped short, turned his cantaloupe-sized head to the left, and listened intently. In a flash he was through the bushes and scaling a nearby tree like a spooked squirrel. Seconds later, he was so high in the branches of the tree I lost sight of him. I looked back down the mountain and saw the thin, endless snakes of the walls far below. I imagined I could flick them with my finger and knock them all down.

When I turned back to the trail, Yipes was standing at attention, not winded in the slightest, with the same calm manner as before. "So sorry. I thought I heard something in the bushes. Can't be too careful now, can we? Important cargo. Yes, very important cargo." He led me to a stream where we drank. I began gulping and Yipes told me to drink only a little or I might become ill and weak. He gave me dried meat from his pouch and told me to sit and rest. Another sip of the icy water and a few minutes more rest, then we were off again.

"Not far now. Not far at all," said Yipes as we meandered farther up the mountain, our pace much faster than it had been. The trees grew thick, but the heat remained stifling as we approached midafternoon. The minutes turned into another hour of treading time behind my stalwart companion. My feet ached with open blisters and my legs burned with every step, but I was determined to keep going without complaint.

The stream we had rested at earlier now ran alongside of us as we walked its bank. Only a few feet wide with a bright green underbelly, it offered the refreshing sound of water flowing over rocks. I saw flashes here and there in its depths — fish moving and reflecting as they sensed our presence along the edge. I was so tired I thought I might pass out, and again I lost track of Yipes in my delirious wondering.

"Excuse me. You can stop now," said Yipes. He was sitting on a large rock a few feet behind me, lacing his leather sandal, which had come undone. He looked annoyingly refreshed, as if the massive trek we had just made was nothing more than a sightseeing stroll.

"I'm afraid this is as far as I can take you. The rest you have to do on your own," said Yipes, now lapping up water from the stream, which had shrunk to only a couple of feet across.

I hobbled over to the stream, now quiet in its slow movement, and I drank in large gulps until I thought I would burst. Then I sat at the water's edge and felt it all coming back up again. Hunching over, soupy water poured out of my mouth. I fought off a sickly shiver, rinsed my mouth in the stream, and turned to face Yipes. Exhausted, I lurched forward and fell on my face.

Why am I out here in the dark? Something warm is beside me. Warvold, his mouth gaping, rotted teeth dripping yellow goo down his chin. He's grabbing me by the shoulder, shaking me hard. Run, Alexa, run! Get away!

"Wake up, Alexa, wake up now. You must get on with it." Yipes was gently nudging my shoulder with his clam-sized hand. It was late afternoon, maybe four o'clock. I must have slept for at least an hour. I stretched, let out a painful sigh, pulled my knees to my chest, and sat breathing heavy sobs, tears rolling down my kneecaps, running a wet track to the top of my feet. My body ached all over, and my mind continued to struggle with the surroundings. I had an unfortunate dull throb in my head. It felt like a man, one even smaller than Yipes, was standing behind my eyeballs with a club, swinging with all his might to bang his way out.

Bang, bang, bang! "Sorry, Mr. Yipes, sir, she won't budge!" "Put your back into it, man! Give it all you've got!" Bang, bang, bang!

"Alexa, stop that now! Pounding your head against your knees won't make you feel any better. On that, you can trust me," Yipes insisted. "Come on then, on your feet!" He was in the stream now, splashing me with icy cold water. I jerked awake, jumping to a stand, and felt the shearing pain in my legs and feet. The open blisters were screaming back at me to sit down. *Sit down or I'll send the club through your forehead!* I fell to my knees; Yipes continued the chilling barrage of splashes until I finally screamed.

"Enough! I'm up! Just give me a second and I'll be ready to start walking again."

He stopped splashing and watched me as I wrung my hair out with my hands. Then he emerged from the stream and returned to his perch on the rock. I was back on my feet, gaining more confidence that I might have the strength to hobble my weary bones a few more steps into the mountains.

"I think I'm ready for another hour or two," I said. "You're going to have to slow down, though — I've got some remarkable blisters."

Yipes smiled and sat with his elbows on his knees, hands folded. He told me in a soft, slow voice, "Young lady, as I told you before, we've arrived. You're an impressive climber. For a child, and such a small one at that, you did very well.

"Now," he continued, "it is my duty and my privilege to point you in the direction of your destiny. My work is done for now. I've brought you this far, but the next bit of effort is all yours, I'm afraid. What I need you to do is walk up this stream. Get right in the water and walk until you reach a pool. You'll know it when you see it, trust me on that one. This is a special place. You get only one chance to go there in all your life. I cannot tell you what to do when you get there. That you must figure out on your own."

I looked up the stream with its bright green bed. It disappeared from view around a corner into the trees a hundred feet away. "But how will I know when I've arrived in the right spo —" I turned back to look at Yipes and found the rock bare.

I removed my sandals and held them in my hand, dangling them from the straps with my fingers. My feet ached more than ever on the hot sandy dirt at the edge of the stream, so I immediately staggered into the water. The stream was only a few feet wide, and it came to my knees in the middle. It felt cold on my bare legs. My feet felt the heavenly touch of the soft, furry bottom. It was like walking on a perfect feathery pillow, only better because the mossy green came up between my toes and surrounded my feet with a delicate, squishy wrapper. I let out a thankful *ahhhh* and an unexpected smile sprouted on my face. In the heat of the day I dunked my head and body the rest of the way in and exploded out of the stream refreshed and walking, enjoying the velvet whisper of every step on my swollen feet.

The stream narrowed further as I rounded the corner, but it remained a foot deep. The water moved slowly and quietly. As I walked farther and rounded yet another corner, I saw a pool surrounded by rock walls on all sides except for the direction I was coming from. This was the place.

I reached the edge of the pool, which was about ten feet across on all sides. I looked down and found that the water had turned to a murky brown around my legs. Behind me, where I had been walking, an inky darkness inhabited the stream like a plague of locusts in a summer sky. The pool itself glowed in a strange hue I had never seen before. I moved to its center in three quick strides, and for a brief moment I could see the bottom, the water now at my chest. I saw the shimmering outline of a stone bursting with lavish green color. A moment later, my disturbance in the pool brought up a muddy brown thickness around my legs, settling around my chest and leaving me almost chin-deep in dirty water.

I dove down, grabbed a handful of rocks, and brought them up into the air. They were all brown and bland, entirely void of bright color. Had I been dreaming? I dove down again and again, all over the pool until I was exhausted and angry, standing in a dark pool of icky guck.

I slapped my arms against the water with a loud pop and let out a grunt of frustration. "I don't understand! What am I supposed to do in here?" I yelled, hoping to see Yipes climb down the rock wall with an answer. But I was utterly alone. As I stood motionless in the water, the blackness turned a shade lighter. Maybe if I could stay completely still the dirt would settle down enough so that I could see the glowing emerald rock clearly again. Then, if I reached down ever so slowly, maybe I could pick out the right rock and it would be glowing green in my hand. While it may not be the end of the test, it seemed like a good place to start, and so I stood, still as a statue, in a pool of murky water, patiently waiting.

It took a lot longer than I thought it might for the water to change. It stayed just the same for an excruciatingly long time. Was it a lighter shade of brown? Could I see the outline of shapes at the bottom of the pool? I couldn't be sure, and I continued to wait and wait. It felt an awful lot like when I stood on the sill in my room for hours on end looking out the window for a sign of life in The Dark Hills. I wondered how Father and Ganesh were doing. I missed them terribly.

A thousand other random thoughts filled my head as I tried my best to stay perfectly motionless. The water was definitely getting lighter now. Unfortunately, the day was getting darker almost as fast. The water had been exhilarating at first, but I was starting to shiver as the heat of the day began to wane. Surely my feet were prunes by now, and worse, my arches were precariously close to cramping, which would cause me to move and stir up the water all over again. Night was coming, and with it a cruel coldness that would force me out of the pool.

I closed my eyes and concentrated hard. I imagined I was sitting next to Father, he with his pipe billowing sweet smoke around the room. The fire was a raging monster, stacked high with crackling wood, sending an orange shimmer across the faces in the room — Ganesh, Grayson, Silas Hardy, Nicolas, and my father, all ranting in their usual way — *that rancid tobacco is about as welcome as a skunk at a dinner party . . . you think the sun comes up just to hear you crow* — all the nonsense that made the evening flow like thick honey into the wee hours.

I opened my eyes and looked up. It was night in the sky, stars sparkling in clusters across my line of sight. And yet it was not as dark as the dark of an unlit night ought to be, the way the streets of Bridewell were after the lamps were extinguished and all was black but for the dim lamplight at the towers. The three rock walls shimmered unnaturally, like the pages of a book under flitting candlelight. I gazed along the wall and down into the water below me. The pool was aglow with radiant green light, pulsing from a single thumb-sized rock a few inches from my big toe. My feet and legs reflected the fuzzy lime flame, which worked its diminishing magic to the edges of the pool in a soft, smoldering finish.

My shivering was rabid now, goaded on by the dreaded thought of reaching down into the water, submerging my head, neck, and shoulders in the icy glow. The more I shivered, the weaker the glow became, and I could see that if I waited much longer, the dirt would rise again and put out the light from the stone entirely. I slowly descended to my neck, yelping in slow bursts as the sting of cold took my breath away. Then I gulped a big breath of air, held it against my will, and plunged all the way under.

I could see the stone clearly now, surrounded by other stones that remained brown and black and lifeless. It was just the one, the one by my big toe that shone like a tiny green sun in a liquid sky. I reached down slowly and grasped its warm surface in my hand, then rose, blasting out of the water, my body frozen in the night air.

"Well done, little lady." It was the unmistakable high-pitched voice of Yipes. "Come on out of there now. I don't want you catching a cold."

I was smiling through my chattering teeth, delighted at the sight of my little friend hanging by the stone wall a few feet above me like a monkey on a tree trunk. He climbed around the wall and down to the stream's edge a few feet away, motioning me repeatedly with his arm.

"I'm f-f-f-rozen, Y-Y-Yipes!" I hobbled as best I could out of the pool and onto the mossy edge of the stream. I was greeted with a warm blanket, which I eagerly wrapped around my shoulders as I sat on the soft, dry bank. Out of the confines of the pool, we were drenched in a welcome bath of moonlight.

"Where are your shoes?" Yipes asked as he placed a leather string around my neck with a pouch at the end.

I cursed, surprising Yipes and myself with the outburst. "I must have dropped them in the p-p-pool. I had them in my hand when I went in, but I've l-l-lost them now," I said.

"No worries, no worries. Put the gem in the pouch around your neck. I'll be right back." Before I could protest, he was gone, headfirst into the water and out of sight. Then with a *whoosh* he was out of the water at the center of the pool, holding my sandals over his head. "These yours?" he asked with a grin on his face, water dripping down his mustache.

He swam back and held my sandals out to me, but I was busy turning the stone in my hands. It maintained a radiant glow. It was smooth, about half the size of a chicken egg, and heavier than it ought to have been for its size. The color was astonishing, a tasty lime cream that made me want to smell it, expecting a tart zing in my nostrils.

"Still holding that thing?" asked Yipes. "You really should put it in the pouch for safekeeping. That's one stone you don't want to lose." And so I did, pulling the drawstring tightly shut after dropping it into its new home: a dry, coarse chamber very different from its previous watery environment. I found myself strangely concerned for its well-being.

"The thing is to keep moving now. I know your feet are hurting you, but the worst is over. Just a little bit farther and you can take a break," said Yipes, wet from head to toe but standing at attention without a sign of discomfort.

I was up without complaint and ready to go. Yipes was starting to grow on me and I was happy to follow his orders if he wouldn't leave me behind. We walked away from the stream into the silence of the night, the moon lighting our way, Renny Lodge somewhere off in the distant hollow of evening.

CHAPTER 12

DARIUS

After Yipes and I had walked for half an hour, I heard the sound of fast-moving water. We approached a stream, which was about twenty feet wide. Along its sides and through its middle, it held fat, formless boulders like freckles on the descending arm of a giant mountain creature. On the other side of the stream, the moon shone down on an odd little house, leaning precariously on stilts, half over the water and half on land. It was small and jutted three miniature stories into the night sky. Puffs of smoke rose from its chimney.

Yipes hopped a path of boulders across the stream, and I followed dutifully to the other side, half enjoying the challenge and half scared I might feel the cold sting of a misplaced footing. He was across and awaiting my arrival before I reached the third of twelve boulders.

"You're a decent hopper," he said as I jumped down from my last rock. "And you followed my path exactly. That's good, very good. A talent such as that will come in handy."

He turned and walked up the path toward the odd three-story house. I followed him, curious what the inside would look like. The nearby stream persisted with its pleasant, crisp sound. We came to the front porch and

Yipes stopped. Perched on the ledge of the porch rail was the hawk. Yipes gave it a soft scratch on the neck.

"This is my house, Alexa. I'll accommodate you as best as I can until morning. Then Darius will be here to take you to the meeting," he said as he opened the door, which stood about three feet tall and a foot and a half wide.

I had to enter on my knees with my shoulders turned sideways, but I stood only four and a half feet tall myself, so it wasn't as small as I thought it might be. I imagined Grayson trying to get in, sucking his gut tight, mercilessly wedged like a cork with his plump belly against the doorjambs; or Pervis Kotcher crouched inside the front room and turning his behind into the fireplace, banging his head against the low rafters as he whooped and howled. Once inside, I took the room to be on the order of twelve feet side to side, four feet from floor to ceiling.

It was cozy and warm, even though I had to remain seated to avoid hitting my head. There was a table at the center of the room, which was filled with bread, nuts, fruit, and fresh water. I hadn't thought of food all day, but seeing the spread in front of me made my stomach quake with hunger. "Yipes, can I —"

"No need to ask. You are my honored guest; the food is for you, of course." He licked his lips and brushed his mustache with his hand.

"I refuse to eat unless you join me in the feast," I said.

"Well, I suppose if you insist," he said, pulling a wonderful little nutcracker out of his pocket and advancing on the table. A broad smile covered his face, hiding his mouth almost entirely with the delicate fuzz from his mustache.

I reclined on my elbow, and he sat at the table on a rickety wooden chair. We ate our fill while the warm glow of the fire danced on the walls. A spiral staircase wound up to the second floor, but it was clear I would have difficulty making the climb. By the looks of it, there was a reasonable chance of altogether lodging myself in the passageway, so I decided not to ask if I could see the rest of his fine little home. Instead, I probed him with questions.

"You're sworn to secrecy, not a word out of you about this man Darius or the mysterious meeting I'm to attend?" I asked, already well into a large, juicy apple.

"Soon enough you'll know everything, soon enough indeed."

"Can you tell me why you live in the mountains and where you came from?" I asked.

He puzzled awhile, fiddling with his nutcracker, then cleaned out a walnut shell. Nibbling its contents, he offered, "I can't tell you much — not allowed, I'm afraid. I did live in Bridewell for a time, a long while ago. When my parents realized I was never going to grow to a normal size, they left me on the streets." He paused, then added,

"You can disappear easily when nobody notices you to begin with." Then *crack,* he was busy on another walnut.

"I'm small, and I can't disappear easily at all," I said.

"Well now, that's because you're special. You're small, but very special indeed."

I think we talked a while longer, but the heat of the room and my full stomach made me so tired, I really can't remember how I got on the floor or when I began sleeping. I only remember waking up, the room in the early glow of morning, crisp and cool. I was crumpled up on the floor like a baby, with a blanket over my body. A quilted pillow nestled my head. I was half asleep, half awake.

She's bigger than I thought she would be.

Oh, she's just fine. Even I can see that.

All right, all right. No need to get excited. She'll do just fine, I agree. You've done a wonderful job getting her this far.

She did it all by herself. No help needed from the likes of me. She's the one you want. She's the one.

The voices became clearer as I sat up. For a timeless moment I thought I was in my room at Renny Lodge and everything I had experienced the previous day had merely been a dream. Then I turned and saw a full-grown wolf standing next to Yipes, razor-sharp white teeth an inch long in its panting mouth.

I jolted back against the wall and felt a familiar cold fear digging into my bones. I rubbed my eyes to make sure I was awake, and found with unfortunate clarity that

I was indeed alert and fully conscious. I began to feel a strange awareness all around me. It felt as though I somehow understood what the trees were saying as the wind blew through the branches outside and what the water rolling over the rocks in the stream meant to express.

"Allow me to introduce myself," said the wolf. "I am Darius." His lips did not move to speak like a human, but I comprehended him entirely. The way he moved from side to side, his paws shuffling on the floor. The tilt of his head, the subtle noises from his throat, and a hundred other things combined to form a language I understood with perfect accuracy. What was happening to me?

"I'm sorry, did I just hear you introduce yourself?" I gasped.

"Yes, you did. And I understand you are Alexa Daley of Bridewell Common. I am ever so pleased to make your acquaintance."

"Likewise," I said in a flat, quiet tone.

Yipes said nothing and remained stiff at attention against the far wall. The wolf advanced in liquid strides and stopped a few feet in front of me.

"I know you're confused and in need of answers. I also know that you have only today and tomorrow before you must return to Bridewell. I know about your father, Grayson, Ganesh, and Pervis Kotcher. I know about your mother, about Nicolas, about Warvold, and a great many other things you don't know about.

"You have been chosen for a special purpose, Alexa. The birth of Warvold set in motion events that his death must now bring to a close. He chose you to accomplish this task, and so you must.

"Yipes has been kind enough to bring you this far. Now it is my duty to escort you to a meeting with the forest ruler and his council. I can take you as far as the tunnel, where you will continue your journey with Malcolm. He will take you the rest of the way."

Forest ruler, council, more tunnels — my head swam with facts I could not begin to comprehend. Naturally, my first instinct was to back out of any false sense of duty I might have stumbled into.

"But I'm just a child — a *small* child," I protested. "I can get my father, he'll believe me; you can talk to him about whatever you need."

"Alexa." It was Yipes whispering from across the room. I could barely hear him utter my name. He continued in a soft voice, "Your size is your strength. Without it, you could not have been chosen. Look at me — I'm half your size. And yet without me, you would still be bumping your head against a tunnel door, locked away inside Bridewell. The size of your body is just right, Alexa. The only question is whether you're big enough *inside*."

Then Darius added, "By nightfall, I promise, everything will be clear, and I'll have you on your way home by morning."

I looked at Yipes and longed to sit with him and chat the day away. He was standing at perfect attention, letting a tear run down his cheek without wiping it away.

"All right, I'll go," I said, and I understood the broad, sweet smile of the wild wolf. It was clear that Darius was in a rush to get things moving along, for just as soon as I agreed to the meeting he was next to me, nudging me toward the door with his powerful head.

"Will I see you again?" I asked Yipes as we made our way out the door and off the porch. He was hanging a satchel packed with dried food around my neck.

"I think so," he said, tears welling up again in his eyes. "Darius will take good care of you. You can trust him." Then he turned away from me to tend to his hawk, embarrassed. I ran back and picked him up like a big stuffed doll and hugged him. Then I spun him in a circle and set him back down on his porch. Without another look back, I began walking with Darius, the sound of the stream farther and farther away until it was lost in the rustle of the trees overhead.

As we walked, I began to think, had Warvold *really* chosen me as Darius had said? Yes, he asked me to go on his last walk with him. But it wasn't just that. He could have given me the key . . . but instead he gave me one last test. I had to find it. And when I did, I would make myself worthy of the choice.

CHAPTER 13

THE TERRIBLE SECRET

I had the distinct feeling we were going the wrong way. I knew the general location of the wall and the three gated roads, and I was sure we were heading toward the Lathbury road, which was opposite from where we should have been going. The road to Lathbury split the mountains from The Dark Hills, not Mount Norwood from Fenwick Forest.

"Darius?" I said.

"Yes, Alexa, what is it?"

"I haven't as keen a sense of direction as you must have, but it seems to me we're heading in the wrong direction."

"Very good, Alexa. You are correct. We're making a slight detour before the meeting. Something I need you to see that won't take but a moment."

Darius was friendly enough, but he had not mentioned this unscheduled diversion when we were with Yipes. It made me suspicious and edgy. Besides, he was a wolf, and I was as lost and helpless as a sheep. I would keep my guard up, and if things continued to feel wrong, I would cut off the trail and go back to find Yipes.

Darius was a big wolf, not at all like the small ones I'd seen in books. On all fours, he reached my shoulders, and his head was the size of the ripe watermelons in my mother's garden. His thick salt-and-pepper coat looked soft and full, though I'd not had the occasion to touch it. Placed against my hand, his massive paws would surely run the full distance of my fingers and thumb. His powerful jaws looked as though they could cut through a wagon wheel.

"Here we are," he said.

"Where is here?" I asked, apprehensive about what the answer would be. Then I looked past Darius and realized we were standing in a thicket, with only twenty yards between the Lathbury road and us.

"How far to the right is the Lathbury gate?" I questioned.

"Not far, about two hundred yards. But we're safely tucked away where the guards cannot see us. And besides, we've got hawks doing double duty this morning. They will let us know if danger is anywhere nearby."

"Why have you brought me here, Darius — to test me? To see if I'll run for the tower and tell everyone the animals can talk and that this place really *is* haunted?"

"Goodness me, no! They would think you were crazy. Besides, they can't understand us. Only you can," he said.

Darius let that information sink in, then continued, "There was a tunnel carved a long while ago that goes under this wall. It's small, almost too small for me to fit — and anyway, I can't stand tunnels. I refuse to go in them, no matter the size.

"This tunnel is about a hundred yards long, and it goes gradually deeper into the ground. At the end is a row of wood planks, and on the other side of the wood planks is packed dirt, though I'm told there is a spot where you can see through if you look just right. Badgers built the tunnel, and Yipes constructed the planks and packed dirt at the end. He's smaller than you and spent a lot of time down there working.

"You must crawl down to the end before I take you to Malcolm. It's the one other thing you must do."

Darius stepped aside, and indeed there was a small hole, about two feet around, staring up at me.

"I'm not sure I can fit in that hole," I said, even though I was nearly positive I could.

Darius walked a few paces until he was standing in the shade at the base of a large tree. He lay down and closed his eyes, his large head resting on soft front paws. "You can help us because you are small, Alexa. I think you'll fit." Then he became quiet, breathing steadily, as though he had fallen asleep.

I peered down into the hole, and I was unhappy to find it going dark rather quickly. Was I expected to climb down into a dark hole and stumble into a den of badgers, thrashing and clawing until they tore me to shreds in a silent underground grave? Darius could be plotting to have me killed for any number of reasons. I barely knew him, and he was the *only* wolf I knew. Could I trust a wolf? I looked over at Darius, who appeared to be perfectly content to nap the morning away in the shade of the trees.

It was true I could run straight for the tower, screaming and yelling and throwing my arms around. Or I might be able to find my way back to the secret tunnel leading to the library. That was a bit more of a stretch, since I really had no idea where it was. With Darius sleeping, I could probably sneak away and get Yipes to help me. But then, how much did I really know about Yipes? Not much more than I knew about Darius.

I paced back and forth in front of the hole, unsure of what to do.

"You are right for other reasons as well." It was Darius, his head up and alert now, and his piercing dark eyes staring at me. "We have been watching you with interest for quite some time. You plot and scheme in search of a way outside the wall. You have always known there was a higher purpose for your life, some mysterious duty, maybe even a mysterious past you can't remember. Your searching has not been as aimless as you might think. It's brought you this far, hasn't it?" Darius rose and took four powerful strides toward me. I imagined he could stand his own against any man or beast I knew of.

"Do you know where the rock in the pool came from, and why it allows you to understand what I'm saying? Have you any idea what happened to Renny Warvold? Who Elyon is and where he can be found? I think the answers to these questions, and many more, would surprise

105

you. But first things first — you won't understand why you are here until you go down that dark hole and see for yourself.

"Your adventure begins or ends here, Alexa."

I hesitated for a moment longer, taking in a big breath of the fresh mountain air and looking up into the light blue of the morning sky. Leaves danced in the wind; a hawk circled overhead. I wondered if Yipes had sent it to watch over me.

I got down on all fours and poked my head into the hole, knowing already that I would soon find myself deep under the earth. I was unable to resist the temptation of discovery that Darius had so aptly placed in front of me.

My hands were next. Touching the cool floor sent a rush of dirt rolling down into the shadows. Once my shoulders were in, I could not turn back to look behind me without knocking loose dirt off the walls. It was claustrophobic, much smaller than it had looked. My body blocked what little of the sun's rays had been streaming into the hole, and only a few shards of light poorly illuminated the space in front of me. With my knees inside I encountered an additional discomfort. The hunch of my back bumped against the top of the tunnel as I waddled from side to side. I could get my front half down by bending my elbows, but my rear end was a protrusion that was hard to control in the tight underground space — keeping it down required me to bend back on my ankles and move forward in short, awkward shuffles.

When I was all the way in and only a few feet down the hole, a cold, dry darkness surrounded me.

How far did Darius say it was? A hundred feet, a hundred yards? I could not remember, but whatever the distance, I was sure it would seem like a hundred miles. The farther I shuffled in, the darker it became. After a while, I closed my eyes to keep the dirt from stinging them. Within twenty minutes, my back and knees began to ache, and a horrible fear gripped me. I opened my eyes and had the strange effect of a dream from which I could not wake; blackness turned to blackness as I opened and shut my eyes, and a dark terror welled up in my throat.

It occurred to me at that moment that I could not turn around. Would not, in fact, be able to turn around when it came time to retreat out of the tunnel. Shuffling forward was hard enough, but backward would be impossible. I would die underground, exhausted and bawling in the end, probably wedged sideways in an ill-fated attempt to turn around. I began to hyperventilate and see a rainbow of colored stars in the darkness. Another moment and I was sure I would pass out with my face in the dirt.

I leaned back on my ankles and tried to calm down. *Twenty minutes in. Why hadn't I counted each of my shuffles forward?* If each of my advances was a foot in length, then I was moving at a rate of twenty feet per minute, which would put me four hundred feet into the tunnel. That would mean Darius was lying, since I had already gone at least a hundred yards. He had probably already covered the entryway with dirt and wandered off into the woods, looking for a hapless victim to devour for lunch. I lay down on my belly against the cold black dirt of my tomb, unsure of what to do next.

I knew I could not turn around or go backward all the way out. I reasoned that the only choices I had were to keep going forward or lie where I was and starve to death. Three shuffles into my decision to go on, my hand encountered air where it should have found floor.

I lowered onto my belly again and tried to reach down and feel the bottom with both arms dangling, but it was too far down to touch. The walls to the sides were also gone, and I perceived a faint light creeping into the space. I took a pebble and dropped it over the edge and heard it pop at the bottom a few feet below. I slithered down into the new open space like a dry snake, then stood.

Maybe Darius had only been bad with distance, not bad altogether.

I felt around for walls and found open air all around me for several paces. Then I reached a wall that was clearly made of wood planks, and I felt along its surface to the ceiling a foot above my head. The faint glow I had discerned earlier was not enough to illuminate the darkness, but the sliver of light it created was clear against the grain of the wood. A small opening, no more than an inch, allowed in a weak beam of dusty light.

I stood with my back against one of the walls and

stared at the sliver of light. As I approached the wall and placed one eye over the small opening, I could not imagine what I might see on the other side.

It was a room. A lamp hung on the far wall, and another to my right, from which I could see only light glittering here and there. A table and two chairs, a map on the facing wall with locations I had never seen, winding in a yarn of twists and turns of brown and black. It was a dimly lit room with earth walls, and I could not see a door.

I heard voices, distant echoes at first, like sounds from the meeting room at Renny Lodge when I tried to listen from outside closed doors. I had that same heart-racing fear as the voices came closer. It was two men, arguing about something. As they approached, their words became clearer, in a muffled language I knew well.

"I don't care about what he says; we've waited far too long already," said the first man impatiently.

"I know you want to go — a lot of us do. What do you want *me* to do about it? He'll go when he's good and ready to go," said the other man. They were in the room now, to my left. Out of my direct sight, but close.

"Why can't we tell him we need to get on with it?" the first man angrily replied. "Our time has come. The men are waiting."

They passed in front of me, and I jerked away from the hole with a yelp, falling back with a dull, earthy thud. I was afraid they might have heard me, and I cringed at the thought of seeing another eye staring back at me through the hole, the boards flying in great splinters as these men broke through and discovered my hiding place.

Soft light was still finding its way through the tiny opening, and the voices moved a little farther away. When I was sure they hadn't heard me, I silently positioned my eye to the hole, and saw that they had settled at the desk to continue their discussion as they reviewed the map hanging above them on the wall. Their tone was quieter, and with the added distance I was allowed only a word here or a fragment there. "Too long." "I understand." An emphatic "No!"

Most of what I heard was a garble of useless words I could not tie together into any meaning. But from the way they spoke and the way they conspired, I could tell that something sinister was going on.

One of the men rose from the desk and began walking toward me, apparently to retrieve something from my side of the room. He was a big man, and as he approached I could see his hair was unkempt and his beard overgrown. I held my breath as he came closer still, almost right in front of me. He struck a matchstick and lit another lamp that hung just to the right of the opening I was looking through. As the light flickered to life, I saw without a doubt what Darius had sent me to see.

This ragged-looking man had a *C* branded squarely on his forehead.

A convict!

CHAPTER 14
THE FOREST COUNCIL

It took me half as long to get out of the tunnel as it had taken me to crawl all the way in. The trip out was much harder on my body as I bumped my elbows, knees, and back in a race for the exit. When I emerged from the hole, the light and heat hit me full force, and it took me several seconds to see anything but sheets of flaming white and yellow. I was exhausted and lay on my back, hands over my eyes, listening to the wind rushing through the leaves on the trees.

"You must be hungry. How about we open up that bag of yours and have something to eat?" It was Darius. He stood a few feet away. I rolled over on my side and looked at him through narrowed eyes.

"What are those men doing down there?" I asked. "I saw one of them up close; he had a *C* branded on his forehead. I thought all the convicts who built the walls were gone. How can they still be here?" I said.

"Oh, I know what they're doing down there, and so will you shortly. But first some lunch, shall we?"

I tried to question him further, but he wouldn't budge. Finally I gave him some dried meat, which he ate in a flash of teeth and slaver. I chomped indifferently on bread as we walked, slowly making our way back in the direction of the Turlock wall that divided the mountains from the forest. I kept asking Darius about the men I had seen, but he seemed content to continue on quietly, winding his way through thick underbrush and around the occasional fallen tree. Finally, in frustration, I yelled at him, "Can't you just stop for a minute and tell me *something*?"

Darius did stop, turning back at me. "I am responsible for two things today: getting you down that hole and having you in Malcolm's capable hands by midday. So far I've accomplished only one of those tasks. All of your questions will be answered before the sun sets tonight, but for now I can't tell you anything more." He turned and started walking again, and though I felt completely exasperated I followed, trailing a few feet behind him down the path.

It was a long, hot journey, but at midday we were standing in a grove of cottonwood trees fifty yards from the Turlock wall. The gate to Bridewell was now safely in the distance, and looking overhead, I could see that several hawks were patrolling the area from above, dodging a storm of white floating fluff from the trees. As I stood catching my breath with Darius, I saw rustling under the brush in the distance, a zing of gray, then more rustling.

"Ah, here he comes. Not much good for sleuthing, but a nice fellow still the same," said Darius. We watched as the formless gray ball of fur continued to weave in and out of view. After a while it became clear that it was a rabbit darting toward us between hiding places in the undergrowth. It was taking quite a long time for him to find his way to us.

"Will you *please* stop the secret spy routine and get over here!" Darius cried. "You'll make us all late." For a moment there was no movement at all.

"Is that you, Darius?" came a tiny, uncertain voice from somewhere in the thicket.

"Yes, it's me, the big wolf come to eat the helpless bunny. The longer you take getting over here, the hungrier I get," said Darius.

A gray head topped with floppy ears popped up about twenty yards away. "Coming!" said the rabbit with great exuberance, and he was standing at my feet a few seconds later.

"No need to get hostile," chided the rabbit, who I took to be Malcolm. "Ah, but I see you've got the girl, and on time. Nicely done."

"All in a day's work for someone on his own," said Darius. He became quiet and looked at Malcolm with a terrible sadness. "Have you any word from Odessa and Sherwin?"

"Stop your pouting — it's pathetic for a creature of your size. This will all be over before you know it, Darius. Trust me," said Malcolm. "Now, how about a proper introduction?"

Darius growled and then introduced me. Malcolm held out his foot in an effort to shake my hand. He said it was human custom to shake, and he wanted to make me feel at home. I bent down, took his furry gray foot between my thumb and forefinger, and awkwardly bobbed it up and down a few times. Malcolm chuckled nervously and we both looked at Darius, who rolled his eyes. I laughed, and for the first time I felt a little less like a guest outside the wall, and a little more like these might actually be my friends.

Darius and Malcolm huddled together and talked while I relieved myself behind a tree. This produced a whole new conversation about when to go to the bathroom, where to go to the bathroom, and whether or not one should cover up when finished.

After several minutes of arguing, Darius said, "I suggest we continue this conversation when we have more time. Though I will concede Malcolm's views on marking trees over rocks make a compelling argument."

Malcolm looked up at me and I nodded my readiness to move on.

"I'll go straight to see Yipes and tell him of our progress. He will be pleased to hear you've come this far," said Darius. Then, with a slight bow of his head, he added, "Malcolm, always a great pleasure. Take care of our girl now, and tell everyone I'm doing fine." Then he walked off, and I was left with nothing to protect me but a smiling ball of fur with poor scouting skills. I felt suddenly alone and missed my father and friends back in Bridewell. I think I even missed Pervis, or at least the morbid comfort of his rude behavior.

"You've grown some from what I was told about your size. It must have been quite a squeeze getting down that tunnel over at Lathbury," said Malcolm. "The next one's not so bad."

"The *next* one?" I said.

"Sure, the next one. Didn't Darius tell you? We've got a big meeting over in the forest tonight. Lots to discuss."

We walked — or, I should say, *I* walked and Malcolm hopped toward the Turlock wall. We arrived at an odd-looking hole surrounded by stone on all sides. It was slanted at an angle, and it looked as though it ran under the wall.

"This is a strange-looking tunnel, Malcolm," I said.

"That's because animals didn't make it. Humans did, and humans are always doing things in very strange ways. No offense to you, of course." He seemed flustered now that he'd said it, as if he wished he could take it back.

"No offense taken," I offered.

"This is a culvert," Malcolm continued. "They appear every few miles along the walls. In the springtime the water runs off the mountain and then through these tunnels to Fenwick Forest and out into The Dark Hills, where it creates something of a marshland in the early months of spring."

Malcolm went on to explain that the culverts were encased in stone, running down five feet under the huge stone blocks of the buried part of the wall, then gradually rising back up into Fenwick Forest and The Dark Hills.

Malcolm easily fit inside. I followed and found that it was a very tight fit. I could move slowly forward on my belly, but the stone walls of the culvert were all around me and it was rough going all the way. I continually grazed my shoulders and elbows along the walls. This tunnel descended faster, leveled out, and then began to rise again slowly, presumably on the other side of the wall. Pretty soon I saw light streaming down, and shortly after that we were outside again in an open field. We were in Fenwick Forest.

"Who are Odessa and Sherwin?" I asked, turning my head to the side and shaking the dirt out of my hair.

Malcolm didn't answer at first, but then he stopped hopping and looked at me. "Odessa is Darius's wife and Sherwin is his son."

I knew there had to be more to the story, and soon Malcolm was telling it. "Darius was off hunting for several weeks," he explained. "They put the wall up so fast, and there were so many humans about, he got caught on the mountain side. Like so many animals, he's far too big to fit through a culvert, and there's no way to dig deep enough to go under the buried part of the wall. He can't walk around the wall, because both ends lead to jagged cliffs that drop off into The Lonely Sea. The water and walls keep them apart. He hasn't seen his family in quite some time."

I thought a moment, trying to consider the consequences of what Malcolm had said.

"Are there other stories like his?" I asked.

116

He turned on the path and began hopping again, his floppy back feet kicking up tiny storms of dust as he went.

"More than a few," he said.

We continued to make our way deeper into the woods. It was turning dark and cooling down. Fenwick Forest was vastly different from where I had just spent two days. The terrain around Mount Norwood had been far more open and arid, with tiny streams crisscrossing and connecting all over. Twenty minutes into our walk away from the wall put us deep in a forest of fir, pine, cottonwood, and aspen trees. The lush forest floor was alive and danced with shadows cast from an endless parade of swaying trees. As we approached early evening it was cool and peaceful. The sound of the trees moving in the wind high above seemed like a friendly traveling companion, calling us farther and farther into the depths of the forest.

As we walked, I kept thinking about the face of that suspicious man with the *C* on his forehead. How these men had escaped into The Dark Hills remained a biting question I couldn't get out of my mind.

I began to have a creepy sense that we were being watched and I started to hear what sounded like whispers all around me. I kept shaking the cobwebs loose from my head, trying to refocus, but the strange whispering sound persisted, and I reasoned that it was the wind in the trees playing tricks on me.

"Malcolm, do you hear anything strange?" I asked.

117

Malcolm stopped and sniffed at the air with his front legs up. "Oh, yes, we've got quite a procession going already. You're famous, Alexa. Every animal within twenty miles is hiding behind a bush or a tree limb trying to get a peek at you."

Things were getting stranger all the time.

We wound through the forest for another five minutes and then came to a stop where the trail split off into two directions, one straight ahead and one veering off to the left and down toward the Lunenburg wall; both were covered by a thick canopy of low-hanging tree branches.

"It looks like we've arrived, Alexa. Go on now, go straight ahead up that trail and don't stop until you see Ander."

"What's an Ander?" I asked.

"You mean *who* is Ander," chortled Malcolm. "Go on then — you'll get all your questions answered once you reach the end of that path."

I did as I was told, too tired to complain or argue with a rabbit. A few minutes later the path widened into a circular area about forty feet wide, bordered by large rocks and dead tree trunks. The rocks and trees were covered with animals, more animals than I had ever seen before — squirrels, rabbits, mountain lions, bears, wolves, beavers, badgers, porcupines, skunks, and a smattering of wildlife I could not identify from my own limited knowledge. It was a frightening sight, made worse by the swarm of whispering I continued to hear buzzing in my head.

Straight ahead, right up the middle of all the animals, was a ferocious-looking grizzly bear. Its head was like a boulder on its massive shoulders, and it swayed back and forth as the beast walked toward me. The whispering stopped. I was about to turn and run for my life when I spotted Yipes sitting on a rock to my right. I was so happy to see him again, I couldn't keep the big smile off my worn-out face. I read his lips as he mouthed the words "It's okay, stay calm."

The grizzly stopped so close in front of me that its wet nostrils sent a gentle wind through my hair. I looked down and saw where its enormous paws smashed the mossy green grass at my feet. It stood on four legs, its head a foot above my own. I knew from what I had read about grizzly bears that one quick swipe from his paw would break my bones and shred my skin. I remained perfectly still, breathing in and out in choppy waves.

"We have waited for you a long, long time, my dear," said the grizzly. His voice was deep, sorrowful, and slow in my head. He seemed old, though I had no idea how old by the looks of him. "I am Ander, the forest king, and I have a lot to tell you.

"Bring the food!" he commanded, and a parade of animals came out of the woods with offerings of nuts, fruits, and fresh water. "Now, let's sit down and have a nice long chat, shall we, Alexa?"

We walked to the center of the grove and sat down. I drank until I thought I would throw up, and then I pulled some leftover meat out of my bag to eat with the nuts and the fruit.

"If you don't mind, Alexa, could you get by without the meat for now? Mixed company, you know. It sets them off." Ander looked around at all the animals. They were all staring at me with wide eyes, and some of the larger animals were dripping saliva and acting strange.

I put my food away and began eating a pear, which suited me fine. Ander proceeded to introduce me to a number of important animals in attendance.

I met Murphy, a lively squirrel who kept zipping back and forth and twirling around in circles after his name was called. It took a while to get him calmed down, and he continued doing backflips and whirling spins every time Ander introduced another animal. There was Beaker, a raccoon. Ander said he was "scientific for a coon, a problem solver." A badger named Henry was complimented on his fierce fighting skills. Picardy was a beautiful female black bear who had not seen her mate in a very long time; he had been off in the mountains looking for a den when the wall came rising into existence. I met Boone, a crafty bobcat, who often came up with outlandish ideas that, for some unknown reason, actually worked most of the time. There was a quick and sneaky fox named Raymond, and a nervous woodchuck named Vesper. Chopper and Whip were an agreeable pair of buck-toothed beavers.

The sun was beginning to set and I was getting cold. It must have shown, because Ander took a break from his introductions to call Yipes over, who presented me with a blanket out of his pack. I draped it around my shoulders and curled my legs up to my chest, wrapping my arms around my knees. Soon it would be night, but for now dusk coated the grove with a soft blend of velvety gold and green. It was heavenly.

Ander finished the introductions with Odessa and Sherwin, the wife and son of Darius. Sherwin approached me cautiously, swaying his head back and forth. He was every bit the powerful beast his father was, but his features were more juvenile and his coat was a lighter shade of gray.

"You've met my father?" he questioned me.

"Yes, I've met Darius. He's impressive," I said. I felt a wave of compassion for Sherwin, wondering what it must be like to lose your father in such an unjust way. I added, "When did you last see him?"

"I don't remember ever seeing him. I was only a few months old when he was caught behind the wall, and by the time I was old enough to travel through the culvert I was already too large. I probably could have done it as a child, but I was too afraid. When I was smaller I thought many times about sneaking under to find him, but I never did. Now I'm so big I can barely get my head into the tunnel."

He paused and looked off toward the Turlock wall in the distance.

"At night, my father howls at me, and I howl back at him. We dream of hunting together and of he and my

121

mother being side by side again. He often sounds sad and, in recent times, even a little old, like the long lonely nights are beginning to wear on him. Sometimes he howls at me and my mother for hours and hours, until his voice is shredded and cracking. On those nights I often go to the culvert and I put my front paws in, imagining I'm small again. Then I look to the wall and beat my head against the same spot until blood is oozing out of my fur and into my eyes.

"My story is not so different from what many of these animals here would tell you. Most of the large animals have lost a son or daughter, a mate, a close friend, or a parent. Others feel the terrible loss of the mountains and the lush wild streams lined with fruit trees and blackberry patches. The smaller animals, the ones who can use the tunnels, have maintained a relatively normal life after the walls."

"What makes you think dragging me out here will make any difference?" I said. "I'm only a child, and I command no special importance in Bridewell. I create more bad than good back there. Ask anyone."

Sherwin looked down for a long moment, then straight into my eyes with a heartbreaking look on his face. "Then we have clearly thought wrong, and we should send you back. You're small enough to use the tunnels and you have the right breeding, those things are true. What you lack is *belief*. If bringing down the wall would require you to fly, you must believe that you can fly. Otherwise, when the decisive moment comes, you will surely discover you have no wings."

He turned and walked back to stand at his mother's side. The whispers and the sun were both gone. The sounds of owls, crickets, and frogs blended together to form a thick soup of mystifying night music. The full moon rose out of the trees from the east, pouring a bucket of soft white into the grove. And again I felt the discomforting loneliness that so often haunted me.

"I see you've got quite a scratch there on your arm," said Ander, his deep voice jerking me out of my self-pity. "I do apologize. Domesticated animals can be rather pesky at times. That's not to say Sam and Pepper are bad cats — they've actually been helpful in our attempts to get you out here. But they can be, shall we say, *spirited*.

"Now then, I believe you have a stone in your possession, which I must now ask you to produce. That is, if you don't mind. It may be that you are not the person for the job at hand, even if I'm quite convinced that you are. In any case, the stone will tell us a lot about what your future holds."

With all that was going on, I had completely forgotten about the stone hanging around my neck in the small leather pouch. I clutched it under the blanket, afraid at first to give it up. What if I never got it back?

I wiggled open the string at the top and removed the

stone. When I held it out to Ander, the feathery green glow illuminated the space between the two of us, and the crowd of animals let out a meandering collection of *ooh*s and *ah*s. I set the stone down on a large flat rock that sat between us, and it continued to throb liquid green light like the steady time of a beating drum. *Boom, boom, boom.*

"Beautiful, isn't it?" said Ander as he gazed at its strange throbbing radiance. *Boom, boom, boom.*

"This entire area, including the forest, mountains, and hills, was at one time full of Elyon's enchantment. It was a marvelous place indeed. The stone you chose is what allows you to communicate with us, just as we communicate with one another.

"At one time there were six stones like this in the pool. Yipes found the first, then another was taken, then the convicts came and took all but this one." He nodded toward the pulsating green mass sitting between us. "In these stones lie the answer to why Elyon created us, why he created this place, and where he's gone."

Ander sat silent then for a long time, his heavy breathing filling the air. It seemed as though he was searching for something in the silence he couldn't quite find. And then he came back to life again.

"Unfortunately, we haven't the time to talk about all that right now," he said. "Elyon is on the move, his plans are unfolding in this very age, and we shall all be witnesses to his triumphant return in the days to come. One thing I can tell you: Someone known to you was responsible for bringing the stones here, but that is about all we have time for."

"Thomas Warvold," I said, without the slightest hesitation.

"An excellent guess. He is responsible for a great many things that, in his death, we are all left to consider. But he did not bring the stones. They were placed in the pool by his wife, Renny."

Ander looked at the sky and sniffed at the air, then continued.

"When things settle down, you can come see me again and I'll tell you all about the mysterious Warvolds. For now, we really must be getting on with things."

I started to protest. I asked about Elyon, whom I had never thought of as more than a legend. But at every turn Ander insisted we stay on his choice of topics, that the time for those answers had not yet come. I wasn't about to have it out with a thousand-pound grizzly, but his comments left me terribly curious to learn more about Thomas, Renny, and in particular, Elyon.

"All magic runs out sometime, Alexa, and this place has been running out for some time now. We used to be able to communicate with the birds; now they understand us but we do not understand them. We can send them off to do things, but we cannot be sure if they have done what we asked them to. Oh, they can tell us a little by the way they move and the sounds they make. But it's as if we speak completely different languages now.

"Some of the animals are beginning to experience the same problems," Ander continued. "We can comprehend one another most of the time, but occasionally our voices become garbled for a morning or an afternoon, only to return again some hours later. This process accelerated after the wall went up."

Ander touched the stone with the edge of his paw and gently pushed it two or three inches along the flat rock. The fluid green light continued to pulsate between the two of us.

"With humans, the stone gives you two important things," he continued, putting his paw back on the ground. "The ability to communicate with animals and a glimpse into the future. In other words, it gives new insight in two ways: present and future. Just like any magical effect, this one comes with its own set of rules. For instance, the ability to talk with animals works only if you stay in the wild. As soon as you leave, the power begins to drift away. Once this process starts, it cannot be reversed, and there are no more stones to be had. Once you leave the wild, the stone will start its gradual descent into dim regularity. It will throb more slowly — and with less intensity — over a period of undetermined time.

"As you can probably imagine, Yipes has never left the wild of the forest and the mountains, and so he continues to enjoy the questionable benefits of speaking with animals." Ander took a moment to look over at Yipes with a nod and a wink, and then he continued.

"I said before that a stone was taken by someone other than Yipes or the convicts. That person set a stone right where you've just set yours, and it glowed like a small but glorious orange sun at the tail end of a hot day. Can you guess who might have sat where you sit now, Alexa?"

I thought for a moment about the possible answers to the question, but I was sure I knew whom Ander was talking about.

"Warvold," I said.

"Absolutely! It was none other than Mr. Warvold himself, the great adventurer. Would you like to hear what his stone revealed about his future?"

I nodded and he leaned forward over the table, the green glow from my stone wafting through his bushy fur with a watery glow.

"Warvold's stone revealed that one day terrible forces from this enchanted land would rise up and cause the destruction of everything he had created," said Ander. "He took this to mean that dark monsters lived out here and would someday enter his kingdom and kill everyone. But he badly misread the meaning of his future."

"He was mistaken, just like he told me," I interjected. "When he sat with me that last night with our backs against the wall, he told me he'd gotten it all wrong." My

127

head was reeling as I tried to put it all together. "His future wasn't about dark enchanted monsters at all. He made his own monsters, then let them loose in The Dark Hills to —"

"Now don't get too far ahead of yourself, Alexa. You're only half right. Allow me the indulgence of giving you the whole story, if you would," said Ander. "When Warvold was told about his future, he was terrified for his wife, Renny, and all the people streaming into Lunenburg. He was beside himself with grief. We tried to explain to him that the Jocasta could be misinterpreted to mean something it did not, and we assured him that we knew of no evil monsters lurking about."

"Did you say Jocasta?" I asked.

"Yes. That's what the messages etched on the stones are called," Ander replied.

"How much did Renny Warvold have to do with all this?"

"A lot, and she was smarter than you can imagine. She brought the enchanted stones here. She started everything." Ander hunched his enormous back up and let out a low rumbling growl. "I'm not as young as I once was, and we're approaching my bedtime," he said absentmindedly. "Where was I? Oh, yes — when Warvold returned to Lunenburg he hatched a plan to build a wall before there was any further expansion. He added more guards and made the arrangement with the leaders in Ainsworth. Everything went as planned, and during the span of the next several years Warvold completed not one but three walled roads, along with three new walled principalities. By the time he'd gone this far, he'd figured out how to use three hundred convicts and hundreds more of his own men to build quickly. The wall between the forest and the mountains was the last. First he built it only eight feet high, then his own people followed behind to finish the rest. It was remarkable, really — sometimes a thousand feet a day were walled in, quickly cutting off the passage between the forest and the mountains. By all accounts the operation was a marvel of speed and efficiency.

"But Warvold made one important miscalculation in his plan: He trusted the leaders in Ainsworth to take back the criminals. Further, he took them at their word when they said they had indeed taken them back. You see, until that night when you sat with him, Warvold never knew that the leaders in Ainsworth had set those men free in The Dark Hills. They never thought Warvold would actually give them back, and they had planned poorly for their return. The officials in Ainsworth had no place to put them, so they delivered them into The Dark Hills and banished them to the caves. The way the Ainsworth officials figured it, nobody would ever be the wiser."

"What caves are you talking about, Ander? I never heard of any caves out there," I said.

"The caves were formed when all the materials for the wall were dug up, of course. My dear, there are miles of giant tunnels out there in The Dark Hills, and miles more on the surface made of thick, thorny underbrush. That's how the convicts get around both above- and belowground without being seen. Where do you think almost three hundred men are going to go?

"Those walls — those miles and miles of walls — are made from a clay that could only be found underground. Clay is a plentiful substance out there in The Dark Hills and easy to harvest. All one has to do is dig a few feet under the ground and start tunneling. Everything in the tunnel's path will be pure clay, which was the primary ingredient Warvold wanted for the building blocks.

"It really isn't all Warvold's fault things have developed as they have. Nonetheless, it was his fear that drove him to create a monster. The monster he created is not the collection of criminals who live in The Dark Hills. The monster is the wall itself. But I suppose that would be a debate for another time."

Everything was becoming clear now. It was like a giant puzzle with interlocking pieces, and Ander had just fit everything together on one moonlit evening. Only it seemed in the telling that one piece was left missing.

"Ander, why am I out here?" I said.

The whispers started up again, and Murphy did backflips and spins. It was exhausting to watch the little squirrel expend so much energy. Ander lifted his head up, and the grove went still and quiet again.

"We believe that Warvold's death set in motion the beginning of the end of this age. We have no idea if this eventual end will take five days or five years, but we know it is coming. For better or for worse, you are the chosen one, and not just by us, but by Warvold himself. There is just a tad more I must tell you now, and then we really must get on with reading your stone and shuffling you off to bed. It's getting late, very late indeed.

"Alexa, all that you are being told must be kept a secret until the time is right to reveal what you know. Someone in Bridewell is not what he seems. That someone is the one the convicts call Sebastian. We have heard them mention him and his plans. He is living inside Bridewell, giving the orders, making things ready for a time when the convicts will invade all of Bridewell and bring Warvold's future to pass. Who is Sebastian? I'm sure the birds could tell us if we could understand them, but we have no idea. None whatsoever. I can tell you but one thing: The convicts left the last stone for a reason. They meant it for their leader, and when they find it has been taken, it will enrage them even more.

"Sebastian must be found out and revealed for the serpent that he is, and the vile criminals must be stopped from invading Bridewell. Cut off the serpent's head and the whole serpent dies. The convicts are not brilliant men, Alexa. However, they are extremely vengeful, and Sebastian *is* brilliant. At present, this is a lethal combination.

"If power is transferred to the criminals, war will be upon us, and the wall will become a military stronghold. Once set in motion, violence will rain down on Bridewell and the wall will remain, possibly forever. We must reveal and remove the danger, and in so doing convince people that the danger is past. That's our only hope of bringing down the wall." Ander was skirting around the point he was trying to make, then he stammered and got right to the heart of the matter.

"You cannot tell anyone about what has taken place here tonight. *Especially* about Sebastian," he said.

"You think Sebastian might be my own father?" I said. The remark was met with a cold, silent stare from Ander. "But my father doesn't have a *C* branded on his face," I yelled.

"True, but we can't be certain that Sebastian was a convict," Ander continued. "It could be someone on the inside who knows more than they are telling and has a motive to side with them. Perhaps it's someone looking for more power, like a disgruntled son or a crafty guard with wicked ambitions. Maybe it's an old man who fixes books, or a simple mail carrier with timely access to powerful people. It could be anyone. That is why you can't tell what you know.

"Alexa, you know how to work alone and maintain secrecy. You're small and easily hidden. You have connections to important people, but you're not important enough yourself to be scrutinized too closely. Face it, Alexa — you're perfect for the task."

I couldn't argue with Ander's reasoning.

"Only one thing left to do — read your Jocasta," said Ander.

"What if I don't want it revealed? What if I'd rather not know my future?" I said.

"That is your choice to make and we will honor it. But in this case, I must say, I think your Jocasta will give you much-needed clarity for the days to come," said Ander.

I sat silent for a long moment, and then I looked straight into the grizzly's powerful face.

"Read it," I said.

Yipes jumped down off his perch and walked toward us. He crawled right up on the big, flat rock and removed a magnifying glass from his vest. Then he held the glass against his eye and put his face less than an inch from the rhythmically pulsating stone. *Boom, boom, boom.* After a moment, he rose into a sitting position and looked at Ander. Ander nodded and Yipes looked at me.

"You will be the one to find the serpent," he said.

PART 2

CHAPTER 15

AN UNEXPECTED ENEMY

The trapdoor wavered in the air while Yipes held it up as best he could. I think he pretended to make it look more difficult than it was so he could more easily avoid eye contact with me. We were both sad that I was going back to Bridewell that morning.

"You have a visitor, Alexa," said Yipes. I looked back over my shoulder into the heat of the morning sun. Standing motionless off in the distance was the silhouette of a large wolf. I waved to him and he turned to the west and headed up into the mountains.

"I've got to go," I said.

I started down the ladder into the dark tunnel.

"Wait!" yelled Yipes. "I almost forgot to give you this." He reached into his vest pocket and pulled out a small tube. "Not to be shared until *you know who* is found out. And one other thing." He wagged his finger at me, trying to balance the heavy door with his other hand. "Be careful who you talk to from here on out. Trust *no one*."

As he said this, it was clear he was losing control of the trapdoor, and it swayed dangerously above me. I scrambled down another three rungs as fast as I could and the door came swinging down with its full force, slamming and showering me with a storm of dirt. I lost my grip and hung by three fingers from the ladder. A few more inches and the door would have hammered me like a nail into a thirty-foot free fall.

I regained my footing and my grip on the ladder and shook the dirt from my hair and shoulders. It was pitch-black in the tunnel. I waited and waited for Yipes to open the door, but it remained dark and quiet. "Yipes!" I yelled, but received no answer. I removed a wooden match from my pouch and struck it against the ladder. The light revealed the lamp I had left hanging on the third rung down. Thankfully it had not plunged to the floor and smashed into useless pieces.

I lit the lamp and felt much better once I could see my surroundings. I held it out over the open air, but I could not see the bottom. The darkness swallowed up the light about ten feet down. I waited until the intense pain in my hands threatened my grip on the ladder. I called again for Yipes but got no answer. Then I started the slow descent to the floor of the tunnel, moving the lamp down three rungs at a time as I went.

When I reached the bottom I found the book I had left behind, covered in dirt. "I bet you never thought you'd see me again," I said to Cabeza de Vaca. "You're looking well these days. Travels treating you all right?" A sparkle from the corner of the tunnel caught my eye and I held the lamp over it. There in the dirt was the tube

Yipes had given me. It was about four inches long and an inch around, with jewels embedded across its wood surface. The top was closed with a wooden cork.

I removed the cork with a pop and took out a paper scroll. Attached was a note, which read *Make sure you don't accidentally give this to the wrong person,* signed by Yipes. I unrolled the paper and revealed what looked to be an exact copy of the map I had seen hanging on the underground wall where the convicts were. This must have been what Yipes was working on when he spent time down in that secret passageway.

The map showed both black and brown lines, along with notations about some of them. The black lines represented belowground tunnels, the brown ones aboveground passageways created by thick brush. I'd have to give the map careful review when I had more light and could make sure it didn't fall into the wrong hands.

I looked up once more, hoping I would see a crack of light and Yipes's little face peering down at me. Seeing only darkness, I turned and started walking for Bridewell. My pace quickened when I thought of seeing my father, Grayson, Ganesh, Nicolas, and Silas. I slowed down when I thought of Pervis. The idea of sleeping in my own bed or talking to Sam and Pepper for the first time or searching for a good book in the library got me moving faster again. I knew that the second I opened the trapdoor back into the library my stone would start weakening and my ability to talk with the animals would slowly disappear.

This made me shuffle slowly and look over my shoulder in the direction I'd come from. It was a bittersweet journey, to say the least.

Eventually I stood on the ladder at the top of the tunnel in the stairwell, listening for any sign of movement in the library. It seemed to me that I had been gone a lifetime, seen a whole new world, and returned as an altogether different person.

"Is that you, Alexa?" came a feline voice from the other side.

Be careful who you talk to from here on out. Trust no one. Yipes's words clanged around in my head like a dinner bell.

"It's me, Sam," came the cat's voice again. It was strange to understand his meowing, but its meaning was crystal clear. "Pepper is keeping an eye on Grayson. It's all clear for you to come out."

I opened the trapdoor toward me, blew out the lamp, hung it on a rung, and then pushed the chair out of the way. The light was bright at first and I saw only the silhouette of Sam looking down at me from his roost on the back of the chair. I smiled and said, "Hey, Sam! How are you doing?"

"Alexa, answer me. Can you understand what I'm saying, Alexa?" Sam demanded, his dark outline held motionless against the dusty light streaming in behind him.

I pretended not to hear him, which aggravated him more.

"Come on, Alexa, let's have it!" he shouted. "I know

you can understand me. I want to hear the latest from Ander."

Sam jumped down and leaned against my legs, staring up at me with his penetrating gray eyes. Time seemed to stand still as he purred and paced back and forth. He took a long, final look at me and then jumped back up on the chair.

"Stupid girl," he said. "As useless as ever. All you hear is purring and meowing all the livelong day. I should have expected as much." I turned away from Sam toward the bookshelf and fanned my hands over the rows of books to hide the shock on my face.

As I stood and thought nervously about what to do next, a flash of shadows moved about the room and the sound of beating wings filled the small space. I had not noticed the perfectly still hawk sitting in the sill, waiting for information. As I turned to look I saw the bird flying off into the bright morning sun.

"Off to tell Sebastian of Alexa's return, no doubt," said Sam.

I tried desperately to remember all the things Sam and Pepper would have seen me doing or heard me saying. How many times had hawks watched me? Were they watching when Warvold died and I took the key? I absentmindedly ran my hand along my forearm, feeling the wicked scratch Pepper had given me when I'd tried to take his amulet in my hands. *Traitors, both of them.* I could hardly believe it. And the hawk — it was also a traitor. I had to get a message to Ander.

"No more time for petting right now, Sam, I've got lots to do," I said with false cheer. Then I moved the chair back into its proper place and dusted myself off as best I could. I was dirty, so sneaking up to my room for a quick cleanup before anyone saw me was essential. I quietly wound my way through the corridors of books, creaking the floorboards here and there as I continued cautiously in the direction of Grayson's office. I peeked around the last corner and saw that his door was ajar, Pepper's long tail flicking up and down at the floor. I had a momentary feeling of fear as Sam purred up against my leg unexpectedly.

"Pepper!" Sam said. "She's as dumb as a post, not a word out of her." Pepper's head came whipping around in the doorjamb.

"That you, Sam?" came Grayson's voice. Things were getting complicated in a hurry and I'd been back in Bridewell for only a few minutes.

I crept down the hallway as quietly as I could while Sam held back in front of Grayson's door.

"That's it, slink off to your room for a nice long nap," Sam jeered.

The floorboards creaked a few paces from the library door, and I froze for a brief moment.

"Who's there? . . . Alexa, is that you?" It was Grayson, but I was safely on the other side of the door and out of sight a second later.

My room had never looked so wonderful. I hid my

stone, the tube Yipes had given me, and the other trinkets I had been carrying around. I put on a fresh set of clothes and performed a healthy bit of primping on myself, then flopped down on my bed and felt as though I could sleep for a month. I thought of all the events of the past three days and drifted off into dreams of talking animals and men with brands on their faces.

I awoke at midday, sweaty and hot. I had been dreaming of a hawk at my window. It was scratching and clawing to get inside, and in my dream I let the bird in and it chased me around my room, landed on my head, and ripped chunks of my hair out with its monstrous claws. As I sat up in my bed, all wet and clammy from the heat and the awful dream, I heard scraping at the shutter. Was I still dreaming or had I actually awoke? I cautiously got out of bed.

Everything hurt, and my feet felt as though they were walking on a bed of nails. As I hobbled over to the window, I realized that whatever was banging and scratching to get in was much smaller than a hawk, and it was scampering around from side to side outside the shutter. It could be only one animal: Murphy, the hyperactive squirrel from the grove. I swung the shutters open and he spilled into the room, bouncing from place to place, sniffing everything and whipping his tail from side to side.

"This is an unexpected surprise," I said.

He was behind my bed between the bathroom and the nightstand, and I had to walk around the room to find him.

"I think it would be best if we stayed away from the

window," he said. "You never know who might be watching us."

I lay down on my stomach and propped myself up at the elbows. It felt good to be off my feet. Murphy remained lively, darting under the bed, flying out with a leap, and landing on my back — then running down my legs and circling back.

"Murphy, if you can calm down a minute, I have news."

"What sort of news? Is it good or bad?"

"Well, to be honest, I think it's mostly bad," I said.

Murphy's cavorting turned to twitching and quick jerks from side to side. Given his nature, I think it took more effort for him to stay still than to scuttle half crazed around the room.

"Let's have it then — no point putting off the inevitable." He closed his eyes tightly and turned his head slightly to the left, as if this would somehow soften the blow of whatever I was about to say.

I was getting sore on my elbows so I dropped down with my chin on my hands. I was eye to eye with him, only a few inches between us, and for no apparent reason I whispered when I spoke. "Sam and Pepper are traitors. On top of that, I think some of the birds might be against us. I know for sure of at least one hawk who's working for Sebastian. I haven't had time to find out much else. Just getting to my room was an adventure in itself, and I've been sleeping most of the day."

Murphy looked stunned as his eyes squeaked back open. He was still for the first time since I'd met him. "That is bad news now, isn't it? We've had our suspicions about the birds, but Sam and Pepper? I can hardly believe it."

"Believe it," I assured him.

"Ander will want to know about this right away," said Murphy. "I suppose I should go and tell him."

He started to leave, then stopped. "Oh, I almost forgot — it was Yipes who sent me. He said to tell you he was sorry for slamming the door on your head. It made rather a loud noise when it came down, and he ran off into the trees to hide, afraid someone or something might have heard. By the time he came back to check, you were gone. He will be pleased to hear that you're not injured in any way."

Murphy bolted for the window. He was sitting in the sill by the time I had my wretched, sore body up to its knees, leaning over my bed.

"How's the stone looking?" he asked.

"I haven't looked, but we're talking, so I guess it must still be all right."

"Best to keep an eye on it every few hours if you can," said Murphy. He was fidgeting back and forth, looking out the window and then back at me. "It will be a shame to lose you. Maybe we'll get lucky and it won't wear out." And then, with a final flip of his tail, he was gone.

Just as well — I had a busy afternoon planned.

CHAPTER 16

PERVIS RETURNS FROM HOLIDAY

My first encounter with just about everyone occurred in the main dining area. I arrived shortly before dinner, and it was bustling as usual with activity. Servants were bringing out food for the buffet — meats, cheeses, fresh fruits, and vegetables, most imported from Ainsworth and all on gorgeous white china. My father was the first to greet me as I pranced into the room.

"Alexa! How's my girl? We arrived only a few minutes ago." He embraced me, lifted me high off the floor, and whispered in my ear, "Let's have a little talk after dinner."

I gave him a reassuring nod and straightened my shirt when he put me down. "You must go to Turlock more often. It brings out your sentimental side."

Father amply countered, "I'm just happy to be back so I can give you all my washing. I was down to my last clean shirt."

"Poppycock! You missed our little lady as much as I did." It was Ganesh, pulling me close to his side and rubbing my head with the knuckles of his other hand. "Next time, we're taking you with us. Any excitement while we were gone?" Ganesh released me and bent down on one knee so that we were eye to eye.

"I wandered around town looking for trouble, but I couldn't find any, so I read a book about a man who got lost in a mist."

Ganesh laughed and looked over at Grayson. "What kinds of books are you letting into our library these days?" Grayson replied with only a grunt and a shrug of his shoulders.

I made my way to the table of food. It all looked so good, I snatched a plate and filled it with fresh bread, blackberries, and apple slices. Grayson was holed up over the strawberries, plucking them out with a tiny fork one by one and popping them into his mouth.

"I haven't seen you much in your father's absence," he said to me. "Come to think of it, I haven't seen you at all." He looked around the room and then whispered to me. "Let's keep that between you and me, shall we?" He put another strawberry in his mouth and continued to talk while he chewed. "Say, did you stop by the library this morning? I had the strangest encounter with the cats, and someone was about the place but ran off."

"Not me. It must have been one of the students from downstairs playing a prank on you or trying to steal books," I said. I was getting far too comfortable with lying to everyone, and it bothered me. Was there ever a time when lying was a good thing? Without knowing who I should trust and who I shouldn't, I couldn't just blurt out the whole adventure and hope Sebastian wasn't in the room. My father, Ganesh, Grayson, Nicolas, Silas — they were all here, and I could not conceive of any one of them being Sebastian. The only person missing was Pervis.

"Where's my favorite man in uniform, Mr. Kotcher?" I asked.

"Still on holiday in Lunenburg visiting friends. He's due back tonight, though, so don't get too awfully excited," said Nicolas. He was looking as handsome as ever.

"Wait just one minute. You mean Pervis has friends?" I asked.

"Apparently so," chuckled Nicolas. "Absence makes the heart grow fonder and all that. Move it along, Grayson — I'd like at least one strawberry to garnish my plate with."

Grayson just kept on poking berries with his little fork and ignored Nicolas entirely.

We sat around the table and enjoyed a lovely dinner. I ate and ate and ate, my hunger satisfied for the first time in days. My body was much less sore now and my strength edged back to within range of normal.

I was seated next to Silas, who leaned over and whispered in my ear, "I must speak with you privately after dinner."

I nodded my agreement but added, "My father first, then I'm yours."

"A game of chess after dinner, Alexa?" said Silas a few minutes later.

"Sorry, Silas, she's already promised me a stroll around Bridewell. Maybe after that," said Father.

I replied to Silas, "Yes, that would be nice. But I warn you, chess is my game. Father and I started playing when I was only three."

"Well then, maybe you won't mind playing me sometime, now that I'm back from visiting my chums." It was the familiar slippery voice of Pervis Kotcher, coming from the entryway where he had meandered in, unnoticed. His face was smeared with an awful smirk, and he was advancing on the buffet with an annoying saunter. He was clearly drunk. "That is, if you're willing to *wager*. I play chess only when something of value is at stake. I find it adds a whole new dimension to an otherwise boring diversion." He was piling meat and potatoes enough for a family of four onto his plate.

"But enough about a silly game," he continued. "On to more important topics, shall we? Say, for instance, the attitude over in Ainsworth toward Bridewell these days. Getting a bit hot under the collar around those parts now, aren't they?" Pervis seated himself opposite my father at the end of the table, swaying to and fro, using his fork to poke and stab as he continued his tirade.

Ganesh interjected, "Pervis, we're in mixed company. I'm warning you —"

"Warning me to *what*? To keep my mouth shut about the discord you and the rest of the idiots running this place have caused with Ainsworth? All of Lunenburg is talking about it! The people in Ainsworth are ready to run this place over, and they've got plenty of manpower to do it."

"Pervis!" shouted my father, but he would not be stopped.

"I could give Ainsworth the keys to our beloved Bridewell with what I know, so you might start treating me with a little more respect."

Ganesh rose, standing over Pervis like a giant oak tree over a craning woodchuck. "That's it, Pervis. You just crossed over the line to a place from which you will never return." Six guards rounded the corner and positioned themselves inside the room; two remained at either side of him.

"Hold on now, I was just running off at the mouth — really now, this is ridiculous. I can help you defend this place — really I can, I —" Two guards lifted Pervis out of his chair against his will. He kicked and screamed obscenities, flipping his plate of food into the air. Around and around the plate went, sending food everywhere, then smashing into bits against a stone pitcher of water on the table.

"Take him to a holding cell and search his room," Father said. It appeared that Pervis had pushed things too far, but somehow the whole scene seemed wrong. Pervis

150

certainly was out of line, but he wasn't anything more than a drunken buffoon returning from holiday. While it was true his behavior was beneath even him, he was hardly a threat in his current condition. Maybe Ganesh and Father had finally become so tired of his ranting they couldn't take another outburst. One thing was for sure — the animals were right. Warvold's death had sent things rapidly spinning out of control. A cyclone was building, and Bridewell was at its center.

After Pervis's crazed dinner antics, I was ready to walk around town with my father and breathe some fresh air, although, strangely enough, I felt a measure of discontent knowing our head guard was drunk and detained while danger swirled around Bridewell. If the convicts were to advance tonight, I'd want Pervis sober and at the main tower barking orders to his men. Unless, of course, he was Sebastian, in which case things were going rather well.

"What was that all about?" I started the conversation as we paced the cobblestone pathway along one of Bridewell's winding side streets.

"We've been talking about locking him up for a while now, Alexa. Ever since Warvold died, he's been *totally* impossible. We all thought — I mean Ganesh and Nicolas and I — we thought a few days away would calm him down. But showing up drunk and filling the room with all that rubbish was the last straw. We'll have to find a way to get by without him."

"You'll get no argument from me about Pervis, though I do worry about our safety with our head guard behind bars. Especially if what he said was true." The one man I loathed more than any other . . . and I was practically advocating his release! It was strange how circumstances were having a way of changing the way I felt about people.

"He's just trying to stir up trouble. I can't tell you much about our dealings with Ainsworth. True, things have been somewhat tense with them. With Warvold passing, they've tried to assert more control. But it's nothing we can't handle." Father sounded confident that everything was fine, but given what I knew, it was not comfort I was feeling. I knew problems were afoot, bigger problems than even he was aware of.

"So you stayed out of trouble while I was gone? No trying to jump over the wall?"

Trust no one. But this was my father, how could I not trust him?

"I stayed out of trouble like you asked," I said. "But now that you've returned, I really must get back to breaking things. I have a reputation to protect."

Father stopped walking and smiled while he rubbed his chin. He seemed exhausted from worry and lack of sleep. I felt sorry for him just then, which was something I had never felt for him before.

"Just be careful, all right? And don't go snooping around where you know you shouldn't. Agreed?"

"I'll do my best." It was not the answer he was looking for, but he accepted it. We held hands a moment longer and then he returned to the lodge.

I walked to the center of town where the main courtyard was. Along the way, I passed three hawks. They were circling closer than usual. Could it be that Ander had sent them to watch over? Or were they on patrol for Sebastian? In either case, it seemed unlikely that the birds could communicate much with either party, so they didn't alarm me a great deal. Silas awaited my arrival as promised and wasted no time getting straight to the point.

"Alexa, thank you for coming," he said. He was nervous, edgy, unsure of how to approach the subject he was trying to delve into. "Here's the thing, Alexa — I've been working for your father for a little while now. I admire the man — Ganesh and Nicolas, too. I think they will do great things for us all. The thing is, Alexa, I don't want to get you into any trouble with your father, but I feel I have an obligation to him." He was *really* nervous, looking down and around in circles, hardly catching my eye.

"What is it, Silas?" I asked.

He looked up at me with his deep brown eyes, a frown on his face, clearly having trouble forming the words he needed to. "I saw your mother yesterday morning when I was delivering mail in Lathbury, and I picked up a letter for you. I knew how much you wanted to hear from her, so I was excited to find you as soon as I could. I looked everywhere. I even asked Grayson, but he just shrugged me off and said you were probably spying around the lodge somewhere. I called your name all over the lodge and walked down nearly every street in town, but I couldn't find you. I was planning to tell your father I thought you were missing when he returned, but I checked your room this morning and there you were, sound asleep." He paused, advanced to a bench, and sat down. "Naturally, I'm wondering where you were."

Silas was a kind person, and I liked him very much. He was what you might call simple, but not stupid simple. He liked easy answers to life's complications, and he was unaccustomed to confrontation in any form. These things were clear from my brief encounters with him, and I thought humor was my best chance to give him an answer he could live with.

"I travel alone in secret, for I am Alexa, the spy of Bridewell!" I proclaimed in my best comic voice, but he didn't laugh. Instead he glared at me, and I began to feel uneasy about his motives. I tried my next tactic. "It might be hard to understand, but Grayson and I have an unwritten rule when my father travels and I'm stuck in Bridewell. He pretends to watch over me, and I play spy as much as I want. It's a game, you see? I thought Grayson sent you to flush me out. He's used that trick before, but obviously not this time. Sorry to have worried you."

Silas looked relieved. "Next time I call for you and

you hear me, do me a favor and assume I'm not playing a game."

"It's a deal. And I really am sorry," I said. I hated lying to everyone, and I think the extra apology was more for me than Silas. I knew the day was coming when all my lies would be revealed, and each time I told one I felt worse.

We talked a spell longer and then Silas got up and started to leave. "Oh, I almost forgot," he said, reaching into his breast pocket. "Here's that letter from your mother." He handed it to me and walked off, the lightness of his step clearly showing the weight of the world lifted off his shoulders.

I sat thinking a moment longer, twirling the unopened letter with my fingers. I thought back on everything that had just happened, and I couldn't help but feel that Pervis's imprisonment had been too sudden — and perhaps even wrong. I was surprised by this thought, and by my next thought, too:

I had to go see him.

CHAPTER 17

THE CHESS MATCH

The emotional distraction I expected my mother's letter to create forced me to shove it into my back pocket unread. I started off in the direction of Renny Lodge, intent on visiting Pervis, but completely unsure of how such a meeting would go. I stopped in one of the classrooms and grabbed a wooden chessboard and a leather bag of matching pieces.

The holding cells were in an area of Renny Lodge that was dark and uninviting. There was one advantage, though, which I found refreshing just now — it was belowground, in the basement, and thus cool. Even as dusk approached in Bridewell, the soggy air belowground was a welcome change from the dusty, dry air above. It reminded me of how it felt to be in the tunnels, which in turn reminded me of Yipes, Darius, and the rest. I found myself missing them.

Turning the corner at the last step, I held back and reviewed the scene. Two guards were present, one at the door into the cellblock, the other at a desk, busy with reports of one kind or another. I recognized the man at the desk, but not the other.

"Hello, Mr. Martin. It's been a while since you've had any business down here. How's our guest doing?" I said.

"Alexa, what are you doing here? This is no place for you to be roaming around. You should go exploring somewhere else, especially given the cargo this place is holding," said Mr. Martin. The man at the door stood motionless and said nothing.

"Has he sobered up yet?" I asked. The man guarding the door smirked and let out a small laugh.

"Let's just say he's been spending a lot of time with his face in a bucket," said the guard.

"Can I see him? He enjoys playing chess, and I thought a game might take his mind off his troubles."

"Now why would you want to make Mr. Kotcher feel better? Everyone knows you two hate each other," said Mr. Martin.

"I know he's a brute, I just —"

"Hold it right there," Mr. Martin interrupted. He was offended, out of his chair and leaning against his desk with both hands in front of him. "We work for him, so as you can imagine we've got mixed feelings about the current state of affairs. A lot of people think he's difficult to deal with, and he surely can be. But he's got his good points, too, not the least of which is an everlasting love for Bridewell and all it stands for. If we lose him we lose a measure of security, especially if he leaves and stirs up trouble in Ainsworth. Just you remember that when your father runs him out of town."

"I'm sorry, Mr. Martin. I'll try to choose my words more carefully in the future."

157

"You sound more like a politician every day," said Mr. Martin.

"So, can I go in and see him? I promise not to do anything stupid," I said.

Mr. Martin rolled his eyes. "Oh, *all right*. But behave yourself — if you only desire to cause him more misery, I won't hesitate to report you to your father."

"Yes, sir."

"Step aside, Raymond. Let her through."

The guard opened the door and cool air escaped out into the hallway. It had the subtle sweet smell of vomit hanging over it, just enough to make me gag for a brief moment. Upon entering the cellblock, the guard slammed the door shut behind me.

The cellblock contained four rooms with rows of bars, two rooms on each side. There were hard floors, bunks, and nothing on the cold stone walls. The two cells in the rear had small windows high up on the farthest wall back, which let in a faint mist of light. The windows were only about a foot in diameter and had bars running across them.

I heard soft moaning from one of the back cells. A three-legged stool sat next to the doorway and I picked it up. With some difficulty I held the stool, the chessboard, and the bag of chess pieces, and I made my way slowly to the back of the cellblock. Three of the cells were empty; the fourth, on my right in the back, held Pervis Kotcher. He looked dreadful.

At first he did not see me. He was rocking back and forth, sitting on the edge of a cot facing the back wall, staring down into a bucket that was surely full of something unspeakably gross. I dropped the three-legged stool with a bang and began setting up the chessboard a few inches away from the bars to the cell.

The sound of the stool hitting the stone floor had an interesting effect. Pervis attempted to turn around quickly with an impaired wrenching of his neck. It was clear that the sudden jerk of his head sent unearthly pain shooting through his skull. In the next moment, he was on the floor holding his head, writhing in pain, and muttering something about "that dim-witted girl." Then, as quick as a rabbit, he was back on his knees, holding the bucket, making a sickening, echoey noise. The quick rise from floor to knees had clearly given him a jolting head rush, and no sooner was he finished with his work at the bucket than he was flat on his back again, moaning quietly.

"Hi, Pervis, how are you doing?" I said, not meaning to be sarcastic, but realizing it sounded that way as soon as I'd said it.

He continued moaning for a few seconds more, then turned toward me and rolled his eyes open. "Whatever it is that you want, please come back for it later. I've no patience for dealing with you today."

"Actually, I thought you might like some company. I brought a chessboard. Want to play?" I said this in my most exuberant voice, undoubtedly irritating Pervis even more.

Pervis opened his mouth and started to curse at me, and then he seemed to think twice about the idea. He closed his eyes, slowly rose on one elbow, and winced in pain. With his right hand he grabbed the bucket and slid it along the floor with a screech, producing an awful slushy sound from the contents. He spat into the bucket, and then began the slow process of dragging his body off the bed and along the floor. First the arm pushing the bucket forward, and then pulling the rest of his body behind him. Inch by grinding inch Pervis made his way over to the bars while I set up the game. When he finally arrived, he slowly moved to a seated position, hurled a mighty discharge into the bucket, and inquired calmly, "What shall we wager?"

Sitting on the stool, I had a bird's-eye view of the contents of the bucket, so I retreated to the clammy dirt floor and crossed my legs. For a twelve-year-old I was a marvelous chess player. It was a game that came naturally to me. Pervis would not be the first adult I'd made haste of with little or no effort.

"Funny you should ask — I was just wondering the same thing," I said. "If I win, I get to ask you five questions that you must answer honestly, on your honor. If you win, I'll do the same for you."

With some effort, Pervis replied, "What could you possibly know that I would care about?"

I stared at him long and hard.

"A lot," I said.

At some level he seemed to believe me, and a typical Pervis Kotcher smirk crept onto his face. He was looking a measure better, though it might have just been an act to rattle me.

"All right, then, you've got yourself a game. On your honor, five questions, answered honestly," he said.

"Deal."

There wasn't much about Pervis I trusted — close to nothing actually. He was a shameless opportunist, a shifty-eyed leader to his men, and probably the lousiest drunk I'd ever laid eyes on. But it was known around Bridewell Common that people, even bad people, never wavered from telling the truth once they gave their word. It was this knowledge that made my lying so difficult, even if the lies were intended for good. I believed Pervis would tell me the truth if I got the chance to ask him five questions, because that was just the way of things around these parts. In any case, it was a risk I was willing to take.

"White first. That would be you," I said.

Pervis moved his pawn to g4, a typically meaningless first move for an amateur. This was going to be easier than I thought.

I moved my pawn to b6, playing a waiting game to sniff out his next move. Now the board looked like this, with me at black and Pervis at white:

161

One of my useful tactics was to distract my opponent with offhand remarks or questions.

"I've never seen you drunk before. Why the sudden downward spiral?"

"Sorry, no honest answers — and no talking — until you beat me," Pervis said. Okay, so he was focused, unwilling to partake of my little distractions. Fine, I'll just finish him off faster that way.

The next three moves put me in a good position to start taking pieces with my bishop and my kingside knight, and I was beginning to understand his tactics, however juvenile they might be. Now the board looked like this:

From the look of it, Pervis had no plan of attack. He
was simply countering my moves while he waited for me
to reveal a power piece (something I never did early). Unfortunately for Pervis, this strategy was leaving his king
wide-open for attack with no protection from the center.
Yes, this was definitely starting to shape up nicely. At this
point in the game we had each moved five times. I gave
myself a personal challenge to finish him off in fewer
than twenty moves.

Pervis took my pawn at d5. I countered by taking his
pawn with mine at d5, followed by Pervis taking my
pawn at d5 with his knight from c3. Two moves later,
Pervis moved his queen to e2, directly in front of his

king. That was odd. He was trying to create a situation where my king would be pinned down by my own pieces. Slightly flustered, I moved my knight to e7.

Pervis moved his knight to f6, leaving the board looking like this:

"Checkmate," said Pervis, which he followed by hacking a big gob of phlegm into the bucket.

"You tricked me. You played dumb and I fell for it." I was in a state of disbelief, and I was angry. He'd beaten me in only nine moves. That hadn't happened since I was seven years old.

"I'll go you double or nothing. Ten questions!" I said.

"No, thank you. I'll take what I've won and cash out

if you don't mind." He shuffled back to the cot, dragging that disgusting bucket as he went. After a monumental effort, he was laying flat on the cot, head on the dirty old pillow that had probably been a fixture of this cell for as long as Renny Lodge had been standing.

"Good old Grob, works every time against over-confident players," said Pervis, a new air of satisfaction in his voice.

"What's a Grob? Are you telling me you cheated?" I said.

"No, cheating would have been much harder than the Grob," said Pervis. He was back up on one elbow, look-ing as if he were past the peak of his incapacitation.

He continued, "The Grob opening begins with an ugly-looking pawn to g4. Many players would not dream of making such a revolting first move in a serious game of chess. It wrecks the kingside pawn structure with an un-protected advanced flank. But, as you have seen, it offers many tactical shots along unusual opening lines. I began playing the Grob as an opportunity to exercise my tacti-cal skills, but found that a lot of my stronger opponents in Lunenburg would fall for it over and over again."

I had badly misjudged Pervis in regard to his chess-playing skills.

"The Grob," he went on, "is an excellent surprise weapon against good players who know and expect all the common openings. I played a Grob blitz against one A-class player at the Lunenburg Chess Club. I won the game in a few moves. Appalled, he demanded that I play the ugly opening again. I did, and I won again. This cycle continued for five games. The Grob won each game to the horror of my stunned opponent." Pervis struggled into a sitting position, obviously encouraged by the sheer enjoyment of beating me so badly. Strangely enough, I had a new respect for him. He was clearly intelligent and very good at a game that takes cunning and skill to be great at.

"Let's see, first question needs to be a real eye-opener, something to set the tone, don't you think?" he said. He rubbed the weak stubble on his nearly nonexistent chin, spat into the bucket, which was now sitting between his legs on the floor, and looked up at me with a big grin on his face.

"Ever kissed a boy before?"

I looked at him with total disrespect.

"I'm twelve years old, Pervis. *Of course* I've kissed a boy before." I said this with an air of indignation, even though it wasn't true.

"Like I said before," said Pervis, a little flushed, "I can't imagine you knowing anything I don't already know that I'd want to know."

He ran his hands through his unwashed hair and rubbed the back of his neck. Then he looked up at me.

"All right, I've got one," he said. I braced myself for whatever sick idea he could come up with. I imagined he might ask me if I'd ever eaten my boogers, sucked on my big toe, or sniffed my armpits — all of which I had done.

"That night when Warvold died, you were out there a long time. On your honor, now, tell me what happened out there for real."

I thought seriously about lying, but something stopped me. I don't suppose it was any honorable streak I could claim. Something else altogether prompted me to tell the truth. Maybe it was the first signs of desperation from everything swirling out of control around me.

"He died," I began. "He was dead awhile before I noticed. I was upset about sitting in the dark with his lifeless body, but I pulled myself together. Not long after I figured out he was dead I ran back to Renny Lodge, but not before I opened his amulet and took the silver key that was inside."

"I knew it! I knew you were lying about that night!"

"I never lied — I just omitted certain facts. I'm only telling you this because I need your help, because for some reason I either trust you or think you're too dense to be the person I'm looking for," I countered.

"What are you talking about — 'person you're looking for.' What's that supposed to mean?"

"Is that one of your questions?" I asked.

Pervis bit his lip and took a moment to answer. "Yes, it's one of my questions," he finally said.

"In that case, I'm looking for a man named Sebastian."

"Who's Sebastian?" Pervis was clearly confused beyond all hope. He was either a gifted actor even after a long night of drinking, or he was quickly becoming someone I might be able to trust based on his apparent lack of knowledge.

"How about that one — is that one of your questions?" I asked.

"No, no — wait, that's not my question."

After a moment of awkward hesitation, he said sheepishly, "Okay, yes, it is my question."

"Sebastian is, as far as I can tell, an escaped convict posing as a citizen of Bridewell," I said matter-of-factly.

After a moment of reflection on what I'd said, Pervis asked, "So you think this is a game, coming down here and making up stories to torment me, is that it?"

"Would that be your final question?" I said.

"No! And quit doing that!" He was yelling now, having a hard time keeping control of himself. I was glad for the bars, seeing as it was unclear what Pervis might do if he could get ahold of me.

"Everything all right in here?" It was the guard from outside, with his head all the way in the room from where he'd opened the entrance about a foot.

"Everything is fine, sir. Pervis is just upset I beat him at chess. Can I have a few more minutes, please?"

"Only a little longer. We've got to move him and

168

clean out that cell," said the guard, closing the door with a sour look on his face.

Pervis was thinking hard, trying to log all the possible questions he could ask, trying to figure out if I was telling the truth or just trying to drive him crazy. I think the drinking had hurt his mental processing power quite a bit, because he sat there mumbling and thinking for a long time. After a while he pushed the bucket out of the way with his foot and looked up at me.

"If what you're saying is true, then I want you to listen carefully. You may not like me much, and to be perfectly honest, I have never thought much of you. You're small, clever, and spirited, which is exactly what I was when I was your age." With an irritated look on his face, he paused, held his stomach, and let out a ferocious, gurgling belch.

"Do you know what happens to a tiny, energetic child who has no money, no promise, and no important associations?" he continued, wiping his mouth with a forearm. "He gets beaten. First by a drunken father, then, living on the street, by bigger children. And at some point it's just life itself that starts kicking that child around. Pretty soon he turns bitter, angry, willing to do anything to gain respect. And who do you think that child, when he grows up, hates more than anyone else? Of course it's the same youngster who he was, only this one's got the money, the powerful parents, all the opportunity in the world. This one gets it handed to her on a plate. That's a lot for a man to overcome."

Pervis got up and walked over to the bars, putting both hands on them to hold his weary body up.

"This place is peaceful when you're not around, Alexa. Every summer it gets a little harder, and I get a little angrier. Maybe I'm simply unwilling to see anything good in you. The fact is, I haven't had a holiday in twenty years, and it has been longer still since I've been drunk. The thought of coming back here to face another three weeks with you and the rest of them in Bridewell was more than I could take." He slipped down, and for a terrible moment I thought he would crash to the ground unconscious. He caught himself halfway to the floor and struggled back up, leaning heavily on the bars for support.

He continued, evidently about to pass out. "If what you say is true, then understand this, Alexa: I can protect this place better than anyone. I've put my whole life into it, and I'm telling you, I'm your man. So if you're interested and you're telling the truth, here's my last question —

"Can you get me out of here?"

"I don't know," I said, and then I told Pervis Kotcher everything.

CHAPTER 18

A NIGHT ERRAND IN THE LIBRARY

After leaving the cellblock, I went to my room. Night had fallen on Bridewell while I was talking with Pervis, and a full moon was on the rise. I pulled my Jocasta out of its leather pouch. It was beating like a tiny emerald heart — the same as the last time I had checked it. I was anxious to speak with the animals. I wondered if it would wear out faster if I didn't talk to them for a while. Were there any animals around here besides those traitorous cats?

"I think you were right to trust Pervis." It was a voice from the window.

"Murphy!" I yelled.

"Yes, ma'am, back with news from the forest," he said, flipping down off the sill, across the floor, and onto my lap like a hairball on a windy day.

"How did you know about Pervis?" I said.

"I was there the whole time, watching through the little window. You deserve an award for staying down there as long as you did. The smell coming up from that place made me run gagging for fresh air more than once."

"You're a regular guardian angel, aren't you, Murphy?"

"Actually, that would be Yipes. He's the one who

keeps sending me to watch out for you. He remains concerned for your safety."

"How is he?"

"Doing fine, and he's a lot closer than you might think, hanging in the shadows near the wall. We have a chain of communication that starts with me, goes through Yipes, then Darius, Malcolm, some of the others in the forest that you met, and finally to Ander and the council. Then the messages come back up the line to Yipes, me, and now you." Murphy's tail was twitching back and forth. He darted off to the door with a listening ear, then back to the windowsill, and finally over to the bathroom that separated my father's room from mine. Within a few seconds he was back on my lap.

"I have word from Ander," he said. "He was surprised about Sam and Pepper, but as they are domesticated, he understood how it could happen. After all, they depend on humans for food and water. As to the hawks, Ander thinks the one you saw might be an isolated case, and that the rest of the hawks are still with us. He asked if you knew of anyone in Bridewell who might keep such an animal as a pet."

I thought about everyone I knew who might keep a hawk in Bridewell. But I could think of no one. Other than Yipes, I had never known of anyone keeping a hawk as a pet, let alone anyone around these parts.

"I'm sorry, Murphy, I don't know of anyone with a pet like that. Did Ander say anything else?"

"Only one thing: 'We're running out of time, so get on with it.' Those are his words, not mine. I for one think you're doing a splendid job. Though I will admit, it does seem to be going a bit slow, don't you think?"

"I have an idea that might help get things moving along, but I'll need your help," I said.

"Absolutely! Pleased to help any way I can."

I spent the next few minutes filling him in on the details of my plan, and then we started for the library. The first order of business would be getting inside the locked doors. A few years back, a small cat door was added on the wall just left of the double-door entryway. No human could fit through the opening with its hinged wood flap, but Murphy would have no trouble navigating what for him would be a wide berth.

It was only around ten o'clock, so people were still milling around Renny Lodge. The smoking room had its usual collection of late-night attendants, and I could hear the cooks cleaning the kitchen and preparing things for the next morning. Murphy slinked alongside of me down the stairs, looking every which way, his slight feet making a quiet mist of noise like small pebbles dropped onto sand. An occasional creak on a step from my comparatively ample weight was the only noticeable sound the two of us made until we reached the double doors.

I whispered, "There's the cat door. Remember, no noise. Turn the latch on the door slowly or it will make a loud pop when it comes open."

Murphy said nothing as he sized up the cat door. With his diminutive front foot, he pushed the wood flap slightly, then let it swing back. No rubbing on the edges, no squeaky hinges, it swung free and silent. He placed his head against the flap and made his way through the space, letting the flap down slowly from the other side with his long tail. I hardly noticed a sound as he leaped to the knob, balanced on his hind legs, and slowly turned the latch. It made an audible click as it came unlocked, like the sound of a peanut shell cracking open between a thumb and knuckle.

I had told Murphy not to jump down off the knob because I thought the sound of his thud on the floor might wake the cats. He would be waiting patiently, balanced on the other side of the door. I turned the knob slowly, and I could hear the tiny mechanisms inside quietly move around. I could not see Murphy, but I imagined he looked a lot like a circus clown rolling around on a big round ball, quick feet doing small hops as the knob turned and turned under him.

Finally the door swung free and I reached my hand around and grabbed Murphy by his surprisingly bony midsection. He was thinner than I had thought under all that fur, certainly no match for either Sam or Pepper, let alone both of them at one time. I set him down on the floor and carefully closed the door behind me.

The library was on the third level, and it had wood flooring. Creaking as I walked was likely to be a problem, so it was up to Murphy to do the hunting. He was light enough not to make a sound while he padded about the aisles to find what we had come for. It would be my job to patiently sit and wait while Murphy found Pepper — hopefully sleeping — and cut off the medallion around his neck. This would be no small feat. The medallion dangled from a thick leather collar attached by a solid gold ring. His only chance would be to cut the leather collar and slide the ring off, then run for the cat door with the ring and the medallion between his teeth, two screeching and clawing cats chasing him all the way. It would have to be a quick operation — *cut, grab, run.* It was the only way.

I signaled Murphy and he nodded and started away from me in the direction of Grayson's office. It was darker in the library than I had expected, and I lost Murphy in the shadows almost immediately. Seconds turned into minutes as I waited. Finally, Murphy returned with news.

I lifted him to my ear. "I found them both curled together in the chair," he whispered. "No sign of any hawks outside the window. With the light it's hard to tell which is which. I know Pepper is darker, but other than that, they're a close match."

"I don't know of any other markings," I whispered back. "If you're not sure, just take the one you can cut off the easiest and get out fast."

I set Murphy down and reached into my pocket to

find the tool I'd fashioned for him. It was a small block of wood. With some effort, I had snapped off the smallest blade on my pocketknife, carved out a slit in the block, and jammed the butt of the small blade into the wood. I took the makeshift leather cutter and placed the wood block into Murphy's mouth. He bit down hard, and I ran my shirt against the sharp edge of the blade as he pushed his head up. It ripped cleanly through.

"If you don't have a clear shot at the medallion, keep the blade in your mouth. It will be your only defense against them," I whispered. Then Murphy turned and was gone, swallowed by the black night of the library. I was immediately sorry I had sent him.

Minutes passed. I heard voices in the distance, the echo of laughter, a clang of a pot or a pan being placed in a sink. Water running. And then I heard an unearthly screech from one of the cats, a sound I could not translate into words. I was terrified for Murphy and I thought my capacity to understand animals had already begun to fade. Without thought I grabbed for the leather pouch around my neck with the stone inside and clutched it tightly.

And then the voices returned. "Stop him! He has the medallion! Kill him!"

It was time for me to move. I opened the door and returned to the hallway. I closed the door firmly behind me, and lifted the flap to the cat door in my direction. All the while I heard a mix of screeching and words and claws on wood. I got down on all fours and placed my head on the floor so I could look through the small opening. There was still no sign of Murphy in the dark.

The sounds were much closer now: "*Mrrrrooooeeew*!! Don't let it get away!"

A moment later I had to move out of the way as a blast of sliding fur came shooting through the door. It was Murphy, gold ring between his teeth, the medallion dangling below. As soon as he was through, I dropped the swinging door and sat down right in front of it. Murphy tried to stop but continued to slide on the waxed floor. He hit the wall opposite the library with a thud; the gold ring released from his teeth and flew into the air, landing with a loud clang between the two of us. The lead cat in the chase came crashing into the door behind me. The second landed on top of him and screamed from inside the library. It was Sam, yelling, "Get away from the door! Who are you? Return the medallion!" and other nasty remarks that billowed through the air.

Murphy came to as loud footsteps started from the staircase below.

"Oh, no," I whispered. "Murphy! Get up, Murphy!" Holding the flap down with one hand I took my knife out of my pocket with the other and opened the largest blade with my teeth. The cats were clawing and pushing against the flap, screeching all the while. I pushed the flap as hard as I could and sent them flipping backward into the air. With one hard thrust, I slammed my knife into the jamb

177

of the little opening. The flap swung down and stopped hard against the blade, locking the cats in for the night.

The approaching footsteps were almost right on top of us. I darted across the floor, grabbed the medallion, and whisked Murphy into my arms, then I tossed Murphy down the hall toward my room, where he hit with a thud. I turned and faced the approaching footsteps coming around the corner.

It was Althia, one of the cooks, and she was holding a saucepan in one hand looking as though she might hit me over the head with it.

"Alexa!" she shouted. "What on earth are you doing out here at this hour making such a racket? You scared me half to death."

"I'm sorry, Althia, really I am." I needed to get her back to the kitchen so I could attend to Murphy, but the cats were still wailing and clawing at the door trying to get out.

"The cats were making this awful noise so I came down to see what all the fuss was about," I said. "I think Grayson has them locked in for the night and they want to get out. I'll tell him in the morning to check the cat door. It seems to be blocked — probably a stack of old books or something."

I stood between Althia and the cat door in the dim light of the hallway and she seemed to believe me.

"I'm just glad it was only you," she said with some relief. "I'm going back to my soufflé before it falls to pieces. You best get back to your room."

She wandered down the stairs muttering about the cats and waving her saucepan to and fro.

I stood dazed in the hallway for a moment, shaking my head and replaying the scene in my mind, hoping Althia wouldn't return with more questions. I quickly advanced down the creaking hall to find Murphy and get back to my room. To my horror, he remained unconscious, breathing uneasily, blood oozing slowly from a wicked scratch across the front of his head. I carefully picked him up and went to my room, cursing myself for sending him into the library with those awful cats.

CHAPTER 19

MY MOTHER'S LETTER

I went to the bathroom and got a wet washrag. Murphy was lying on my bed, shivering and twitching as if dreams of fighting off maniacal cats were racing through his head. I dabbed his wound and cleaned the fur matted with blood around his eyes and nose. What really bothered me was the considerable bump I found on his forehead. It was either from his crash into the wall after the chase or, heaven forbid, from the impact of being thrown onto the landing.

While Murphy remained quiet I dug into my pocket and removed the medallion and the gold ring. Like the one from Sam's neck, this one had a beautiful pattern etched on its surface. I hoped the Jocasta hidden beneath would grant me some new insight I desperately needed. I lifted the throw rug beneath my bed. Under it was a loose floorboard, which I popped out. In the small space below the floorboard I kept my tools, Warvold's silver key, his favorite book, my mother's broken spyglass, and the printer's glass with its damaged lens.

I removed the printer's glass and covered the hole again with the board and the carpet. When I came back up to the bed, Murphy was sitting up straight, licking one of his paws.

"You're all right!" I placed my hand on his head and petted him gently.

"Couldn't be better. Most excitement I've had since a coyote chased me up a tree a month ago. Quite a good headache, but otherwise, all in one piece," he said.

I was ecstatic to see him up and about. "What happened? Tell me everything," I said.

"Well, let me think — it was dark, hard to get a read on things at first. I decided my best chance was to wrap my hind legs around Pepper's neck and sit on his head all in one quick motion, then cut the collar, grab the gold ring, and hightail it for the door." He was up on his hind legs acting dramatic.

"As soon as I jumped on his head he jerked and jangled all over the place. I was flying around the room so fast it was dumb luck I was able to hold on at all. I cut the collar, which sent the ring and the medallion soaring across the floor and down the hall. Unfortunately, I also gave the cat a sharp poke in the neck, and he jerked his head back so hard it threw me in the air like a rag doll. There was a lot of confusion when I landed, but I was closest to the medallion. I ran across the floor, grabbed the gold ring between my teeth, and bolted for the door with both cats behind me."

"Amazing!" I said. Murphy beamed, the proud aura of mythical battle status hanging all about him. The story needed no embellishment; it was first-class legend all on its own, and I had a feeling Murphy would be telling the story to children and grandchildren for years to come.

"You got the right one, too — the one from Pepper. He was fighting mad when I locked him in the library," I said.

I took the printer's glass and set it against the medallion. What I saw rippled like a kaleidoscope in every direction. The broken glass would make it difficult to read the Jocasta. I pulled back, reviewed the glass, and found the largest unbroken piece. Then I got down on the floor on my knees and pushed the broken lens out of the metal frame. It fell in bits and pieces onto the floor. I took the largest shard of what was left, about a quarter of the whole lens, and sat back up on the bed.

"Do you think it will work?" asked Murphy.

"I think it will, but it may take a while to see everything," I replied.

As it turned out, it was a simple Jocasta — a diagram of three boxes. Two had a line joining them; the third was unattached. The end of the line formed an arrow, which pointed to the third box. It looked like this:

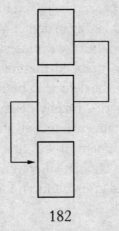

I wrote the diagram down on a piece of paper and cleaned up the glass on the floor. Murphy and I puzzled over the diagram for a few minutes without any idea what it might mean.

Finally, Murphy said, "I'm sorry, Alexa, but I must go report to Yipes. He'll be worried I haven't checked in, and Ander will want an update." He jumped down, ran across the floor, and popped up onto the windowsill. "What do you say I coat our progress with a little honey?"

"Fine by me," I replied. "Though I'm at a dead end as far as I can tell, and I have no idea what to try next. This Jocasta was my big hope, and it was a failure. Sorry I sent you into all that trouble for no reason."

"Not to worry, I enjoyed it immensely. I'm a wartime hero; they'll probably decorate me with medals and give me a parade when this is all over with. What more could a squirrel ask for?"

He darted out the window and I was alone with my thoughts in the deepest part of the night. It was past one in the morning, and I was utterly exhausted. I reclined on the bed and felt a poke in my back pocket. It was my mother's letter, and now was as good a time as any to get the reading of it over with. With some good fortune I thought it might lull me to sleep.

Alexa,

   Thank you for your letter. I miss you and your
father very much, and even a few lines make me
feel closer to you. The daisies are coming up all
over town and the garden is full of tomatoes. I told
your father not to plant so many, but he wouldn't
listen. Now I'm off to the neighbors every three
days giving them away and having them for
breakfast, lunch, and dinner. No matter how
many tomatoes I eat or give away there are always
more the next day. Tell your father I said, "I told
you so."
   I was sorry to hear that you had taken my
spyglass to Bridewell. It's hard to discipline you
from far away, but you can be sure I'll have you
clearing out all the tomato plants from the garden
when you get home. I understand the temptation
was great, but you really must learn to make
better choices. The spyglass was a gift from Renny
Warvold. It's the only thing I have to remember
her by, so it's special to me. Just bring it home
with you and be careful with it. I'll get the lens
fixed and you can work off the expense around
the house.
   How's the weather in Bridewell? I'm sure it's
as hot as ever. The River Roland runs even

higher than usual this year and keeps Lathbury
cool by late afternoon.
  Write again! See you and Father soon.

Love,
Mother

The beautiful, ornate three-piece spyglass. As soon as I learned it was a gift from Renny, I began to understand things in a new light. Maybe the three boxes on Pepper's medallion were the three sections of the spyglass. The images on the first two could equal whatever was on the third. I scrambled off my bed and ran to the window, looking all around for Murphy, hoping I could catch him. But he was already long gone.

I returned to my hiding spot and removed the rug and the wood panel. My hands shaking, I picked up the broken spyglass and returned to my bed. I extended the sections and revealed all the wonderful paisley patterns that adorned the tubes. Every section was like a vibrant forest of color, and finding the Jocastas hidden within seemed an impossible task, especially given that I had only a shard of magnifying glass to work with. I began scanning the large, outer tube with the splinter of glass, and quickly realized that it would take hours just to scan the one part. I was already so tired I could barely keep my eyes open.

I went to the bathroom and listened for my father's steady snoring. It swept into the night, a quaint little snore, not too loud, almost soothing. I took water from the basin and wet my face and neck, hoping the water would revive me. Then I returned to bed and began scanning again.

It was hopeless. At the rate I was going it would take days to find the hidden Jocastas, and I was already bobbing my head as I tried to stay awake; before long I would collapse from exhaustion and wake up with Sam in my face and Sebastian towering over me with a sledgehammer. I pulled back and rubbed my eyes. There had to be another way. It was past two in the morning and I couldn't stay alert for much longer.

I held the spyglass at arm's length and turned it slowly in my hand, looking for a pattern that might join the three tubes together. I placed one hand under the largest tube and one on top of the smallest tube and continued spinning the whole thing around. The three patterns did seem to have a point at which they matched, but they were not lined up between the three sections. I took the top and bottom tubes in hand and, to my surprise, with a fair amount of effort I was able to slowly twist them in opposite directions. When the patterns lined up, the tubes snapped into place and stopped. It had never occurred to me to turn the tubes in this way before.

Now I could see a line of commonly shaped paisley swirls, one on top of the other, each slightly larger than the last, in a row down the three tubes. The color also ran light to dark from the first pattern to the last. At the center of each paisley pattern was a symbol, which looked like a flash of yellow light. I picked up my shard of glass and moved in tight to view the center of the pattern on the first tube. I had found the first of three Jocastas.

It was an image of a man, eyes missing, groping his arm up and out against an invisible object. I immediately recalled the fable Warvold had shared with me on the night of his death about the blind men and the elephant, and I understood the invisible object to be the elephant in Warvold's story.

My heart was racing and I was all at once wide-awake as I moved to the next tube. The Jocasta on this tube depicted a man on his knees, arms raised in worship to an unseen god.

I moved to the last tube, and found an even simpler Jocasta than the one on Pepper's medallion. It was nothing more than a capital letter S.

Elephant + Worship = Sebastian.

I was more confused than ever.

CHAPTER 20

THE MEETING ROOM

Extreme fatigue is an overpowering force. Under the right circumstances it blankets its captive under heavy layers of deep sleep, layers that must be peeled away to reach beneath. As voices and light from the wakeful world pound to get in, they fight against a thick film to wrench the weary back to life.

"Wake up, Alexa. Wake up!" How long had I been out? How long had a squirrel been screaming at me in his squeaky voice? This was all a dream, all of it — the talking animals, the wall, and the rodent doing cartwheels on my chest — all a delightful dream.

The squirrel had his face in mine now, his mouth wide open, revealing a surprisingly stout set of teeth. He bit down softly, then harder, right over my nose, and I was awake.

"Murphy!" I yelled as I jerked up into a sitting position, sending him head over heels off the end of the bed with a harsh thud. The first soft light of morning crept over the wall into the room. I had slept for almost four hours.

Murphy climbed onto the bed looking dazed. "You're getting into a bad habit of tossing me around rooms."

"All in a day's work for a hero," I countered, and then added a profound apology.

"There's trouble, Alexa. The convicts are on the move."

"Then we must hurry." I spent the next few minutes telling Murphy what I had discovered during his absence. Once wound up, it takes a great deal of effort to get him calmed down again, and news of my progress sent Murphy into a fit of enthusiasm. I finally had to grab him by the midsection and hold him in midair to calm him down. After a few seconds, he hung there, limbs dangling, chest heaving up and down.

"Let's not get too excited," I said. "We still don't know Sebastian's real identity, and I fear we've run out of time. I think what we've discovered can still do some good, but I'll need your help to make sure."

I knew he would be willing to go on another errand, and I quickly explained what I needed him to do and sent him on his way. He would be gone for more than an hour. As for me, the sun was coming up and the time had come to talk with my father.

I crept into the bathroom, quietly opened the door to his room, and peeked inside. His room was dark except for the ray of light pouring in from where I stood. The light turned everything a glowing shade of shallow orange. His familiar deep breathing filled the space. I tiptoed to the other side of the bed and crawled over the covers.

It was warm, and I had to overcome the urge to sleep again.

"Father?" I whispered. Then again, only louder, "*Father?*"

He stirred and rolled to his side facing me, smacking his lips and rubbing his eyes. His hair was formed into a high golden arch, which made me laugh out loud. Father opened his eyes.

"Alexa. How nice to see you," he said in a dreamy voice, and then his eyes slowly shut once more. I called his name again and this time he sat up, fully awake.

"Is everything all right?" he asked.

"I'm tired, but yes, I'm fine."

We looked at each other for a long moment.

"I have a lot to tell you," I continued.

"What do you mean?"

I sat up and wrapped the thick blanket from the bed around my shoulders and told my father all the details of the previous few days. Well, almost all the details. Midway through I decided the notion of talking animals was something I would keep a secret. It served no purpose to tell him, and I had grave concerns about how the knowledge might be put to use once word spread in and around Bridewell.

When I was finished, I asked him the question I had been asking myself all morning: "Who do you think Sebastian is?"

He rubbed the stubble on his flushed cheeks and gazed thoughtfully across the room.

"I don't know, but we must share what you've learned with the others," he said. "Get dressed and be in the meeting room in half an hour." He rose from the bed and walked to the bathroom, stretching his arms over his head and lowering them again as he went. I remained motionless, afraid to move, the warm blanket still surrounding me. He splashed water on his face, then turned to me, water dripping from his thick beard. "Get up, Alexa. There's no time to waste." It was an order, not a request.

I crawled out of the big bed and touched my feet on the chilly wooden floor. As I walked past him into my own room, I brushed up against his legs and he knelt down beside me. He placed his giant hands on my shoulders, and I realized something new about my father, something I had never thought of before. If he chose to, he could crush me with those monstrous hands; it would take him almost no effort at all. Instead, as if aware of my new understanding, he pulled me close and hugged me for a long time, my small head in his hand, and he whispered in my ear, "What am I to do with you, my crafty little girl?" And then he released me and returned to his work at the washbasin, running both hands through his golden funnel of hair.

With my bathroom door closed, I dressed and prepared myself for the meeting. I wore my green long-sleeved shirt, a red button-up vest, and a brown armless tunic with a brightly colored hem down the front. I topped it off with my snug leather cap and tucked my hair behind my ears. A short while later I heard the door to my father's room open and close, his footsteps pounding in the hall and down the stairs until I could discern his movements no more. I opened my window and looked all around for Murphy, but an hour into his task he was nowhere to be found.

I picked up my bag and trudged down the hall in the direction of a mysterious room I had never stepped foot in.

One day last summer I had been so bored that I began sneaking around Renny Lodge, hiding under tables and behind couches near the walls. It was a fun diversion on an otherwise dull afternoon, and I found myself enjoying the thrill of pretending to be a spy. I had turned every person in the lodge into an evil character in my plot to find some make-believe hidden treasure. Lost in my own world, I found myself concealed behind a thick purple curtain near the meeting room. To my surprise, the door to this mystifying room opened and Ganesh appeared, followed by Warvold and then my father. I pulled the curtain back a little more and peeked inside as the door began to shut. I saw only a sheet of light streaming in from an enormous window, glaring against silhouettes of objects in the room. As the door creaked closed, a large hand touched my shoulder, locked down, and pulled me from behind the curtain.

"I've told you not to sneak around. It's for your own good, so please obey me." It was Father. The way he'd said it wasn't mean, but it was forceful and stern. He wandered off toward the kitchen then and left me with my heart racing. I had never since gone near that room.

And here I was, being invited into that very place only a year later, a shiver trembling through my body as I stood at the closed door. I looked to my left and saw the heavy velvet curtain hanging in a bunch against the wall. Then I grabbed the handle, opened the door, and went inside.

The meeting room was brisk and humorless with dark tile flooring and shadowy walls with nothing on them. Inkwells and worn old pens adorned two long facing tables in the middle of the room. Stark terra-cotta water pitchers and cups were placed on the tables along the edges. It was a plain room, a business room, a room without character or charm. I closed the door behind me, leaving only natural light from the imposing window on one side. Morning dust was in the air, golden and swirling in the sunlight, dancing about as people became quiet and moved into their seats behind the tables.

Everyone was present: Silas, Ganesh, Nicolas, Father, Grayson, and even Pervis, chained to a chair, hands in shackles, dutifully overseen from behind by a club-wielding guard.

We moved to our seats, my father with Ganesh on his left and me on his right. Nicolas sat next to me, and across from us at the opposite table were Silas, Grayson, and the shackled Pervis.

The last thing I remember hearing before Father began was the unfortunate sound of Pervis shifting in his wooden chair and moving the chains around his ankles. This produced a chilling clang that echoed off the high ceiling, reminding us all of his grim circumstance.

"Thank you for coming to such an early meeting," Father began. "It means a great deal to me that you would accommodate my desire to talk with you. Assuming Pervis is adequately secured, I must now ask the guard to leave us to our privacy." The guard checked over Pervis to be sure of his handiwork, then made his way toward the door.

"Guard," said my father, "leave me the keys." The guard returned and stood before my father, unhitched the keys from his belt, and placed them on the desk. Then he turned and left the room.

The chamber sufficiently sealed, Father continued.

"As you all know, losing Warvold has been a serious blow to Bridewell. Ainsworth senses our new weakness, and they may take advantage of the situation. More and more people are trying to settle here, and we have nowhere to put them. Our head guard is in shackles, leaving us vulnerable to attack and his soldiers without a leader. And there are other, more sinister plots afoot that we may not even be fully aware of.

"Grayson has been here longer than anyone; he is an old and dear friend. Silas is a new addition to this group, but someone I feel we can trust. Nicolas is new as well, but he is clearly a gifted leader and someone who will no doubt be an important part of our future. My dear friend Ganesh — words cannot express how important you are to Bridewell and what will become of it. I have also invited Alexa to join us this morning. The need for her presence here will become clear in a moment."

He paused and looked at our chained companion. "And Pervis. What will become of you? I fear we have made a mistake in locking you up, but I can't bring myself to set you free."

As Father poured a glass of water from a pitcher on the table, I became aware of a strange movement from the edge of the large facing window. It was small, almost unnoticeable, like a twig caught in a spider's web, dangling on a puff of air. Murphy was back.

His body was hanging outside the sill by one paw, and he was waving with his other paw to get my attention. He kept waving and waving. Then the little leg shot out of sight and I heard a faint *flit* as he lost his grip and scraped along the outer wall.

"Father, may I stand at the window for some fresh air? The dust is a bit thick," I said. He nodded and continued talking.

"A week ago Alexa discovered a way outside the wall, and she just completed two days in the mountains and the forest before returning here yesterday."

A collective gasp filled the room.

"Have you lost your mind? She could have been killed

195

out there!" Ganesh cried. Grayson looked as though he would rather have been under the table where no one could see him, and poor Silas stared at me as if my lies had broken his heart.

While the group asked questions of my father, I arrived at the window, placed my back against the wall, and felt blindly along the edge for a furry mass. Murphy was gone, but he had left me a gift on the flat of the stone sill. I picked it up.

"Listen to me," Father said with a raised voice, and the room grew quiet again. "Alexa did this on her own accord without my knowledge or permission. But I think we will all be thanking her before this meeting is over." He shot an accusing look at Grayson, who sat slack-jawed and gazing across the room.

"While Alexa was outside the wall she discovered a narrow tunnel that led to a position from which she could see an underground chamber," Father continued. "The chamber is part of a labyrinth of underground tunnels created from the mining effort to build our walls. The tunnels and chambers wind all around The Dark Hills and even directly under Bridewell itself. A group of people, people with Cs branded on their faces, live within these tunnels."

"Why, that's preposterous!" yelled Nicolas. "Do you realize what that would mean?"

Everyone else sat motionless, some with mouths hanging open, calculating the implications of such a fact.

I was back in my seat, and my father nodded to me. I removed a wooden tube from my bag and handed it to him.

"I'm afraid it's true," he said. "I have a map here that shows the layout of all the tunnels and chambers. Another collection of tunnels resides aboveground covered by thick brush, which is how these criminals maneuver without detection, scrounging for food and water.

"These men are angry, and for years they have been plotting to enter Bridewell and take it over. They could attack the city as early as tomorrow night, and we are inadequately prepared to deal with such an attack."

"This can't be possible," said Ganesh. "We sent those prisoners back. Warvold escorted them all the way to Ainsworth. I tell you this *cannot* be possible!"

"I'm sorry, Ganesh, but as much as I wish none of this were true, I don't think Alexa is making these things up. Please, just let me finish. I have more I need to tell you, and then you can ask all the questions you want." Everyone went momentarily quiet and still. The faces across from me expressed shock and confusion.

"Warvold was a mysterious man, and his wife, Renny, was maybe even a little more baffling than he was. As you know from our conversations with Nicolas, she was fond of a certain kind of artwork called a Jocasta. She was kind enough to leave these veiled treasures hidden all around us, and Alexa has used them to help solve a puzzle I think both Renny and Warvold wanted us to figure out after they were gone. We have to face the fact that

197

Warvold's death set in motion the end of Bridewell as we know it. What that means is still a mystery, but one thing is certain — we're not all on the same side in the battles that will soon be waged."

I pulled a piece of paper from my pack and handed it to Father. "This is a drawing of a Jocasta Alexa found hidden within a medallion on one of the library cats' collars. For those of you who may not know, those cats used to belong to Renny Warvold. As you can see from Alexa's drawing, the image shows three boxes, two connected, that when joined together clearly equal the third." I pulled the spyglass out of my pack, extended the three sections, and handed it to my father.

"The three boxes on the Jocasta represent the three sections of this spyglass, which was given to my wife as a gift from Renny Warvold. Each of the three sections on this spyglass contains another Jocasta, and it is within these that an important message is revealed."

My father pointed his finger to the first tube in the spyglass. "The Jocasta on the first section depicts a man groping at an object above and to his side." Pointing to the second tube, he continued, "The Jocasta on the second section reveals a human figure, kneeling with arms raised, praying to an unseen god. And here, on the third section, the Jocasta is nothing more than a simple letter S."

My father paused and looked around the room at the confused faces staring back at him.

"Fascinating," said Nicolas. "The convicts, the labyrinth of spooky tunnels, the messages all hooked together through my mother's art projects. It's a bit far-fetched, to say the least. Nonetheless, your daughter spins a mighty good tale, and I can't help but want to hear the outcome."

Without further comment, and with the reassurance of a nod from Grayson and Silas, Father went on with what I had shared with him earlier that same morning.

"On the night when Warvold died, he told Alexa a story. It was about six blind men who all felt an elephant and thought it was something different because of the part they were touching. One touched the tail, another the side, yet another the head, and so on. Thus the depiction in the first Jocasta stands for an elephant. The symbol on the second Jocasta is self-explanatory — it represents the worship of some unknown god. The letter S on the final section might have held no meaning to Alexa had it not been for her encounter with the convicts."

It was here that my father motioned me to rise and speak, and I lied to protect the animals. "According to two convicts I watched and listened to in the underground chamber, there is a traitor living among us," I said. "This man is their leader and goes by the secret name Sebastian, thus the letter S."

A burst of gasps again filled the room, not the least of which was from Ganesh, as he looked at me with horror on his face.

"You've gone too far now, Daley. Stop with this nonsense!" he shouted.

"Really, you two, this is too much," said Grayson.

There was a mixture of mumbling around the room, and then a voice was heard that no one expected.

"I personally helped escort the convicts to Ainsworth." It was Pervis, his head down, facing the floor.

He looked up then, and surveyed the room from side to side. "Only thing is, Warvold stayed in Ainsworth for several days after my guards and I returned to Bridewell. It could be that he bought their freedom, or otherwise persuaded Ainsworth to set them free outside. He was a peculiar man and he often made secret, unusual decisions with implications only he understood. Don't think for a minute that he didn't expect things to unravel as they have. We may yet see his wisdom in all this before we're through." He scraped his chains across the table, turned, and gestured toward the window. "In any event, we've known for a long time that creatures move around in The Dark Hills. My guards and I see them all the time. Maybe now we know what they are."

"Oh, come on, Pervis, this is simply ridiculous!" Nicolas exploded. "Are you telling me you believe the fantasies of a child?"

For the first time since I had entered the meeting room, I felt conviction and courage and even some anger. So much at stake, and such closed minds. It would take something more concrete to get this group to believe. I pushed my chair out and walked to the window. I stood for a moment with my back to the group and observed the sickening stone wall. It looked almost alive with its green ivy veins shooting in all directions. When I turned around to address the men, I had a new passion in my eyes.

"I have more to tell."

CHAPTER 21

THE DARK HILLS DIVIDE

All my hesitation was gone. The people sitting at the tables, the things I knew were true about the convicts, the meeting room itself — none of it scared me any longer. Years behind the wall had blinded these men to the world outside. But the wall had taken more than their freedom to experience the outer world. I could see that it had stolen their ability to figure out the truth.

I unfolded the paper Murphy had left for me on the windowsill.

"When I ventured outside the wall I met a remarkable man. This man has lived in the mountains for many years, and he has extraordinary abilities with animals. He has been watching the convicts, and he gave me this note."

"Did this man tell you his name?" asked Grayson. I nodded and told him the man's name was Yipes. He questioned me again, this time about the man's size, and I told him he was the smallest man I'd ever seen. Grayson turned a ghostly white and looked at me with a blank stare. Then he put his elbows on the table and dropped his head into his hands.

"What is it, Grayson?" Ganesh asked. Grayson looked up, scanned the faces in the room, and answered.

"I think she might be telling the truth," he said. Everyone was looking at him now, trying to figure out what he was talking about.

"Yipes is no legend," he continued. "He's real. He's a very small man, more than likely able to communicate with animals, and he lives in the wild." Grayson continued his stammering and began shaking his head. He stood up and looked around as though he was trying to recall a distant memory and remember it properly before speaking.

"When he was a boy he lived in Bridewell for a time. He arrived from Ainsworth, and wandered the streets until he was hungry enough to steal bread." Grayson stopped and looked directly at me, then continued. "He stole that bread from me, and I caught him. After that, I let him stay in the library and sleep on the chair in the corner. He was so small, nobody ever took notice of him. When people came in, he hid in the shadows. I brought him scraps from the kitchen and read him books." Grayson walked to the window, drawing out the memory, gazing at the ever-present stone and vine of the wall.

"One day I rounded the corner to the chair and found him sitting in Warvold's lap. I was shocked, afraid old Warvold would get rid of both the boy and me. But I could not have been more wrong. Warvold loved the boy. He would sit and read to him and they would talk of things I heard only in whispers, of talking animals, of things in the wild outside the wall, of secret passages and mysteries of the distant past only Warvold understood. I thought it was all rubbish."

He turned and faced the room, leaning against the windowsill, his body outlined against the morning light. "I went about my business, cared for the boy, and taught him what I knew. Warvold was a busy man in those days, and often he would be absent for weeks on end before returning. Yipes was remarkably agile and strong for his size. He would stack books on the top shelves when no one was about. He could scale a tall bookshelf in an instant, hang by one hand, and stack volume after volume perfectly.

"I don't know how old he was when he arrived, nor have I any idea what his age was when he disappeared a year later. I only know that he told me he would find a way outside, and that when he did, he would live in the wild with animals and learn to communicate with them. Warvold told him so, and he believed. He was treated badly by humans, forgotten, discarded. In the wild, he believed things would be different."

Grayson was visibly moved by his own recollections. He seemed overcome by the idea that this boy he once cared for was still alive, living out his days in the mountains and the forest.

"One day I came into the library and Warvold was sitting in the chair sobbing, holding a strange silver key between his fingers. 'He's gone,' he said, 'never to return.' I guess Warvold was right, because I have not seen Yipes since."

The room was quiet. I felt it was my best chance to reveal what little else I knew, to convince them that trouble was indeed on the way. So I read the note from Yipes I had sent Murphy to get. And in the reading, I felt a chill in my bones.

"'The Dark Hills divide cannot protect you from an evil that lurks within. At twelve o'clock this very night he will signal them, and they will come for you. Your only hope is to tear down what you have built.'

"It's signed by Yipes," I said. After that, there was a look on the faces in the room I had never seen before in all my visits to Bridewell.

Suspicion.

CHAPTER 22

A SECRET PLAN

After I read the note from Yipes, the meeting room was quiet for a long time. It was as if nobody knew what to say or do next, or even how to act. My father was the one to finally break the silence.

"It seems we are all having trouble coming to grips with the situation at hand. Unless anyone objects, I suggest we let Alexa tell us everything else she knows. If what she has already explained to us is true, and it appears that it is, then we have almost no time to prepare for a possible invasion." Pervis shifted in his chair and started the chains jingling between his legs. I was glad to have him in our midst.

I rose and advanced to the far end of the room where a large wooden table surrounded by chairs was kept. My father unhitched Pervis and escorted him to a chair at the new table, then locked him to one of the legs. I invited everyone else to join us and sit down, and I unrolled the map onto the middle of the table. I used heavy brass candlesticks to keep the map flat against the wood.

"We haven't got a lot of time and we lack proper defenses," Father said. "Most of those who normally reside in Bridewell are conducting business in other parts of the kingdom, which is both good and bad. Fewer people are at risk, but it puts us drastically short of men. No doubt this is precisely why the convicts have chosen to attack now."

Father looked across the table at Pervis and said, "We have the six of us. How many guards do we have?"

"We have fourteen, fifteen if you take these shackles off of me, plus sixty or so men, women, and children scattered around town," said Pervis.

"Fourteen guards?" asked Silas, assuming we would not be letting Pervis go. "There could be hundreds of convicts out in those hills. There's no way we could handle them all, especially since we don't know how or when exactly they will strike. And worse, one of them is inside the wall. It could be anyone. Even one of us."

Silas had voiced what all of us were thinking but were afraid to say: What if Sebastian was someone in this very room?

"I refuse to believe that," Father said. "The only one of us who hasn't been in this group for years and years is you, and you don't strike me as an evil mastermind. Besides, whoever this Sebastian is, if he is at all, he would have to keep a low profile to last this long in Bridewell. I suggest we not worry so much about the spy and stay focused on the invasion, which is coming whether a spy exists or not."

What Father was saying resonated with the group. "My hunch is we've already locked up Sebastian anyway," added Nicolas, with a weary eye toward Pervis.

The implication bothered me, and Nicolas had caught me at a time when I was ready to stand up for Pervis when no one else was. This was the opportunity I was looking for to try to get him out of his shackles.

"I don't think pointing fingers at Pervis will solve anything," I protested. "We have no evidence to suggest that he is Sebastian. In fact, he is probably the last person among us who we should distrust. He's the only one who was working directly with Warvold before the convicts even arrived in Bridewell. Besides, we have a much better chance of success if he is free to lead our few trained guards in a battle plan."

"She's right," said Grayson. "I've been in Bridewell longer than he has, but when I started working in the library, Pervis was already a part of Warvold's inner circle."

Within a few minutes the group agreed that it was exceedingly unrealistic to think Pervis could be Sebastian. It was further agreed that he was indeed worth more to the cause as a free man than as one imprisoned. The group agreed on a simplified charge against him, drunken and disorderly conduct, and he was released with a stern warning to behave himself.

"Glad to have you back," I said as Pervis rubbed his wrists where the harsh metal of the shackles had worn his skin raw.

"Happy to be back at work. I hate holidays," he replied.

We were ready to review the map and begin forming a plan, and I leaned over the table so I could better see the details in the natural light pouring in from outside.

"If you look at the map, you'll see that the brown-colored lines represent the aboveground paths," I said. "The black lines represent the ones belowground. A number of black lines run below Bridewell, but only one seems to have any strategic significance. That one there." I placed my finger on a black line out in The Dark Hills and ran my finger along the map, winding my way toward the center until the line ended. "I believe this spot represents the courtyard in the center of town and the convicts have continued digging until this tunnel ends a few feet beneath the cobblestones. When the time is right for them to strike, I think they will break through the cobblestone and pour into Bridewell like so many rats out of a sewer."

Nicolas took his turn at leaning over the map and tried to calculate the distance and direction of the line I was pointing to. "I do believe she's right on that one," he said. "That does look like the center of town. You see the lodge is here with the adjoining wall along its side. Either Alexa is right, or it's somewhere close to the courtyard." He looked up and smiled at me, and my anger over his accusation of Pervis subsided considerably.

"There's more," I continued. "As long as we move quickly and secure the city so that no potential spies are allowed out, the convicts have no way of knowing that we've discovered their plan. I believe Sebastian and the convicts communicate using a hawk to carry messages back and forth. It gets complicated with the animals, but Yipes has a hawk of his own."

I went on to explain that during the past few hours, Yipes's hawk had been flying over The Dark Hills, looking for signs of a place where the convicts might rendezvous with their own hawk to send and receive messages.

"My hope is that by now the hawk the criminals and Sebastian were using to communicate has been apprehended. If Sebastian does try to correspond further, his hawk will be difficult to find, since Yipes should have it caged up in the mountains by now."

A look around the room revealed wide eyes and drooping jaws. It was nice for now that they had no knowledge of the army of animals who were responsible for most of the progress I had made.

"Our best chance is to allow the convicts to continue with their plans to attack the city and to allow for this attack to take place at night. If Yipes is right, and our location guess is correct, the convicts will attack at the center of town at midnight tonight."

"But that's not enough time to mount a plan against them, Alexa," my father said. "We should contact Yipes and see if the attack can be thwarted from the outside."

"No, I disagree," Pervis argued. "Right now we have the element of surprise working against them. It may be our only chance to catch them off guard. What we need is a plan, and I think I'm onto something that will work." Pervis looked at the map thoughtfully, then asked for the note from Yipes and re-read part of it aloud. "*'Your only hope is to tear down what you have built.'* I can't get that out of my mind, and I think I know what he means for us to do."

The next hour was spent planning our strategy and working out everything that could go wrong. Everyone agreed it was a brilliant plan, but there was a great deal of anxiety about whether it could be done in time. It was noon when we finished our planning, leaving us about twelve hours until the invasion was expected to begin.

A town meeting was held in the main hall of Renny Lodge, and everyone in Bridewell was put to work on projects relating to the scheduled assault. We had eighty people, including the guards. All four of the gates into Bridewell were locked and heavily guarded, and the library door would be kept locked to prevent the tunnel from being used. If a spy did live among us, it was essential to our plan that his ability to communicate with the convicts and move about freely be eliminated.

The town was in a fever of activity by the time night arrived. Everyone was engaged in the effort. I became so tired after darkness enveloped the town that I fell fast asleep sitting up against a wall. Father wanted to carry me to my room and put me into my bed, but I refused.

"How are you doing?" I asked in a sleepy voice.

"All things considered, not bad. It's a lot to process so quickly."

"I know what you mean," I said. "How are the preparations coming along?"

"Just fine. It will be close, but I think we'll make it."

He turned to leave, then turned back as if to say something more. Instead he just looked at me, and I saw that his thick hair had swished into the shape of a C against his forehead. He brushed it away with his brawny left hand and walked off as I drifted back to sleep against the wall.

CHAPTER 23

A MYTHICAL CREATURE

"Blast that Pervis! All the strawberry jam is gone. He must have snuck in here and finished it off last night."

It was only a few hours until midnight and I was in the kitchen, energized by the approaching invasion. Grayson was in a sour mood, and I was trying my best to cheer him up.

"Tell you what, Grayson. If things go well tonight, I'll get Silas to bring in a cart full of strawberries and you can eat jam all day long if you like."

The smell of fresh-baked breads and tangy slices of red and green apples filled the kitchen. While I stacked my plate with both, Grayson picked up a biscuit and contemplated its size and shape.

"My irritation is made complete by the perfection of biscuits just out of the oven," he said. "It would be sinful to eat them plain." He tossed the biscuit onto the table with disgust, sending sparks of crumbs flying in every direction.

I ate ravenously and drank milk in great gulps, my body still searching for fuel to fill some unknown reserve.

When I looked up again from my plate, Grayson was inspecting something new he had pulled from his pocket.

"I believe this belongs to you, does it not?" he said, holding my pocketknife. "I assume you had a reason for leaving it where it was, so I pushed a bookshelf in front of the cat door before I removed it. The cats seem agitated and they whine and scratch at the door a lot. Any idea why that might be?"

I had completely forgotten about Sam and Pepper. I took a drink from my glass to buy some time and consider a good answer.

"Keeping them locked up for now would be a good idea," I replied, wiping away a milk mustache with the back of my hand. "It's hard to explain, but they could cause us trouble if you release them. Maybe once everything settles down I'll tell you more, but I can't right now."

Grayson nodded his approval and jammed a big spoonful of slimy-looking oatmeal into his mouth, then he handed me the knife and looked down at his bowl, rolling his spoon around in its soupy contents.

"You know, he had no name," said Grayson.

"Who?"

"Yipes. He had no name when I met him. His parents, whoever they might be, left him in the streets. He told me he lived in the Ainsworth Orphanage for a while, but they never bothered to name him. He was nothing more than a number in that hideous place, and a small number at that."

"It's a very strange name he decided on," I said.

"That it is," said Grayson through a mouthful of food. "But I'm partial to it, since I helped him pick it out."

As Grayson remembered it, the two of them had been stacking books on a frosty winter day in the library when Grayson came upon a very old volume that was broken and cracking at the seams. He took it to his office and began restoring it while Yipes watched from his perch on the desk. When he finished with his mending, Grayson flopped the book open and began turning the pages to inspect the repaired joint. They came upon a particular page and Yipes exclaimed, "Read that one to me," for though he was good at putting away books, he could not read them when he arrived in Bridewell.

The book itself was filled with mythical creatures and beasts, pure fantasy from cover to cover. Some pages included pen drawings of monsters and strange beings from even stranger places. The page that Grayson had landed on included a picture of a bizarre creature — small, and apparently half monkey, half man. As Grayson read, it became clear that this thing they had stumbled upon had, oddly enough, many qualities in common with our little friend. The creature was undersized and could climb and jump with amazing agility. It did not trust humans and remained hidden whenever men were about.

"Those odd, mythical creatures in the book were called 'Yipes.' As soon as I finished reading that section, we both agreed it was the perfect name for him."

Grayson observed his bowl with a blank stare. The story had brought a rush of memories back.

"He's doing well, Grayson," I offered. "Life outside is what he told you it would be, only better."

Grayson raised his head and looked at me with deep appreciation. Our conversation had renewed his strength in ways that food could not, and we were both ready to get back to work.

We left the kitchen together and walked through the center of town, which bustled with activity in every direction. The men and women looked tired and beaten. The work was steady but slow. Even Pervis barely stood, leaning against a wall, as he shouted orders. I approached him cautiously and asked how things were going.

"Not well, Alexa," he said. "We underestimated the work this would take. At the rate we're going, we'll never finish by midnight. Ganesh and your father talked it over, and they gave me orders an hour ago. I've sent Silas to quietly round up more men in Lathbury, and Nicolas is doing the same in Lunenburg. Another guard is trying the same in Turlock. Still, it's doubtful they will return in time to bring reinforcements." Neither of us voiced the obvious concerns about the risks of sending them off on

216

their own; we just looked at each other and shrugged, hoping for the best.

Grayson grabbed hold of two shovels and handed one to me. "Time to make some blisters," he said, and the rest of the evening was lost in a haze of sweat and dust.

Hours later, with midnight approaching Bridewell, a heavy wind was whipping through the courtyard, stinging tired eyes and clogging heaving lungs with thick dust. Despite the conditions and fatigue, the people who had worked around the clock continued with an inhuman stamina.

"Storm's coming," I observed. Grayson rose from his work and stood beside me, leaning hard against the wall as the wind parted his meager head of hair. We saw Pervis coming from the direction of Renny Lodge. He approached us slowly, shirt flapping uncontrollably at his sides, the wind directly in his face in great gusts.

"We'll make it by midnight. Just finishing things up now," he yelled through the wind. He looked beaten but alert, alternately watching the guards at the near tower and the work on the ground.

An hour short of midnight, we finished the work. No streetlamps were fired; only a blush of soft moonlight remained on the town square. Families hunkered down in their homes as tired men milled around the completed work with anticipation. The kitchen staff prepared kettles of soup and fresh loaves of bread, and people formed a line outside Renny Lodge. At the door they took a bowl and a spoon, then my father poured the soup and handed each person a small loaf of bread. Inside, tables were set in the smoking room, and a great fire raged in the fireplace.

There was a strange aura that hung over the room as we sat elbow to elbow sipping from our bowls, listening to the wind buffet the shutters that had been closed over the windows. It was a harrowing sound, as though the convicts were pounding to get in and tear the place apart. A few sips into our late dinner all the townspeople went back outside clutching lumps of bread, too skittish to sit inside making chitchat over bowls of broth.

Only Father and I remained.

"You've been working hard," Father said.

"I don't mind," I replied.

"I think it's time for you to go, Alexa. I want you sealed up tight in your room, door locked, until this thing is over. No more running around," he said. The thought of what was coming scared me and I was happy to obey his request. We hugged, and then I retreated to my room and locked the door behind me.

CHAPTER 24

THE PAPER STORM

It was ten minutes to midnight when I arrived at my open window, door locked behind me, a thick wind tossing my hair. I hadn't been paying any attention, but clouds were rolling in. Storm clouds. Within a few moments, the moon was gone, and the unlit town of Bridewell below was as black as The Dark Hills had ever been. I could not differentiate between the inside and the outside of the wall, and for a brief moment it seemed as though the wall itself were a myth, and Bridewell was open, sprawling into the hills uncontained. But the clouds continued to move, and part of the moon cast its revealing light against the ivy-covered wall. As quickly as the wall had disappeared, it was back in all its awful glory.

I was holding Warvold's favorite old book, *Myths and Legends in the Land of Elyon*, the one I'd gotten from Grayson. After my visit outside the wall, its title was newly intriguing. I had never thought of our land as Elyon's land. *Elyon* was just what we called it, nothing more. Flipping through its ragged pages was somehow comforting, and I began to think about having Grayson repair it so it would stop falling to pieces every time I picked it up. While I was lost in my thoughts, the clouds once again moved over the moon, and the blackness of the unlit night returned. Gusts of wind continued to blow; the first drops of rain pelted my hands on the sill, and I closed the book to protect it.

"Alexa!"

I jumped back from the window, lost my balance, and fell to the floor, all the while clutching the precious old book.

"Well, I guess that's one for me." It was Murphy climbing through the open window. His presence was a bad sign.

"Why are you here, Murphy? I need you to stay on the lookout," I said, getting back on my feet.

"That's just it, Alexa. I left an hour ago to check in with Yipes, and when I returned, it had been opened."

"Are you absolutely sure?" I asked. It appeared that my fears had come to pass.

"I'm positive. The chair was put back, but I marked the footings on the floor, and they no longer match up." Murphy was staring at me wide-eyed. "Either someone's got in through the secret door or someone's got out. I can't be sure which."

A gust of wind slammed through the window and racked the shutters back and forth against the wall. Wind rushed into the room and blew Warvold's book clean out of my hand, bursting the spine loose anew and blowing pages all over the room.

"Oh no!" I cried. Some of the pages were sucked out the window as the wind changed directions; the rest were flying around the room in a blizzard of paper. I ran to the window and grabbed the shutters to close them. The rain was coming harder now and the handles on the shutters were slick. I saw pages from Warvold's book dancing on the wind outside. One was caught in the ivy clutches of the wall, another was stuck to the wet sill, and still another fluttered over the divide and out into the dark night beyond my sight. I grabbed the page stuck to the sill and threw it behind me, then secured the shutters and turned to face the room.

It was worse than I thought possible. Pages were everywhere, and Murphy was dragging an empty spine across the floor by his teeth for my inspection. The book was forever destroyed.

"This is terrible, Murphy. We'll never get it back together, no matter how hard we try."

He dropped the spine on my feet and looked up at me.

"I'm sorry," he said.

I sat down with my back against the wall, and Murphy hopped up on my lap. I picked up what was left of the book and opened it up. Not a single page remained. The spine was not only empty of pages, but torn at the stitching on the inside cover, revealing the inner board beneath the fabric. It had always been this way, at least ever since the book came into my possession. But with the pages gone the fault was more obvious and accessible. I ran my fingers along the edge absently. Then I tucked my finger under the fabric and felt along the board. It was a mindless gesture, and when I felt a ridge where one should not have been, I ignored it. Then I realized the ridge felt more like paper than board or fabric, and I looked closely at the broken cover. Something was inside. Something secret.

I looked at Murphy with astonishment, then ripped the fabric off the cover and revealed a folded piece of paper. I set the mangled book aside and unfolded the treasure, my hands trembling with anticipation. It was one page, torn from Warvold's journal. The date and time of the entry indicated the night of his arrival in Bridewell for the summer meetings, probably between dinner and the stroll with me from which he never returned.

As the shutters buckled back and forth in opposition to the wind, I read the entry aloud to Murphy.

> *I have wondered ever since Renny was taken from me if Sebastian is real. My arrival back in Bridewell makes me wonder more than ever. Were Renny's suspicions imagined? "He's not quite right," she would say upon our arrival. And who is this Sebastian anyway? Is he anything more than a mere legend heard in whispers? To tell the rest of them I must be utterly sure.*
>
> *Grayson — I'm getting old and mischief follows me everywhere. If I am dead when you go to repair my favorite book (I know you won't be*

able to help yourself), you'll surely find this note.
If events surrounding my death seem suspicious,
read page 194. Otherwise, burn the book
immediately and go about your day in peace.

W.

"Why did Grayson have to give me the book? For all we know, page 194 is flying around outside somewhere!" I yelled. Murphy scrambled off my lap and began sifting through pages on the floor while I checked the ones that had landed on my bed. Five minutes into our search we were still looking, and all the pages in sight were piled in a heap in the corner of the room. It seemed likely that one of the pages outside, probably the one long gone over the wall, was the page we were looking for.

"Alexa!" came a muffled cry from under my bed, and a moment later Murphy came out, pushing page 194 along the floor with his nose. I reached down and picked it up.

A moment later, with water pooling on my windowsill and dripping into the room, we huddled together in the corner near the pages we had piled up and I read page 194 aloud to Murphy.

Immediately, we knew who Sebastian was, and Murphy said what we were both thinking:

"We have to catch him."

CHAPTER 25

A TĪGHT SPOT

I unlocked my door and ran down the hall with Murphy close behind. When we arrived at the landing on the second floor, I stopped and gazed out the window toward the center of town where a shard of moonlight cut through the night. The rain began coming down in sheets, and the moon disappeared again behind ominous clouds, this time for the duration of the storm. I lost sight of the town square.

I would need a weapon, so I went to the smoking room and took the iron poker from where it stood next to the great fireplace. Then I motioned Murphy in the direction of the library. On the way out of the smoking room I picked up a lamp from the table, lit it, and trimmed it so the flame was low.

We passed through the kitchen, went up the creaking steps, and stood at the landing in front of the library doors. As I suspected, the doors had been locked from the inside, and the bookcase remained firmly backed against the wall in front of the cat door.

"I wonder if Sam and Pepper are still in there, watching for intruders," I said.

"If they are, then they're hiding," Murphy replied. He hadn't seen them while he watched for activity in the library. We began to wonder if they might have jumped out the open window by the chair, but it was a long way down. Murphy could hold on and descend a twenty-foot wall, but the cats would have to free-fall to the ground. No cat would willingly leap out a window that high.

The sound of thunderclaps and driving rain magnified the sinister darkness of Renny Lodge. I crouched down by the cat door and swung it toward me into the hall, inspecting the weight and size of the bookcase blocking the way. Already, there was almost enough room for Murphy to squeeze through, so I turned and put my foot through the small door against the bookcase. I pushed, just a little at first, then as hard as I could, but it would not budge. I held the door open with my hand, pulled my foot back, and waited for the next thunderclap. When it came, I thrust the flat of my heel into the bookcase. This produced a shooting pain up my leg, and the shelf remained in the exact same spot.

We sat motionless for a moment, and then without warning, Murphy moved quickly past my foot and sideways through the little door. He struggled mightily to squeeze into the small space as I spun around to where I could see.

He spoke in a muffled whisper I could hardly understand.

"Awfully tight in here. Can you push me through?"

I put my hand next to his furry side and started pushing. The wood against the back of the bookcase was slick, and his fur was soft, but the stone wall was rough. The coarseness of the wall combined with the slippery fur and wood made him twist as he went. I pushed; Murphy spun, alternately facing the stone wall, the exit, the bookcase, and me. It was hard not to laugh as I imagined his poor little face squashed against the wall, nose all flattened out, followed by a dazed look as he rotated free in my direction. I moved him as far as I could, but when my elbow reached the edge of the cat door, I could push no further, and Murphy had yet to reach the edge of the bookshelf.

He was stuck.

"Alexa?" he whispered.

"Yes?" I answered, the subtle beginnings of hysteria in my voice.

"Cat," he said.

And then I heard Sam's menacing laugh fill the library.

"How sad for you, Murphy — stuck in such an uncompromising position. And no one to save you," said Sam.

The time for quiet deliberation had passed, and I threw my body full force into the library door over and over again trying to get in.

"It's no use, Alexa. He's finished, Bridewell is finished, and Sebastian has escaped undiscovered and unharmed. You have failed at every turn." This time it was Pepper, standing behind the door, taunting me.

I spun the fire poker in my hand and examined it, thinking of all that had gone wrong, and believing for a moment that I was defeated.

The cats were inspecting the bookcase, enjoying their little moment, continuing to taunt and jab as they decided who would rip into Murphy's flesh with a bare claw and yank him out.

"I think you should do the honors," joked Sam.

For no particular reason, I leaned against the library door, and continued examining the fire poker. It was a solid metal device with a sharp tip.

"I almost wish I could let you in, Alexa. This is going to be quite a sight to behold," said Pepper.

I quietly moved to the cat door and opened it.

"Enough of this. Get him out," said Sam.

I jammed the fire poker under the bookcase as hard as I could, and I lifted the handle up off the floor with all my strength. The bookcase tilted out slowly, then faster, then it was crashing into another shelf in front of it, spraying books everywhere. I could hear shelves falling like dominoes out into the library, pounding the floor with books.

When all the shelves in the row had been toppled, I waited to hear the cats going after Murphy, but all I heard were random books slipping off tipped shelves and popping on the floor like giant raindrops at the end of a storm.

Then I heard a magical sound. The lock on the library

door creaked, and I watched as it slowly turned and snapped open. I carefully turned the handle and pushed the door open a few inches.

"Close call," said Murphy. He had already jumped down from the doorknob, and he was standing at my feet.

"Where are they?" I asked.

Murphy motioned me in and I followed him into the library. In the dim light it looked as though nine or ten shelves had tumbled over. Hanging out from under one of them were two lifeless cat tails.

"Oh my," I said. Murphy climbed over a bookshelf and started in the direction of the chair and the secret tunnel. I followed him into the dark recesses of the library.

CHAPTER 26

SEBASTIAN

The shutters had not been closed and water was everywhere. Books, shelves, and the old chair — all were soaking wet. Rain continued to pour into the space as I pulled the chair back and revealed the secret entry. I removed the silver key from my pocket, unlocked the small door, and swung it open. A gust of wind blew it shut again with a bang, and I worried over who might have heard from down below in the darkness.

I reopened the door and held it tighter this time. The lamp that had hung on the ladder was gone, and I hung mine where it had been.

"Ready?" I asked Murphy. He nodded, and I picked him up and put him in my pack along with the fire poker. I descended the ladder as I had done before. When we arrived at the bottom, I released Murphy and set him on the dirt floor.

To my surprise, five of the boards that once lined the wall behind the ladder were strewn about the floor at my feet. Where the boards had been, the opening to a threatening dark corridor remained, staring at us like a giant black eye. I stepped through the opening and Murphy followed.

The brown walls reflected weak light from my lamp,

and I had the creepy sense that Sebastian could jump out from a hiding spot at any moment and attack me. I turned the lamp down, just enough to see in front of me, and began running the length of the tunnel. After a while it turned and widened, and then I saw light flickering in the distance. I stopped and turned my lamp as low as I could and set it aside; then I sent Murphy ahead to scout the situation. He returned breathless and agitated.

"We've reached the main tunnel," he said. "It shoots off in two directions, one back toward Bridewell by another route, and one out toward The Dark Hills. There's a torch lit at the corner. What do you want to do?"

Without answering I began running toward the flickering light as fast as I could. When I arrived at the torch I removed it from its holder and rammed it into the dirt floor until it was out. "What are you doing, Alexa?" yelled Murphy.

"Quiet down — you'll give us away," I whispered. I pulled a piece of paper from my sack and held it down to the light. It was a crude copy of the map of the tunnels, something I'd thought I might find a use for after relinquishing the original.

"He would have tried to find his men, which means he would have taken this tunnel here." I pointed out a long, twisting black line that started from the hub we were standing at. My finger followed along the map as I spoke. "After that, he would intersect with this tunnel and drop down under Bridewell here. If our plan works, he will encounter a dirt wall near the end. The only way back out is through the hub we're standing at." I paused a moment and looked at Murphy.

"He's separated from his men and looking for a way out. He knows he won't make it before the passage is blocked," he concluded.

We sat motionless in the dark, the dim light from my lamp covered between my back and the wall of the cave. We waited quietly, which was difficult for Murphy. He kept flipping and flopping as he continued whispering. "What if we're too late?"

Before I could respond, we both saw a flicker of light coming from out of the darkness. It was moving fast. I hunched down at the edge of the adjoining tunnel and pulled the fire poker from my pack. The light bounced brighter and brighter off the walls, and then the shadow of a man came into view. I could hear his labored breathing and his steps as he moved across the dirt floor. Thunder clapped from outside in a muffled tone, and I peeked around the corner to see how close he was. Only about ten yards off, Sebastian had slowed to a brisk walk. I slipped back into the darkness, and as he passed in front of me I swung the fire poker with all my might, hitting him square on the bone of his lower leg. He screamed in pain and threw his lamp to the ground, hopping on one leg over to the side of the tunnel with his back to me, holding himself up with one hand. I'd broken the skin at the bone, and blood began to stream down his leg.

I picked up my lamp and turned it up, holding the fire poker in one hand. Sebastian, still turned away from me, winced in pain, his hand over the wound feeling for broken bones.

"You stupid girl!" he shouted, throwing a handful of loose dirt into my face. I was blinded but kept a firm grip on my weapon as I went down and tried to rub the dust out of my eyes. I felt a forceful blow to my ribs and the wind was knocked out of me. Then I was thrown over on my back, and the fire poker was wrenched out of my hands. I waited for something awful to happen, something painful. Instead I heard a voice.

"If you follow me one step farther, I'll drive this fire poker into your heart," he whispered, grotesquely close to my ear, dripping sweat in my hair. Then he moved away from me and I heard the sound of smashing glass as he destroyed my lamp.

"He's got the light and our weapon and he's heading for The Dark Hills," yelled Murphy. I could hear Sebastian dragging his bad leg as he went. I sat up and tried desperately to clean the dirt out of my eyes. They stung badly, and I could see only a blurry view of the light dancing off into the distance.

"I have no protection and no light, and I can hardly see. This is going well, wouldn't you say?"

"We can catch him if we hurry," countered Murphy. He raced down the tunnel before I could stop him, so I followed as fast as I could. My ribs were on fire where

232

Sebastian had kicked me, and I was having trouble catching my breath. Another fifty yards and I'd be finished. The light was getting closer again as I rounded a corner and slowed down. I crept a little farther and saw that Sebastian was in a familiar underground room. The map of the tunnels hung on the wall and he was studying it, looking for the way out.

I knew this room.

I crept in behind him against the wall and looked all around for some sort of weapon I could use. A lighted torch was all I could find, and I quietly moved toward it. Murphy hid in the shadows and waited.

"I told you not to follow me," said Sebastian. His voice shocked me, and I stumbled over my feet, landing beneath the torch. He remained with his back to me, unmoving.

"I wouldn't have believed it was you if not for the clues that were left behind," I said, my voice shaking with fear. "Renny had you figured out first, but Warvold had to be convinced. The clues he left me led to a page in his favorite book describing a mythical elephant god from a fanciful story set on the other side of Mount Laythen at the edge of the sea." I stood up and groped along the wall for the torch. "An imaginary god called Ganesh."

There was a long moment of silence in the room. I pulled my hand away from the torch and waited, not sure what he would do. He remained facing away from me, and began to speak in a tired old voice.

"I was lazy, brash, and I didn't want to work. In Ainsworth a young man with those characteristics had better either shape up or leave town," he said. Then he turned and looked at me for the first time with his hollow eyes, old before their time. "I did neither, and by the time I was nineteen, I had this." He pulled his shirt aside and revealed a *V* branded to his chest. V for vagabond.

"On the inside, we joked that the *V* was for victory, but the guards in Ainsworth were ruthless. A few vagabonds were killed; many others were beaten within an inch of their lives." He paused and his eyes went glassy for a moment before he continued. "It's not as though I really cared — most of the criminals I met were very bad men who'd done awful things. Still, if Warvold had not come along, I am quite sure we would all be long since dead." He shuffled closer with his injured leg and stood before me.

"But he did emerge, and the officials in Ainsworth were thrilled to rid themselves of us. Warvold was no softy, but as long as we worked hard and obeyed, he took care of us. We ate well, worked hard, and enjoyed a bed to sleep in at night. For many of us, this was as good a life as we'd ever known." Ganesh turned my fire poker in his hand and examined it absently. There was a strange, leisurely madness about him.

"When the wall was finished, Warvold and his guards escorted us back to Ainsworth as promised. We were all thirty or thirty-five years old by then, beaten down from years of hard labor. We were no longer strong-willed, able young men, and this terrified us.

"Ainsworth never expected Warvold to return us, and they surely didn't plan for it. After a week of life back in the prison I thought I might go insane. The place was full when we got there, and we nearly doubled the number overnight.

"I talked with one of the guards, and I told him if they released all of the convicts that had worked in Bridewell into the wilderness, I could guarantee that no one would ever see or hear from us again. We would remain in the wild where no one would find us, and if any of us were found, we would expect nothing short of death. Seeing this as a way to rid themselves of us once and for all without having to kill us, the officials agreed to the plan, and shortly after that, under cover of night, they released us into The Dark Hills." He was growing weary from the pain in his leg, which appeared to have been shattered at the bone from my swing — the pain must have been unbearable. He rocked back and forth and caught himself like a drunk, but he was determined to finish the story.

"Once released, we began planning a takeover of the walled city. Bridewell is a marvelous fortress, and with it under our control, we could bargain with Ainsworth as equals, and turn Bridewell into a trade route between Ainsworth and the sea towns of Turlock and Lathbury.

"Those of us with brands on our cheeks hoped to

cover them up with beards. My *C* brand was conveniently low, and my beard grew very thick, so I was an obvious choice to send out.

"Shortly after our arrival in The Dark Hills, I moved to Turlock. It had just been settled, and only a few hundred people lived there. I immediately went to work on constructing houses and other buildings, and I involved myself in all forms of planning for the town. Within a year, it grew to several thousand people, and I was elected mayor. With no family to speak of, working sometimes twenty hours a day to build the community, I was a natural selection.

"The rest is fairly obvious. You know all about talking to animals, so there's no sense in my hiding it now. Some of the other convicts discovered the pool and its strange powers. They befriended the hawk, and the hawk befriended the cats.

"I began making trips to Bridewell and started planning the invasion. We needed information that would take time to attain, and there was years of work to expand the already extensive tunnel system. But here we are, many years later, and the invasion is upon us."

"What will you do now?" I questioned, trying to keep him talking. "You're cut off from your men, wounded, and found out."

Ganesh looked at me with a cold stare, the fire poker glistening in his hand, blood oozing down his damaged leg. "It's refreshing to cleanse the soul in telling my story, but the situation remains obvious: Nobody else knows I'm down here, and there are many ways out. I'll have to kill you, just like I killed Warvold. With him it was poison, not too messy. Funny how he had no idea — maybe he wasn't as smart as you all thought he was." He lost his balance for a moment, then regained it and spoke once more. "With you I'm afraid I'll have to draw some blood." I leaped for the torch and grabbed ahold with both hands, waving it in front of me.

"You really think that dried-out piece of wood is going to save you? I think not." His mood had turned dark and threatening. This was not Ganesh; this was Sebastian. He advanced on me and I began to move to one side, swishing the flame back and forth between us.

He was just close enough to bat the torch out of my hands and drive the fire poker into me when Murphy darted out of the shadows, jumped onto Sebastian's leg, and chomped down with all his force, driving his teeth deep into flesh. Sebastian screamed fiercely, looked down, and with one brute swing batted Murphy across the room. I was up against the wall opposite the map, nowhere to hide, and Sebastian, fuming with rage, focused all of his years of anger squarely on me. He advanced quickly, ripped the flaming torch from my hands, and pinned me to the wall with his forearm.

"Aaaaarrrrgggggh!" He screamed and pulled back to drive the fire poker into me. I closed my eyes and waited for the impact.

237

But the impact never came. I heard the sound of wood splintering and I was thrown to the ground. Dirt flew everywhere and I lost sight of Sebastian altogether.

"Murphy, what have you done?" I slid down against the wall and held my knees to my chest.

As the dust settled to the ground I saw Sebastian lying flat on the ground. Standing over him, covered in dirt from top to bottom, was a little man. Next to him was Darius, dripping saliva, his massive gaping mouth hovering over Sebastian's neck, ready to drive razor-sharp teeth into flesh upon the slightest movement from Sebastian's body. But the precaution was unnecessary. Sebastian was dead, his neck turned hideously, broken in the fall by the fierce charge of a huge wolf.

"Yipes!" I screamed. I jumped up and grabbed him around the waist, hugging him mercilessly. Then I turned to Darius, touched his ominous head, and pulled him close.

"It's all right now. It's all right," said Yipes. I looked back over my head and saw that Yipes and Darius had crashed through the hiding spot, a big gaping hole where once there was dirt wall. Splintered boards dangled aimlessly into the air of the chamber.

"How did you know?" I said.

"Just a hunch, a hunch is all," he said. "But Darius is the real hero. He worked tirelessly for hours and hours to crawl down the tunnel and make sure you were safe. The big brute wouldn't fit, so he had to dig as he went and widen the tunnel. Without him we could not have broken through the wall. He's as strong as an ox."

Murphy came hobbling up beside us. He seemed dazed but unharmed.

"Good to see you all back together again," he said. And then, in a comic whisper to Yipes, "Keep an eye on her, old boy — she's got a reputation for throwing us small ones around."

Yipes reached into his vest pocket and pulled out a small, sharp-looking knife. He approached Sebastian with caution, turned his lifeless head to the side, and placed the edge of the knife against his face. He looked back at me and motioned me closer, then he pulled down on the knife and revealed the dark crest of the letter *C* branded beneath Sebastian's thick beard.

"I guess that settles it for good."

I could hardly hear him say it, and then I was adrift somewhere far away where no one could find me, deeper into the tunnels, all the way out under The Dark Hills and into darker tunnels still, until I was so far and deep I could never be found again. And it was very dark indeed.

"Wake up, Alexa. Wake up."

I felt as though pulled by a cord out into the light, and I awoke to see Father's familiar, comforting eyes staring down at me. I reached up and grabbed him around the neck. Even with the pain in my side, I held him longer and tighter than I ever had before.

"You passed out," he said. "Yipes tried to revive you, but couldn't. He came looking for help in Bridewell."

I looked over and saw that Pervis was inspecting Sebastian's dead body. Then he looked at the mess of splintered boards and the opening into the tunnel, and finally with a look of astonishment his eyes fell upon the smiling little man standing before him.

In the silence of that moment it occurred to me for the first time what had happened. Yipes had been in Bridewell, with people — civilized people — which meant it was only a matter of time before he would lose his gift to speak with animals.

"It can't be," I said. "Please say you didn't do it." I reached for his hand and he took mine, but he wouldn't look at me.

"It's been worth it, Alexa. Really it has," he said. "It's all been worth it. Besides, I have a good feeling things were about to change out there anyway. This just speeds things up a bit."

I held on to his tiny hand a long time, my eyes filling with tears, and I whispered quietly, "Thank you."

Murphy came over and jumped up into the new opening that led out into the wild, and he balanced on one of the boards that had been broken free. Darius was nowhere to be seen. I could only assume that he'd traveled back through the tunnel when Yipes ran off to get help, in fear of being seen by men.

"Come on, Yipes, it's time for us to go," said Murphy.

I nodded my approval and let go of Yipes's hand.

"We'll see each other again," he said, and then he hopped up into the hole and I watched him vanish into the darkness. Murphy reappeared, leaped from the edge of the hole, and landed confidently in my outstretched arms.

"You're a hero," he said. "Not quite the hero I am, but a hero nonetheless."

I held him close, rose to my feet, and set him in the hole, and then he too was gone.

"We've got to get aboveground, Alexa. This isn't over yet," said Pervis.

We left the small, dingy room with its gaping wound, my father on one side and Pervis on the other. It was comforting to have them with me.

"Who's the rodent?" said Pervis, putting his arm around my shoulder.

"He's a squirrel, actually — a good one. Talks a little too much, but a nice fellow."

Pervis laughed and I managed a smile. He had no idea that I was being perfectly truthful.

CHAPTER 27

BEYOND BRIDEWELL

As I emerged from Renny Lodge the rain was pouring down in sheets and the wind was whipping through the town square. Through the clatter of the storm I heard another, more ominous noise. It was the muffled sound of metal and men. The invasion was upon us.

Though I could hear the menacing sound of the enemy coming, I could not see them. They were hidden, and it seemed as though our plan might actually work. During the previous twelve hours every able-bodied person in Bridewell had worked tirelessly to build a wall within a wall. We knew the enemy would come from The Dark Hills' side, and so, stone by stone, the top half of the wall separating Bridewell from the forest was taken down and put back together again twenty feet high, all the way around the town square. The enemy was trapped inside a prison of stone, not unlike the one I'd been trapped within my whole life.

As soon as all the convicts were inside, ready to pounce on Bridewell in the stormy black night, the explosions were set off at locations coinciding with the map. I felt the cobblestones rumble under my feet as the earth pounded beneath me. The detonations were used to be sure the tunnel would cave in and trap the convicts, a

242

few belowground, but most already out of the tunnel, completely unaware of the trick that had been played on them.

"They will try to scale the walls. We must hurry!" cried Pervis. With a fierce look my father motioned me to return to the lodge, and then he turned and disappeared into the night.

I stood motionless with rain pouring over me, fear gripping my bones. I was terrified that the enemy would escape over the wall and overrun Bridewell, that I might be taken prisoner or worse. A heavy wind gust tore through the town square and I had to brace myself from falling back.

Ladders had been placed all around the wall, and guards were stationed here and there upon the stone shelf on top of the wall. With the wind and the rain they were having trouble holding on, and I feared they might be blown off and tumble to their deaths. Without thinking I began walking, then running toward one of the ladders. I scaled the wall in the driving rain, the pain in my side reminding me with every step of the blow from Ganesh. And then I stood on the top of the wall and I looked down over the edge.

Convicts were standing on shoulders, grabbing hold of the seams in the rock, and scaling the wall. To my left was a pile of rocks, each the size of a large apple, placed there to use as weapons for just such a time as this.

"You there!" a guard yelled from my left. "What are

you doing? Get down from the wall!" But convicts were climbing right beneath him as they were beneath me. I couldn't see across the enclosure, but I could only assume that men were trying to scale the wall all the way around.

I picked up a rock and hurled it straight down, where it bounced off a man's shoulder a few feet below. He screamed but held his grip, then looked up at me and growled through clenched teeth. I picked up another stone and threw again, this time hitting him on the head, and he toppled over and fell to the ground, alive but injured.

The rain began to lessen and the noise from the enemy drew back. They were gathering in the center of the enclosure, crowding together like shimmering black boulders.

"Alexa!" It was Pervis, running along the top of the wall toward me. When he arrived he sat me down. I hadn't even realized I was standing on the edge, a gust of wind away from falling to my death.

"What on earth are you doing up here?" he asked. "You could have been killed!"

I looked out into the center of the prison we had built and I realized something wasn't right. They'd given up their attempt to scale the wall and they were rushing to huddle in the center of the town square. Where were the rest?

"What's going on, Pervis? Have they retreated into the tunnel?"

Pervis looked at me for a long, silent moment before answering. "We've sent men in to check, Alexa, and that's all there is."

"Where have they all gone?"

Pervis looked at me, blocking the rain from his eyes with one hand. "They're all dead, Alexa. Most have been dead for years. The ones in the square are all that remain. Let's get down from here before the rain and wind pick up again." He descended partway down the ladder first and I followed, glad to have him watching my steps on each slippery rung. When we arrived at the bottom I noticed a thin bead of blood running down the side of Pervis's face.

"Why the gash on your forehead? Don't tell me one of them actually took a swipe at you," I said. He touched his temple with his hand and wiped away some of the watery blood, grimacing as he did so.

"Slipped on the way up the ladder and bashed my head against the wall." He placed his hand against one of the massive stones in the structure we'd just spent two days building. "It seems as though the only things causing pain around here are these ridiculous walls we'd just spent so much effort building."

As it turned out, there were fifty-seven convicts who tried to invade Bridewell that night. All the rest had died waiting for Sebastian or Ganesh or whoever he was to give them orders to attack. He had taken terrible advantage of their willingness to follow blindly someone, anyone,

245

who would just lead them. While he lived a life of royalty for many long years, they hid in tunnels, scrounged for food, and watched their lot die of disease. Most of them were barely adults when they entered the prison at Ainsworth, and cowering there in the town square that night, I got the feeling they only wanted a place they could call home. I was scared to death of what was to become of them. But I needn't have worried.

A few days later, after things calmed down, my father and Nicolas decided to send twenty of the remaining convicts to Lunenburg, twenty to Turlock, and seventeen to Lathbury. It was easier to handle them in small numbers and each town was willing to do their part. The resolve to fight had left most of the convicts, especially once they understood what Ganesh had done to them. Some of them, though not all, were rehabilitated and lived productive lives after a time, and there were even a few that seemed out of place as convicts to begin with. One of these, a man named John Christopher, would become my friend (but that's a story for a different time).

A few days after the convicts were moved, my father and I took a group of men to the midway point on the road from Bridewell to Turlock, and we smashed six-foot holes in the walls on both sides of the road. Before we left, I looked out into the mountains with my father and watched as Darius came into view. Then I looked into Fenwick Forest on the other side and saw two more wolves creep out from behind the trees, Odessa and Sher-win. They would finally be reunited on that very day. I waved in both directions and the three of them howled: "Thank you."

It was the last thing I ever understood the animals to say.

EPİLOGUE

A month after the invasion the people of Bridewell voted to tear down the walls. Six months after that, the giant blocks that once formed the massive walls were strewn across the valley floor in thousands of pieces, weeds and flowers alike growing between the shattered stones, like an endless broken tombstone. The only walls that remain are those that surround Bridewell, a decision made by my father and Nicolas at Pervis's insistence. It sits alone now as a walled fortress at the center of everything. Maybe those walls will be of some use in a distant future I can't see, but for now they only remind me of an imprisoned past I'm happy to have behind me.

Life is better without the walls, everyone agrees. Still, sometimes I'm afraid of the outside world, and every so often in my private thoughts I wish the walls were still there to protect me. It feels like growing up, as if the safety of childhood has been stripped away, and I've woken up on the edge of something dangerous. The walls are gone and I can do as I please. It's a freedom I'm not so sure I'm ready for.

These days, when I make the trip from Lathbury to Bridewell, I see animals all along the way. I no longer understand what they say, and it makes me feel old, as if all the child has gone out of me. But I still get a funny look now and then from a squirrel or a wolf or a fox, and I remember the thrill of those days and all that was at stake, so much that nobody will ever know or understand. For a passing moment I feel like I'm twelve again, the magic filling the forest, and I can almost hear the animals talking.

The last time I visited Bridewell I spent hours and hours in the library, walking the aisles of books, looking for the volume I've missed that would make for the perfect companion. Grayson and I sat quietly reading all day, sometimes nodding off to sleep, other times sharing a favorite passage, as only old friends can.

Pervis is still the head guard. With so many walls down, he seems a tad more jumpy, forever casting a wary eye toward Ainsworth and The Dark Hills.

Yipes moved to Lathbury for almost a month, but he missed the wild of the mountains so much he returned to his house on the river. He seems content to live out his days mostly alone, and he goes back to the pool and looks for stones all the time. I know, because sometimes I go with him and I look, too, but we never find any. The ones we find are as dull and lifeless as the one I carry in a leather pouch around my neck.

In fact, as far as I can tell, all of Elyon's magic has drained out of the valley, leaving a dry and barren void even when the rainy season is upon us. I suppose the wall had its own way of holding the enchanting beauty of the wild away from us for a time, but eventually we found a way to snuff out what little magic remained. Maybe that's just what people do, or maybe Elyon, if he's real at all, is getting farther away from us as Ander had suggested in the forest. How I wished I had pushed Ander for more answers when I had had the chance. I fear the great silence between us will forever make Elyon a mystery to me.

Lately I've been wondering whether or not I could go off searching for a place where you could stand in a pool of icy water and come out talking to animals. A place where secret messages could be found, and squirrels are full of comic bravery. Sometimes I think I could ask Yipes and he would go with me, and we could travel the world just like Warvold did, looking for pockets of magic where Elyon's presence still remained. But then I'm not twelve anymore, and sometimes I'm almost sure adventures like that only happen when you're a child.

My thoughts keep returning to Elyon and all that Ander had said about him. The mystery of this mythical "creator" has drifted into my head and I can't get it out. My world has always been so small, hidden behind walls. I'm beginning to think this Land of Elyon is bigger and more dangerous than anything I could have imagined. How many more mysteries are waiting for me beyond the walls?

I wonder what would happen if I drove my cart through Bridewell, on to Ainsworth, and beyond — a girl of thirteen and not a wall in sight to hold me back.

Was that a rabbit that just winked at me? I think I just saw Ander in the mist, and I hear Darius howling through the windswept trees. Could it be that Elyon is in the shadows, waiting for us, longing to be with us once again? Maybe an unscheduled visit to see Yipes with a big bag of tomatoes would be a good idea.

To be continued . . .

AUTHOR'S NOTES

The Dark Hills Divide was originally constructed as a weekly serial for my two daughters. If you should run across them in your travels, cover your ears, and run the other way. They are talkative little darlings, and we are always somewhere beyond the reader in Alexa's adventures.

Bridewell was a real place: a prison in England, where they really did brand *V*s on vagabonds.

Renny Lodge was the name of one of the buildings at the historic Bridewell prison.

Lunenburg (the first town Warvold settled) is the name of a town from the Robert Frost poem "The Mountain."

The Grob is a genuine chess strategy used for precisely the reasons outlined in this story.

Cabeza de Vaca (which translates as *cow head*) was a real person, a Spanish explorer of the sixteenth century.

COMING SOON

The Land of Elyon Book 2

Beyond the Valley of Thorns

Alexa Daley has been keeping quiet, living out what remains of her life in the city of Lathbury, mending books and daydreaming about faraway places. But all that changes when a mysterious letter arrives from an old friend beckoning her to the caves, a dark and ominous place, the one place she doesn't want to go.

Thus begins the second installment in The Land of Elyon series, in which Alexa leaves the safe confines of Bridewell Common and travels into The Dark Hills and beyond. She discovers stunning new lands, finds extraordinary new friends, and encounters a strange new evil with the power to destroy The Land of Elyon.

Full of excitement and peril, *Beyond the Valley of Thorns* will redefine everything Alexa believes about the world she inhabits. She will discover the dark unseen forces at work all around her, and she will carry a burden she alone was meant for, a burden that will determine the fate of The Land of Elyon and all who reside there.

ABOUT THE AUTHOR

PATRICK CARMAN began *The Dark Hills Divide* as a story to tell in the night. The characters and places soon took on a life of their own, and The Land of Elyon was born.

Before writing this, his first novel, Carman helped to create board games, Web sites, a mentoring program, and a music show heard on hundreds of radio stations across the country and around the world. He currently lives in the Pacific Northwest with his wife and two daughters.

To learn more about
Patrick Carman and The Land of Elyon,
visit:

www.scholastic.com/landofelyon

THE THRILLING STORY OF HOW IT ALL STARTED!

BEFORE ALEXA. BEFORE THE WALLS. THOMAS WARVOLD JOURNEYED...

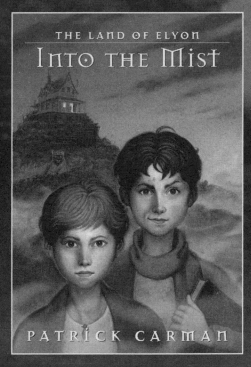

THE LAND OF ELYON
INTO THE MIST

PATRICK CARMAN

Follow Thomas Warvold and his brother as they travel through Elyon, discovering new mysteries, new challenges, and new magical creatures that will alter the history of the land.

BEYOND THE
VALLEY OF
THORNS

THE LAND OF ELYON BOOK 2

BEYOND THE VALLEY OF THORNS

PATRICK CARMAN

SCHOLASTIC INC.
NEW YORK   TORONTO   LONDON   AUCKLAND   SYDNEY
MEXICO CITY   NEW DELHI   HONG KONG   BUENOS AIRES

In addition to the people I thanked in *The Dark Hills Divide,* I would like to add the following: Charisse Meloto for her boundless energy and leadership; Jennifer Pasenan, Rachel Coun, and Katy Coyle—their enthusiasm and hard work make me wonder how I got anything done before I met them; Barbara Marcus and Jean Feiwel, for making me feel at home in an unfamiliar place; Remy Wilcox for her critical eye and unwavering support; and to Jeremy Gonzalez, who risked everything on my behalf.

ISBN-13: 978-0-439-89121-9
ISBN-10: 0-439-89121-3

12 11 10 9 8 7 6 5 4 3 2   7 8 9 10 11 12/0

Printed in the U.S.A.   40

First Scholastic Book Club printing, March 2007

For Sierra

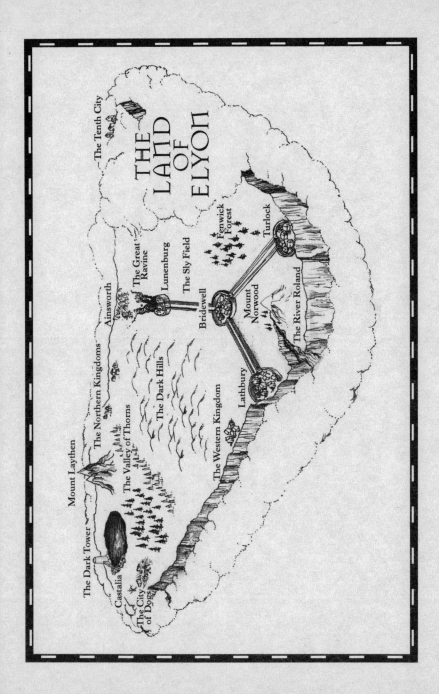

THE LAND OF ELYON

The Tenth City

The Northern Kingdoms

Ainsworth

The Great Ravine

Lunenburg

The Sly Field

Fenwick Forest

Turlock

Bridewell

Mount Norwood

The River Roland

Mount Laython

The Dark Tower

The Valley of Thorns

The Dark Hills

Lathbury

The Western Kingdom

Castalia

The City of Dogs

As evening approaches and the shadows begin their descent into Bridewell, the same frightening thoughts always disturb me. Darkness sends its shadows to draw all men back into itself, for it is in the shadows that darkness plays. And what of the man who stays in the shadows too long, at play with sinister thoughts?

Darkness will surely overtake him.

FROM THE DIARY OF THOMAS WARVOLD

To be surprised, to wonder, is to begin to understand.

The Revolt of the Masses,
JOSÉ ORTEGA Y GASSET

PART I

CHAPTER I

MY ARRIVAL IN BRIDEWELL

Yesterday I left Lathbury behind. I traveled with Father and he let me drive the cart on the road to Bridewell. The journey could not have been more different from the one I took on the same road only a year ago, before the walls that surrounded it were taken down. The ride is still hot, but yesterday I could see in every direction — the Dark Hills to my left, the valley floor and Mount Norwood to my right, Fenwick Forest a green mass in the distance. As I looked around and smelled the air thick with blooms, I couldn't help but daydream about the adventures that might be had in the faraway corners of The Land of Elyon.

Driving along the dusty road, I kept a lookout for animals I might recognize or hawks flying overhead, but it seemed the animals had been sent into hiding by the noisy grinding of our wagon wheels on the road.

"So, can you tell me the rules once more?" I asked my father. After all the events of the previous summer he was more protective than ever, and I wanted to be sure I knew the rules I'd likely break once we arrived in Bridewell.

"Ah, yes, the rules," he replied, whittling on a stick with his knife. "First and foremost, absolutely no leaving the confines of Bridewell unless accompanied by an adult, and even then I want to know exactly where you're going and why. There's plenty to keep you busy in town without milling around outside unsupervised. And no sneaking around the lodge, listening in on conversations you shouldn't be hearing. Also, you're to join me for dinner each evening. It's time I started grooming you for leadership. A few more years and your visits to Bridewell will be less play and more work."

I could feel my childhood slipping away with each of his statements, most notably the last remark about becoming a leader in our community. It made me long for the days when Warvold had told me stories and I'd been off on adventures in the mountains with Yipes and Murphy. I wished my father wasn't so important, that I was an unknown girl drifting through towns on my way to one place or another, free to travel The Land of Elyon as I pleased.

"Sounds exciting," I replied, faking enthusiasm a bit more than I should have. My father looked at me as if my tone was not what he had hoped for. We settled into a silence, he no doubt thinking of how he might keep an eye on me and still get his work done over the summer, me dreaming of adventures to be had in faraway places.

Half an hour passed with little talk between us, and then the walls of Bridewell came into view a long way down the road. These were the only walls that remained, and their presence seemed to appear out of nowhere, like a giant limbless tree cut to a stump, sitting cold and alone in the wild. I suddenly felt unprotected out in the open, a feeling that had come and gone ever since the walls had been removed everywhere else. Even in the safety of my home along the towering jagged cliffs by the sea, I couldn't seem to shake the feeling that I was somehow unsafe without the walls that I'd been so eager to be rid of only a summer ago.

The horses picked up their pace upon seeing their destination. It wasn't long before we arrived at the huge wooden gate where Pervis Kotcher stood high above in the guard tower. Even at a distance I could see his wiry face and thin mustache. His eyes, always dark and pene-trating, watched carefully as my horses came to an abrupt stop in front of the entrance to Bridewell.

"Oh, no. Trouble has arrived along with Mr. Daley," Pervis said to the man at his side. "Best we keep double watch at the towers until she takes her leave."

I smiled up at him, and a flood of memories swirled around in my head. I was back in Bridewell for another summer and my adventurous spirit was newly flamed.

"Nice to see you, too, Pervis," I said. "I'm looking forward to eluding you day after day, all summer long."

We entered Bridewell and the day was filled with the business of settling in at Renny Lodge, unpacking my one bag, and enjoying meals with my father, Nicolas,

Grayson, Silas Hardy, and Pervis. Each of these men had played an important part in my life, especially during the eventful previous summer in Bridewell. My father, ever the leader, was already busy with endless meetings. Nicolas looked trim and handsome as usual, but he was more serious now, and he seemed to have aged more than the year since his own father's death. What can be said of Grayson for those who might have forgotten him? He remained plump, forever sneaking to the kitchen, and I still loved visiting him in the library where he worked at mending books. Silas continued his duties as mail carrier for my father and other important folks, but he had grown into something of a confidant to my father, the two of them often walking together and talking quietly. Pervis had stopped following me around trying to catch me escaping, but I'd never known him to be more alert and cautious of the outside. He spent most of his time at the guard towers, and he seemed to be waiting nervously for something I could only imagine. The only person missing was Ganesh. A year later it was still hard to believe how he had deceived us all.

A day later, with the journey and the greetings behind me, I was able to sit on the sill of the window in my room and think. The walled confines of Bridewell were oddly comforting to me now. To see them from the window in my room or walk around the town square and see the walls all around produced in me a very different feeling than it used to. A year before I could not imagine anything better than escaping those walls; now I couldn't help but enjoy their strong arms encircling me in safety. I could take pleasure in them now as I could not before, especially since I hadn't seen them in a year's time. My hometown of Lathbury was so different, all out in the open, lounging at the edge of the cliffs with room to grow and expand wherever it wanted to. I wondered if I had misjudged these walls as something to fear rather than embrace. When you get what you wish for, it's never quite what you think it will be.

And yet, despite the comfort of the walls, I also wondered what I would find in the Dark Hills, past where I could see. I wondered what lay in the mist beyond Fenwick Forest, if anything at all. The adventurer in me dreamed of escaping once again, only this time I would go much farther, past where our kingdom ended, into lands that only Warvold had traveled and explored.

My daydreaming got me to thinking about the library and my old chair, so I stepped down from the windowsill and headed there. The door to the library was open so I walked in and smelled that old familiar scent of books, heard the creaking of the floors, and saw the twisting, turning rows of shelves. These things made Bridewell feel like home again, like somewhere I belonged.

"Who's visiting?" came a voice from the library office, the messy little room where Grayson spent most of his time mending books and dreaming of strawberry jam.

"It's only me, Grayson," I said. "Just coming to browse and sit a spell before it gets too hot." I'd already seen him at dinner the night before so there was no need for a grand entrance.

Grayson peered around the corner of his office and smiled at me. He was the same plump and happy person I'd left behind the previous summer.

"It's so good to have you back in the library, Alexa. Things have been a mite boring around here in your absence. Maybe you can liven things up a bit." Grayson looked at me sideways, thinking about what he'd said, then added, "Just don't liven things up too much, agreed?" I nodded and smiled, then slowly made my way deeper into the cavernous library.

Walking along the dusty rows of books, my finger scanning the titles, I was struck by the feeling of routine creeping into my bones. The floor still made the same noises as I walked the winding pathway through the library to my favorite chair in the hidden corner, surrounded by towering shelves of books. I tidied the shelves on my way, making for a long meandering journey down many of the aisles. When I arrived at the place where my chair sat I stopped at the windowsill and looked at the wall staring back at me — a blank, unmoving mass of rock brought to life only by the green ivy climbing up and over its top.

My gaze fell on the chair, and I was tempted to move it away and try to open the secret door behind it. I could sneak down into the tunnels below and make my escape into the wild. I could run free. But it would be no use. My father had taken the door's silver key from me and had forbidden me from ever going into the tunnels again. So instead I flopped down in the chair and looked at the books on the shelf next to me. I'd seen them all before and had read and enjoyed many of them. But this time I was looking for one in particular — the one I'd dropped down into the opening behind the secret door last summer, the one called *Adventures at the Border of the Tenth City*. I searched all along the rows of books, moving some out and nudging others in to straighten them perfectly on the shelf. I finally found the book and pulled it out, then settled into the chair and put my feet up on the old wooden box that always served as my footrest.

I flipped open the book and began reading, the breeze outside the window making the ivy leaves along the wall dance and sing as only leaves can do.

And then I heard a different noise. A strange noise. It was a faint, almost unnoticeable, knocking.

Knock, knock, knock.

I looked all around, then stood up with the book in

my hand and leaned out the window to listen for the sound again.

Knock, knock, knock.

Louder now, but not from outside. I turned and faced the shelves of books and remained very still.

Knock, knock, knock.

The book I held slipped out of my hand and fell to the floor with a pop. I remained motionless, not even breathing.

Knock, knock, knock.

The sound was coming from behind my chair, from the other side of the secret door.

CHAPTER 2
AN UNEXPECTED MESSAGE

I walked back through the library, crisscrossing down several aisles, listening for Grayson to see if he was anywhere nearby. Finding no one, I quickly returned to my chair and began pulling it away from the wall as quietly as I could. Even though I was a year older, I was still as scrawny as ever, hardly a muscle on my bony little arms, and it took all my effort to wrench the chair away from the secret door. I crouched down and listened. Was I hearing things? I started to think I was so desperate for adventure that I'd made up the knocking in my head. But then I heard a soft *click* and the little door swung in slowly on squeaky hinges, revealing only darkness inside.

I held back, too afraid to peer inside. Then a tiny head popped out into the room, accompanied by a high-pitched voice I knew well.

"I was beginning to wonder if you'd leave me hanging here all morning." It was Yipes, dangling on the old ladder that led down into the darkness, a big grin on his small face.

"Yipes!" I said. "What on earth are you doing in there? I can't believe it's you!"

11

He popped out of the tunnel and crouched down next to me behind the chair, then put his finger to his lips.

"*Shhhhhh.* There's no telling who might be milling about the library," he whispered.

"But why are you sneaking around in the old tunnels?" I asked.

He crawled up the back of the chair, scaled one of the tall bookshelves, and disappeared over the top. I could hear him hop from one shelf to another, a quiet, almost imperceptible flitting of his feet. I stayed behind the chair, staring at the shelf he'd disappeared over the top of, wondering where he'd gone and when he might return.

"You can come out now." It was Yipes, sitting on the windowsill behind me. His voice startled me.

"Must you sneak up on me like that? You're worse than Murphy with his slinking around."

"He and I have an agreement," he answered. "It's just too much fun startling you not to try it whenever possible. In any case, Grayson has gone off to the kitchen and the library is empty for the moment. We can talk in peace."

I moved around to the front of the chair and sat down facing the window where Yipes sat on his feet, ready to spring to life should he hear even the smallest disturbance in the library. No matter how many times I saw him, I was always taken aback at how tiny he was. His deeply tanned face was worn and friendly, and he had a smile beneath a pointy little nose that gave away how happy he was to see me.

"It's wonderful to see you, but you shouldn't be sneaking around down there in the tunnels," I said. "They send guards, you know, every hour or so, to make sure people aren't creeping around where they shouldn't be."

Pervis had long ago devised an entrance from within the courtyard, housed in a small stone room, leading down into the tunnels. He'd spent days and days going from chamber to chamber, making sure no one was hiding. The guards knew every way in or out, all of which they had already permanently blocked.

"I don't understand how you even got in there," I continued. "I thought Pervis had sealed off the tunnels from the outside."

Yipes smiled mischievously and leaned closer to me.

"There is still a way for those of us who are small enough." He seemed quite proud of himself, and I was all of a sudden very interested in hearing more about this secret exit and where it might lead.

"There's something important I need to tell you," Yipes went on. He took one last look around, leaning his head from side to side to listen carefully for any noise. "When you were only a few years old, after Renny died, Warvold went on a journey. He was away for quite a long time and nobody knew where he went. When he returned he stopped in to see me, not long after I'd made my home in the wild. He seemed concerned in a way I'd

13

never known him to be, and he gave me something I was to take special care of."

Yipes opened up his vest and dug his little hand inside, fishing around for something. He pulled out a very old and pitiful-looking envelope and held it out to me. The envelope was dirty and torn at the edges, and the writing on the front was smudged with a dried red substance, probably wine from a glass spilled long ago. On the outside were scribbled these eight words:

For Alexa Daley, one year after I've gone

I moved into the light of the window and stood next to Yipes. It felt very strange to be holding a message from Warvold. Just hearing his and Renny's names sent shivers of excitement through my bones. But there was another emotion as well. It was odd, but whenever I heard the names of Renny or Warvold, I felt an unusually strong longing to be with them once again.

"Why didn't you give this to me sooner? He's been dead for a year already," I asked.

Yipes shifted back and forth on his feet and looked away from me before answering.

"It's only just been a year since his death," he said. "As you can see by the letter, it says to wait a year. I promise you it was hard not to give it to you sooner. I spent many a night holding it by candlelight trying to read what it says, but the envelope was too thick."

He paused and scratched at his knees.

"In any case, it's in your hand now," he said, "so you had best open it up and see what it says. I have a feeling the time has come for something he intended you to do."

I looked at the envelope, my hand shaking as I held it, and a thousand thoughts ran through my head about what it might contain. I turned it over and carefully tore at the wax seal. Inside was a piece of yellowed paper, folded at the center and ragged on the edges. There was also a smaller envelope enclosed, addressed to my father. I set the smaller envelope aside, opened the first sheet of paper, and began reading aloud.

Alexa,

> *I have known Yipes for quite some time and he was the only one I could trust with this letter. There is much you need to know but only a little that I can tell you now. If I told you everything I'm afraid you wouldn't have enough courage to undertake what you must, and so I'll only tell you one thing to get you on your way.*
>
> *There is a secret cave in the Dark Hills, beyond anyplace you can see from Bridewell. Within this cave there is something you must retrieve, something very important and very special. This something is for you alone, Alexa, and you must find it. I have taken the liberty of*

including a letter for your father. Leave it for
him, and he won't follow after you. This is a
secret journey that he can have no part in. He is
aware of certain facts, certain situations, and you
can be sure he will understand why you must go
into the Dark Hills.

Off with you now. Go!

Warvold

Beneath the words was an intricate map. The map led to an entrance I knew nothing of, but beneath the entrance on the map was a squiggly double line clearly marking the place I was to go: *Dark Hills Caves, Secret Far East Chamber.*

I looked up at Yipes, and though I should have been feeling a sense of dread, instead I felt an overwhelming joy at the prospect of adventure. From the grave, Warvold was calling me to do something unexpected and scary, but in my heart I felt as though I'd anticipated just such a development. A big grin spread across my face.

"Yipes, this is incredible," I said. "Will you go with me?"

"I wouldn't have it any other way," he replied.

I could tell he was just as excited as I was at the prospect of what we might find in the Dark Hills.

CHAPTER 3

THE SECRET CAVE

I ventured back to my room and packed my leather bag with everything I could think of that I might need. On the way back to the library I stopped in the kitchen. It was midmorning and the cooks were taking their break in the smoking room. I went to the large pantry and hoarded all the dried meats and fruits my bag would hold.

When I returned to the library, Grayson was back in his office, mending an especially large book. I peeked in, knowing I couldn't avoid him on my way back to my chair. He turned away from his work and looked up at me.

"Off on a journey, are we?" he said, seeing the bag over my shoulder.

"Just some snacks and books for an afternoon of reading and strolling around town."

"Ahhh. Sounds wonderful. I only wish I could join you. The mending on this book is past due and Silas is scheduled to take it to Ainsworth tonight. I'm afraid I'll be slumped over my desk for some time yet." He turned back to his work and shifted in his chair, his big stomach rubbing against the desk. I was relieved — what if he'd wanted to come with me?

"Happy reading to you," he said, and then I walked away toward the back of the library.

17

When I arrived back at the chair it was just as I'd left it — back in place, with the secret door shut tight behind it. Yipes was nowhere to be seen, and I began to think again that I'd imagined everything.

I pulled the letter for my father out of my bag and set it on the chair. Then I heard the quiet knocking once more.

Knock, knock, knock.

This time I knew it was Yipes, waiting for me on the ladder in the tunnel. I went about the grueling business of pulling the chair out again, and there he was, dangling from the ladder, hiding in case Grayson came to find me. Yipes moved down on the ladder, and I stepped inside, the cool earthen air refreshing on my skin. I took one last look into the library and shut the secret door behind me.

It was darker than I remembered it, the light from the lantern only a faint glow against the smothering blackness all around us. I felt like a tiny firefly, caught all alone in the depths of the night.

"We need to be very quiet," whispered Yipes. "No telling if one of the guards is doing rounds within the tunnels."

I nodded in agreement and we descended to the dirt floor in silence. Yipes led the way as we walked along the tunnel, the light dangling in his tiny hand, shadows thrown along the walls. We walked for some time, twisting and turning into places I'd never been before. As we came upon a sharp turn to the right, Yipes stopped, turned back, and crouched down. Then he blew out the light, and we sat motionless against the tunnel wall.

"What is it?" I whispered. I couldn't see Yipes in the dark, and he made no reply. He only touched my shoulder, moved his hand along my face, and put his fingers over my mouth. A moment later I saw light dancing on the wall, coming from a distance and moving toward us.

My instincts told me to run back before the guard discovered us, but Yipes held me down at my shoulder, as if to tell me we should stay perfectly still. The light came closer, until it was almost on top of us, and I heard the footsteps approaching.

I was fighting the urge to get up and escape as Yipes continued to hold me there, breathless, against the wall. Just about the time I expected to see the guard come around the corner, the light from his lamp began to diminish, and his footsteps became harder to hear, until finally it was all darkness and quiet again.

"Where did he go?" I whispered.

"Another tunnel shoots off to the right, just around the corner. I've been watching the guards as they make their way through the tunnels, and they always turn there, then double back and come this way. We've got only a moment to get across before he returns."

We stood up in the dark and felt along the wall. I followed Yipes as we turned the corner and made our way past the opening where light was moving down the tunnel the guard had entered. Near blind, I stumbled over a rock on the ground, letting out a small gasp as Yipes steadied me and pulled me along more quickly.

"Who's there?" yelled the guard, footsteps sounding toward us.

Yipes hurried me along the floor in the dark, then turned to the left.

"Show yourself!" the guard commanded. But then he went past where we had turned, continuing on in the wrong direction. With the careful silence of cats, Yipes and I moved far enough ahead in our own direction that I began to feel we'd lost the guard in the maze of tunnels.

"That was close," Yipes said, after a time. "But we're almost there now. Just hold my hand — I know the way in the dark."

A few twists and turns later, Yipes stopped and let go of my hand. I couldn't tell where he was, and then a shaft of light appeared near the floor. Yipes had removed the boards from the wall, and with the light from the opening, I found I could see the dimly lit space around me. We had entered a room, surrounded by wood planks on the walls. It looked as though it might have once been sleeping quarters for the escaped convicts who'd hidden in the tunnels before the walls had come down.

"In you go, then," said Yipes. "It's a tight fit, but it's not far to the surface."

Once again, Yipes was pushing me forward. Sometimes

it seemed that forward was the only direction he knew. He'd already pushed me through tunnels and forests. Now he was clearly determined to lead me forward beyond those earlier adventures. He was my friend and I trusted him, so I followed. I moved in front of Yipes and looked into the hole, then I put my arms in front of me as if I were about to dive into a pool of water. It was truly a challenge to move once I was inside, but I managed to slowly inch my way along until my head popped out aboveground in the bright, hot sunlight.

Yipes followed and we found ourselves out in the Dark Hills, the walls of Bridewell standing closer than I'd hoped in the distance. But we were hidden by the thick underbrush, which formed something like a tunnel above the ground, leading away from Bridewell, deeper into the wild.

"That guard might have gone back to bring help," Yipes warned. "They'll be looking for trouble, so we'd best move quickly."

We turned and walked as fast as we could down the hidden pathway. It was hot and cramped as we went, winding our way farther and farther into territory I'd never dreamed I'd be brave enough to venture into. After a long while, Yipes stopped where the pathway split in three directions.

"This is it. This is where the map begins," he said.

I took the map from my bag and laid it flat on the ground. There was indeed a fork on the map with three pathways leading in different directions. The map indicated that we should take the middle fork and follow it until we met with a giant stone somewhere down the way. It was there that we would find an open space and the entrance to the secret cave.

"We're not too far off, maybe a mile," said Yipes. "Let's get on with it. No telling what we'll find when we get there."

About a half hour later we emerged from the confines of the brush, into lands that were more rocky and desolate. We were in a long, skinny ravine, the ground gnarled with deep green brush and sharp, dead trees. It was a dim and gloomy atmosphere. Everything was brittle and hard underfoot. Large, colorless boulders spotted the landscape in every direction.

I sat on the warm ground and spread the map out before me.

"There are rocks all around this place," I said. "But that one is definitely the biggest."

I pointed to a large stone mass protruding from the ground in front of us. It was red and brown and shaped like an enormous nose poking out of the earth.

I wiped my forehead, dripping with sweat, and drank a bit of water from my wineskin. We walked around the rock and the thick brush, looking for an entrance to the cave or a sign that one existed. White cotton clouds crept over the sun, and shadows filled the ravine.

Yipes scampered up the rock and stood at the very tip

22

of the nose. He seemed to be thinking about the way things looked around him, measuring the dead trees and the brush to see if they were where they ought to be. A moment later he bounded across the rock and jumped down to the ground a few feet across from me.

When he landed it didn't sound like I'd expected it to. I anticipated a hard, solid thud, but instead I heard a hollow emptiness beneath the dirt, as if very little was holding Yipes up. He jumped up and landed on the dirt again, and I had the uneasy feeling that all was not right with this patch of earth. Yipes jumped again and again as he moved away from the rock, and eventually he landed on ground that sounded more like it ought to.

He turned around and faced the rock, crouching down on his knees. At the same time, we both saw with some surprise a small piece of crudely twisted rope, half buried in the dirt. Yipes picked it up and looked at it, then turned and faced me, holding the rope out in his hand.

"You do the honors," he said.

I grabbed the rope and pulled, throwing a dirt-covered wooden door up into the air, bugs and spiders scurrying around its underbelly. A gust of cool, dank air rose from the black hole beneath.

CHAPTER 4

JOHN CHRISTOPHER

Yipes and I sat down and let our feet dangle into the hole; the air, though musty, felt refreshing. I ran my hands along the sides of the opening, where the earth was hard. The lower I felt, the cooler the wall became. I let my feet and arms dangle down into the opening for a moment longer, then I felt a spider crawling along my fingers and quickly jerked all my limbs back into the heat of the ravine.

"There's not much choice," said Yipes. "We're going to have to go down in there, and the sooner we do it, the better. At least it won't be as hot as it is out here."

There was no ladder along any of the sides, and though the light poured into the hole, I could not be sure if I was seeing the floor of the tunnel or not. At first I thought the bottom was only seven or eight feet down, a distance I could manage if I jumped in. But then my eyes began to play tricks on me. I wiped the sweat from my face and dropped a rock the size of my fist into the opening while I watched and listened. To my relief it landed quickly and within sight, its gray mass outlined in the shadows less than ten feet below. Yipes jumped first and seemed to have no problem whatsoever with the landing. This gave me the courage I needed to do the same, and though my landing sent me careening across the floor on my hands and knees, we'd made it safely into the secret cave.

I picked up the rock I had tossed into the hole, thinking it might suit me as a weapon should the need arise. The tunnel went in one direction only, and the ceiling was lower than I'd hoped, so low that I had to stoop to manage it. Six steps into this new underground world left me in near-total darkness with Yipes close behind. Something small, probably a field mouse, scurried at my feet as I pushed cobwebs away with my hand. Without thinking, I felt for the dirt ceiling above. As I'd moved along, the tunnel had widened and risen in height, and I realized that I was able to stand upright in the chilly air. In front of me I saw what I expected to see behind me: the light from the opening, looking more like a faraway lamp than light pouring in from outside. I felt along the cold earthen wall and turned back in the other direction. It wasn't until then that I realized the spot we'd gotten ourselves into.

Down the expanse of the tunnel there was a round spot of light — the opening we had come through. I turned and looked again in the direction we were moving and saw the far-off light that looked like a flickering lamp. Then I heard a loud bang off in the distance and turned to see that the round spot of light had disappeared. Someone or something had closed us in.

"That's an unfortunate development," said Yipes.

"We don't have any choice now," I said. "Whatever

Warvold wanted us to find is down here somewhere. I just hope it doesn't have claws and sharp teeth."

A small furry creature brushed against my ankle and I yelped, hopping off the ground, bumping my head against the ceiling, and showering myself with crumbling earth.

"There's something in here with us, Yipes. Something at my feet."

"It's probably just a field mouse or a rat," he replied. "I wouldn't worry too much until you feel a nibble on your toes."

I brushed myself off, then continued walking in the direction of the flickering light, slowly inching my way along in the darkness, my hands held out to gather the cobwebs and feel for obstacles in my path.

"Hello?" I said quietly. "Anyone there?"

"I'm here," Yipes teased.

I smiled in the darkness and asked out loud if anyone besides Yipes was there, but no one answered.

Ten feet away were three wide candles nestled close together on a large stone table. A shadow darted across the wall and my breath was caught in my throat. I leaned flat against the right side of the tunnel and remained still, the cold of the wall gripping the back of my neck. Again I felt the scuffle on my ankle as something moved over my sandals. This time the light from the candles illuminated the floor just enough to make out shapes, and I saw the silhouette of a large rat walking across my left foot. I screamed and kicked the beastly thing across the tunnel. It crashed into the wall with a thud, then scuttled off out of sight.

"Well, come on, then, we haven't got all day. Lots to do and a short time to do it in."

It was a voice I didn't recognize, deep but friendly, coming from somewhere up ahead. Yipes was the first to answer.

"Who are you? What are you doing down here?"

There was a long silence, and then the voice answered.

"My name is John Christopher. Warvold asked me to be here when you arrived. And if that doesn't comfort you, maybe another friend of yours will." The voice was quiet for a moment, and then it spoke again. "That poor beast you've been kicking back and forth in the dark is a rodent that's been driving me half out of my mind down here for hours. He won't stop running around and flitting all over the cave. I believe you both know Murphy."

I came out into the open, and the squirrel ran across the cave in front of me, then leaped into my arms.

"Murphy!" I cried. "What a splendid surprise!"

Yipes walked the rest of the way into the light, and I followed, running my hand over Murphy's soft fur as I went. We found ourselves in a small underground chamber, softly lit by the three large candles.

"It is awfully good to see you again," I whispered to Murphy. "If only I had a Jocasta so we could talk to one another."

27

"You should get used to stumbling around in the dark," said John. "There will be much of that in the coming days." Candlelight flickered across his face, the glow just enough to make out his bright eyes and the shape of his face. He was a tall man, thin but powerful, and to my surprise he had the letter *C* branded on his forehead. He was a former convict, and I was suddenly very uncomfortable in the confines of the cave.

"I see you've noticed my forehead," said John. "That's good. We might just as well get that out in the open before we do anything more."

I set Murphy down and tapped him on the head, then he scampered a few steps and leaped onto the stone table in the middle of the room. His big furry tail twitched up and down nervously, casting erratic shadows across the walls.

"Murphy!" Yipes cried. "Calm down, will you? You'll give us all a headache." Murphy moved away from the candles, did a backflip, and caught his long tail between two front paws on the way down. He continued to shake and move about nervously, his big black eyes bulging comically, a silly look on his kind little face.

"I don't know what we are to do with him," said John. "The poor thing can't bring himself to sit still. Have you ever spied him sleeping? It's more of the same, twitching and carrying on. I tell you, I don't know how much longer I can stay down here with him. One day is enough to last me a lifetime."

Everyone looked at Murphy, and he sneezed three times in the course of five seconds, all the while trying not to let go of his tail and having quite a time of it. As Yipes tried to calm him down, John began speaking again.

"Where were we?" asked John. "Oh, yes, this letter *C* on my forehead. It's true I was once a convict in the service of Mr. Warvold. But he and I had a special relationship. I was what you might call a petty criminal. I only took what we absolutely needed to survive: a little bread here, a chicken there, the free lodging of a barn or a shed. Warvold saw in me someone he could put to some use, someone he could trust with an important, secret task. It is this task that we must turn our attention to now."

"Why did you close the secret door we entered through?" I blurted out. Come to think of it, I wondered *how* he'd done it as well.

"This is a dangerous place you've stumbled into. You never know who or what might be lurking about in the Dark Hills, what might have found its way down here had I not sealed us in."

"Yes, but how did you close it from way back here?" I asked. I wasn't sure I trusted John Christopher yet.

"Let's just say there is more than one way into this room, and I was aware of your arrival when you opened the door to get in."

Murphy let go of his tail, and it darted up and down again, casting shadows all over the room.

"Murphy!" yelled Yipes. This time the squirrel jumped off the table and back into my arms, burying its head next to my elbow. There was a deep silence in the room. I watched in disbelief as John leaned over and blew out the candles, leaving us in complete darkness.

There was no protection now.

CHAPTER 5

WHAT WARVOLD
LEFT BEHIND

A cold blackness enveloped the space. I was afraid, and I stepped back for a wall to lean against while I called into the darkness for Yipes. Murphy became restless in my arms and darted up to my shoulder, where he sat flicking his tail against the back of my head. I turned to look at him, my nose touching his, but I could not make out his face.

"Take my hand," said John. "Come on, reach out and take it. We've very little time, and certainly none to be wasted on meandering about like the blind."

I felt uneasy about putting my hand in his. I hardly knew him at all and he was much bigger than I was. In the dark of the cave I felt my hands shaking, and I felt trapped, as though I had no choice but to do as I was told.

I kept one hand on the wall and reached out in the air of the cave with the other. When I touched John's hand I realized how comparatively small mine was. The coarse texture of his skin felt like an old knotted rope. I held tight to his hand, and he pulled me along the wall of the cave until I was unclear where we were.

"Sit down, Alexa," he said. I felt the cool dirt floor

beneath me with my free hand and slowly sat down. Murphy remained on my shoulder, holding my thick hair between his front paws and shivering with fright. Yipes was somewhere in the room, but he was quiet, so I couldn't be sure where he was or what he was doing.

I sat in the black cave only a moment longer, and I listened as the sound of rock sliding against rock came from a short distance away. Then, miraculously, the cave was aglow in watery light, much brighter than the candlelight had been. As the sound of sliding rock persisted, a kaleidoscope of fiery colors ran liquid all around us. I crawled over to the source as Murphy scampered onto my back, and I peered over the edge of a large boulder. Its top was flat, and the inside had been cut into a bowl. Within the bowl lay a foot of water, and at the bottom sat a glowing stone, pulsating red and yellow like embers in a fire.

"A Jocasta," I whispered.

"The last one," said John, his face aglow as he gazed over the edge of the pool looking as though he'd found the greatest of long-lost treasures.

"It was placed here years ago under Warvold's direction," he continued. "The cave entrance used to be there, but it was easily seen, so he covered it up." John pointed to a pile of rocks a few feet away, obscuring what had clearly been an opening at one time.

"We are well past where the convicts dug their tunnels near Bridewell. They never came out so far into the

Dark Hills. At least most of them didn't." Here John paused, reached over, and tapped Murphy on the head. "Warvold appointed me the task of digging the short tunnel that leads to this cave, as well as blocking the old entrance. It was me who chose the soft stone that would hold the last of the Jocastas, chiseled out its middle, and found a slab of rock that would perfectly cover the top of the secret pool. It was a task that required many years, as you might imagine."

Yipes leaned over the edge of the pool and looked into the water, the glow of the Jocasta shimmering across his face. He had a deep longing in his face, as though he'd found something he was sure no longer existed. It would take him but a moment to snatch it in his miniature hands.

"This stone was appointed for you, Alexa," said John. Yipes looked at me and nodded his agreement with a smile. "We don't know why this is so, but it's what Warvold told me to tell you both. There is something more to this stone, something more than all the rest."

All of this had been done for me? All the careful planning and work to protect this one stone. It was hard to imagine. Warvold had trusted John Christopher with quite a lot, and suddenly I felt I could trust him as well.

"If you don't take it soon, Murphy's head will explode," said Yipes. "He must be very excited to talk with you."

The last Jocasta. Yipes and I had been back to the glowing pool upon Mount Norwood many times hoping to find one. And all this time one had been waiting, hidden by Warvold in the cave. Murphy began scratching at my back, and I reached down into the clear, cold water. I put my fingers around the smooth, plum-sized stone and pulled it out into the air.

"Murphy the brave, at your disposal!" said the squirrel on my back.

The magic of the Jocastas remained. What followed were a few minutes of chatter between old friends, mostly catching up on where we had been and what we had been doing. Murphy had been sitting down to a nice walnut for supper when John came calling.

"John has lived in the wild since before the walls went up, and he visited the glowing pool quite a long time before you did," Murphy told me.

John opened a leather pouch around his neck and removed a glowing blue stone.

"It's not the last stone, but it will do," said John. We both looked at Yipes and wished he could go back in time and have his own Jocasta restored. But he seemed perfectly content to have us do the translating for him.

"I'm just happy to be a part of the adventure," he said.

"There's no more time to waste yapping in the cave," John broke in. "You two can talk all you want aboveground."

By the light of the Jocastas we walked the length of the tunnel, John in front.

"How did you know we would arrive here today?" I asked our guide.

John laughed out loud.

"You can't imagine how many times I wanted to tell Yipes to give you the letter. It's been my sole duty to watch and wait for him to deliver it to you. The boredom was excruciating. As soon as he went off to get you, I gathered Murphy and another friend as Warvold had instructed and came straight here. We've been waiting for you since last night."

We arrived where the secret door had been thrown shut. I had brought my first Jocasta with me, now dull and lifeless in its pouch around my neck. John instructed me to remove the old stone and place the new Jocasta inside. This command I obeyed, and when John placed his Jocasta back in its hiding place, all was dark once more.

I heard a pop above my head, the sound of a stone hitting against the bottom of the wood door. A moment later the door flew open and stinging bright light enveloped the space. I had to shield my eyes before looking up through the opening. A silhouette peered over the edge, but it wasn't that of a person.

"She's grown quite a lot. Not the little girl she once was." It was a gentle growling of words, the mystic voice of a wolf, the outline of its huge head glaring down upon me.

"That she has," said John, pulling a ladder from the shadows in the corner and placing it against the wall of the tunnel.

"Darius, is that you?" I asked as I scampered onto the edge of the opening, and Murphy jumped free of my shoulder.

"I'm afraid his adventuring days are over, so you'll have to settle for the likes of me." It was Odessa, Darius's wife. She was every bit the hulking figure Darius was, with piercing blue eyes and massive white teeth. She was a powerful creature, and even though I knew instinctively that she was my ally, her presence was so frightening I had trouble standing next to her. Not so for Murphy, who had already leaped onto Odessa's back and was busy jumping up and down and squeaking for no particular reason. (Odessa seemed not to care.)

Yipes came up the ladder and stood beside me, then John slammed the door shut and sealed off the cave below. As we stood in the ravine, the wind began to blow, and a hawk drifted down to earth and sat upon Yipes's shoulder.

"I was wondering when you would return, you rascal. Out hunting again, are we?" said Yipes. "And stop looking at Murphy like that. He's not a meal, he's a member of our party." Murphy clung tightly to Odessa's fur, and his tiny eyes were wide and dark.

Thus the group was assembled: Yipes, John Christopher, Murphy, Odessa the wolf, the hawk (named Squire), and me. It was a strange assortment of animals

36

and humans, and it struck me then that Warvold saw far beyond what the eye beholds in its view of a creature. For who would think to leave this world entrusting a grand unfinished quest to a mere child, a former convict, a grown man no larger than a five-year-old boy, and an odd assortment of animals?

John had prepared well. There were three leather packs, one large and two small, along with a supply of water held within four good-sized wineskins. The wineskins were laced together, two on each side, and the whole water supply was set upon Odessa's back and secured around her waist and neck. The skins held a gallon or more of water each, but dangling at Odessa's enormous sides they seemed more than manageable. She would have no trouble with her duty.

I found my pack to be quite heavy and hot against my sweating back. Murphy added a pound or two by making his home in the leather where the drawstring was pulled behind my head. Squire was off again, flying in front of us in the clouds, and my two human companions appeared ready to depart.

"Just one more thing, Alexa," said Yipes as he pulled a small magnifying glass from a pocket in his vest. "You know the stones are inscribed with a message for the person they choose. Shall we take a look and see?"

I had a strange, uncertain feeling about the stone now in my hand, and for reasons I can't explain, I didn't want to know what it might say.

"I think I'll wait, if you don't mind," I said.

Yipes puzzled over my decision, shrugged, and began gathering the last of his things. When he was ready he ran his fingers over his mustache and looked around at the group of us.

"Now what?" he asked, and we all looked at John, hoping he had some idea what we were meant to do next.

CHAPTER 6

THE BLACK SWARM

Standing in the open space of the Dark Hills was uncomfortable, with the sun beating down and a growing fear that someone might come looking for us.

"Yipes," I said, "do you think that guard would come all the way out here trying to find us?"

Yipes thought a moment and replied, "I don't imagine so. They're probably busy searching through the tunnels. They won't think we've gotten so far out into the Dark Hills."

We were all standing together, wondering what we should do now that I'd accomplished the task Warvold had set out for me in his letter.

"I don't understand," I said. "Why would Warvold send me here to get the last stone and then leave no other instructions? Do you suppose he just wanted me to have it?"

John and Murphy exchanged glances, and then John knelt down and inspected his pack to be sure everything was secure.

"There are a few things I know," he said. "Things that Warvold shared with me over the years — clues to why we're here and where we're meant to go."

He looked up at us and wiped his brow with the back of his hand. Then he spoke.

"Somewhere past the Dark Hills lies the Valley of Thorns. At the end of the valley is a lake of unusual depth and darkness, and at its distant shore sits the Dark Tower."

This sounded like the start of one of Warvold's spooky stories. John took a long breath and continued.

"Though no one from Bridewell Common ever travels there, more than once Warvold journeyed to the Dark Tower and the poor town it rules. He spoke to me in whispers of these places and their history. There is more I can tell you about it as we make our way, but we can't stay here any longer. There are unseen dangers in this place."

He rose once again and threw his pack over his shoulder, then pointed deeper into the Dark Hills.

"What I can tell you right now is this: We must travel beyond the Valley of Thorns, to the places where Warvold ventured. Only there will we find the answers we're looking for."

For the first time I began to wonder what I'd gotten myself into. This sounded far too dangerous for a girl of thirteen, especially without the permission of her parents.

"Are you sure about this?" I asked. "I can't imagine what my father would say if he were to find out I'd gone off so far from home. He'd be furious." But even as I said it I remembered the letter from Warvold. *This is a secret journey that he can have no part in. He is aware of certain facts, certain situations, and you can be sure he will understand why you must go into the Dark Hills.*

"It's your decision, Alexa," said John. "Either way, we have to be moving along. We can't stay here any longer."

My hand instinctively went to the leather pouch around my neck, and I felt the Jocasta hidden inside. *The last Jocasta.* It was in my possession, and Warvold wanted it taken somewhere for some purpose. If I returned to Bridewell, that something would be left unfinished, with terrible consequences I couldn't begin to understand.

"Lead the way," I said to John.

It wasn't long before we all realized why the Dark Hills was a place that, once visited, was rarely returned to with fond memories. Only an hour into our journey, we were forced to stop as the sun pounded us with crippling heat. I felt most sorry for Odessa and Murphy, who was out of my pack and walking now; covered with thick fur, they were almost certainly suffering from exhaustion. But neither of them complained, and though our conversations lagged, they continued on in good spirits.

41

The real problem with the Dark Hills was the lack of shelter. The farther we traveled, the more desolate the terrain became. Other than the occasional boulder casting a droplet of shade, it was a dead stretch of dry dirt and gnarly underbrush that cut and grabbed at your legs like sharp claws. Amid all of this uninhabited bleakness we found a rather large rock, and this we sat next to, opposite the sun. The ground had been heating up all day, as had the rock, and these facts, as well as the meager shade the rock provided, gave our moment of rest a sense of hopelessness. We did enjoy a drink of water and a bite of dried fruit, and these were taken with great pleasure and a measure of relief. But the reality of the situation was beginning to set in: Our adventure would be hard and dangerous work that would push us beyond our limits.

"How are you holding up, Alexa?" Odessa asked. "This is difficult terrain on four feet — I can't imagine how hard it must be on two."

I was reminded of the journey I'd taken up Mount Norwood when I'd first met Yipes, how that journey had ended at the glowing pool with my feet blistered and sore.

"I think I'll manage," I answered. "I only wish it wasn't so very hot."

"We're nearing sunset," said Yipes. "Things will cool down soon."

John looked at the lot of us, weary from the day's travel.

"Have any of you heard of something they call the black swarm?" he asked.

We all looked at one another, wondering what he was talking about. It was clear we'd never heard of such a thing.

"We have a ways to go before we reach shelter," he continued. "I've been out past here before, and there is a place we must find."

John paused and took a quick drink from one of our wineskins of water.

"I haven't been there for a very long time, but I think we can reach it by nightfall. Best we do — the swarm comes out at night."

"John," Yipes began, nervous fear growing in his voice, "what's the black swarm?"

John took one more drink before answering.

"Bats," he said. "But not the kind that feed on bugs. These bats stay together in a giant, swirling mass, and they look for prey to devour. I've only seen them once, from a distance, but Warvold was familiar with them. If they find us, our journey will come to a quick end."

We were all on our feet then, ready to make for shelter before nightfall without another word of encouragement from John.

The next two hours were hard fought against the elements. Though my body was drenched in sweat and my back was sore, it was my ankles that really began to bother me. I had brushed against countless sharp, dry bushes and thistles. My legs burned and itched from my knees all the way down to my feet, and within my sandals, dirt and tiny stones grated and stung as I walked.

Night was falling as we arrived at a large dead tree, broken in the middle and charred from a past fire, its top section fallen against a grouping of fat red stones.

Murphy hopped to the top of the broken tree, scanning the horizon for Squire, who we hadn't seen for over an hour. She was the aloof one of the group, partly due to her natural tendencies as a hawk, but probably more because none of us could talk with her. For whatever reason, the Jocastas had no effect with birds.

"Over here," said John. He had gone around the other side of the tree and was crouching in the dirt. I came around the corner and bent down next to him. There on the ground was a large rock, John's hand running along its smooth surface. I was beginning to have trouble seeing as the night crept in.

I heard Squire shriek from the air, a long way off. I turned to look for her, but she was lost in the darkening sky.

"Squire has rejoined us," said Murphy, and he jumped off the tree onto Odessa's back, shivering with fright.

"That's not Squire," said Yipes. "That's something else."

John stood and scanned the horizon, and then he spoke a single word that sent a chill down my spine.

"Bats."

CHAPTER 7
CLUES İN THE DARKNESS

"Everyone, against the rock!" John shouted. He was leaning all his weight into the large stone he'd been touching. It was tilting up off the ground a few inches, then crashing back down with a thud.

Yipes was the first to join him, then Odessa placed her head against the stone, pushing with her legs. A moment later the three of them had the large stone rolled over on its side, revealing the entrance to an underground space. It looked awfully dark and small from where I was standing.

The bats shrieked once more, and I turned toward the sound. But in the darkness of night I could not make out shapes in the air. They were closer — close enough to see us if we didn't hide quickly.

"In you go," said John, looking at me.

"When was the last time you were down there?" I asked. "Maybe something crawled in, and it's waiting for the first of us to step inside." I was reminded of the first time I'd gone into the tunnels in Bridewell, how it felt like walking into the mouth of a giant.

Murphy scampered past me and down into the space, then squeaked from inside.

"It's no problem," he said. "Just a barren space, nothing much to look at."

The shrieking of the bats was very close, and I was sure anything would be better than being chewed apart by them. I descended, and the others followed quickly behind me.

I found that I could not stand upright, so I crouched down against a wall, where Murphy jumped into my lap. At the bottom of the small opening to the space was another large stone, this one rounder in its shape than the other had been. John immediately put his shoulder against the stone and began rolling it in front of the opening. As it covered the last of the entrance I could hear the flapping of leathery wings and the deafening sound of bats flying in a swarm overhead. It sounded as though some of them were beating their wings against the other side of the rock, swirling around in the space just above us. And then they were gone, the sound of them nothing but a shrill whisper. I realized how very dark it was.

Everyone remained quiet, still afraid a lone bat was hanging behind the stone, waiting to hear us so it might chase after the swarm and bring it back. But there was nothing, only the sound of our breathing and the flit of Murphy's tail as he tried to keep still.

I heard John fumbling for something, and then the room was aglow with soft blue light, cast from the Jocasta he held in his hand. He held the light out in front of him, and I was able to see for the first time the place where we'd arrived.

It was a small, low, covered room without furnishings of any kind. There were, however, two oddities I immediately spied — a wooden cup, chipped and scuffed, resting atop a neatly folded blanket. These items sat alone in the middle of the room.

"We can talk now. They've passed on," said John. I could see Yipes as I crawled over next to the cup and the blanket and sat down. He, Odessa, and Murphy were the only ones who could stand upright in the room, and Odessa just barely.

"This is my kind of place," Yipes joked. "Cozy, and the ceiling is just the right height."

He smiled and looked around the room happily, the watery blue light from the stone dancing in his eyes.

"We'll have to stay here for the night," said John. "I can move the stone back a little to let in fresh air, but only after we've put the Jocasta away."

Yipes removed the wineskins from Odessa's back, and John began setting out nuts and fruit and dried meat. I took the old cup that was sitting on the blanket in my hand and turned it, wondering who might have left it behind.

"Warvold journeyed here," said John. "More than once is my guess. He told me of this place a long while ago. I'm a bit surprised I was able to lead us here without too much trouble."

Sometime in the distant past, Warvold had drunk from this cup. He'd been here, sitting in this very spot, hiding from the black swarm just as we were.

I took the corner of the folded blanket and began wiping the dust from the inside of the cup.

"What's this?" asked Murphy. He'd been scampering all around the room, running up and down the walls, sniffing everywhere he went. He'd arrived at the blanket, his nose beneath where I'd lifted the corner to clean the cup. When he emerged he held pieces of paper between his teeth. I snatched them out of his mouth and set down the cup.

It was a marvelous discovery, and everyone gathered closer to see them, excited about what the pages might contain. I flipped the pages over in my hands and realized what a treasure Murphy had found.

"This is Warvold's writing!" I cried out. Murphy could hardly contain himself, flipping and scuffling all around. There were five pages, covered in words on both sides, all in Warvold's familiar scrawl.

John held his Jocasta closer and everyone crowded

together. Odessa lay down next to me, gnawing on a chunk of dried meat, and Murphy jumped onto her back.

I filled the wooden cup with water and took a long drink, then cleared my throat and read what the pages said so everyone could hear.

CHAPTER 8

CASTALIA

"There is only one other person, alive or dead, who I've told about this secret place. I made this shelter many years ago, and I've taken refuge here often as I've traveled between the far reaches of The Land of Elyon. I fear this is the last time I will ever see these walls, and there are things I must write down, should I meet unexpectedly with my demise.

John Christopher, I do hope you've managed to find this letter. More important, I hope you have Alexa with you and that she carries the last stone.

Have patience as I tell you a brief history of the places beyond the Valley of Thorns."

I looked at the faces glowing blue all around me. Everyone had stopped eating, even Odessa.

"This ought to be interesting," said Yipes. Then he tossed a nut into his mouth and leaned forward like a child about to hear a wonderful story. I drank again from the old wooden cup and began reading once more.

"Some three hundred years ago there arose a small king-dom at the edge of a wide lake. The lake they called Castalia, and soon after, the kingdom itself took the same name.

The Castalians thrived for a hundred years. The water

from the lake fed their crops, and their numbers grew until many thousands lived along the shore. But then the Castalians had an unfortunate bit of bad luck.

They were visited by a man named Victor Grindall. Though of average size and modest appearance himself, he had with him a band of a hundred men very large in stature, more than twice the size of anyone in Castalia.

The Castalians were a timid people, never having been bothered by anyone, and they knew little of weapons or war. Grindall's men, though pleasant in appearance, were intimidating because of their size. Grindall gave the Castalians a choice: either make him their ruler or his giants would overrun the city and take it by force.

Many years later, the descendants of Grindall and the giants remain, and even now Castalia lies in the hands of an evil man and the dark forces that guide him."

I looked up, confused by the strange story Warvold had begun.

"Warvold was a teller of tall tales," I said, trying to lighten my own mood. "This sounds like something he would write."

But even as I said it, I somehow got the feeling that this story was not like the others.

"Would you like me to finish reading it?" asked Yipes. "Whether it's true or not, I want to know what happens!" He reached out his hand and I gave him the pages. Then I took the wooden cup in both hands and held it, running my thumb along the chipped edge, hoping to feel Warvold's presence in the room.

Yipes continued on at a merry pace, his high voice bouncing off the walls.

"Not so long ago, two sisters lived in Castalia. The elder was named Catherine and her younger sister was named Laura. The two of them lived in secret among the poor of Castalia, during the ninth reign of Grindall. Few can tell of how they came to live in hiding and what they discovered in the dead of night, but I will tell you a little of the story.

The girls were orphans. Catherine was thirteen and Laura was eleven, and they were forced to take care of each other and find food and shelter amid the poverty of the town square. Castalia had long since become a sprawling peasant village. The Dark Tower loomed high above — an ominous, dark spire in which generation after generation of Grindall men had forged their cruelest intentions.

The girls were determined to escape Castalia and find a new home, even though the gates were guarded by giants. Catherine was a crafty girl, always watching, and she discovered a way out. Together the sisters hid within the confines of a garbage cart and were rolled through the gate and out of the city to the dumping grounds.

The girls found themselves in a space overgrown with trees and brush, and most of the structures around them had walls that had fallen in and were now filled with rubbish. A terrible smell haunted the air. They had been dumped into an area once inhabited by Castalians but now used as the place where all the refuse was thrown. This place had long been called the City of Dogs, because large packs of wild dogs roamed there, living off what they could find among the mire in which the girls now found themselves.

They came upon an old, vine-covered clock tower — a stone relic at the corner of a forgotten street near the edge of the dump — that had long since been left in ruin. The clock tower was to become their home.

On that first night they remained on the ground floor, too afraid to climb the ladder on the wall and push on the door in the ceiling. But the next morning, hungry and bored, the girls climbed the seven steps and pushed on the wooden door that led to the clock tower. The door was blocked and would not move, and though I was not there and only heard the story secondhand, it was told to me that at precisely this moment a pack of wild dogs began sniffing around the base of the old structure, growling menacingly at the smell of new inhabitants."

"Slow down, Yipes," said John. "I can hardly make out what you're saying."

Yipes was breathless, reading at a frantic pace, overcome with anticipation as the story became more and more perilous. He stopped and held the pages out to me.

"You'd better finish it, Alexa," he said. "I won't be able to stop myself from racing to the end. But don't go *too* slowly, all right?"

I nodded and took the pages in my hand, scanning them until I found the place where Yipes had been interrupted. I was frightened of where the story might lead, but I was also terribly curious about a great many things. What would happen to Catherine and Laura? Why did Warvold leave a note about them? Who were they? And what of these giants and Victor Grindall — were they real or imagined?

I steadied my shaking hands, took a deep breath, and read on.

"The girls looked down from their perch on the ladder and realized the stone they had removed to enter the building had not been replaced. The wild dogs were coming in, a pack of them, frothing and snarling as they approached the ladder. And then something very curious happened.

The door at the top of the ladder opened.

Seeing no other choice, Catherine and Laura scampered inside and stood against the wall. There was only a faint light in the space, but it was clear that something was hiding there. A match was struck and a fat old candle was lit in a corner. A creature sat hunched against the wall, arms folded around bent knees.

It was a giant."

CHAPTER 9

WHAT THE GIANT TOLD

We had read half of what Warvold wrote, the room turning stale from lack of fresh air. But that didn't matter. We were all caught up in the story.

"Wait just a moment while I let in a bit of air," said John.

He crawled over to the stone, unable to stand upright in the room, and then he put his Jocasta back inside its leather pouch.

The room was suddenly dark, so dark that I couldn't see the pages in my hand as I heard the rock move against the opening. Warm air crept slowly into the room, whipping tiny specks of dust on a soft evening breeze. We sat silent in the darkness, waiting for the light of the Jocasta to return.

John Christopher was as curious as we were to finish the story Warvold had left for us, and we didn't wait long to hear the stone rolling back and see the room aglow once more in blue light.

"Only a few pages to go," I said, flipping the papers in my hand. "Shall I continue?" Everyone nodded eagerly, and my voice filled the room with the rest of Warvold's tale.

"And here we find ourselves before a creature with knowledge of things no peasant of Castalia or ruler of Bridewell could know. On that first evening, Catherine, Laura, and the giant became acquainted, and in the days that followed, the giant told them a great many secrets about himself, his race, and the history of the Grindalls. What I am going to tell you now will draw you into a conflict from which you cannot turn. Your enemy, who prowls as close as the Valley of Thorns, will become clear as crystal on this very night.

When Elyon created the world and the human race he also created something else — a hundred powerful beings he called Seraphs. These beings were made to protect The Land of Elyon from within the realm of the Tenth City, a secret place where Elyon made his home and everything could be seen. While the Seraphs were created to oversee the human race, they were forbidden to ever leave the Tenth City.

One of the Seraphs was called Abaddon, and he was more powerful than all the rest. Abaddon was overcome with jealousy and wanted to rule The Land of Elyon. In secret, he convinced the Seraphs that they must enter the realm of men and women to protect them. When the Seraphs arrived in The Land of Elyon they took the form of giants, larger than normal men, stronger, and still with some lingering powers.

57

When Elyon discovered what the Seraphs had done, he was enraged and he banished them from the Tenth City forever. Abaddon, his power growing uncontrollable, was harder to contain than the other ninety-nine. A great battle ensued between Elyon and Abaddon, and in the end Abaddon was chained down in a great pit at the edge of the Tenth City.

Elyon uses a great deal of his own strength to keep Abaddon in the pit. Still, even though Abaddon cannot leave the pit, he is able to assert his will in various ways. He is able to corrupt men from afar, encouraging their evil for his purposes. And then there are the bats. Innocently present in the pit when Abaddon arrived, they are now poisoned by his will, swarming The Land of Elyon.

Abaddon wants to destroy The Land of Elyon along with the Tenth City, so he can rule everything and drive Elyon away.

To do this, Abaddon must prey on the evil and the weak, using them to achieve his goals. Victor Grindall is the most powerful man to have fallen under Abaddon's spell. Abaddon can bend Grindall's will to do his bidding.

In this case, he is using Grindall to search for the stones.

Where, you may ask, do the stones come from? There once was a place in The Land of Elyon that no longer exists, a place that was only known by Elyon and the Seraphs. This was a magical place, where creation began and the first voices were heard. Long ago there was only one language between the animals and humans, and even Elyon's voice could be heard and understood by a few. Unable to return to the Tenth City, it was in this place that the Seraphs first made their home, hidden from people.

This place was supposed to be a secret. But Abaddon used Grindall to make his way there, saying things the Seraphs seemed to understand. Something about Grindall made them follow. Little did they know it was the voice of Abaddon, calling them from the pit to do his bidding.

Through Grindall, Abaddon instructed the giants to gather the stones that lay in a pool in this secret place, stones that would contain the power to hear the original language of Elyon. And then the Seraphs left, following the only voice that sounded anything like home. And Victor Grindall led them to Castalia.

But Abaddon was deceived, for some of the stones were enchanted by Elyon so that they might only fall into the hands of those he chose."

"There's only one more page," I said. Everyone in the room looked as confused and amazed as I felt.

"Read the last of it, Alexa," said John. "I have a feeling we haven't heard the most important part yet."

Somehow I felt the same, like something dreadful was about to happen. I held the last page closer to the light of the Jocasta and started reading.

"*Two hundred years after the first Grindall was dead and gone, Armon the giant was appointed keeper of the*

59

stones. The line of Grindall was in its ninth reign, and the remaining stones were kept in a pool in the deepest part of the Dark Tower, in the darkest corner of the dungeon, where Armon guarded them.

Day after day, Armon watched the stones as they sat quietly in a pool of water, until one day a single stone began glowing faintly. Overcome with curiosity, Armon picked up the stone and for a brief moment heard the forgotten sound of Elyon's voice, distant but clear, coming from the Tenth City. From that moment on, Armon was compelled to protect the remaining stones, to remove them, and to leave Castalia. He escaped into the City of Dogs, hid in the clock tower, and was discovered by Catherine and Laura.

When Armon touched the stone, Abaddon at last realized what Elyon had done. He understood that the remaining stones had the power to destroy him if they were carried to those Elyon had chosen. And so Abaddon infected the reigning Grindall with all his might, giving him an unquenchable thirst for the stones.

We find ourselves now in the depth of the tenth reign of Grindall, and if things have gone as I've hoped, Alexa holds the very last of the stones. From the beginning Elyon has chosen her, and he has left the fate of the world in her hands.

It falls to Alexa now to defeat Abaddon."

CHAPTER 10

JOURNEY ACROSS THE DARK HILLS

As you might imagine, I was speechless. I sat silently contemplating what it all meant. If this tale was true then I held the last Jocasta, and this band of misfits I'd surrounded myself with was all I had to help me. It struck me then that this was the same sort of group that had managed to bring down the walls around my kingdom and save Bridewell from the evil plot set against it. John Christopher, Yipes, Murphy, Odessa, and Squire — whatever trouble I'd fallen into, I had to believe these companions would protect and help me to the end. As I looked around at the faces before me I was comforted — even excited — to walk the paths old Warvold had tread, into places I could only imagine. I smiled.

"BOO!" I yelled.

Yipes jumped up so fast he bumped his head on the ceiling, while Murphy spun and rolled off Odessa's back, landed on his feet, and scampered into a corner of the room. John and Odessa only flinched and remained where they were.

"Why must you do things like that?" pleaded Yipes. "You've scared poor Murphy half out of his wits."

I chuckled, then John joined in, and pretty soon we were all laughing, our nervous energy released into the small room. When everyone became calm and quiet again, I showed the back of the last page of Warvold's notes.

"There's another map here," I said. "It looks as though it will be our guide for the next few days."

It was a crude drawing of markers and lines with a title scribbled across the top that read *Across the Dark Hills to the Valley of Thorns — route void of BATS.*

"That's encouraging," said Murphy from his new perch atop my shoulder. Squirrels have surprisingly sharp claws, and he was digging in more than usual.

"You're holding on a bit tight, Murphy," I said. "Not scared, are you?"

Murphy loosened his grip and put his wet nose in my ear, something he did when he'd had enough of my pestering.

"Best to get some rest," said John. "By the looks of that map, we've got at least three days of travel through harsh lands in front of us. We should get some sleep while we have the safety of this room."

Everyone seemed to agree. The Jocasta was put away and the rock rolled back just enough to let in a trickle of fresh air again. Before long I was the only one awake. The deep darkness of the room scared me. To comfort myself I thought about my desk back home in Lathbury — its top the color of walnut shells, the aged wood somehow

62

soft and hard at the same time, the smell of old books all around me. I rolled onto my side and held Murphy against my chest with one arm, his slight breathing and warm coat comforting me. It wasn't long before I, too, was fast asleep like the rest.

The predawn hours were colder than expected, and everyone woke early the next morning. We packed our few belongings quickly and began walking north, the presence of the sun known only by a delicate tint of orange along the horizon. Right away I felt the first burning scratches of dried brush along my legs, the dusty earth beneath my feet. Murphy sat on my pack, nibbling on a few nuts while I ate from a handful of dried apples and figs.

For the next three days we followed the map, ever wary of intruders, an endless trek into barren lands. I could only guess, but by the end of the fourth day I thought we must have been a hundred miles from Bridewell, miles that would have been impossible to cross on horseback with the many crevices and climbs. As the sun was setting I looked back toward where we'd come and realized with some astonishment how far away from home I was.

"We should keep moving as best we can until night falls," said Yipes. "We're nearing the end of the map, but we're also running low on food and water."

I'd forgotten how determined Yipes could be when he set his mind to something. By the look of the map we would arrive at the edge of the Valley of Thorns sometime the next day. We were all terribly curious what the Valley of Thorns was, but the mere sound of it worried me.

"The days get easier for me as we go," said Odessa. "Less water is less for me to carry — that and Murphy every now and then, but he's as light as a feather."

The evening light passed quietly as the heat let go of its grip on the land. Squire rejoined us, alighting on John's pack and looking around nervously for field mice she might have the good fortune to discover. John took a piece of dried meat from a small pocket on the side of his tunic and held it behind his head. Squire immediately snapped it away and ripped it into small bits between her claws and her beak. Not long after that she flew off again. I made a game with Murphy of trying to track where Squire had gone, until she flew into the horizon and we both lost her.

Soon after, we fell into a conversation about the merits of having a body covered with hair. It became quite lively, the two animals extolling a lengthy list of reasons why hair upon one's body was to be envied and insisting that a hairless beast walking upright on two feet was a disgusting thing indeed, a sight which had been largely spared them by the use of clothing. Yipes, John, and I were victorious in the end, but only because the oppressive heat emphasized the inherent problem of having a coat you could never take off.

When I looked up again the sun was only a far-off sliver, and we found a clearing surrounded by a thicket to shelter us for the night. We were now only hours from the Valley of Thorns, and everyone was concerned about what we might encounter there.

"The sooner we get to the Valley of Thorns, the sooner we can find out what all this means," said John. "The best we can do now is rest and rise early. By tomorrow afternoon we'll be there."

"I wonder what became of the girls," I said, already lying down with my head resting on my pack.

"Catherine and Laura," I whispered, already drifting off to sleep, exhausted from the long day. "I wonder where they went, or if we'll ever find out." I tried to stay awake and think more about the mystery, but a moment more and I fell into a deep sleep.

Sometime later, in the full of night, I was awakened by Odessa. She had been guarding the camp for several hours, and it was my turn to do the same. The night air had gone cold and I shivered in my effort to sit up, placing my arms around my knees.

"All's quiet?" I whispered.

"Squire flew in an hour ago and startled me, but she's resting by Yipes now," the wolf answered. "Otherwise it's been silent but for John. He's more restless than usual tonight, waking often and looking around to see if I am still at my duty."

I got up and walked to the edge of our camp, looking out across what remained of the Dark Hills. So bleak, so desolate. Even in the night I clearly understood its awful barrenness. I looked back and saw that Odessa had curled up next to John, the two of them whispering. And then I saw Murphy sneak slowly across the camp and curl into a ball of fur at John's feet. The hours of my watch drifted by, filled with thoughts of Castalia and all its strange wonders, until the first orange glow of morning touched our camp and all at once everyone was stirring, wakeful, slowly preparing their things for our final walk on the ground of the Dark Hills.

CHAPTER 11

MY SPYGLASS GETS SOME USE

"Someone is near," said John.

"What do you mean?" asked Odessa, sniffing at the air to catch an unknown scent. But John continued ahead without offering an answer. When I probed him further he turned and addressed all of us at once.

"There's something not right about this place. It's like the feeling I have when it's dark outside and I think maybe there is someone watching me. And then I hear a twig snap and my heart jumps. That's the feeling I've had all morning."

"What do you suppose it is, John?" Yipes asked. His voice expressed the concern we were all feeling.

John shrugged, turned, and began walking again. "I haven't the slightest idea."

We had been walking all morning, mostly in silence, and the anxiety we felt was only heightened by what John had said. I wished then that John had kept his feelings to himself. But he hadn't, and I was left to imagine all manner of beastly monsters overtaking us in the gloom of the Dark Hills.

We had been moving in the direction of a great hill

for some time, and in due course we found ourselves at its edge in a dry ravine. Though I would not call it a mountain, the hill before us was both steep and of great length from side to side, running off at both ends well beyond where we could see. Since we couldn't see a way to get around it, we knew we'd have to go over the top. We thought it best to stop and review the map while we indulged in a few minutes of rest before starting the climb.

I looked across the parched earth and watched as Murphy cleaned between his paws and ran his little forelegs over his head and back again. Standing as I was between Yipes and John, it struck me how filthy they were. Stubble marked their faces and dirty hair hung down on their heads. Also, they stank. It occurred to me then that I had to look and smell as awful as my companions, and I became momentarily depressed.

"We smell bad," I said.

Yipes and John looked at each other. Then each raised an arm and sniffed in the general direction of the exposed area. Unsatisfied, they stepped closer to me, sniffed at the air once again, and turned away.

"I'm afraid it's you, my dear," said Yipes. "You're as ripe as a July tomato."

John nodded his approval.

"Really?" I said, and I began sniffing the air around me.

Murphy, who was always my advocate in such matters, immediately darted up Yipes's leg, grabbed hold of his vest with all four claws, and dug his little head into

Yipes's armpit. Yipes squirmed about, spinning this way and that, until at last Murphy came up for air, a look of disgust on his little face.

"This one smells *terrible*," cried Murphy. "And *that* one." He looked over at John, whose arms were folded firmly across his chest. "That one there is three times the size of Yipes and sweats by the bucketful."

At least I wasn't the only one in need of a bath. This was a small if meaningless comfort.

We were all looking at the map when John spun around and looked up to the right on the barren hill in front of us.

"I feel it again," he said. "Someone or something is near."

He pointed across the ravine at a clump of half-dead bushes next to a small rise of dirt. "Let's huddle down beneath the brush and stay out of sight until we figure out what to do. I fear the Valley of Thorns may be just over that hill."

We hurried to where the bushes were and crouched together in the dirt. The cover it provided was not sufficient to hide us entirely, but at least we were out of the wide-open space of the ravine. The day had crept into early afternoon and the sun was hot, but not so much as it had been thus far on our journey. There was a faint breeze, and though it was not altogether cool, it had a freshness unlike the baking heat of past days, as if this wind had its origin in a colder place.

"If it's true that we find ourselves at the base of the Valley of Thorns, do we have any idea what to do now?" asked Odessa, the ears upon her mighty gray head sticking straight up and alert.

"Where's Murphy?" I asked, not finding him among us in the thicket. We were all looking back and forth when the sound of pebbles sliding down the hill came from above us. At first I was terrified of what I might see, but when I looked up, I saw that Murphy had darted away and was scampering up the hill, his tiny legs sending him on a zigzag course as he hid beneath tufts of weeds. He was quickly halfway up, where he looked back, jumped, and waved his limbs all around. Then he turned and raced off again.

"I don't know what to do with him," said Yipes, shaking his head slowly. "He hasn't a shred of common sense."

"Maybe the smell of your armpit scrambled his brains," I said.

"Quiet, you two," said John. "I've lost him in the brush near the top."

I removed my spyglass, the same one I'd taken from my mother and used in Bridewell the summer before. The lens that Pervis had broken out had been replaced, and it seemed as good as new when my mother offered it to me as a gift on my thirteenth birthday. I slid it open with a snap and handed it to John. The spyglass had been of some use along the way already, but this was the first time I was truly relieved to have brought it with me.

We were all quiet for a moment while John tried to find Murphy on the hill.

"There, I have him. He's just reaching the top now."

I waited in silence, watching as Yipes secretly raised his right arm and smelled the air beneath it, and then I could hold my tongue no longer in my worry over Murphy.

"What's happening? Can you still see him?" Just then we all heard a shriek from above and looked into the sky. Squire was circling the air, watching as the scene unfolded. I wished then that I, too, could fly, if only for a moment, so that I could see everything that lay before us on the other side of the hill.

"You know, this really makes very good sense, now that I've had a moment to consider it," said Yipes.

"What's happening?" I asked, ignoring Yipes in my worry over the plight of our friend.

"No, really," Yipes continued. "I don't think he's gone mad, at least not completely. When you think it through, who or whatever lies beyond the hill might well be watching for intruders. A squirrel poses no threat. In fact, he probably goes entirely unnoticed. I only wish he would have let us come to that conclusion together before dashing off on his own."

John closed the spyglass and held it out to me without looking in my direction.

"He's halfway back down. There," he said, pointing to a small brown clump flitting this way and that down the hill.

Murphy rejoined us, completely out of breath and momentarily unable to speak. We gathered close around him until finally he was able to tell us what he had seen in a single well-chosen word.

"Giants," he said. He took a few more labored breaths, looked around at the group, and added a bit more.

"Lots of them."

CHAPTER 12

THE VALLEY OF THORNS

We all sat silent and still as Murphy told us what he'd seen from the top of the hill, a long pause every now and then as I shared this information with Yipes. Though Yipes seemed perfectly happy to hear the details second-hand, I felt bad for him only hearing a long trail of squeaks as Murphy spoke.

There was a steep drop-off on the other side, followed by a hundred yards of valley with terrain much like the Dark Hills. After this came a large swath of what appeared to be thin tree stumps sticking up out of the earth from side to side as far as Murphy could see. Beneath the stumps was a gathering of brown stubble, and walking upon the stubble were ten or so men of remarkable size, who Murphy took to be giants. In his further description, it appeared to Murphy that the trees had not been cut where they stood, for they were too closely placed together and arranged in a perfect pattern. The trees or wooden poles — Murphy was less sure of their nature the longer he spoke — stuck out of the ground at varying heights, some so low to the ground that one would measure them in inches, others several feet high, and still more that were five feet and above. In all cases, the stumps or poles were black at the base and carved to a sharp point at the top, where the tips were the color of blood.

The stumps continued along the valley floor for something on the order of a hundred yards more, and past these the valley became alive with abundant shades of green. Not far beyond the green was the striking presence of a bright blue lake. Murphy called it "magnificent in its size and color."

"Castalia," said Odessa. The word hung in the air until it was pushed away by a question from John.

"Are the giants too far from the edge of the hill to be reached with a well-placed arrow?"

Murphy looked thoughtfully back up at the hill, trying to remember how far off they had really been.

"You might be able to hit the edge, but the giants walked among the poles toward the middle. Plus I thought I saw a head appear from the earth, so they might have dug trenches, too. Either that or there are some very short giants down there scattered among the big ones. I think a sky filled with arrows, shot down from the top of the hill, would only fall wasted in the valley."

John and Yipes were the only ones with bows and a small reserve of arrows, so it didn't seem likely that we'd be able to fend off even a single giant.

"One thing is for sure: We have to find a place to

hide," said Odessa. "They must be in the habit of sending scouts to the very ground we stand on."

We looked as far as we could in every direction and found with unfortunate clarity that the only shelter to be had was back in the direction from which we had come. We'd be seen by anyone patrolling the top of the hill.

"There are at least three good sets of large rocks a half mile back," said Yipes. "We could stay here until night and move back to one of them, or take our chances in broad daylight."

Neither option sounded very appealing to me. Where we sat, we only had a few miserable bushes to hide behind. And yet venturing out into the wide open of the Dark Hills in the middle of the day seemed foolhardy with giants milling around so close by.

"Can you hail Squire?" John asked Yipes.

"I believe I can," said Yipes. "But to what purpose?"

"I have an idea she might be useful."

Yipes stood up and pulled a red cotton handkerchief from his vest pocket. He held it over his head and waved it to and fro for some time, careful to stay behind a bush so he could only be seen from the sky. Squire ignored him entirely and continued circling high in the air above us.

"You've trained that one well," said Odessa. "Can you make her roll over and play dead?"

Yipes waved the red handkerchief more furiously until at last he agreed that Squire was indeed ignoring him. He looked around nervously until he caught sight of

Murphy, who was absently working on a walnut I'd given him upon his return.

"There is one way that almost always works," said Yipes, and then he knelt down next to Murphy and looked at us as if he were about to do something under-handed.

"How is the nut?" he asked.

"Fine, thank you," said Murphy, though Yipes only heard him squeaking.

"I'm so glad you're enjoying it."

Just then Yipes tapped Murphy upon the head, ran his hand along his back, and grabbed hold of his tail.

There is one thing a squirrel cannot stand, and Yipes had just perpetrated it on our little friend. Instinct will send a squirrel caught by the tail into a fit of biting, scratching, and screaming, and Yipes was well aware of this. He quickly moved out into the open, away from the bushes, and began swinging Murphy in circles over his head, which kept the sharp teeth from whipping around and finding his forearm. All the while Murphy was screaming his head off, and though this was not the loud-est sound one might hear, a hawk has exceptional hearing (not to mention outstanding sight), and Squire dived into the ravine looking for a trapped squirrel almost immedi-ately.

As soon as Squire started for us, Yipes stopped spin-ning Murphy, crouched near the ground, and let go of his tail. Murphy rolled several times and landed punch-drunk on his feet in the wide open. He wobbled back and forth and then fell on his side, the twirling having dizzied his mind.

"Grab him!" yelled Yipes. Squire was within a hundred feet of us and heading straight for Murphy. I was the closest, so I bolted the two steps I needed to and crouched down over Murphy, covering him with my back. Squire pulled up short and circled low, then landed on Yipes's outstretched arm.

"That went rather well, don't you think?" said Yipes.

Murphy recovered, and I cradled him with one arm while I handed him back his nut. He grabbed hold of it and began working at the shell again.

John approached the hawk and put a hand near his head. Squire remained calm as John slowly moved the hand closer and finally touched her with two fingers on the neck. None of us, John included, could know what Squire was thinking or if she really understood the things we said. Still, John spoke to the stately creature in a quiet voice.

"Can you tell us if they are coming?" He ran his two fingers along the neck to the top of the wing, picked up the fingers, and started again at the neck, then softly spoke to the bird one more time.

"Will you warn us if they move for the hill?" He took his hand away, reached into his pocket, and presented a bit of dried meat to Squire.

"Let her go," he said. Yipes threw his arm up, and

Squire's powerful wings moved her off toward the distant sky. We watched until she resumed her circular motion over the hill, quietly floating above the earth, watching all that lay beneath her on the ground.

"We could also leave Murphy to watch," Odessa said. "I'm a prize they are likely to come after with arrows, but Murphy they would ignore."

"He wouldn't make it through the day," said Yipes. "It's amazing he's not dead already."

At first I was puzzled by his reply, and then all at once I understood.

"Squire," I said.

"Indeed," said Yipes. "She's a lovely bird, but a rodent is a rodent and nature is nature." He looked up into the sky. "That bird will devour Murphy if we leave him all alone at the top of the hill. Look at him, he can't sit still, and in this case his life would depend on it. We can't risk it."

I could feel Murphy trying to wriggle free from me, to escape and run back up the hill. As Yipes had observed, he had no fear, so I kept him close and calmed him down until he agreed that he should stay with us.

"We must run with all our might back to the rocks, the largest of the three groupings to the right, and we must do it now and trust Squire to warn us if the giants emerge," said John.

It was quickly agreed, and after a brief glance up to see that Squire was still circling, we began running back into the Dark Hills. Odessa was by far the fastest among us, and she raced out ahead. The rest of us stayed clumped together and tried not to trample the brush too much for fear that a scout might see where we'd been and become alerted to our presence.

I listened for Squire over labored breathing and the noise of packs bouncing upon backs and feet scuffling over dried earth. We were a few minutes into our run, all of us tiring badly, when Odessa reached the rocks in front of us. The rest of us still had a hundred yards to go, and though most of the work was behind us, that last stretch seemed like miles and miles in my exhaustion.

With fifty yards left to go it seemed as though I could almost touch the rocks with an outstretched hand. The group of us caught our second wind. This was further helped along by Squire, who began screeching from the expanse behind us, a sound that scared me into a full sprint until I fell to my knees breathless behind the rocks.

No one spoke while we recovered from the run, which made Squire's screeching all the more terrifying. I hoped, as did the rest, that she'd only been happy to see us reach our destination or that she'd caught sight of another hawk and they were alerting each other of their presence.

The rocks were not as protective as we'd hoped, and we had to sit or lie down to avoid being seen from the top of the hill. The situation was further complicated by the discovery that two of the rocks sat together and one was several feet to the left and all alone in the dirt. Each of the stones was large enough to hide a body or two, but not much more. Odessa had arrived in front of the lone rock, and there she stayed. The rest of us were crumpled together behind the two remaining rocks, which were barely big enough to conceal us. Murphy darted across the three feet that lay between us and jumped onto Odessa's back.

"She's stopped her shrieking," I whispered, and then I realized how unnecessary whispering was since we'd gone so far out into the Dark Hills. I continued in a normal tone of voice. "Murphy, jump up on the rock and tell us what you see."

This he did, nervously flitting from side to side on the fat stone.

"Stop moving around so much," said Yipes. "You'll only draw their attention."

"I don't see anything moving on the hill. It's perfectly still," said Murphy, and then he jumped back down onto Odessa's back.

Yipes, John, and I rose slowly until the tops of our heads peeked out over the rocks and the hill came into view. It was true — no one was on the hilltop. We all breathed a sigh of relief.

We became momentarily relaxed and raised our heads a bit more over the edge of the rocks. Then Squire landed directly in front of us, her powerful wings flapping her to a stop. The three of us were so startled we fell back from the rocks and landed on our elbows.

"Maybe you could give a little warning before you arrive next time," said Yipes, beginning to stand so he might be able to wipe himself off.

"Wait," I said. Then I turned to Murphy and asked him to jump on the rock and look once again. Squire flew off, her wings so powerful they stirred the dust beneath the rocks, and we waited on our backs.

"Don't move," said Murphy. "Three giants, all with spyglasses aimed this way, are standing on the hilltop." Sweat dripped down my temple and I quietly relayed this information to the others. I stayed completely still and out of sight along with the rest.

Murphy jumped down off the rock and ran off somewhere I could not see. The seconds turned to minutes.

"I'm scared," I said aloud. I felt like I might begin to cry, the weight of our circumstances quickly becoming more than I could handle. I took a few strands of my hair into my mouth and chewed them, a nervous habit I hadn't fallen into for a long time. John took hold of my hand and rubbed the backs of my fingers. His thumb was incredibly worn and rough. It had a protective, powerful way about it, as if it had been through much worse and survived.

"They've gone." It was Murphy, who had returned to the rock. "The hilltop is empty and Squire is circling again."

"It would seem that our winged companion has become quite useful," said John. I brushed the strands of hair out of my mouth and let go of his hand so I could sit up without trouble. Then we all gathered behind the two rocks and quietly prepared the small bit of food and water that remained.

We sat hidden behind the rocks until the sun set behind the hill. Not long after that, everything was quiet and dark. It was nighttime in the Dark Hills, and we were without food, water, or shelter.

CHAPTER 13

AN UNEXPECTED DEVELOPMENT

The lights were moving swiftly down the face of the hill, but they did not bob and jump as they might if men were running with torches. They were giants, and they were simply walking toward us. It frightened me to think how quickly they could overtake us on foot if they chose to. Odessa began a deep, low growl as we watched the torches continue their descent.

"Try to stay calm, Odessa. You'll give us away," whispered Yipes. He and John had both set arrows into their bows to try to protect us. We had come with little weaponry; a few small knives and two bows were the whole of our defense.

A hurried conversation ensued. Should we stay hidden behind the rocks? Should we run into the Dark Hills where no protection could be found, hoping they turned and went back? All the while, the lights kept coming, slowly closing the gap between us.

"I feel it again, the same presence I've felt all day," said John.

"Of course you do," said Yipes. "The giants are right there in front of us."

While they spoke I realized that Murphy had disappeared once again. Could he have darted out ahead to bite the legs of those awful creatures? The giants were off the hill and walking in the open expanse between us now, Murphy was missing, and we had nowhere to hide. I whispered Murphy's name and when he didn't answer I began to panic. Odessa uttered a low, barely audible growl. We all looked hopelessly at one another, and a distinct feeling of despair hung in the air.

"Quiet," said John.

Odessa stopped growling, and there was no noise but for our breathing. Then I heard the scamper of tiny feet, and all at once Murphy was among us again, shouting incoherently in his squeaky voice, excited beyond words and unable to contain himself.

"Calm down," whispered Yipes. "Can't you see the giants are coming toward us?"

Murphy tried desperately to calm himself until finally he was able to form a few simple words.

"Don't be afraid," he said. "Just stay quiet."

This was a strange thing to say, especially given that Murphy himself was so agitated he could hardly calm himself long enough to put together a plain sentence. Our confusion was further heightened when he darted out into the Dark Hills, away from the advancing giants. We lost sight of him again.

"He's finally gone completely out of his mind," said Yipes, his head shaking back and forth. "I suppose it was only a matter of time." Then he went back to preparing his bow and watching the torches in the distance.

Odessa turned and growled in the direction Murphy had gone, after which Murphy came darting out of the blackness again, his small frame like a formless shadow rushing along the ground.

I had a sensation then that wasn't quite feeling or hearing but a mix of both at the same time. I looked into the night and pressed against the rocks, the feeling growing more scary and real as the seconds passed. And then I saw him coming out of the darkness — an immense, formless mass. Out of the night came a giant, and before we could think to run, he towered over us not unlike the walls of Bridewell had in years past. He was gigantic, beyond comprehension in his magnificent size. A sword was sheathed in his belt.

"The arrows will do you no good," said the giant. "You should put them away." His voice was surprisingly soothing and aged; this was not a young giant but an old one. His face was difficult to see in the darkness.

"Armon?" questioned John. "Could it be?"

"The very one," replied the giant. "Come to save you in your hour of need, just as Warvold instructed."

There was very little light, but the moon was on the rise and the stars were thickening by the minute. I began to distinguish his face. It was just as I'd hoped it would be: very wise and very kind; old, but not ancient; strong in a graceful way.

85

"Gather your things and move as quietly as you can," he told us. "They place the rocks here on purpose. As you see they are the only places to hide, and it is here as always that they will come looking for intruders."

Armon reached down and picked up our empty wineskins, which seemed extraordinarily small slung over his shoulder. On the other shoulder hung a large leather pack, three feet wide and five or more feet in length. I wondered what might be inside.

Yipes walked up to Armon and stood in amazement at his feet. He looked at John and said, "Now you know how I feel." Then he reached out and touched the giant's knee.

"Move away from the rocks, if you would," said the giant. We all obeyed without hesitation.

He proceeded to pick up each of the gigantic stones one by one, the largest of them almost as big as my desk back home, and moved them four giant steps closer to the hill. This he did with great care and speed, placing the stones in the same formation they had been in, dusting his tracks after each trip out. Not the least bit out of breath from the effort, he stood before us and pointed into the Dark Hills, away from the oncoming lights.

"Run, but go quietly as you do," he said.

Armon walked slowly behind us, covering tracks as best he could as we went. A short while later he told us to stop, kneel down, and remain silent.

"They have arrived at the rocks," he whispered. The

torches had split into three, one at each of the formations we had seen earlier in the day. We paid careful attention to the rocks we had hidden behind as the light danced along the ground, rose into the air, and started moving back toward the hill. We watched as the three torches came together once again and moved away from us into the night.

Armon knelt before me, his wonderful face close enough now to see clearly, wrinkled with the years and yet somehow ageless. His skin had no beard or stubble like a man's — it was clean and perfect. Waves of black hair ran over his ears and onto his shoulders.

"You must be Alexa," he said. He placed his fingers on the side of my face, each as thick as five of my own and more than twice as long. I was overcome with emotion; his presence among us was like we were in a real fairy tale, bringing hope to a hopeless situation. Could it be that Elyon was among us? If so, Armon was the greatest gift he could have given. With Armon's touch my fear melted away. The mighty giant had arrived to protect us. He was the one giant among them all who was bound to Elyon and so bound to us.

He rose again to his feet without another word and looked up at the stars in search of direction.

"I have prepared a place where we can rest," Armon said. "It's not far from here."

"What's it like up there?" asked Yipes, standing again at the foot of the giant. He seemed terribly curious about

Armon, as though the opposing nature of their size gave them something in common. Armon put one hand around Yipes's middle and lifted him ten feet off the ground into the night sky, where he looked him straight in the eye.

"I have heard about you," said Armon.

"Somehow that doesn't surprise me," Yipes replied, his short legs dangling helplessly over the ground.

Armon set Yipes down and began walking parallel to the great hill. Murphy leaped onto the giant's leg, ran the length of his body, and sat on his shoulder. Armon paid Murphy no attention other than to gently tap him twice on the head with his big finger.

"The last of the stones," he said, as if reading from an ancient text. "I had another stone long ago, but its powers have been erased by time. I hear only squeaking when the squirrel opens his mouth, but I gather you hear much more."

He looked at me then and, though it was dark, I could tell he was smiling.

Armon slowed and put his hand on John, covering his back entirely with the palm, his fingers wrapping around John's arm on the other side.

"Warvold spoke highly of you," said Armon, still looking forward as he walked. "You and Yipes and Alexa. There were times the three of you were all he talked about for days on end." And then Armon looked down at

John. "He was of the opinion that behind your weathered face lies untold wisdom."

John put his hand on Armon's great forearm and squeezed what little of it he could get his fingers around.

"I'm delighted to have you among us," said John. "With Warvold's story unfolding these past days, I've hoped for some help. This is beyond my wildest dreams."

While they spoke, a thousand questions ran through my head. I was beginning to have some trouble keeping them to myself.

"What became of Catherine and Laura?" I asked.

Armon looked at Yipes and found that he was having some difficulty keeping up with the rest of us. We were all walking faster than normal, and even though Yipes was energetic, the fact remained that his legs were tiny compared to Armon's. Armon removed his hand from John's back, picked up Yipes, and placed him on his shoulder, which put Yipes's head at something on the order of twelve feet in the air.

"You're too kind," said Yipes, while Murphy scampered even higher than he had been and sat on Yipes's shoulder. Murphy on Yipes on Armon — it was beginning to look like a circus act from where I stood below, and it further illuminated the unique nature of our group. I was beginning to see fewer of our weaknesses and more of our strengths; the events of the day were a reminder of how each of us had certain abilities that the rest did not.

It was as if we were each a part of a whole body — one the hands, another the legs, and so on — dependent on one another and working best when we performed in unity. I felt inadequate then, unsure what part of this body I might be.

"We have only another hour to walk, and then we shall rest and talk of how to overcome the Valley of Thorns," said Armon. "I must warn you that we will only have a short while to sleep, a few hours at the most. We must rise before dawn and set our plan into motion."

He looked at my pleading face and saw how much I wanted to hear about Catherine and Laura.

"There will be plenty of time to address our plans after I tell you what became of the girls," he said.

And then he spoke of what Warvold had left untold, a steady breeze in our faces as we went.

CHAPTER 14

WHAT REMAINS OF THE STORY IS TOLD

Everything changed for me in the passing of that hour. Armon spoke with an incredible authority, in such a way that all the story's pieces fell delicately into place. As we walked I knew nothing of the fearful things that awaited us — Victor Grindall and his line of sons, the torches I'd seen on the hill, the wild dogs of Castalia's dumping grounds. For that hour Armon's commanding presence was all my world could hold.

"Not long after Catherine and Laura arrived in the clock tower, it became clear that the three of us would need to leave the region," he began. "We needed to travel far away, to a place where we could not be found. We had to take the stones with us and protect them from Grindall and the evil forces that guided him.

"Already Grindall was sending out his men and his giants to search for me and the stones. Soon enough their searching would lead them into the City of Dogs, and our hiding place would be found."

Murphy scurried down from his perch on Yipes's shoulder and landed on the ground. He took two quick strides and leaped into my arms where I held him against my chest, glad to have him near me.

"Two days after arriving at the clock tower, at the darkest point of moonlessness, we ventured into the night. We encountered one of the packs of wild dogs, twenty or more in number, and I placed the girls high on my back, out of danger."

Armon set his hand on the butt of his sword, a weapon more than six feet in length, the end dangling at his ankles in its sheath.

"My sword was of much use on that night," he said. "The first pack of dogs relented, but others crept in as we traveled the length of the old city and its piles of debris. On that night we counted over a hundred dogs, some in packs as large as thirty, others in groups as small as five, all of them ravaged with disease and rage. A single bite from one of these sickly creatures would surely bring illness, madness, and eventually even death.

"At the edge of the City of Dogs is a large forest that runs for several miles along the western shore of the lake. As we made our escape, the forest was crawling with giants and men in search of me and the stones. But Grindall made a grievous error, for at that time giants were in service to both Grindall and those of their own race. There in the forest, two men saw us. These two called a warning with a horn, and help arrived in the form of three giants. The giants took hold of the men and threw them against a tree, dashing out their brains in the process."

"This story keeps getting better and better," said Yipes, a grin hiding his lips beneath his mustache as he looked down at me on the ground.

"I spoke to the three giants," continued Armon. "And it was agreed that they would set us free of Castalia to roam the wide reaches of The Land of Elyon in search of a new home, and that we would keep the remaining stones with us and protect them. We were taken to the Valley of Thorns, a place where only giants roam, and we were each of us seen by yet more giants who agreed to set us free. Over the great hill into the Dark Hills we ventured, with no idea where the journey might end.

"We had no food or water and precious little time to escape. So I took the girls once again on my back and ran through the night into the Dark Hills. In the morning I slept an hour and then continued in the same way until night fell once more. In two days' time we stood at the base of Mount Norwood, a place we would call home for many years thereafter."

"You lived on the mountain near Lathbury?" I asked, astounded at how close he'd been.

"The very one," Armon answered. It struck me then how I might have walked right past places Armon had been while I was on my first journey with Yipes outside the walls of Bridewell.

"We traveled high into the lush green of the mountain and made for ourselves a home there where we watched and waited. On very clear days, far across the Dark Hills, we could see the outline of the other great mountain that stands upright to the east of Castalia."

It was Mount Laythen that Armon spoke of, a mountain much taller and wider than Mount Norwood, not so different in size than Armon was to Yipes. Mount Laythen was the highest peak in The Land of Elyon, with a fat round bottom fifty miles wide.

"Catherine developed a deep fascination with all of the stones that remained," said Armon. "Especially the one that she took herself. She was completely obsessed with protecting it and understanding what she could of the rest. Soon she took advantage of their power and befriended all sorts of wild animals, one of which was an exquisite mountain lion. In the past Catherine had been unwilling to show the remaining stones to her animal friends, but something about the lion was different, and so she took him to where the stones were hidden. Together they examined the remaining twenty stones, and the lion was able to see something Catherine could not. Some of the stones were different, inscribed with an ancient language. With the help of the lion, Catherine separated the stones and found that only six were marked in this special way. The fourteen that were not marked were taken to a small pond near the base of the mountain and left at the edge for those who might find them, while

94

the other six were taken to a secret pool high atop Mount Norwood, mixed among ordinary stones, and left to be found by those who might stumble onto them as Elyon had ordained.

"Catherine and the mountain lion spent much time together, and the lion told Catherine all that he had seen in the stones, what the ancient language looked like, and how he was able to understand what was written. From this knowledge, Catherine made a habit of finding objects and carving patterns on them with secret hidden messages and pictures. In time she would learn to do such things with intricate tools on smaller and smaller items, until finally, much later, Catherine was able to do these etchings on items as small as a stone that might be carried around the neck of an ordinary library cat. She liked to call them Jocastas."

"It can't be so," I said.

"Catherine was Renny Warvold," said John, not as if he'd known all along but as though he'd figured it out just then, as I had.

Armon looked at us both with kindness and nodded slowly, a strange, sad hope in his eyes.

"Some time after she etched Elyon's words on each of the six stones, it came to pass that a young adventurer, many years of wandering behind him, came to rest on Mount Norwood. He had explored the land to the farthest cliffs, beyond Ainsworth to the northern side, and to the heights of Mount Laythen where he looked down on the plight of Castalia. He had traveled through the Dark Hills, the magnificent forests, and even into the haunting lair of the Sly Field. He had visited each of the two cities along the northern cliffs and the one to the west. In all his travels he never found a place more peaceful and joyous than Mount Norwood, and it was here that he returned after Catherine, Laura, and I had already been living there for a dozen years."

"Thomas Warvold," I whispered, the pieces of the puzzle coming together now.

"As Elyon would have it, the young Warvold stumbled onto the pool of Jocastas, quite sure that he had found the greatest treasure in The Land of Elyon. The girls were now grown women, and together with them I met Warvold for the first time at the edge of the pool. Warvold had seen giants before, but I was very different from all the others. Having had quite a lot of experience with seeing all manner of oddities, he was not so startled as you might suppose. Very quickly the four of us became acquainted. We went about the ritual of presenting Warvold with a Jocasta, and spent a time enjoying one another's company in the surrounding beauty of Mount Norwood.

"As you might have guessed, Catherine and Warvold fell in love, and soon thereafter the two of them began to tire of living alone in the mountains. It was decided that Warvold would go to Ainsworth and find those among the city that he might recruit into building a new kingdom past the Great Ravine, a city surrounded entirely by walls, which would afford protection from the dangers of the wild. It was further decided that before accompanying him, Catherine would change her name to Renny, in the event that anyone within the settled world knew of her and the legend of Armon."

I was at once astounded by all that Renny had been through. I tried desperately to remember her, but I had been only a small child when she passed away, and I could dig up no images to remind me of her. I only knew that I missed her more than I thought I should. I wished she were still alive.

"In the years that followed, Lunenburg came into being, Nicolas was born to Renny and Thomas, and the kingdom of Bridewell surfaced in The Land of Elyon."

Armon stopped then and knelt down so I could see his expression clearly.

"Shortly after the walls were completed, I began to feel a terrible dark presence from the distant land of Castalia. So I traveled there — or here, I should say — to where we now find ourselves. In the dead of night I crept to the top of the hill. What I saw there I must now, unfortunately, share with you."

He motioned everyone closer, and we stood before the kneeling giant.

"From the very beginning there have been stories among the giants — sacred stories, many of which have become more fable than truth as the human side of us dominates more and more. Our former home — the Tenth City — has been forgotten in the passing of time."

Armon paused, digging up the past in his head. He seemed to be weighing what he should and shouldn't say.

"Humans are a forgetful and doubtful race of beings," he continued. "To remember things of a distant past is something of a difficulty for them, and so it is with my own kind in the tenth reign of Grindall, our memories of the Tenth City washing away."

Armon stopped again and looked at the great hill, searching for signs of life in the moonlight. Then he turned back to us and went on, his face downcast.

"Do you know about the bats?" he asked.

He was surprised to find that we knew of them and had even encountered them in the Dark Hills. He seemed concerned about this.

"Where did you see them? Was it near?" he asked.

"No, it wasn't near," said Yipes with a soothing tone. "It was many miles back, closer to Bridewell than here."

Armon seemed to listen very carefully, still agitated.

"I can never be seen by them," he said, and then he told us why.

"There is a swarm of a thousand bats, sent by Abaddon from where he dwells, and these bats have but one purpose — to peck and tear at the heads of the giants, to infect them with Abaddon's will.

"Imagine a giant the same size as me with its skull emptied of hair but for clumps and strands growing sickly around the rim and over the ears. Imagine the head and face marked with scabs and open sores that never run dry, the teeth rotted out and missing or blackened — a hideous, disfigured creature answering to Abaddon's will."

Armon stood up then and towered over us.

"That's what happens to giants who are found by the swarm of bats."

He closed his eyes, letting the words sink in. I got the feeling things were about to get even scarier.

"I am the last of what remains of my race. The rest have already been found by the swarm," he said, opening his eyes. "What lies beyond the great hill is not more of my kind, but the darkest evil in The Land of Elyon — ninety-eight gargantuan monsters with but one goal before them: to destroy us so Elyon can never return."

"The swarm has narrowed its hunt to only one?" John asked, his worrisome question hanging in the air like thick black tar until Armon gazed into the Dark Hills and spoke once more.

"They move in the night, forever searching until they discover me and infect me like the rest." He looked at us then with a glimmer of hope. "We must win the battle before they find me."

He started walking again into the darkness, and I found myself running to be near him and find comfort in his presence. I was happy when Armon started talking again, his peaceful voice pushing my visions of dreadful beasts away.

"There is some good news among all the bad," he began again. "I have not quite finished with the story. The infected giants are no more powerful than they were before, and although forceful, they can be defeated if one knows how. Further, and of far more importance, to kill all the giants would be to destroy Abaddon's vast army and leave him exposed, furious, and reckless."

"But ninety-eight of them?" I said.

"It is a bit daunting," said Armon. "But you must never forget that Elyon, in his own mysterious way, a way which we cannot understand, is on our side. The creator of both human and Seraph has chosen us, and I can only hope that in his vast wisdom he will show us how we might prevail against all odds."

We had been walking for a while. Armon looked around in all directions.

"This will do," he said. "I've brought some food and water. Set out your things and eat if you like. You will have only a short while to sleep."

We were still out in the open and the great hill lay before us.

"Isn't this more exposed than we'd like?" asked Odessa, which I in turn translated to Armon.

"There's no other place to be had, I'm afraid. I'll watch through the night, but I don't expect to see anyone near here."

I set my small pack on the crusty dirt and took a

100

handful of nuts and berries out from the stash Armon provided.

"If you're not too tired I'd like to tell you the last of the story. I believe it may help to properly motivate you in the coming days."

Armon sat down among us and gathered his thoughts to speak a final time about the things of the past. While he considered what to say, I watched the night sky with its countless stars and its moon, and I wondered about the universe and all that had been created, why the stars and the moon rose at night and the sun in the day, how vast it must be, how I could never understand the infinite measure of its size.

Odessa rarely chose me when it came time to rest, but on this night she did, and she lay down along my side with her head next to mine. Murphy hopped onto her back and made a bed of her soft gray hair, and the three of us were comforted by one another.

"The tenth reign of Grindall came into existence not long after I departed Castalia," Armon began. "I know this prince of darkness, this tenth Victor Grindall. His reign began through trickery and murder, and immediately he focused everything on finding the remaining stones.

"But in all his efforts Victor Grindall failed to recover the missing treasure. This greatly displeased Abaddon. So it came to pass that Grindall sent the giants beyond

101

the Dark Hills to find the stones, to places they'd never searched before.

"Before long the giants were within reach of the wall at Bridewell. Pervis Kotcher, the head of the guards, was the first to see them from his tower at the Lunenburg gate. This was a moment he understood might come, for Thomas and Renny had told him if giants were ever seen in the Dark Hills, he should hide the fact and send all the guards off the towers. If other guards had seen, Pervis was to collect them and bring them before Warvold, and the rest of the kingdom was to remain unaware of the horrible danger beyond the wall.

"Renny was the first person Pervis found as he searched the lodge for either of the Warvolds, and he told her of the giants approaching in the distance. Renny instructed Pervis to find Thomas. Then, without delay, she ran to the library and entered the secret tunnel that leads under the city and into the mountains."

Armon leaned back on his mighty hands while the rest of us sat wide-eyed before him.

"Once in the tunnel, there is a hidden door that, when opened, leads the short distance out into the Dark Hills. This door Renny opened, and not long after that the giants arrived at the wall. She stood alone and unprotected among them."

"Why, Armon? Why would she do such a thing?" I asked.

"She thought, quite rightly, that if she could offer herself it might appease the giants. Capturing the one who had taken the stones might be a good enough reason to return to the Dark Tower. It would certainly be a noteworthy find. And so Renny offered to go with them, insisting that she would only tell what she knew to Victor Grindall himself.

"About this time, Warvold and Pervis arrived at the Lunenburg tower. The giants, who Warvold would later say were already possessed by Abaddon, were big enough to break through the wall if they wanted to. But they only wanted the remaining stones, and this they demanded of Warvold. They would have the remaining stones or the whole of Bridewell would be overrun and everything within the kingdom would be destroyed.

"Weaponry was not advanced in Bridewell, and the city relied almost entirely on archers for defense. The giants carried two things that worried Warvold greatly — large metal shields and bags filled with stones the size of watermelons, which he rightly guessed they could throw with great accuracy. The hideous giant heads dripping with sweat and open sores, the shields combined with great black armor — these things conspired against Warvold and the armament he possessed. These were huge creatures, well armed and adequately protected. A hundred of them would wipe out everyone in Bridewell and move on to Turlock and Lathbury when they were through."

Armon looked at Yipes, who was sitting upright, eyes almost comically wide, completely enthralled by the story. Like so many of us from Bridewell Common, our little friend simply loved to hear a good tale. I'm not sure he fully grasped that the story included us, the dangers looming larger every time Armon opened his mouth.

"Thomas saw the moment for what it was," continued Armon. "A pivotal encounter in the fight over which forces would control The Land of Elyon, forces of evil or good. But the price was higher than he had imagined it could be. His own life he would have gladly given, but he had great difficulty sacrificing those of his people or his beloved wife. He knew where the six stones lay hidden in the secret pool on Mount Norwood. He could lead these awful creatures there and they would disappear once again into the Dark Hills. But what evil would overcome the land if he allowed this to happen, and how quickly would an even darker force return and bound over the walls if he gave away the secret?

"Warvold would not reveal what he knew, and on that terrible day Catherine was taken from him. It was said that if she could not produce the whereabouts of the stones, she would be locked away in the deepest part of the Dark Tower at Castalia, until the remaining stones were found and returned to pay her ransom.

"I don't know what Catherine told them or how she has kept the giants away from Bridewell these ten years.

Maybe she has sent them searching in the City of Dogs or in the streams of Mount Laythen. But one thing I feel is certain: She remains among us. Catherine, the woman you know as Renny, is alive, locked in the dungeon in the tower across the lake."

PART 2

CHAPTER 15

FIRE AND RAIN

"Wake up, Alexa. The fire is already started." It was dark and cold as I shivered awake, my body aching from yet another night of broken sleep against the floor of the Dark Hills. Everyone else was already stirring or standing, looking across the valley where an orange glow rippled along the top of the hills. This was not the sight of the sun rising over the earth; it was something closer and more dangerous.

"What's happening?" I asked, rubbing sleep out of my eyes as I rose, feeling the toughness of the ground beneath my tender feet. I bent low to itch the scabs on my shins from which I continued to find no relief. It was still night or very early morning, and everything was dark but the fire on the hill and the stars overhead.

"Armon has been busy while we've slept," said Yipes through a yawn and a stretch. I walked to where they stood and gazed at the hill.

"The wind rolls down the mountain and into the valley," said Armon. "And thunderclouds often gather along the rim of the great mountain. Vast brushfires along the hill are not so uncommon during this time of summer. Everything turns black, only to be reborn again in the spring with new underbrush. The cycle continues year after year. Some years there are many fires and some years there are few, but often humans or nature ignites the dead brush."

My eyes had adjusted to the starry light and the distant glow of fire on the hill. Armon knelt next to me, pointing into the darkness.

"I started the fire there with my flint, at the base of Mount Laythen, and the wind carried it along the hill and over to the other side." Already the fire had spread over the top of the hill and along its front to the valley where we stood. I could only assume it had spread to the other side of the hill as well.

"There are thousands of poles that make up the Valley of Thorns. They are covered in thick tar at the base, and the brush beneath them will burn through as it always does. The giants will pull back from the Valley of Thorns and stand at its edge, protecting the forest in case the flames come too close, until the fire passes through. Then they will walk through and stamp out any glowing embers that remain. By morning our opportunity will have passed."

The orange glow of the fire line was mesmerizing in the darkness, like a twisted snake upon the land, writhing and devouring everything in its path. It glowed hot and wide when the wind gusted through, and sat low and patient when the billows ceased.

"Gather your things and breathe deeply while there is

110

fresh air. The smoke that provides our cover will make the going difficult," Armon warned.

"How far away is the great mountain?" asked John, trying to get his bearings and understand where we would enter the city.

"From here, probably twenty miles," Armon answered.

"You couldn't have traveled that far while we slept, Armon. Forty miles in only a few hours is hard to imagine, even for you," said Yipes.

"Two hours and twelve minutes, to be exact," said Armon. "And you thought I'd only been eating blackberries and lounging about in the mountains all these years, getting fat and happy."

"Yes, but *forty miles?*" Yipes objected. Armon had nothing more to say on the subject, and the night air stood silent, a cool breeze driving the flames closer still.

We walked away from the flames, in line with the hill. The fire had not yet drawn close, but it was traveling fast, and it seemed to me that within an hour it would be right on top of us. Already the oddly appealing smell of smoke hung heavy in the air, and the stars were obscured from the haze pouring into the sky.

"We must move quickly, until we are but a mile off the southern cliffs, then take the hill as the flames dance at our feet," said Armon. "We shall hope the giants who remain will not see us through the haze as we pass into the forest on the other side."

We walked on, our pace stronger as the wind increased, and the fire seemed to halve its distance from us in no time at all. Twenty minutes later the flames were closer than we'd hoped they would be.

"We must run!" Armon yelled. He knelt down and instructed me to jump onto the great leather bag on his back and hang on. Then he took Yipes and Murphy on his shoulders and stood erect. John and Odessa were left to run of their own power, goaded on by Armon's colossal steps behind them, like the cracking of a whip at their heels. I was astonished at the size of Armon's back, the breadth of his neck, how high in the air I was, the power of everything about him. It felt as though I were riding a great bull with magnificent strength, that I might be thrown high into the night air and trampled underfoot.

"Follow me the rest of the way," Armon said to our running companions. "We must turn to the hill now and overcome its face. Stay as quiet as you can, muffle your coughing. No matter how tired you become, don't stop until I tell you."

The smoke was much thicker now, coming in waves. A mere fifty yards to our right lay the slithering snake of fire. As it approached us I was surprised by the height of the flames. I had thought they would be only a foot off the ground, but when the wind took them, they darted seven or eight feet up, licking against the night sky.

We had already been moving diagonally against the hill under Armon's lead, and before long we were at its base. I looked back and saw that John and Odessa were right behind us. Ahead lay the most difficult part of the night's journey, and Armon had timed it perfectly. The heat from the fire was growing steadily, and smoke ran in formless white rivers all around us. I kept looking back to see our companions. Finally, about halfway up the side of the hill, the smoke came thick enough between us that I lost sight of them entirely.

"Armon, we've lost them!" I said, and then I looked to my right and found that the fire was no longer a safe distance away. Hidden in the smoke it had crept up on us, the flames dancing now at Armon's leather-clad feet.

Armon darted to the left and continued running up the hill toward the smoke-filled sky. He was moving faster now, bounding in great strides up the hill and moving to the left as he avoided the flames.

"Armon, you're losing them!" I said. "They can't keep up."

But he just kept running, faster and faster, until we reached the edge where the hill topped out, flattened, and tumbled down the other side. He dropped us from his back and shoulders quickly and descended the hill into the smoke from where we had come.

"Keep moving away from the flames and stay just this side of the top," he said as he went. "Don't go down the hill on either side."

At the top of the hill the smoke was not as thick, but breathing was still difficult. Yipes, Murphy, and I stayed in front of the flames as they approached us, slipping down the side of the hill occasionally as we tried to stay off the top and out of sight. I looked down the hill where the smoke was thickest and saw nothing of our two companions.

"I hope they're all right," squeaked Murphy.

Seconds turned to minutes, and we moved at least thirty feet along the edge to stay out of the flames. I glanced up at the sky and realized with some astonishment that a low ceiling of smoke hung all around us in the air, obscuring anything more than a few feet overhead. I was alarmed at how completely the smoke had taken the sky. I also began to wonder how close to the southern cliffs we were, where the hill would taper down and eventually meet with the steep drop-off that ended in jagged rocks and the Lonely Sea below.

While my head was turned toward the cliffs, Odessa came sniffing and pawing at my feet. I knelt down and embraced her around her big bushy neck.

"Armon's got John, right behind me," she said, and no sooner than it was out of her mouth, Armon arrived with John flung over his shoulder. He dropped John to the ground with a thud, and I was happy to see that he was conscious and alert.

"The clouds have moved in," said Armon. "Soon the rain will come and our cover will be lost." He said nothing else, only crouched low and moved to the top of the hill. It was flat for twenty feet, then it dropped off even more steeply than the side we had been on. Looking out over the edge I saw the lights of Castalia's wharf in the distance, but everything else was shrouded in smoke and darkness.

"You must follow me precisely," Armon told us. "Don't veer off my trail to the left or to the right. Hold onto one another so we stay together through the smoke."

Armon began to descend the hill on the opposite side, Yipes and Murphy once again on his shoulders, me holding tightly to the bag on his back. John held Armon by his leather vest, which hung down behind him. With his other hand he grabbed hold of Odessa's mane.

The descent was steep, full of brush and small rocks. I winced every time the pebbles shot out from under Armon's huge feet, fearing the noise would give us away and a monstrous giant would suddenly appear before us. I was glad when we reached the bottom, although the smoke was terribly thick and gray, and I was only able to see a few feet in front of me. My lungs screamed for fresh air, and I could hear myself wheezing as my body tried to adjust. The first drops of rain began to fall and the wind began to swirl around us, the smoke following its master and thinning out as it spun in circles.

"Behold the Valley of Thorns," said Armon. Through the swirling smoke a vast graveyard of poles emerged. "Don't touch anything and move carefully. Delicate wires connect many of the poles, so we must be careful to go around them. The top of every pole is

115

lathered with poison. Imagine this field of venomous tips as you would a labyrinth. Follow me closely. If we leave a trace, they will surely find us."

Armon zigzagged between poles, some of them short and some at my eye level atop Armon's back, all razor sharp at the tip and shining bloodred with poison. I held tightly to the big leather bag and hoped it wouldn't be flung from Armon's back, me with it, impaled onto a pole. The smoke whipped through like a great fog, swirling all around us, and the poles, like hollow bones, stood erect in the thin light of dawn. All the while the rain fell thicker, first only a few drops, then larger and more frequent. Before long the sky would let go all at once, the flames would be snuffed out, and with them the smoke that hid us.

Armon stopped abruptly and remained still and quiet. We were approaching the far edge of the Valley of Thorns, and I could see the outline of trees in the forest before us. But there was something more, movement to the right through what remained of the thin layer of smoke. In the haze of morning my heart pounded against Armon's back, and the sky let go of the rain altogether. The gleaming back of a giant's head appeared, his monstrous, misaligned shoulders swaying to and fro as if working at something in front of him. And then another giant appeared to my right, walking toward the first. This one I saw completely as he passed before us in the murky light only ten feet away, streams of water flowing over his misshapen face, the smell of him so close that even in the cleansing rain I felt my insides quake and sour. He pushed the first giant, and they barked at each other in a language I could not understand. It was guttural and wet and low, as though they were spitting up gobs of phlegm with every word. They marched off into the rain, leaving behind them a tall pole bent a little to the left, as if it were not held in place like the rest.

With the rain coming in sheets and the smoke all but washed away, Armon began to move forward, then pushed John and Odessa into the gloom of the forest. A group of giants was gathering to the right with the two we had seen. Just as they turned to survey the area we occupied, Armon slipped into the trees, taking me with him upon his mighty back.

We remained still a moment, smoke hanging like a deep mist in the trees, and we breathed the forest air. It was a thick section of trees buried in wiry underbrush. I was glad to be on Armon's back, out of reach of the scratches to be had on the forest floor.

"We have yet to pass through the wood, but the haze of smoke will help hide us," Armon said quietly. "Soon we will reach a wooded path that forks off in different directions. One of these forks will lead us to the place where we must hide."

Armon whispered more, telling John and Odessa to watch him and be ready to leave the path and hide in the wood if he should do the same, for the paths were patrolled by Grindall's giants. We moved silently through the gloom and Odessa seemed to struggle the most, her legs tangled often in the deep underbrush. Before long we came upon a winding path. In a place where such death and despair were expected, I was taken aback by the beauty of the simple curves, the smoky mist overhead, light shooting through the clouds that were already moving on and revealing spots of pale blue, the rain now a mist of tiny droplets all around us. Armon set me, Murphy, and Yipes down, and I felt the soft, wet earth beneath my feet. We walked on, curving this way and that, Armon peering forward, then back in search of our enemy.

"Why do they smell so bad?" I whispered. Armon put his finger to his lips and motioned me to be quiet, then he leaned down and whispered back.

"They are rotting from the inside out," he explained. My face soured, and he dropped to one knee, bending low and facing the lot of us.

"My race is all but wiped out," Armon said, and I saw his sadness at admitting he was the last of them. "What remains are not giants. They are transformed, entirely possessed by evil, not a trace of light remains in them. Best we call them ogres from now on, for that is what they have become. I have no kinship with them."

The morning was fully awake now, wet leaves and plants dancing gently in the slight breeze. The sky above was sapphire blue and only a few light clouds remained.

The trees rose high above us on both sides of the path, swaying lazily in the first breath of day.

A racket of noise startled us from behind. I nearly jumped off the path entirely. It was Squire coming to a stop on a tree that lined the path.

"Squire!" whispered Yipes. "Must you be so dramatic?"

But Squire only screeched in reply, an angry look in her eyes.

"Off the path," said Armon, and before I could turn to see him he had taken me by the waist and lifted me off the ground, my face and arms running through thick brush as he carried me away. Squire flew into the air again, and the rest of us crouched in the thicket off the path. All except Murphy, who had found for himself a nut that had fallen from one of the trees. He was absorbed entirely by the crunchy morsel, nibbling aimlessly in the middle of the path, until two dreadful ogres were only a few strides from where he stood. Their shadows overtook Murphy. Looking up, he screamed, ran back and forth as if he'd lost his mind, and then darted up a tree where he looked down on the two ogres in time to see what remained of his breakfast trampled underfoot.

Again there was the unpleasant smell as the ogres passed by, ripe and wet, a loathsome odor of dying flesh raised on the wind and carried to where we crouched motionless in the thicket. They hardly took notice of

Murphy as they moved on. Ahead, where the trail split in two, the ogres went along in opposite directions, one passing deeper into the forest, the other veering off toward the lake.

"Why didn't I think of that?" said Yipes after they had passed. "He'll make a fine lookout from up there — if we can keep him from eating his way through the forest."

And so it was decided that Murphy would remain in the trees above, scouting our way as we passed through the wood. It was really quite beautiful, surprisingly full of birds and other small creatures that scurried away in the brush. The wood ran along the south side of the lake and at a certain point I was able to see through the trees and behold the vast expanse of cobalt blue, the mirror image of Mount Laythen shimmering on its surface. It was unlike anything I could have ever imagined seeing in Bridewell.

For a long while we encountered no other ogres, though Murphy ordered us off the path once when a group of three women passed by in a rickety old cart pulled by a meager-looking horse. I was startled to see other people in the woods, and became newly aware that we were nearing Castalia. I saw the women through the brush, especially the one sitting closest to me on the edge of the cart. She was not pretty, but it seemed as though she might have been once. She appeared tired. Her two companions spoke quietly as they passed, but she remained silent. I rose up in the brush and watched the three dark bonnets on their heads bobbing up and down with the bumps on the trail. Something about the one woman struck me, and I felt as though someone was telling me to remember her face.

We continued on, and soon a new stench was in the air, just as bad as the smell of ogres, yet different, more like rotting garbage. Murphy scampered down a tree, and we all gathered off the trail once more.

There were only four words spoken, but they were words that brought a new feeling of alarm.

"The City of Dogs," said John, and Armon nodded his agreement.

CHAPTER 16

İNT⊙ THE CİTY

⊙F D⊙GS

"Just around the bend and in the clearing," said Armon, "the forest thins out and the dumping grounds begin. Within them we shall find the wild dogs, their packs grown larger and more violent with the passing of the years." He paused and sniffed at the air, concentrating, no doubt trying to remember the place as it had been when he had last seen it.

"Take out your weapons and prepare for the worst," he whispered, unsheathing his own massive sword as quietly as he could. Then he eyed Odessa closely, the two of them staring at one another in the stillness.

"You might be of some use to us here," said Armon. "It is possible they might see you as one of their own and let us pass through. But there will be no avoiding them. They know we are here."

We moved down what remained of the path before us, Odessa and Armon striding confidently beside each other at the front. As we came around the one remaining wooded corner the stench almost knocked me off my feet, a gentle breeze carrying with it an omen of what lay ahead.

It was a good deal as I'd expected it would be, a vast expanse of broken-down houses and mountains of flowing debris. Trails shot off in various directions, the hard earth grooved deeply with wheel marks pooling from the rains. Piles of garbage steamed with the morning sun, and the breeze sent a continual flow of pungent new odors over us.

We walked on, following Armon's lead, careful to listen for humans or ogres who might be roaming about. It wasn't long before we were deep in the City of Dogs, and howls could be heard from both near and far. Odessa began to growl as she moved forward with increasing hesitation, her ears pointed and alert for the dogs that might jump out and attack us.

"Where are they, Odessa?" asked Yipes, an arrow pulled and ready to shoot from his small bow.

"They keep moving," she replied, and I translated to the others. "And there is more than one pack, at least two. Both are tracking us and watching one another." Then she stopped entirely and looked back at us. "These are both large packs, fifty or more to be sure."

All at once the sound of growling and barking was all around us, and a moment later we were trapped, one pack of dogs emerging around two garbage heaps to the left of the path, and another pack moving in from the right. They encircled us, row upon row of dogs. They were dripping saliva, some with open wounds and sores around their

mouths and noses. Others limped weakly in the row farthest from us.

The group of us came together as the wild dogs
inched closer. Running would be futile; it would be what
they'd hope we would do, so they could separate us and
single us out, take us down at the legs, and rip us to
shreds one by one.

"Can't you talk to them, Odessa?" I pleaded. The
barking and growling was fierce and I was frightened and
shaking. The first row of dogs was just a few feet away.
Where the two packs touched, dogs growled and fought
one another violently, and I felt it was only a matter of
time before we were caught in a storm of teeth and claws
as the two packs fought over who would have us as their
prize.

A very large and surprisingly healthy-looking black
dog with a huge head and a crumpled mane pulled closer
to us still, and I took him to be the leader of one of the
two packs. Odessa darted between him and me, growling
ferociously. The two of them squared off, not attacking
but apparently thinking of little else. From the other
pack came a similar situation — the largest of the dogs, a
brown mixed breed with bushy hair and glaring white
teeth, moving out in front to square off with Armon.
These were scary creatures, ill with diseases that a single
bite could inflict on any one of us.

"You have a choice to make." It was John, his calming
voice sending a wave of sniffs and swaying heads across

the sea of wild dogs. "We can go to war here in the mire. You will surely overcome us in the end, but not before we slay a good many, if not most, of you. Armon's sword alone will cut a large swath of you to the grave. And who knows, we might even kill each and every one of you before we're through. After all, we have blades and arrows and a giant." John paused and looked around him. "Against a hundred dogs it may not be enough, but it will surely be close."

The black lead dog paced back and forth in confusion, uncertain what to make of this man before him.

"How is it that you speak and we understand?" growled the dog. "Do you hear what I'm saying to you?"

John repeated what was said by the dog word for word, and this further confounded both lead dogs. Confused beyond measure and unsure what to do, the rest of the two packs backed up and waited to see what their respective leaders would do.

"If the two of you will listen to me, I will offer you an alternative that I think you'll agree is to your advantage," said John. He bent down on one knee between the two of them and began to explain who we were and why we had come. He left out many details that were of little consequence. He told them we were here to overthrow Grindall, to free the people from the ogres, and to save a prisoner enslaved in the castle.

"If the two of you can control your packs and use them to help us defeat Grindall and his army of beasts, then I give you my word I will do everything in my power to help you," John concluded.

The mangy brown dog licked at his nose and seemed to contemplate the offer.

"Piggott?" he said, looking at the other leader and questioning his intent. "We have long since chosen our territories and formed our armies. But food runs scarcer by the year and our fighting brings less and less benefit. Soon we'll have to move into the wharf to find food, and this will bring the hammer down on us for good. The giants will come and clear us out one by one until none remain."

The black dog eyed us carefully, standing tall and proud, and I noticed for the first time that his ribs were protruding beneath his gangly hair. How long had he gone without food? I wanted to reach out and pet him, but I feared he might snap at me and dig his teeth into my hand.

"Scroggs," he addressed the brown dog, "could it be that this is the giant who took the last of the stones?" Armon remained quiet, watching in wonder as we communicated with the dogs. To him, Piggott and Scroggs only growled and barked and rolled their heads this way and that. It was a language he could not hope to understand.

I took my Jocasta from its pouch and presented it, glowing even in the full light of day. Piggott and Scroggs backed up a step each, and the rest of the dogs retreated even farther back, some out of sight but for their faces, the rest of their bodies hidden behind broken walls and mounds of rubbish.

"It is indeed the giant Armon, the one they look for day and night," said Scroggs, astonished and trembling. "The end must be nearer than I'd thought."

A great deal of discussion followed, with Piggott and Scroggs fighting over who would hold the highest rank and by what method the packs would merge or otherwise work together. They seemed fiercer than ever in their excitement to overthrow Grindall.

It was decided that we must be hidden, and once again the place would be the clock tower on the far end of the dumping grounds. Scroggs and his pack would roam the north side of the City of Dogs, and Piggott and his brood would roam the south. When the time was right, we would call for them, and as one, the hundred dogs would besiege the castle in the dead of night.

"We will require something in return for our help," said Piggott, and all the dogs from both packs began to whine and bark. "There is a butcher on the wharf. Bring us a hundred slabs of fresh meat and we will fight to the death. These beasts deserve one good meal in their lives, and I aim to give it to them."

I looked out upon the two packs. With the ominous growling and barking at bay they were a sad lot indeed. Many of them were large but oddly frail and meek, and most were quite clearly ill. I felt sorry for them then, and though I wished I could save them all, I knew that victory against Grindall would mean little for these creatures. Their lives were marked for a death that would come sooner rather than later. Scroggs and Piggott knew this, and maybe that's why they so willingly joined us in our quest. A heroic end by the knife was a better end than the one both packs faced. They hated Grindall and the ogres and their evil ways, and this was the chance to destroy them, to be of some great purpose at the very end.

"John and I can do it," I said. "We'll get you your meal, more if we can hold it."

The packs stayed to their sides while Scroggs and Piggott led us deeper still into the City of Dogs on our way to the clock tower. There was only one thing more that we lacked, something upon which our ability to succeed almost entirely depended. What we needed was Castalians, and we needed a great many of them.

CHAPTER 17

THE WHARF

The clock tower was just as I'd imagined it when I'd heard the story. It looked mysterious sitting alone among weeds and debris, as though secret things had taken place there in the distant past. It was round and made of stone, lined with ivy, and looked very old. I immediately wanted to touch it and feel something of the place where Laura and Catherine had hidden.

"It's fantastic," I said, looking up at John in the cooling night air. He only nodded, lost in his thoughts of this place in the same way I was.

Both our faces were shrouded by hoods fashioned from blankets. It was common for Castalia's peasants to wear a throw this way, and it helped to make us feel more as though we would not be noticed or picked out as outsiders if we encountered anyone. The rest of our attire was in keeping with that of a commoner; everything we wore was dirty and tattered from our journey, John with his shabby tunic, me with an earth-brown tunic frayed at the ankles and an old pair of weathered leather sandals.

We had left everyone else behind in the clock tower to begin planning how we might rescue Catherine and rid Castalia of Grindall and the ogres. In the tower it was stuffy and hot, and I was glad to be free of it. Even still, the open air of the City of Dogs smelled as though it could be cut like a block of cheese. I longed to be near the lake where the air would smell fresh and clean.

Armon had already thought a great deal about how best to go about our business with Grindall. He had explained in detail how we should approach the wharf without being seen and how to blend in should someone engage us. Both John and I carried our leather satchels on our backs. They were empty, but we hoped to return to the clock tower with as much meat as we could put in them.

"The butcher, he usually takes in three or four pigs in the morning," said Piggott, who was scouting just ahead of us, leading us quietly to the edge of the wharf where he would wait for our return. "In the back of the shop he cures the ham and boils the bones. It is there where you will find what we want. The hams will be heavy, but you can manage it. You can cut them up in the clock tower."

Piggott continued on, John and I following, until we reached the last of the broken-down buildings and piles of trash. Before us lay an open stretch of field. Beyond the field emerged the shimmering edge of the lake, its surface a liquid sea of black, marked by reflections grasped from the stars and the moon above.

"If you cross the field here and stay along the lake, you will find the wharf," said Piggott. He sat down and scratched vigorously against the side of his head. "This stretch is not patrolled by giants, only by humans. They will not be looking for intruders, since no one ever comes.

They look only for those trying to escape. But even these are so few that the guards mostly sleep or gamble in the night. If you are careful you should have no trouble entering the wharf. Getting out could prove a bigger challenge, but if you're watchful and quiet you will get past."

Before our departure, Armon was careful to explain that on the wharf, darkness meant few people would be out and about. We would see occasional guards and ogres, and we might see washmaids dumping dirty water or men hauling out debris, but the streets would be mostly barren until morning.

John was first to venture out into the open of the field; I followed with some hesitation, wishing for once that I might stay in the squalid safety of the City of Dogs. It was not far to the edge of the lake, and as we approached, the air cooled and the night felt calm and peaceful. The sound of water lapping lazily on the rocks soothed my frazzled spirit, and for a moment I was taken back home behind my desk again, bored but happy and safe.

We walked quickly along the water, following it toward the dim lights not far in the distance. I heard voices carried over the lake, and began to wonder who we might encounter and what they might be doing. Two men, probably guards, walked along the lake as we did, making their way toward us, each with a torch in hand. John took my hand and we darted out into the field, then lay perfectly still on the ground in the brush and waited.

The men came only a little farther, then turned back to the wharf without reaching us, talking peaceably as they went.

We rose and followed well behind them until they disappeared around a corner and we stood at the edge of the wharf where houses began to appear. It was nearing eleven o'clock in the evening, and as Armon had suspected, the cobblestone streets were deserted.

Even in the darkness it was clear that the wharf was a dirty place. The houses and the fronts of the small buildings were made of whitewashed stone and wood, but these were simple structures lacking any charm or character, and many were marked with broken facades and crumbling corners. The street was made of small cobblestones, much smaller than the ones at home, and the recent rain had left many of the stones covered with mud. A stone wall, three feet high, ran along the lake side of the wharf, and every twenty feet an opening appeared that led down to the water's edge.

"What shall we do?" I asked.

John motioned me forward and we walked along the edge of the wall until we reached an opening. Then we crossed through the opening and crouched down behind the wall, moving quietly along the lake. Beneath our feet were clumps of brush, pebbles, and rocks, but we were hidden by the little wall along the lake. We passed a group of guards throwing dice and a man rolling a noisy cart down the cobbled street. Lamps lit the night along the street, but we were able to move ahead without notice in the relative darkness next to the lake.

A while later we came upon a group of women standing next to the wall. They were washing clothes and talking quietly. One of them walked through the opening and poured dirty water into the lake, then took her wooden bucket and filled it once again. She wore a blue bonnet, as did the rest of them, and as she turned to go back to her work I saw that she had the same expression as the woman I'd seen passing through the City of Dogs earlier in the day. She was sad and tired, going through her motions as if she were only half-awake.

She rejoined her companions, and the four of them worked and talked quietly. We would have to cross over into the street and pass them in the open to find the butcher's shop. The two of us backtracked and emerged where the light was scarce. We covered our faces and looked down, then walked along the street toward the women in blue bonnets. I could hear another cart rolling down a side street and the guttural voice of an ogre somewhere behind us. The voice was far enough off that I couldn't tell for sure where it had come from as the sound bounced off the lake. We quickened our pace and soon enough we were nearing the women, the sound of wet clothing slapping against soapy stones and the sharp, white smell of detergent hanging in the air.

I kept on with John and listened as the women stopped their work and the street became quiet. Then we passed in front of them, my eyes downcast and watching as the small cobblestones rushed by beneath my feet.

"You should not be about at this hour," came a voice, quiet but firm. "Have you some work you are attending to?"

When I glanced up I saw that it was the woman from the forest, the quiet one on the cart whose face I couldn't forget. How could we meet twice by chance in such a small window of time? I wondered if Elyon was indeed pulling on strings from within the Tenth City, moving people around so they might encounter one another. I instinctively placed my hand over the leather pouch holding my Jocasta, then stopped on the street even as John tried to pull me forward.

I had been surrounded by men my whole life, and the journey to Castalia, with the mostly silent exception of Odessa, had been no different. This was a reality that did not bother me in the least — I lived in what often felt like a man's world, and I'd come to accept this fact and even enjoy my unique place in it. But there was something about this woman's face and the way she'd spoken to us. I understood her in a way John did not. I felt a hidden hope in her questioning — a hope that John and I might be something more than two peasants wandering in the night.

"You work late tonight," I said, still not turning to face her, but letting her know that I was a girl.

"We are behind on the washing, and so we work," answered the woman, the others whispering beside her. The woman's tone remained quiet and measured, as if speaking was something she did only when necessary. "That is the way of things in Castalia. You know this." She was probing me, looking for more.

John pulled on my tunic once again, and this time I took his hand and gently pushed it away. Then I looked up, full into the faces of the four women, and pulled the covering off my head, letting it rest around my shoulders.

"We are not from here," I said, a cold wave of fright washing over me as the words tumbled out of my mouth. There was a moment of silence, and then I reached out my hand and softly touched the closest woman on the arm. "We have come to help you."

And there it was, out in the open. Everything we had risked and all that we hoped for hung in the wind. They could scream for help, and we would be captured and tortured in Grindall's dungeon. All would be lost. Abaddon would gather the stones and Elyon would be overcome.

The voice of the ogre was coming closer, moving in from a side street, wheezing and spitting, his huge feet clomping along the earth as he came.

"The enemy is upon us. What do you say?" I asked. The woman looked at her companions and seemed to consider if any of them were about to give us away. John began tugging at me again, pulling me down the street against my will.

135

"Pack up your things and get back to the house," the woman said. The other three smiled broadly and started to move. The woman reached out her hand to me. I looked at John and he hesitated, then nodded his cautious approval. The moment I took her hand the three of us were racing across the street, and soon we had vanished in the maze of narrow streets, turning first this way and then that. She said nothing as we went. This was not the quiet woman I'd seen in the forest on the cart or at the wharf doing the washing. She was energized, alert, and purposeful.

Somewhere in the twists and turns along the wharf she stopped and peered around a blind corner. Here she squeezed my hand harder and whispered in my ear.

"Do not be afraid," she said, and then she motioned for me to look around the edge with her. Twenty yards off was a high wall made of stone, and within it was fashioned a massive gate of iron. Before the gate stood two ogres armed with enormous swords. Beyond the gate was a dark path, and beyond the path a series of torches that climbed into the darkness. Against the night was a single spire, rising into the stars, a threatening shadow invading the sky.

"It's the Dark Tower," she whispered. "Grindall's castle."

"Why did you bring us here?" I said, unsure as we stood so close to the enemy. She held my hand tighter still. One pull and it would be over; I would be out in the open and helpless.

She turned to both of us, her former beauty clear to me even in the darkness. Though beaten down and aged by poverty, she had a perfect face, and the tears in her eyes made me want to rescue her more than anything I'd ever wanted before.

"He is a wicked man, led by wicked forces," she whispered, her voice trembling with emotion. "No one knows the things that happen in the Dark Tower, only that these things are evil."

She paused and looked around the corner once again, then back at us. "The giants grow angrier and more violent by the day. They grow more ill, more rotten. And Grindall grows more impatient for whatever it is he is searching for. It consumes him."

I looked her squarely in the face, my own voice surprisingly firm and reassuring as I spoke. "I know what it is he searches for, and why," I said, no longer afraid of what I might reveal.

"So do I," said the woman, and then she winked at me and smiled coyly for a moment. I could not help but return the smile at seeing the hope in her face.

"We should go," said John, his hand firmly gripping the sword he had kept hidden, his eyes darting this way and that, searching for trouble from where it might come.

The woman spun me around, and again we were

whipping down the streets back toward the water's edge. While we ran I told her my name and John's, and she told us hers was Margaret. I couldn't say whether Margaret was taking us on the same route or a different one — the narrow streets and passages wound in every direction and the facades all looked familiar, but then everything was a slum built of stone and wood and to see one building was to see them all.

We came to a wooden door with a round knocker shaped like a horseshoe. Margaret took the knocker in her fingers and rapped three times, a thick wooden sound echoing down the street. A moment later the entrance creaked open. We crept inside, and the door was shut and locked behind us.

CHAPTER 18

BALMORAL

There was a fire burning. A few small candles — two of them on a big old table, another one melting on a pile of wood in a corner — also added to the dim light in the small room. A little girl sat on the floor, playing with onion peels dropped from her mother's lap. The girl was carefully tearing the papery peels into dolls and clothing for them to wear. She and her mother stopped what they were doing and stared at us, the girl clinging to her mother's leg, the mother gaping at the sight of us.

There was also a man in the room, skinny with a bushy black beard. He stood next to the fire with a poker in his hand. It was he who had opened the door, after which he had stared in disbelief at Margaret for bringing us. He had big eyes, sallow cheeks, and a mop of dark hair on top of his head.

To our right were the other three women we had seen by the lake. One was washing a brown plate in a wooden barrel, another was plucking the feathers off a small bird, and the third was hanging wet clothing on a wire that passed to the side of the fireplace. A heavy oblong table, marred with age, sat in the very center of the room, strewn with roots and potatoes, wooden dishes and pitchers. Two long, thick benches sat along the table, and

Margaret, who had gone rather pale, motioned for John and me to sit on one of them; then she went over to the man, and the two of them whispered while everyone else in the room pretended to go back to what he or she had been doing.

"I like your dolls," I said to the girl. She seemed the easiest one to approach, even with the mother towering above her. "I never thought of making them that way. You must be a clever girl."

She beamed at me, and then looked at her mother as if to say, "She's nice, may I play with her?" Before she got her answer, the man at the fire moved to the center of the room and looked at us with a wary eye.

"My name is Balmoral and this is my home." He waved his hand around the room in a grand gesture. "Grindall's had us working until after dark most nights, so dinner's come late indeed. You're welcome to stay as long as you like, and if you haven't eaten, we'll have a kettle of onion and magpie soup within the hour."

He placed his hand to the side of his mouth and leaned closer, then whispered, "She's mostly onion and water, but you'll get a nibble of meat here and there if you're at the front of the line." And then he smiled just a little, and I could see that he was a hospitable sort, glad of the unexpected company, curious about the reason for our visit.

"Enid, take your wash bucket and walk down to the lake and back. Make sure nobody saw these two come in."

A young woman, one of the three from before, dashed across the room, picked up an old wooden bucket, and moved toward the door. Margaret removed the wood plank that barred the door and opened it. When Enid had gone, Margaret pushed the door shut and put the plank back on its iron claws, locking us in once again.

When the door was shut I began thinking about the boiled magpie. This, mixed with the strong smell of onions and body odors, made me put my hand over my mouth and lower my head. The whole world smelled thick and pasty. I wished I could get back out in the open air next to the lake and breathe.

"I know, I know. The onions are a bit ripe. Not so ripe as the lot of us, though, don't you think?" Balmoral burst out laughing, and I could see that one of his front teeth was missing. The women in the room seemed to think him quite funny, and they began to laugh along with him. Soon enough I was laughing, too. Even John, still nervous about our predicament, expressed some amusement as he smiled and looked around the room.

"You'll find we're a happy bunch in the nighttime," continued Balmoral, bringing himself under control with a wipe of a tear from his eye and a dying spasm of chuckles. "We've not much to live for, but we have one another and our privacy when the sun goes down. We live as best we can amid the reign of Grindall."

The man walked back over to the fire and poked it with his gaff. Sparks flew up and lit the room for an instant, and then Balmoral put his finger in the black kettle that hung over the fire and pulled his hand away quickly.

"I do believe we're ready for those onions." He wiped his fingers along the brown sleeve of his tunic, then he looked affectionately at the woman peeling onions.

"This here's my wife, Mary," he said, and as he continued I learned that the young girl making onion paper dolls was Julia, his daughter. Margaret was his younger sister by two years, and the other women were Gwen, Rose, and the recently departed Enid. When he finished introducing these last ladies he added, "Them three's widows." Then he bowed reverently, rose, and looked again at them.

"An awful sickness ran through the place a year ago and took one in ten of us." Balmoral was momentarily downcast; clearly some of those who had died had been his friends, and he missed them. But he wasted little time on the sadness of the past, his mood brightening a moment later.

"Well then, if what Margaret tells me is true, we've got a bit of talking to do, haven't we?" he said. Mary stood behind him, dumping onions into the pot with a wet plop.

The next hour passed quickly as John and I told the Castalians everything we knew. We started with Warvold's story and our journey, then the legends of Elyon and Abaddon, and finally our plans to rescue

Renny and overthrow Grindall. All the while Balmoral drank ale and stood by the fire, occasionally taking a large wooden spoon to sample the soup. He was very inquisitive and cheerful as we spoke. "Ogres you call 'em?" "You say his name was Warvold?" "You have a stone, one of the special stones?" — on and on he went with his questions as we waited for the soup to be finished.

Eventually Balmoral took the big black pot from where it hung over the fire and placed it on the stone floor before him.

"The thing about the giants — the ogres — they weren't so bad before they . . . well, I assume you've seen 'em?" Balmoral asked as he looked around the room. John told him the last detail he needed to know, that we had on our side the last of the giants, a true giant, one not possessed by Abaddon, one who would fight to the death to free Castalia.

This bit of information seemed of particular interest to Balmoral. As he scooped up bowls of steaming soup, he looked at John with a seriousness I had not yet seen in him.

"Then it's true," he said, a half-filled bowl of soup in one hand. "The legend comes to pass on this very night."

The flickering light danced in the whites of his enormous, sunken eyes, and Balmoral stared off into the fire for a long moment of contemplation, the big wooden spoon dripping watery soup into the kettle. Then he seemed to awaken from his trance and began pouring more bowls of soup.

We gathered around the table, little Julia making sure to find a spot next to me. I was surprised to hear them offer a prayer to Elyon, lifting up their hands in the air and thanking him, asking for his return. They did not plead for their freedom or cry out in anguish. Instead they were thankful for a watery bowl of magpie soup. When the prayer was finished they ate slowly, drank their ale, and smiled often. I tickled Julia in the ribs and made her jump; she laughed and leaned her head against my arm, and as we played at big and little sister, I ventured a question to the Castalians.

"You believe Elyon is real?"

Balmoral started to answer, but Margaret gently touched his forearm and offered her thoughts instead.

"Thousands have suffered and died to build that castle of beasts," she said, wiping her mouth with the flap of her apron, her voice shaking as it had before. "We have been in the midst of an immense evil for a very long time, and no one has come to help us. But, in its way, the evil has been a comfort, as if by its very presence we know the stories that have been passed on are true. Elyon is among us, close by, waiting in the shadows, until the cruelty runs its course and he returns to claim us."

Even in the midst of her affecting answer I remained unsatisfied. "Yes . . . but how do you know he will return?" I asked. "He's been away an awfully long time. Long enough that many from where I come don't remember him at all."

144

Margaret raised her spoon full of broth and tipped it, the beads of liquid dripping back into her bowl.

"Where does the water come from? Who makes this air I breathe in and breathe out? I don't know how these things are made, and yet I live."

She paused then, thinking, before she continued:

"Evil rules my people, but the giants become monsters just as the stories said they would. And you — you come with the last of the stones around your neck, just as the ancient stories say. And where do these stories come from? Either they are a wicked trick of Abaddon or they are the truth. I choose to believe they are the truth. The time has come for Abaddon to fall, for Elyon to return."

"They can be killed, you know," said Balmoral, smacking his lips between sips of broth. I looked at him, not immediately understanding what he meant. "The ogres, they can be killed." He took another big slurp of soup and a slug from his big metal pint of ale. "Just need to put your blade in the right spot. Only problem is the spot is a bit difficult to get at, since it's at the top of their heads."

I took a mouthful of my own soup, which was not as bad as I feared it might be. Mary had added wildflower, cypress root, and ginger, and I found myself enjoying the sharp flavor of the onions despite the occasional chewy bit of magpie.

"They wear chain mail at their chest and back under all that wretched black clothing, metal plates over the shoulders, legs, and neck," Balmoral continued. "They also have helmets, but their sorry heads are so full of open sores and scabs they can't stand to wear 'em. I've seen an ogre up close when one of 'em was dunking his head into a vat of water. I tell you, it's a bloody mess. That's where the damage is the greatest, on top of their heads. It's just a big open wound up there; near drives them crazy with anger."

He took three more spoonfuls of soup and slurped them loudly before looking up from his bowl to notice we were all staring at him. His bulging, comical eyes darted to and fro, a drop of slippery broth sliding down his hairy chin.

"Oh, yes, a blade in the top of the head would do it, I think. I'm almost sure it would," he said, and then, sensing he had for himself an audience, he went on. "I have a thought that might clarify things a bit more, if you like."

Seeing no objections, Balmoral looked longingly at his half-eaten bowl of broth, set aside his wooden spoon, and ran a ragged sleeve across his mouth.

"The thing you must never forget is the order in which things were made," he began. I was already confused, and Balmoral could tell. He ran his hand over his bearded face and started again.

"If Elyon really did create everything from the start, he would have special knowledge no one else would have. We didn't show up until quite a long while after the Seraphs and the giants and The Land of Elyon itself, so

Elyon certainly knows more about us than we know even about ourselves. But wouldn't that also be true of other things he created, especially the first things?"

Balmoral was beginning to sound wiser than I'd expected when I'd set eyes on him.

"On Abaddon's side are Grindall and the ogres; these are the things of evil, things like rage, malice, and deceit. But we cast our lot on a different side, a side controlled by Elyon, who is just, wise, and kind."

Balmoral looked once again at his bowl, was overcome with hunger, and lifted it to his mouth, neglecting the spoon entirely as he gulped down the last of what remained.

"Ahhhh. So much more pleasant to talk on a full stomach, don't you think?" He picked up his mug of ale, took a mighty swig, and belched outrageously. Then he continued with his thoughts.

"Now, from where we're sitting, Grindall and the ogres look insurmountable. It seems as though taking on such a monstrous foe would be foolhardy. But let me go back to my original statement and show you why things may not be entirely as they seem."

He looked around the room, giving pause to the moment, while Julia squeezed my hand and leaned yet closer to my lap.

"The thing you must never forget is the order in which things were made," he repeated. "For you see, Elyon created not only The Land of Elyon and people like you and me. A long time ago he also created Abaddon, and who is to say that when he did he might not have done something unexpected?"

Balmoral lowered his voice almost to a whisper.

"In the same way that you or I might form a bit of clay into a figure in our hands, Elyon made Abaddon as the brightest of the Seraphs — as a friend and a helper. If Elyon was wise and planned ahead — which I must assume he did — isn't it possible that he planned for the unlikely event that things might spin terribly out of control? That this once great friend of Elyon might turn on him?"

Balmoral got up from his seat and stood in front of the fire, the light dancing off his silhouette. He took a worn old pipe from the charred mantel and lit it with a stick dipped into the fire. Looking longingly around the room, he blew a puff of smoke up over his head.

"Here we stand," he continued, "toe to toe against Grindall and a host of beastly giants ready to dash out our brains. And yet there may still be hope. What if Elyon set a trap that would only be sprung if Abaddon turned on him? I believe that is precisely what has happened, and this has given us the advantage we were meant to have."

We were all riveted by what Balmoral was saying. He was a wise man in peasants' garments, a tooth missing and stinking of sweat, but full of ideas and enthusiasm.

"When Abaddon turned the black swarm on the giants he was lost in a mad rage, and in his cruelty he took

all the evil at his disposal and put it into the most powerful creatures he could find. The giants were actually kind
in the beginning, but now that they are possessed by
Abaddon, what remains in them is only malice, hate, and
blind fury."

We were getting to the end of his tale, and he rushed
to the finish from his place next to the fire.

"Ahhhh, but the trap has sprung! The giants cannot
contain such evil without having the evil pour from them.
It's too great a darkness for their bodies to hold, and so
they are teeming with sores, especially upon the head,
where it dances like a fire in their brains.

"The last of the story is not known — it was not
revealed to us or to Abaddon. We stand at the edge of
what our world was and what it will become. If we do not
defeat the ogres and Grindall here and now, Abaddon will
spread his sickness like a plague across the land, bringing
evil wherever he goes, and his goal will be simple — to
destroy all of humankind and drive Elyon out of the Tenth
City. Only then will Abaddon's work be complete."

"You speak like a man I once knew, a very wise
man," I said, thinking Balmoral sounded something like
Warvold in his more reflective moments.

"I believe that Abaddon has fallen into the trap, a trap
that makes his mighty army vulnerable to a strike. With
a bit of planning I think we can defeat the ogres, all but
the ten who guard the Dark Tower. I'm afraid those
might be a bit of a problem."

"So there are eighty-eight outside the castle and ten inside?" John asked.

"That's right. And we're quite sure where most of the eighty-eight are at any given moment." It was Margaret, speaking out after a long silence. "They run in two shifts, one by day and one by night, and they switch over at dawn and dusk," she continued. "There are usually forty-four that move about at night, forty-four when it's light outside. There are fifteen along the Valley of Thorns, another ten patrolling the forest, and three along the cliffs at the sea; on the wharf are ten more making their rounds, two watch the gate leading up to the tower, and four stand guard around the base of the Dark Tower itself."

"And the sleeping giants?" asked John.

"There is a barracks next to the Dark Tower, down by the lake," said Margaret. "I can only imagine what an awful place it must be. The stench alone is surely wretched beyond imagination."

"There is yet another problem we have neglected to mention," said Balmoral. He turned and grabbed hold of a stone in the mantel of the fireplace, pulled it out, and reached inside. When his hand came out it held what one might call a short sword, about a foot long with a primitive wooden handle.

"This would be one of only a very few fighting blades we have among us in Castalia. Grindall does not stand for a weapon of any kind in the hands of a peasant, and he's been diligent about making sure there are none to be had.

150

We have no armor, no helmets, few swords, and certainly no bows and arrows. What we have is hidden away, and I don't think it numbers more than a few dozen shabby blades."

As Balmoral went on, we discovered there were ways to get hold of things quickly that could be used as weapons, things like axes and small knives used for various tasks on the wharf, but these were few in number and our lack of protective armor remained a problem. We were nearly weaponless with no shields for defense. Our enemy, full of anger and three times the size of a full-grown man, had an almost impossible advantage. It was a hopeless situation.

Just then, a frantic knock came at the door. Margaret was nearest to the entrance and, after looking through the peephole, removed the plank. To our surprise, Enid burst into the room, pushing the door closed behind her. Shaking, she fumbled with the plank and dropped it, then Margaret helped her secure it over the door once more.

Enid turned to us, out of breath, and stammered, "Someone has seen them! The giants are going from door to door looking for intruders on the wharf!"

CHAPTER 19

THE ⊙GRE

We looked at one another for a brief, still moment, faint sounds from the fireplace popping gently through the room. Then there was a terrible, loud bang on the door. Julia buried her head in my arm and I held her close.

"Ogre!" Balmoral whispered. He dropped his pipe where he stood, bound for the table, and grabbed hold of his daughter, then thrust the girl into her mother's arms.

"To the back of the room with you, and cover the poor child's eyes," he said. All of the women obeyed except me. I rose from the table and stood with John in the center of the room. Again there was a pounding at the door, this time so loud and violent the very walls shook and sparks flew up into the chimney.

"Margaret! Come quickly," said Balmoral. "You unhitch the door then run for the back of the room. I'm going for the rooftops to see if I can get a shot at him from above." He was gone into a dark corner of the room and up a makeshift ladder before anyone could stop him, swinging open a trapdoor and disappearing outside.

Margaret was so frightened she could hardly speak. She slowly inched her way toward the door, but when it was pounded again so hard it almost fell off the hinges and into the room, she backed away into the shadows where the others sat trembling against the wall. I looked at John.

"Do you want me to open it?" I asked, my hands shaking as I grabbed an iron and walked toward the entryway. John nodded his approval, holding his small sword out into the air in front of him. A moment later I stood at the door and slid the plank free. There was a final crash against the door and it flew open, the ogre's massive arm throwing me to the floor in the center of the room.

He was so big, so horrible — the small space of the home seemed to magnify everything about him. His huge swollen head, the shoulders hunched over, the awful smell of his rotting body. The women were screaming as he swung wildly around the room, grunting until he stood staring at me, dripping thick green and red from his lower lip. John leaped onto the table and stood with his sword drawn to protect me. As the beast turned to him, I crawled through his enormous legs to safety.

With John on top of the table, he and the ogre were almost the same height. The ogre unsheathed his giant sword and held it out toward John's. It was as though John were holding a butter knife, and from where I lay in the room I knew he had no chance of escape.

"Run for the door, Alexa! Take the women and the child with you. Get them out of here while I have his attention!"

It was a brave thing to ask, knowing he could never escape from the room alive on his own. He was my protector, my friend. I couldn't bear the idea of letting him go.

Just then a guttural noise from outside the room escaped into the night air.

"Aaaaarggghhh!"

Any hope I'd had was taken away completely as I waited for more ogres to enter the room. I clutched my Jocasta and whispered a desperate plea. *"Where are you, Elyon? Will you help us?"*

The ogre turned away from John and in one stride was at the doorjamb. When he turned John jumped from the table and lunged at the beast from behind. There was a loud clang as his blade struck armor. I was overcome with fear, cowering in the dark recesses of the room, watching in frozen horror as the ogre stepped closer to my friend.

"Run, Alexa! You must escape!" John yelled. The ogre took one swing at him — not with the sword, but with his huge hand. I watched with horror as John was thrown into the wall with terrible force. His body fell, slumped against the wall, to the ground.

The ogre turned in our direction and sniffed the air as if he'd smelled something he was looking for. His eyes fell on the leather pouch around my neck.

"Aaaaarggghhh!"

It was the noise from outside the door once more, more ghastly than the last time we'd heard it. I felt certain this was where my life and the adventure would end, torn to pieces by two ogres in a peasant's hovel.

The ogre heard the noise and returned to the door-jamb, lowering his gruesome head to get out. He peered from side to side, then made a terrible sound and began staggering to and fro, ducking his head back into the room. He turned in our direction, and there before us was the wooden handle of a blade sticking out of the top of the ogre's head.

The ogre teetered drunkenly, his eyes bulging and wild, and dropped his huge sword with a loud clang. One of his feet stepped into the fire, sparks igniting up his leg. Then the ogre fell over the table and onto the stone floor in a smelly heap. Balmoral jumped down off the roof and landed in the doorway. With a look of satisfaction on his face, he strode into the room, dusted himself off, and stood over the giant.

"You see there, I told you it would work," Balmoral said, a wide smile across his face. I stood up next to Balmoral and looked at the ogre.

At first the beast lay perfectly still. I could hear the faint, disgusting sound of his insides squishing free, the sound of death permeating the room. But then one of his long arms swept quickly out along the floor and the extended fingers caught hold of me at the ankle and jerked me off my feet in one powerful motion. I kicked with my free leg and Balmoral struck the terrible beast over and over again with his bare fists. The ogre let go of my leg for an instant and then the huge hand was across my chest, wrapping tightly around the leather pouch that held my Jocasta. Balmoral kept on swinging at the ogre with little effect. The ogre seemed to be entirely dead but for its one hand holding tightly to what it had found.

"Out of the way!" It was John, advancing across the room, sword in hand. He swung the sword down on the ogre's arm again and again, but it was like trying to cut through inches of worn leather. As I lay there I looked at the ogre's face, and for a brief moment he opened his eyes and saw John standing over him. The sight of John swinging away with the sword seemed to bring forth some final bit of rage stored up in the ogre. Faster than I thought possible, the hand let go of the Jocasta and the arm shot up. I was free, but the ogre had taken hold of John's neck and pulled him down to the floor.

I scurried away, screaming for Balmoral to do something. John Christopher's eyes caught mine then, and though I expected to see fear, he only looked at me as he always had — peaceful, a faint smile, as if he were doing just the thing he had come to do. Then his eyes closed and everything was quiet but for the faint crying of the women and the child in the room.

I sat stunned, unable to believe what had happened. Balmoral lunged for the blade in the ogre's head and pressed it deeper. I knew I shouldn't do it, but for some reason I moved closer to John, not caring whether or not the ogre would come alive again. I touched John's face, and then I did the only thing I could think of that made any sense at all. I placed both my hands on the pouch around his neck, opened it, and took out the glowing blue Jocasta. The ogre did not stir, all the life now passed out of him.

I held the blue stone in the faint light of the room and listened to Julia whimpering in the corner. The Jocasta was still throbbing, its light like a dying heart beating its last. I walked over to Julia and handed it to her, watching as she took it. She held it in her little hand and it beat three more times. *Boom, boom, boom.* The last of the watery blue light faded away, and I knew for certain that John Christopher was no longer among us.

The last Jocasta hung around my neck. All the rest were gone forever.

CHAPTER 20

THE SECRET IN ARMON'S LEATHER BAG

The whole world seemed to shrink to the one fact: John was dead. I wanted time to stop. I wanted everything to stop. I wanted simply to stay in the same place and mourn my friend's death. But everything kept moving as it always does. I was still alive, and I was still involved in things that wouldn't wait for my needs to be met. The night was late, and I knew I had to gather my things and go.

Balmoral had visited with his friend the butcher and said what needed to be said in order to fill both packs with meat. Hearing of our terrible night and our plans to help liberate Castalia, the butcher had even gone to the trouble of slicing the meat into single portions.

I kissed Julia on the head and we embraced, and I told her to be ready. I promised things were going to get better very soon. Then Balmoral and Margaret called me to the door and it shut behind us, the cool night air a welcome relief from the ghastly scene inside.

"There was nothing you or anyone else could have

done," Balmoral told me. "The ogre had him, and no amount of force was going to set your friend free."

He was carrying one of the packs full of meat and would have carried both had I not insisted on taking the second. I heard his words but didn't listen, my mind racing back to the room where I'd sat over John and wept. I had pulled the terrible dead hand off his throat and tried my best to say good-bye. We would bring him back to Bridewell, but for now I had to leave.

"Something is different," I said. Margaret took hold of my hand and tried to comfort me, said something about how things were going to change, that John's death would not be in vain.

"That's not what I meant," I said. "I feel something I haven't felt before. It started the moment John's Jocasta faded away."

"What do you feel?" asked Balmoral.

And then a long silence followed by words I had never been surer of.

"Elyon is near. It's as if I feel his very presence hanging around my neck."

It was the most unusual feeling, both comforting and frightening at the same time. I felt as though some new presence had moved suddenly closer, a wonderful presence, but a dangerous one as well.

We walked a while more in silence and arrived at the edge of the wharf, the two guards aware of our presence.

As if on cue, they stepped aside, bowed graciously in Balmoral's direction, and let us pass into the night without a word. I looked at Balmoral, and he whispered, "They may work for Grindall, but they are still Castalians." Then he winked at me and we continued on in silence until we reached the edge of the trees, where Piggott stood waiting. As I had expected, he was full of questions. "Who are these people?" "Where is John?" "What took so long?" "Did you get the meat?" I waved him off with my hand and told him he would have to wait for answers until we reached the clock tower. As we entered the forest, Margaret took hold of my hand.

"Balmoral will go with you and meet with Armon," she said, "but I must return home and help clean up before dawn. We have but a few precious hours before light. Before night sets again we must be ready to strike if we are to catch Grindall unaware."

"She's right," said Balmoral. "Either we mobilize and attempt a strike tomorrow night, or we risk losing our advantage. Already an ogre is dead, and he will be missed."

Margaret hugged me, and I think if not for the work I knew lay ahead, I would have wept and wept in her arms. Instead I made it a quick encounter, turned, and left her standing at the edge of the wood.

Before long we arrived and entered the clock tower where we met Murphy and Yipes. We left the two heavy packs of meat in the lower chamber for Piggott and

Scroggs to distribute as they pleased, then we ascended the ladder, Murphy on my shoulder squeaking question after question.

The upper room of the clock tower, suffused with gray light, held the soft glow of night like a cup of warm milk. As soon as I was all the way up the ladder and in the room, I slumped over in a corner, completely exhausted, and I cried uncontrollably. My friend was gone forever, the stress of what remained of our task was heavy on my mind, and I longed for the many comforts of home. The adventure had become something more, something that was no longer fanciful. Already a great cost had been paid, and as I wept, I felt certain much more would be paid before we were through. I looked up to see silent faces all around me, filled with concern, and I was able to compose myself enough to tell them who Balmoral was and let him give the account of the evening.

"It will have to be quick. We've absolutely no time to waste," he said, and then he proceeded to tell them all about our encounter with the ogre, about the weaknesses we had discovered in their defense, and about the death of John.

Yipes gasped when he heard the news, while Murphy came over and curled into a ball in my lap — a perfect, silent gesture. Armon remained still, closed his eyes, and lowered his head. Odessa remained standing and slowly lowered her head, too, until her nose hung only inches from the floor.

"He was brave, very brave," said Balmoral. "He stood his ground to protect the innocent, and if we win the fight before us, his death will forever be remembered as the beginning of the end of the reign of Grindall."

Armon raised his head, looked Balmoral squarely in the face, and questioned him.

"What powers do you have to rally your people?"

"If Grindall allowed a leader among us, I would be that leader," said Balmoral. I looked at this simple, feeble man, and I was stunned. All the while I'd been in the presence of the true ruler of the Castalians, and I'd thought him nothing more than a broken man with some fanciful ideas.

"I can have two hundred men ready to fight by night-fall the next, but our weaponry is primitive — stones, a few dozen knives, no armor to speak of. The fifty Castalian guards who work for Grindall don't even have swords. They have only horns to blow when trouble is afoot, and then the ogres come running. It is a problem for which I have no answer."

Armon looked long and hard at Balmoral, and though he could not stand upright in the space, he did get up on one knee.

"I don't think that will be such a problem," he said. Then he took hold of the massive bag he'd been carrying since we'd met him, untied the rope at the top, and poured the contents into the middle of the room. Sword after sword fell forth. Chain mail, shields, bows, and arrows all tumbled onto the floor. The pack seemed to hold an endless array of armament. It must have weighed hundreds of pounds, and I was newly amazed by Armon's superhuman strength. Balmoral's eyes were as wide as saucers, and he laughed with excitement, touching the different objects, holding them in his hands.

"I think it's time we started planning," said Armon, and then he turned and jumped out the wide window. A moment later we heard whining, and Piggott was raised on giant hands over the windowsill. Scroggs followed, and then Armon climbed back into the clock tower and pushed all the armor aside so we might sit in the center of the room.

The eight of us sat in a circle — me, Armon, Balmoral, Yipes, Murphy, Odessa, Piggott, and Scroggs. Balmoral produced a map he'd been working on for many months and placed it in the center of the circle. It was drawn on parchment paper with black ink, and it detailed the position of each ogre.

"I can't read or write, but this drawing is about as close to perfect as I can get it. I would have shown it to you earlier, but with all the commotion, well —" Balmoral broke off, glanced at me, and looked down at the map. It took him a moment to get going again, but he had so much energy and passion that before long he was enthralled in the plan, taking us with him every step of the way. First he detailed all the events of the evening, giving special attention to the encounter with the ogre and the way it had been destroyed. It was more than a little grotesque, the way Balmoral explained how easily the blade went into the top of the head, as if the skull were made of eggshell instead of bone.

"The first challenge will be hiding the fact that ogres are disappearing throughout the day and night. They check in with one another, not across sections so much, but within the forest or the Valley of Thorns or one of the other areas. They expect to encounter one another regularly. To overcome this problem we'll have to systematically take out each area, one at a time. The easiest areas to clear out will be the wharf and the forest. The housetops and the trees, combined with the weaponry Armon has provided, will give us an advantage.

"The guards that work for Grindall are all Castalians, and they are Castalians first. They have no weapons, but they do have two things we can use to our advantage: mobility and warning signals. I shall address the warning signals in a moment. As to mobility, some of the guards are actually assigned to patrol the forest along with the ogres. Others patrol the wharf, and still more include the City of Dogs in their rounds. To be fair, the rounds through the City of Dogs have been few and far between in recent years, as the dogs have become wilder and the dumping ground more uninhabitable. It's often forgotten for long stretches of time by both ogre and man. This will prove a good piece of luck for us."

Balmoral looked at Piggott and Scroggs uncomfortably, as if the dogs made him nervous or unsure, and then he addressed them directly.

"I can't understand you, but if you can understand me, know that your role in this conquest is of critical importance. Without you and your respective groups, we'll have no chance of winning the day."

Both Piggott and Scroggs sat tall and proud, and I was happy to see them as part of something so big, so important. Balmoral ran his hand along the map as he continued going through his plan.

"You see, here, at the gate to the City of Dogs, I can send a half dozen guards through in the morning. They will tell the ogre at the gate that it has been a while since the dumping grounds have been patrolled, and they plan to spend several hours checking it thoroughly. The ogres will let them go, thinking they are making a reasonable request, and I will send them directly to the clock tower, where they can arm themselves and take up positions in the trees here, near the edge of the forest." He pointed then to the area on the map where the forest met the City of Dogs.

"The rest of the armor should be taken to the active dumping ground and hidden. My people will smuggle the weaponry in the garbage carts as they come back in, leaving just enough debris in the carts to cover whatever they can hold. Dumping runs begin in the early morning

165

every day and there is at least one delivery of debris every hour. By midmorning all the armor will find its way into the wharf. Once inside, a network of peasants will distribute the various items, and by the time the noonday sun is straight overhead, two hundred Castalians will be armed and ready for battle."

Balmoral's plan was beginning to sound like it would at least give us a fighting chance. I nibbled at some dried fruit as he went on, my head bobbing now and then from fatigue. I was very tired, but Balmoral remained so enthusiastic it was hard to imagine falling asleep.

"The forest must be taken first. It's the most critical early victory if we are to succeed. Now, as I promised, we have arrived back at the issue of the warning signals used by the guards. These are horns that can be blown at varying levels of sound. Blow hard, and the whole kingdom of ogres comes running. Blow soft, and only those ogres within a reasonable distance hear the warning. This tool can be used to our great advantage. The ten patrolling the forest are spread out, and we shall blow the horn very softly from the trees at the edge of the City of Dogs. One by one, or maybe two at a time, ogres will come to the rescue of the guard who calls the signal, and when they do, we shall attack them from above in the trees. The ogres carry the horns as well, and it is absolutely critical that we draw them in slowly, one at a time, so we don't encourage suspicion. These ogres have a great deal of arrogance, and they will blow a horn only if the situation is desperate.

"What we ought to be able to do is take out the ten in the forest first, then move to the edge of the forest here, where it meets the Valley of Thorns, and go about the same exercise once again, drawing the ogres along the Valley of Thorns into the forest where we will attack them. In this case, we are as far from the wharf and the Dark Tower as we can be while still finding ogres. These guard the outer perimeter, so we can blow the horn a bit louder, draw several at once, and take them down in groups of three or four."

"Yes, but how can we be sure, in either the City of Dogs or the forest, that the ogres will arrive directly under us so we can strike?" asked Yipes.

"A guard calls them in, and when the ogre or ogres arrive, the guard will guide them to where we are hidden in the trees above. It will simply be a matter of a well-placed diversion," Balmoral answered.

"The wild dogs," said Armon. "We can draw the ogres around a single tree with a pack of three or four wild dogs. All of their attention will be focused on killing the dogs, which will make our attack from directly above all the more surprising."

"Now you've gone and stolen my thunder. Bad giant," said Balmoral. This brought a smile to my face, the first I'd had in quite some time.

"It is unlikely that all of the ogres from the Valley of Thorns will be drawn into the forest," continued Balmoral. "I think we will count ourselves lucky if we get half of them, which would leave seven or eight more roaming around. The Valley of Thorns backs up against the forest trees, and often in the late morning the ogres take refuge from the heat by standing near the trees for shade. Unfortunately, we have no way of knowing which trees the ogres will stand near, so we must use the dogs once again.

"The wild dogs never roam outside the City of Dogs, and seeing a small pack of them attempting to pass into the Valley of Thorns will enrage the ogres. What remains of them will come to the edge of the trees — where we will be waiting. It will certainly be our biggest challenge; if we miss one of them we might just as well have missed them all. That one will blow his horn and the ogre barracks will blow open, unleashing an army we will never be able to overcome."

Everyone looked around the room at one another, sensing the enormity of the odds stacked against us. All I could think about was the ogre in that room with John and the others, how it had smelled and looked, the terrible sounds it had made. Only Balmoral and I had been so close to an ogre and seen its terrible rage. I was glad the others hadn't seen such things.

"This all must take place within a few hours tomorrow morning," Balmoral warned, "between dawn and nine o'clock. If the guards from the wharf are gone much longer, the ogre at the gate will become suspicious. There are other guards in the forest and in the Valley of Thorns who will help you. Once the forest is cleared, you'll have another six fighters. When you reach the last remaining ogres in the Valley of Thorns, you should have a dozen fighters in the trees. Along with Yipes and Alexa, that brings your total to fourteen."

"What about Armon?" I asked. "He's our greatest weapon. Where will he be during all of this?"

Balmoral pointed again to the map, this time to the cliffs beyond the City of Dogs, and looked at Armon.

"I'm afraid you must find a way to destroy the three ogres at the cliffs on your own. This will require straight hand-to-hand combat, three against one. And, worse, you must somehow make sure they cannot blow their horns." Balmoral glanced back at the map, then said, "I have had occasion to see this place. The cliffs rise high above the water, but how high no one knows. Even in the heat of summer the mist rises to hide the water below. The edges of the cliffs are solid underfoot and speckled with sharp rocks."

"I'll take Scroggs with me," Armon said. "Piggott and Odessa, you go with the others. Scroggs, bring six of your most trusted companions. Together we'll divert them one by one, draw them to the edge of the cliffs, and hurl them into the mist."

Armon was so certain, so sure, his voice like a slab of rock. It gave us a new measure of confidence we had previously lacked.

Balmoral nodded his approval of Armon's plan. "While the lot of you are at the business of clearing the forest, the Valley of Thorns, and the cliffs, I will guide my fighters on the wharf. The only way this works is if we strike at the wharf all at once, avoiding the gates to the Dark Tower in the process. The wharf is split into two sections, the forest end and the end nearest the Dark Tower. Five ogres patrol each — four on the castle side, since one was killed tonight. They are fairly regular about how they move around. An hour before dark, we will strike at the nine that remain and move the bodies off the street before darkness falls. I don't think the one we've killed will be missed in the morning. Often they wander into the barracks as a pack, and stragglers arrive later, occupied with some duty that keeps them out a bit longer. Before long, they fall asleep and think nothing of one another. However, by the time the next shift goes out, he will be missed, so we must strike immediately."

"Let's say for the moment that the plan works," I said. "The forty-four that remain in the barracks will wipe out all our effort as soon as they wake up. How will we deal with all of them at once?"

"As long as we stay away from the castle gate, the plan will work," answered Balmoral. "The sleeping ogres follow the same pattern every day. They wake, they eat, they march out to the gate, and then they disperse to the places where they must work and replace the ogres from the shift before them. In doing so, they follow the same road away from the gate and onto the wharf. Once through the gate there are twenty ogre steps, then a sharp turn and a long, narrow walkway with buildings on either side. It is here that we will attack them all at once, all but the ones who exchange places at the gate and around the Dark Tower itself. I have other plans for those fourteen. But the thirty-seven who walk the shadowy narrow road will have no idea what is about to happen to them. I'll have two fighters, each with swords, assigned to each ogre. They will be positioned along the tops of the buildings a few feet apart. A first strike all at once on every beast and a second just in case we miss our mark."

We all looked at Balmoral, his bulging eyes alive with victory, and we believed. We actually began to believe we could defeat the ogres, Grindall, even Abaddon himself. If we could do all that Balmoral suggested, there would only be the six ogres at the gate, the eight from around the castle, both the ones that had been on guard and the new four who had come to replace them. Those fourteen, plus the ten in the castle. With Balmoral's plan, we'd gone from ninety-eight ogres to twenty-four in only one day. Still, even twenty-four ogres was a formidable army given their size and strength.

"I know what you're thinking — we still have fourteen outside and ten inside to deal with," said Balmoral, as if he were reading my mind. "The ogres at the gate will have heard the commotion and they will come running. These will be easy targets for my fighters. But what of the ogres that remain around the Dark Tower? It is at this point we must take the tower by force. Two hundred

171

armed Castalians, a hundred or more wild dogs, a giant of our own, all against what remains — eight giants outside and ten within the Dark Tower."

Balmoral paused and looked around the room, which was faint with light from our dying candle.

"I believe at this point we will have created an even fight, a fair fight, a fight that could go either way."

That was a far cry from no fight at all, and we unanimously agreed to Balmoral's plan. At last our preparations were complete. Balmoral went home to gather his forces, and I was able to lie down on the cold floor of the clock tower. As I lay there, just shy of sleep, thoughts of what we might find in the Dark Tower began to fill my mind. I began to wonder what Catherine would say when she saw me, if she was even alive. And I wondered for the first time what Grindall would look like, how he would act, what he might say.

Murphy stayed with me and we whispered about John for many sad moments, and then we both fell fast asleep, exhausted from all that had transpired since our arrival in the City of Dogs.

CHAPTER 21

THE DARK TOWER

The morning air was cool and pleasant, especially so given our location high in a tree at the edge of the forest, the smells from the City of Dogs somewhere off in the distance. Yipes and I sat next to each other, hidden in the leaves of a monstrous oak tree, fifteen feet above the ground. Murphy was up much higher, thirty feet or more, scouting the area for ogres. I seized my new sword firmly in my right hand and held onto a branch with the other.

I looked over at Yipes, a few branches to my right, and saw that he was preparing his bow. Unlike the Castalians, he was very adept with an arrow. After some deliberation it had been decided that his best weapon would be the bow. I glanced at another large tree across the way and saw that two Castalian guards had taken up their positions and were waiting patiently. Beneath them were three wild dogs milling around the base of the great tree.

Squire circled above, scouting the entire kingdom. I wished again that I could be her, seeing all that she could see, knowing the very position of each and every ogre.

"I knew John a long time," Yipes said, startling me. The two wild dogs below our own tree and Odessa broke their nervous pacing to look up at the sound of his voice.

"He had a hard life," Yipes continued, a little softer, "but he never complained, never once that I can remember. Though he had never met you, he spoke of you often."

"What did he say?" I asked.

"He worried about you. He knew it was his greatest duty to protect you. This was the most important job that Warvold had ever entrusted him with. Until this journey I never understood what John was talking about, but now it seems clear that he knew all along it might cost him his life to make sure you were safe. He died protecting you, protecting the last Jocasta, which is precisely what he expected might happen." Yipes smiled at me then, his wonderful little mustache covering up his lip, and I was suddenly afraid of losing him, too.

"Did he ever tell you why he was imprisoned?" asked Yipes.

"No. I asked him once on our journey but he wouldn't tell me."

Yipes repositioned himself on a limb and fidgeted with his bow.

"There was a group of women and children living in the forest," he quietly explained. "The story goes that John felt especially sorry for the children, so much so that he raided the kitchens and stores of Ainsworth in search of food and clothing for them. This went on for some time, and he was very successful in his pursuits on their behalf — until he was captured and put in with the rest of the convicts."

"Is that really true?" I questioned, maybe a little louder than I should have. Yipes only nodded and before I could question him further one of the dogs beneath us barked in our direction.

"Quiet!" Odessa growled from below. Then we could hear the faint sound of the horn being blown by the guard standing off to our left. My heart was racing, my palms sweating as we waited for what the warning sound would bring.

We were all very still, and then Murphy came scampering down and held firm to the tree trunk at my side.

"Hold tight, here they come," he said. This meant more than one, and I signaled two with my hand, to which Murphy nodded.

It was deathly silent, no wind in the trees, no sound of birds or other animals. The ogres were coming — I could sense them near. I began to hear the snapping of twigs and brush, and then I saw one of the hideous creatures come down the path, clearly irritated and looking around wildly for the guard who had called him. Another came bounding up behind him, scratching his head and grunting furiously. As they approached the guard, I looked over at Yipes. He had already drawn his bow and now held it firm, waiting for the moment when one or both of them stood beneath us.

As the guard and the ogres approached between the two trees, the dogs began barking uncontrollably, just as we had planned. The two ogres split, one taking the opposite tree, the other advancing on ours. He was monstrous, his head only a few feet below us as he approached. The dogs stayed right at the base of the tree, then moved back along its sides, drawing the ogre closer. The ogre drew his huge sword and appeared entertained by what he was seeing, excited about the prospect of putting his blade through these mangy animals.

I looked across the way again and saw that the ogre there had done the same and was directly under the tree jabbing and poking at the dogs with his sword. Down came a guard out of the thick of the tree, five feet over the head of the ogre. He plunged through the air, landing on the ogre's shoulders and thrusting the knife through the beast's head. At almost the same moment, Yipes fired his arrow at the ogre under our tree, but the ogre had glanced back, hearing the other ogre's scream over the incessant barking of the dogs. The arrow glanced off the ogre's head and down into his shoulder. He screamed an awful roar of pain and rage. We only had another moment before he would grab the horn and blow it, so Odessa's two companions went for the ogre's legs and chomped down hard and fast. The ogre kicked and flailed but the dogs were locked on and only death would get them off. The ogre reached down and grabbed both dogs at the neck. I yelled, causing the creature to look up as Yipes fired again, this time hitting the ogre directly in the fore-head. To my astonishment, the arrow disappeared almost entirely into the ogre. He teetered a little to the left as if in slow motion, then fell backwards, crashing to the ground under the tree.

I came down from the tree quickly but kept my distance from the giant body, remembering what had happened to John. I was still surprised to see the ogre slowly sit up, then lean against the tree. He took his horn in his hand and tried to get it to his mouth. An arrow came from above and pierced the ogre's palm. I jumped in, grabbed the horn, and quickly moved away. The ogre wobbled once more and fell back to the ground, the dogs still holding hard at his legs.

I looked across the trail and saw that the guards had been victorious as well, and they were already calling us over to help drag the dead ogre into the thicket. It hadn't gone perfectly, but we had done it. We had defeated two ogres in the span of a few minutes.

The morning went along in much the same manner, the gruesome details of which I will not share in great detail. We were able to lure in all of the forest ogres. Besides the one wayward arrow Yipes had shot, we had other difficulties. Guards were lost, wild dogs were lost, and we arrived at the Valley of Thorns with six ogres still remaining. We had ten guards scattered through the trees and fifty or more dogs roaming beneath us on the ground, but the remaining ogres were not close enough to be taken. Before these ogres could think to blow their own horns, six of our guards made the warning sound, not loud enough for the wharf to hear, but louder than we had dared blow them in the forest. With so many horns going off all at once, the six ogres that remained didn't think to blow their own. Instead they ran to help, sure that every ogre from the forest would come running as well. When they arrived at the trees, the dogs began their barking and the arrows and swords began to rain down on the ogres. A few minutes later we'd taken what remained of the ogres in the Valley of Thorns.

All told, we lost thirteen dogs and two guards. Another guard was badly shaken when an ogre slammed him up against a tree, but he was able to continue on, a few broken ribs not enough to keep him from the important work ahead. It was midmorning and we had achieved something miraculous, setting the stage for what we hoped would be greater victories in the hours to come. We raced back to the clock tower and found Armon and Scroggs waiting for us. They, too, had been victorious at the cliffs by the sea. One was taken while he lay sleeping, the other two lured to the cliffs by the dogs and pushed from behind by Armon.

Balmoral had thought of everything, and when we arrived back at the clock tower, Margaret was waiting for us with fresh uniforms. The guards removed their bloody, stinking clothes and replaced them with new ones. Then those who had joined us earlier in the day ran off toward the gate, no doubt to receive more weaponry and instructions from Balmoral on the wharf.

"I must go quickly," said Margaret. "I will bring word to Balmoral of your success. Stay here until an hour before dark, and then wait at the edge of the wharf in the trees. Remain out of sight until a fire is lit by the lake, and then come as quickly as you can."

We bid her good-bye and offered Piggott and Odessa as escorts through the City of Dogs, which she accepted.

Then we waited as the minutes turned to hours in what seemed an excruciating slowness. We ate and talked of our accomplishment, of what we would do on the wharf. We spoke of the black swarm that remained loose on the wind, hunting for Armon, and our fear for him as we advanced on the castle. The thought of this perfect creature mauled by a thousand bats was unbearable, and I begged him to stay behind. But he was no more willing than I to remain in the City of Dogs while the decisive encounter took place at the Dark Tower.

In due time the hours turned the day to an orange dusk and the whole of our army made way for the edge of the wharf — dozens of wild dogs, a very small man, a squirrel, a girl, a smattering of Castalian guards from the forest and the Valley of Thorns, and one giant. We were not what you might hope to see coming around the corner to save the day, but together we had defeated twenty-eight ogres, and we walked with confidence, knowing we at least had a chance of winning the day. The

179

dogs in particular had a new pride in their step and in the way they held their heads. I was happy for them, for the sense of purpose they enjoyed.

We waited as instructed, quietly looking for the flame against the lake as the day melted away on the horizon. In the distance I could see the Dark Tower, and I imagined Grindall himself standing atop the highest point, looking down on his wretched kingdom, thinking all was well as the sun tipped down and out of sight against the shimmering of the lake.

"There it is, the fire," said Yipes, who sat on Armon's shoulders. With that, we were moving fast, the whole lot of us, the dogs leaping out in front and running with all their might, Armon's huge strides keeping pace, Yipes and Murphy riding on his shoulders. This left me at the rear, running as hard as I could to keep up and falling behind quickly.

"Come on, Alexa! Run!" yelled Yipes. And so I did. With everything I had in me, I ran, sword drawn, onto the wharf and toward the Dark Tower.

I arrived at the narrow road to find ogres and Castalians strewn all about. It was a sea of bodies large and small. From the looks of it, the Castalians had triumphed. As I dodged and ran down the narrow road, I heard the dogs barking and growling. It was a ferocious noise that chilled my bones.

I came around the last corner and saw that the gate blocking the road to the Dark Tower had been breached.

All of the Castalians, dogs, and guards had gone through and were laying siege on the ogres at the base of the tower. All at once I was struck by the evil of this place — the dark spire against the night sky, the single flame from a window far above, and the silhouette of a man who looked down upon the war that raged at his feet.

I was terrified by this place. I had some trouble breathing, and I began to wobble back and forth where I stood. Then the strangest thing happened. I heard a voice, one unlike any I'd heard before, like the wind rolling in one ear and out the other.

It is you who must go, you have I chosen. There is no other.

I heard the words as clear as a bell. They were firm, and they were not a request — they were an order. I began to walk, slowly at first, and then I was running again, to the long line of stone steps that led to the great wooden door of the Dark Tower. While the fighting continued below, I kept running, bounding from step to step. I didn't look back, I only ran and ran until I stood on the last stair and gazed up to see a hulking beast of a door, big enough for an ogre to walk through upright, a layer of iron bars before it, and in front of that a wicked ogre with a spiked maul in his huge left hand.

"Out of the way, Alexa!" It was the booming voice of Armon, who had come up behind me unnoticed. He was standing on the steps, ripping a giant stone from its mortar where it protruded from the Dark Tower and formed

181

part of the entryway. The stone was so big, a square mass he could barely get his huge arms around. He pulled it free and raised it over his head, advancing on the door. Then he threw the stone with all his might into the ogre, knocking him back and smashing him through the bars. With tremendous effort Armon picked up the stunned ogre and hoisted him over his head. With a loud cry he threw the foe over the edge of the stairs.

I crawled up onto the stone banister to look over the edge and saw that the ground lay fifty feet below. Torches lit the night well enough to see that Balmoral, the dogs, and the Castalians were overtaking what remained of the ogres. Soon they would have control of the tower. I jumped down and stood at the door, the bars mangled but standing.

"Step aside, Alexa," Armon said, taking the huge stone and throwing it once more. This time the door itself blew apart at the center.

The entrance to the Dark Tower lay exposed. Inside, darkness and the flickering of torches against barren stone were all that could be seen.

CHAPTER 22

VĬCTOR GRĬNDALL

I stepped carefully inside the doorway, then Armon ripped away what remained of the bars and the door and strode in behind me. It was damp and musty inside, weak flames from a few torches the only light I could see. Everything was dark stone and eerie shadows. I could still hear the dogs barking below, and there was a soft breeze blowing through the exposed opening behind us. Still, there was no mistaking the whispery voice that came on the wind once more.

The black swarm is near. Send Armon away to the cliffs at the edge of the sea.

The thought of Armon morphing into an awful ogre terrified me even more than staying within the Dark Tower alone. I looked up at Armon and beckoned him to lean down to where I stood.

"What is it, Alexa?" he asked, seeing my concerned expression.

"The black swarm is near, Armon," I said. "You must go to the cliffs and wait for us there."

He stared at me a moment and then took my shoulders in his enormous hands.

"It is said that the last stone would bring the word of Elyon himself. That the one who possessed it would hear his very voice," the giant said reverently. "Have you heard this voice?"

I looked down and grabbed hold of the leather pouch that kept my Jocasta hidden.

"I believe I have," I whispered. "You *must* go right now, before they come for you. Run, Armon!"

Armon rose quickly, turned for the door, and lumbered away. As he disappeared into the darkness, I heard voices. At first distant, then closer. I drew my sword . . . only to lower it in relief when I saw two little heads peering around the edge of the broken door. One was furry and twitching, the other mustached. It was Murphy and Yipes, and they bounded into the open space of the tower. Armon dipped his head back into the doorway.

"It's up to the three of you now. You must save Catherine and put an end to Grindall once and for all," he said.

"Go! Go to the cliffs and do it quickly!" I yelled back. Armon nodded, turned away, and disappeared into the darkness, leaving Yipes, Murphy, and me alone in the gloom of the tower.

"A fine mess we've gotten ourselves into," said Yipes. "I suppose there's nothing left but to go as high as the stairs will take us . . . or down into the dungeon."

Murphy was already several paces ahead of us, sniffing at the stone floor and darting from side to side. There were two enormous sets of stairs, one going down and one up. The landing itself was circular, empty except for the two torches that hung along the walls. I immediately thought of going down until we reached the dungeon, rescuing Catherine, and running away. Then I remembered the solitary figure at the top of the spire, standing at the window, watching his kingdom crumble all around him. If we were to put an end to Grindall, we'd have to find him first.

"We're going up," I decided. "He's at the top, only a few flights away. The dungeon can wait." The stone steps outside had led us to the very center of the tower — fifty feet below and fifty feet above. Something told me we were meant to find Grindall waiting for us at the very top of the spire.

Murphy was on the sixth step before I could say another word, moving fast for the next level, staying close to the wall where the shadows lurked. Yipes and I followed quietly, winding around the inside of the tower, the sounds from below growing weaker as we went. After what seemed like a very long time, we came to a landing and yet another door. I thought it odd that the door was ajar, but Murphy thought nothing of it and scampered right through.

I pushed gently on the door and it opened slowly on squeaking hinges. When there was just enough room to put my head through and see inside, I smelled the ogres — that terrible smell of wet, rotting flesh. It was coming from behind us, and as I turned back to look, the door flew open and we were pushed inside. Yipes and I both fell to the floor, surprised. The door was slammed behind us, two of the biggest ogres I'd seen standing before it, placing a huge wooden beam across the middle and barring the door from anyone who might seek to enter.

"I don't see how this can get any worse," Yipes mumbled. But then we both looked into the dimly lit room and saw that eight more ogres, all of them bigger than any we'd seen before, stood in the room. Four of the beasts were against one wall, four against another. Between them stood a single stone chair where a man in a flowing dark purple cape sat, head down, his long black hair cascading over his face so that his features could not be seen.

"Guess you were wrong," I said.

The man in the chair looked up, crazed, his head tilted to the left. His skin was deathly pale, as if he hadn't seen the sun for years and years. His eyes bulged miserably from their sockets, full of rage and deceit, his gaze locked on the leather bag that held my Jocasta. His brow was set low over his eye sockets, and, to my astonishment, when he saw me looking at him he bared his twisted teeth as though he were a wolf or a serpent. His thick lower lip hung down and a twinkle of drool marked the corners of his mouth. I realized then that Grindall — for this had to be Grindall — was not at all in his right mind. He pulled his upper lip back from his teeth in a sinister grin and bolted up from the chair. It was then that the ogres began to speak in their own language, filling the room with the sloppy, guttural sounds of groans and low roars. Grindall spoke to them in their language, and I was amazed to hear the sickening sounds he made as he commanded these creatures in harsh tones. They became still and, though their noisy, wet breathing remained, they were mostly quiet.

"You have caused me a great deal of difficulty, Alexa Daley," Grindall intoned, his voice sultry and deep now, almost hypnotic in its slow cadence. "However, you have also delivered something to me for which I have searched an awfully long time. How convenient that the last Jocasta hangs around the neck of a pitiable little girl, a mere child. I find it amusing that this is the best Elyon could do."

"Are you Victor Grindall?" I asked. He looked at me with such malice I had to turn away, and then his voice slithered out once again.

"Indeed I am. The tenth Victor Grindall, to be exact." His voice was measured and slippery. "And these are my servants, the most powerful of the giants, sworn to serve and go to their death at my choosing. A smelly lot, but as you might imagine, very useful in situations such as these."

Then I heard a glorious sound, for Balmoral and his

men had arrived outside the door, and they began beating on it with all their might.

My confidence surged.

"You're trapped," I said. "You and these few remaining ogres. A very large army is about to break into this room."

"Is that so?" he replied. "How convenient for me, since I intend to bring the whole tower down on top of them. I have no doubt my servants will keep that door shut until you and I finish our business."

He spoke again in that hideous, throaty voice and ordered two more ogres to the door. There were four there now, and though the door bounced on its iron hinges when the men on the other side battered it, it seemed unlikely that they would break through soon enough to save us.

Grindall advanced to the window and looked out, then returned his attention to us and leaned against the sill. Behind him I could hear a terrible sound on the wind. It was the sound of leathery wings and the shrill voices of a thousand dark creatures. The black swarm was coming, searching for Armon.

"You do realize the one who created all this is long since gone," Grindall taunted. "He's not coming back, not *ever*. He fancies other creations now. Humankind has been quite a disappointment to him. I must say, I can certainly understand his position on the matter."

The bats arrived at the window and swirled in the night air behind Grindall, their shrieking almost unbearable. Grindall turned to them and spoke.

"The giant you seek is near, somewhere down below. Find him! Take him captive and bring him to me!"

Grindall turned back into the room with a new look — a sort of delighted rage.

"The only one in command around here is me and the forces I control," he said. "All the violence going on outside that door is utterly pointless. I have long since grown weary of these wretched Castalians. They're dirty, lazy, practically useless to me." He gazed once again at the pouch around my neck. "All that matters is the stone."

"If the tower goes down, you go with it." It was Yipes, his voice startling me. He was showing even more courage than I would have given him credit for in such an unnerving scene. The wild dogs outside were barking and the men were pounding to get in. The smell of the ogres was astonishingly strong in the small space, and Grindall was laughing. It was an awful laugh, sinister and crazed, half human and half something else.

"I believe you are the stupidest little man I've ever seen," Grindall spat, his laughing trailing off and his tone becoming serious once more. He strode over to where Yipes stood and backhanded him hard across the face. Yipes fell to the ground, motionless, his head bleeding from the temple. Grindall stood over him and heckled grotesquely.

"Oh, I say, you really *are* quite impressive. Maybe I should pick you up and toss you out the window. It would be a pleasure to watch you fly through the air and break into pieces. Or maybe my giants would enjoy eating you for dinner. What do you think, Alexa? Shall we toss him to the giants?"

The ogres grunted and moved closer, stirring up the rotten air in the room. Grindall was much stronger than I had anticipated, and he picked up Yipes by the vest and tossed him across the room. An ogre caught him and eyed him hungrily.

"Take out the Jocasta and give it to me, Alexa," Grindall demanded. "Give it to me now or we'll finish your friend." He was out of his mind, looking at the pouch as if it were the only thing in the world he cared about, his arm held back and waiting to signal the ogre to dash Yipes against the stone wall of the room.

Take out the Jocasta and present it to Grindall.

I couldn't believe my ears. It was the whispering voice on the wind. Had Elyon given up? Had I failed him?

"Have I made a mistake coming here? Did I do something wrong?" I asked.

"Who are you talking to? *Give me the Jocasta!*" Grindall screamed, his dark humor gone, nothing left now but desire for the stone around my neck.

190

"Give it to me!" he screamed again. A moment more and he would take it from me by force.

I looked at Yipes, so small and helpless. Then I gazed around the room. All stone; ogres at every turn; one large, open window that faced the lake; a flickering torch at its edge. After everything we'd been through, if Grindall did as he said, the tower would fall and destroy everyone, including Catherine. Elyon would be defeated, once and for all, and the dark reign of Abaddon would travel across the whole of our land, devouring it until nothing good remained.

I took the leather pouch into my hand, opened it, and pulled the glowing Jocasta out for everyone to see. I held it up high, its orange glow filling the room and dancing off the walls.

Victor Grindall looked at it, laughed nervously, and reached out his hand to take it away. And that's when I realized Balmoral was right: Elyon saw everything, even things Abaddon could not see in all his terrible desire for the stone. At the very moment Grindall was about to touch the stone, Squire screeched louder than I have ever heard her screech, and flew into the room, her massive wings flapping, her serious eyes focused entirely on the Jocasta.

Startled, Grindall turned for a moment and saw Squire come in through the window. I watched as Murphy dropped from the beams that ran across the ceiling. As Grindall looked back to the Jocasta, he felt

Murphy's teeth dig deep into his outstretched hand. Grindall screamed and grabbed Murphy, but Murphy would not let go. While they struggled, Squire arrived at the Jocasta, took it in one of her great claws, turned sharp against the back wall, and flapped for the window. As she arrived at the opening to the outside, an ogre slapped down with his sword. Feathers and sparks flew around the windowsill, but it was no use for Grindall. The ogre had only grazed Squire's tail, and the last Jocasta was gone from the room.

Murphy let go and scampered up one of the walls, then perched atop a beam near the ceiling. The sound of dogs barking and men clamoring to get in grew louder. The four ogres were struggling mightily now to keep the door closed.

"The army is about to break in," I said. "Have you any last words before we take the Dark Tower and destroy the last of your evil ogres?"

Grindall looked on me with loathing, trying to hide what must have been extreme pain from the bite Murphy had given him.

"Such a dreadful child," he said, and then his voice rose louder and louder. "You've only made things worse. Elyon is never coming back. What you've done has enraged me even more. I was content to sit here in Castalia and keep Abaddon under control. But look what you've done — you've released Abaddon to the rest of the world. This tower can no longer hold his rage."

Then he turned to his ogres and commanded them.

"Go! Make way for the true king!"

It was unthinkable, but five of the ten ogres — those not guarding the door or holding Yipes — ran to the window and jumped out. The door was about to come down and the remaining four ogres grunted and howled uncontrollably in their effort to keep Balmoral's army out of the room.

"You have unleashed Abaddon, and he will not rest until he rules everything," Grindall vowed. "I would suggest you leave this place now. The Dark Tower will soon crumble into pieces. You must live so you can return the last stone to me."

Then Grindall grunted at the ogre holding Yipes. The beast held Yipes under his arm, went to the window, and jumped out. I screamed for Yipes, but it was no use. He was gone.

Grindall bent down and put his awful face a few inches from my own. He reached out with his bloody hand and touched my cheek, saying, "There is a place I haven't had need of for a long time, especially with Ganesh watching it so closely for me all those years."

"Ganesh worked for you?" I asked, newly amazed at Grindall's reach.

"Well, of course he did, you silly child. What do you

think, that I'm not aware of all that goes on in your pathetic little kingdom beyond the Dark Hills?"

The way he said it made me wonder if there were others under his command within Bridewell. But who?

I shivered.

"I'll give you three days to meet me in Bridewell," Grindall went on. "You bring me my stone and I'll give you back your friend. Trust me, Alexa — Elyon is not coming back. This quest you're on is futile. You can save your friend *and* you can have a place of power with me. Just bring me the stone."

We looked at each other for a long moment, then Grindall rose to his feet and called to the remaining four ogres. He turned for the window, ran, and dove out into the night air like the rest. As soon as he was gone the last of the ogres bolted from the room and ran for the window, leaving the door behind as it splintered and broke open.

I crossed to the window and watched as they fell through the air, falling for such a long time, and then landing in a giant pool behind the Dark Tower. The pool was attached to the lake by a canal, and from beneath the tower I could see torchlight moving, as if on a boat. Grindall and the ten ogres had escaped, and they would cross the lake into the Dark Hills, bringing their evil plans who knew where.

Balmoral was in the room. He knelt down and put his arm around me.

"Are you all right, Alexa? Why did you come up here without us?"

"He's taken Yipes," I said, unable to think of anything else.

Balmoral and a few of his guards advanced to the window just as Squire was returning, which scared them all back for a moment. Squire flew around the room and dropped the Jocasta in my hand, then landed on a beam and screeched loudly.

"She's telling us to get out of here," I said. "Grindall has some way of bringing down the tower. We've got to get everyone out and find the dungeon before the whole thing tumbles down."

"What are you talking about?" Balmoral asked. "He's gone — I can see his boat from here. It's already moving out onto the lake." Then he paused a moment, and we all felt the tower shake and wobble back and forth.

"Oh, no," Balmoral said.

Everyone was running out of the room and down the stairs as quickly as they could. Balmoral was one of the last to go and Scroggs remained at his side.

"Come on, Alexa!" Balmoral urged.

I turned to Murphy and called him to my shoulder. I replaced the Jocasta in its pouch, then jumped onto the windowsill and looked back at Balmoral.

"We're going this way," I said. Murphy looked at me as though I'd lost my mind, and Balmoral yelled back at me to get off the sill. Then I heard Squire come up behind me and I watched as she flew free into the air. Murphy and I followed out the window, into the night. I closed my eyes, hoping the water below would cushion our fall enough to keep us alive. We flew and flew, down toward the ground, and then everything was cold and dark, my body stinging from the impact.

CHAPTER 23

THE DUNGEON

I burst out of the water, the sting from hitting the pool with such force still hanging over my body. I hadn't touched bottom even though my ears felt like they might burst from the depth. The pool was much larger than it looked from above, and clearly it was very deep. I saw Murphy paddling with all his might for the shore, and then I looked down the canal toward the lake and saw that Grindall was already well on his way, the ogres rowing on both sides, the group of them disappearing into the night.

I waded to the edge of the pool and crawled up onto dry land. The hour was late and already the dew had begun to gather on the slope. Early morning would soon come. I was behind the tower, which was guarded by two high walls that ran from the tower to the edge of the water. This was a secret place, a place prepared for just such a day, a day when Grindall might need to escape quickly without being stopped by anyone on foot.

The tower rumbled above and a section of stone broke free into the air, toppling down and banging along the side of the great structure as it went. It was bigger than a grown man and landed with a loud thud behind the wall. It shook the very ground we stood on.

"What could Grindall have done to set the tower to fall?" I asked.

Murphy was running his paws over his tail, wringing the water out of it.

"He must have used the might of the ten ogres at the base of the tower," said Murphy. "Maybe he had this whole thing set up so he could jump and then remove stones that were made ready for just such a night. If the right stones have been pulled out at the base, it's certainly possible he could bring down the whole thing. In any case, we haven't much time before it collapses entirely. We'd better get moving."

We stood and began walking along the edge of the pool toward the tower, where a large opening gaped before us. The sunken cave was completely black inside, the water like a sinister dark syrup hanging low in the space. This must have been where the boat was kept, and it was our only hope of getting into the dungeon before the tower crumbled all around us.

I heard voices and shouting on the other side of the wall and saw the flicker of torchlight against the tower. Then a huge hand grabbed hold of the top edge of the barrier, and what must have been one of the last of the ogres pulled himself up onto the wall and stood upright. He did not see us, he only stood and howled, arrows sticking out from his legs and one arm, blood pouring off him from all over. And then something miraculous happened. Armon, whom I'd sent to the cliffs, jumped onto the edge of the wall and stood toe to toe with the damaged beast. Armon was every bit the powerful fighter and he quickly overcame the ogre. The two fought with swords for a brief moment, and then Armon knocked the ogre back off the wall, away from us, and I could hear the Castalians below overtake him.

"Throw me a torch!" Armon yelled to the people below. A moment later he had the light in his hand. He then jumped down on our side of the wall, and in three quick strides stood towering over Murphy and me.

"Why aren't you hiding at the cliffs?" I asked. I was happy to see him but also worried.

"I stayed there for a while and watched the swarm making its way toward me, but before it reached me it turned," said Armon. "It appears it has fled to the lake, following Grindall and the ten remaining ogres."

Looking out over the water, it did seem as though a black cloud hovered over Grindall's boat, a cloud slightly darker than the rest of the night hanging over the lake.

Armon motioned behind him. "That ogre on the ledge there, he was the last of them remaining here. The Castalians are free at last."

Just then the tower wobbled once more, this time with more force, and another stone tumbled off the top section to the ground, larger this time and accompanied by a group of smaller sections that were torn loose as well. From over the lake I heard the distant laughter of

Victor Grindall, who was roaming free and heading toward my homeland.

"We have to reach the dungeon and save Catherine," I said. "We must hurry!"

Without another word Armon was moving, the torchlight dancing on the walls of the cavernous opening. He stepped into the water and was quickly in past his chest.

"Grab hold of my shoulders!" he yelled.

Murphy scampered up my body and sat on my head and I waded out into the water. I wrapped my hands around Armon's thick neck and he began to swim into the darkness, one hand holding up the torch, the other paddling us into the murky cavern. Before long Armon was walking again, and I dropped down off his shoulders and waded until I could stand. When I reached the place where Armon stood, there was a stout wooden door built into the stone base of the tower. It was marred with age and half decayed from the moisture, but it was still a terribly strong-looking barrier to our entrance.

Armon handed the torch to me and ran his fingers along the edges on the top and sides of the obstacle before us. The tower rumbled once more and dirt showered down on us. I closed my eyes, certain that we'd missed our chance, sure the tower was about to come down on us. But once again it held, not ready to fall to pieces just yet.

"Hold the torch down here," Armon said. I angled it down near his feet and illuminated the muddy earth at the base of the door. There was enough of a gap that Armon could get both of his hands underneath.

"Stand back," he said, crouching down and waiting for me to move away from the door. There was no place else to go, so I backed down into the water until I stood with only my head and arm protruding out. Murphy's paws had hold of clumps of my hair, and he tightened his grip with each step back into the water until I finally had to tell him to stop.

Armon used all his strength to lift the door up and out. He groaned loudly, the sound echoing through the cavern. The door broke free and Armon fell back into the water just in front of me, sending a massive wave of water over my head. Armon caught hold of my arm and dragged me back to the door, both of us dripping wet, the torch a black ball of smoldering ash. Murphy had lost his grip and paddled up behind me.

Through the opening there was a long stone hallway and torches along the walls. I picked up Murphy, whose wet fur felt like a soggy bit of green moss, and I ran through the entrance and down the hallway with its flickering light. Armon was close behind, and as the tower trembled above us we descended the stairs into the dungeon. Huge wooden beams lined the ceiling, creaking under the pressure of the tower. There were no longer any moments of silence — the tower was coming down, and it was coming down in a matter of minutes, if not seconds.

We rounded a corner on the stairs and then landed on a dirt floor in a long room. On either side were arched stone entryways, five on each side, and between each entryway were torches. At the end of the room, there was a large chair and a set of keys hanging low from one of the legs. Next to them was a narrow flight of stone stairs that led up into darkness. Armon took one of the torches and walked along the length of the room, flashing the light toward the entryways, discovering that each was covered with thick iron bars. These had to be the dungeon's cells.

"Catherine!" I screamed, but no one answered. We went a bit farther, past the first two sets of cells, which were empty. And then, at the third cell on the left, we found a body hunched over in the back corner. Armon handed the torch to me and took the thick bars in his hands. He groaned madly, trying with all his might to pull the bars away, but his strength was beginning to diminish with exhaustion. He stepped back with a puzzled look on his face, as though he couldn't imagine such a thing as bars he couldn't bend. He set his brow, grabbed the bars again, and tried once more to pull them apart. Just as the bars began to separate with agonizing slowness, Murphy spoke.

"Theeth wight helph." He held the ring of keys between his teeth, and Armon looked down at little Murphy and smiled.

"You make up for lack of size with impressive resourcefulness." Armon took the keys, inserted one of them into the lock, and swung open the iron gate.

I ran into the small, damp cell, calling Catherine's name over and over. I knelt down beside the frail body, all crumpled over and dirty. Armon bent down and entered the cell with me, his huge presence nearly filling the space on its own.

I touched the body, shook the shoulder, and pulled the rumpled hair back from the face. I knew immediately that it was her. It was the woman I had known as Renny Warvold, who my adventure had taught me was Catherine. She was skinny to the bones and barely breathing, but it was definitely Catherine. She opened her eyes then, and looked at me with such joy I could hardly keep from hugging her frail body. It broke my heart to see her in such agony.

"Alexa?" she whispered.

Armon moved me aside, picked up Catherine, and strode out of the cell. The walls were beginning to crumble and the whole room was filled with the noise of impending doom. I got the message loud and clear: There would be time to reacquaint ourselves later. To my astonishment, Armon turned back toward the cells we had yet to check.

"Armon, where are you going?" I yelled. "We have to get out of here or we'll never make it."

And then it happened. The most miraculous thing I could have imagined in my most fanciful dreams. Murphy had gone out ahead while we tended to Catherine, and he had delivered the keys to another cell, which was now open. As we approached the archway to that last cell on the left, a man slowly walked out into the torchlight. He had a long, white beard, he was thin but strong-looking, and I recognized him immediately.

"Right on time, dear Armon. Although you might have moved it along a pinch given that the tower is about to fall on our heads."

Armon bowed low with Catherine in his arms. "My apologies, Mr. Warvold."

It couldn't be. How could Warvold be alive? Ganesh had poisoned him. He was dead. I had been there — I *knew* he was dead. His notes had led us all the way to where we now stood. Could it be that he had been here waiting for us all along, somehow alive all this time?

"It can't be," I said.

"How is she?" said Warvold, ignoring my quiet plea, staring at Catherine. He touched her softly, probably for the first time in years.

"She'll be fine," said Armon, and he threw Warvold over his shoulder and ran out of the room as fast as he could. I ran behind and caught Warvold's eye in the dancing light, watched his white hair springing up and down over his face as he bounced through the room. He

204

winked at me and smiled his beautiful smile, still the same. He even seemed younger than I'd remembered him. And in that moment I knew his voice like I hadn't known it before. I always knew he loved me, that there was something special about our relationship, but until I heard the words I didn't realize what I'd done.

"I knew you could do this, Alexa! You've turned the tide in our favor!"

As the walls came tumbling down, we ran from the dungeon, outrunning death, Catherine and Thomas Warvold with us once again. We emerged from the tower and swam through the pool, and then we kept on running along the wall toward the lake. When we were just to the edge of the lake, we stopped at the thundering sound of the tower falling, falling in a great heap on the earth. The sound was deafening, like waves crashing against the rocks in a storm. The time it took for the tower to fall seemed like forever, as if it were crawling to oblivion. It tipped to the left of us and then the bottom buckled out and the whole thing came tumbling straight down. As the dust began to clear we could see that the stairs leading up to the tower entrance remained, broken at the edge with a pile of rubble beneath them. And then the men and women of Castalia began to climb the stairs. In the dim light of morning we could see them, rising from the ground and walking up the stairs, waving hands and cheering as they went.

A new day was dawning for Castalia.

Armon set Warvold down and held Catherine out to him. She was awake now, the fresh air and the sound from the crash of the Dark Tower bringing her back to life. With my help she stood, and Warvold embraced her.

I looked across the lake and saw morning coming, and a dot on the horizon — Grindall and his ogres escaping into the Dark Hills.

CHAPTER 24

⊙VER THE CLİFFS

We stood in the clearing a moment longer, Warvold with his arm around me, Murphy jittering on his shoulder. Warvold had a troubled look in his eye and I could guess that our rest would be short-lived.

"We must move quickly. I'm afraid our work has only just begun."

Armon picked up Catherine again and we raced around the wall, hip deep in the lake. On the other side we found Balmoral, who Warvold also seemed to know.

"So nice to see you, Balmoral," Warvold said. "You look as though you've had a mighty good evening."

"That I have, sir, made all the better by the sight of you and Catherine."

"Balmoral, if I might ask a favor, could you bring the longest and strongest rope you can find to the cliffs right away? We'll meet you there and make our departure. Oh, and find John. He'll be coming along with us."

We all looked at Warvold hesitantly, unsure how to proceed. It was an awkward moment, and then Catherine spoke the words that nobody else would say.

"He's dead, isn't he? He died trying to save us."

Nobody could find the right response; we all just

looked at Catherine and Warvold and nodded our heads. But then Balmoral stepped forward.

"No, ma'am. That's not exactly right. He died trying to save more than the two of you alone. He died trying to save Castalia. And by the looks of that tower, he's done it."

Balmoral paused a moment, then continued. "I'm afraid Grindall has taken Mr. Yipes as well, and we don't know whether he's alive or dead."

"He's alive," I said. "Grindall told me he would keep him alive if I brought the last stone to Bridewell in three days."

Warvold was always composed and calm as a leader, but my statement alarmed him.

"We must move quickly," he said. "More than our little friend is in danger. If Grindall means to take Bridewell, the walls that remain around it won't be enough to hold him back."

"There's one thing more I should tell you," I said.

Warvold raised one eyebrow, listening carefully.

"Grindall said something about Ganesh working for him."

"That comes as no surprise," said Warvold.

"Yes, but after that, after he'd told about Ganesh, he said something that made me think there might be someone else working for him. Someone in or around Bridewell."

Warvold furrowed his brow and seemed to think this over while the soft wind blew his white hair back and forth.

"The thought had occurred to me," he said. "But I can't imagine who it might be. We'll have to be careful about who we trust in the days to come."

Warvold looked at Balmoral as if to say, *Shouldn't you be going?*

Balmoral stood a moment more and then all at once he seemed to remember what he was supposed to be doing.

"I'll be getting those ropes for you now," he said and then turned and ran away.

The rest of us walked quickly along the edge of the broken tower and spoke briefly to a few of the Castalians.

As we moved along Warvold kept looking at me, his bright green eyes blazing like I remembered from my childhood. He had such authority and grace. I felt no fear, only anticipation of what was to come in the days that followed.

Then I asked him a question that had been puzzling me.

"Warvold, why are we going to the cliffs? Won't we chase Grindall through the Dark Hills?"

"Too much work for a man of my age," he answered, though he seemed perfectly able by the way he kept up with Armon's pace.

Odessa, Scroggs, and Piggott came alongside us. Odessa had gained their respect and she was the biggest and strongest of the three by a healthy margin. Piggott and Scroggs seemed to have accepted her as the leader.

"It looks as though we've met with some success today," she offered.

"Not as much as we might have hoped for," I replied, and then I told the dogs about Grindall's escape and the unfortunate circumstances with Yipes.

When we arrived at the cliffs, the mist hovered as it always did a few feet below the rocky edge. We were not long in waiting for Balmoral, who arrived with two of his men carrying a long, thick rope between them.

I looked out over the edge. At every locality where ocean meets land there are the cliffs of black jagged rocks. If you look over the edge there lies a mist a few feet below, so thick you can't see the water. As far as the eye can see, nothing but white, puffy mist, as if we hang in the clouds and to step off the edge would leave us falling for days. If not for the violent sound of the waves against the rocks somewhere far below, one might suppose our lands were an island in the sky.

"There you are, then. Enough rope to tie up a herd of sheep," said Balmoral, interrupting my thoughts.

"Tie it to that rock, and make sure the knot is as tight as can be," Warvold ordered. He was pointing to an enormous stone jutting out of the ground about twenty feet back from the edge of the cliff.

Balmoral and his guards, with the help of Armon, did as they were told. A few minutes later they walked over to the rest of us, a few feet from the edge of the cliff and the mist below.

"Now throw the rope over the edge," Warvold continued. Balmoral looked at him as if he'd gone mad, not sure what to do.

"Throw it! We've got no time to lose," Warvold insisted.

Balmoral threw the rope over the edge. It was very long, maybe a hundred feet, and it fell into the mist to places unknown, places none of us had ever seen.

"What's everyone standing around for? Down we go! Roland is waiting!" said Warvold. "Armon, you go first with Odessa under one arm and Catherine on your back. We must get you out of sight before the bats return."

The largest and wildest river in The Land of Elyon was the River Roland, so named for the only person who had ever tried to sail it. Roland spent twenty years building a boat he called the *Warwick Beacon*, then disappeared down the pounding waves of the river into the Lonely Sea before I was even born. Nobody had seen or heard from him since. Everyone assumed he'd failed in the attempt and died long ago, the *Warwick Beacon* smashed into pieces against the rocks.

"Roland?" I asked. "Roland and the *Warwick Beacon*? Is he really down there waiting for us?"

"Well, he'd better be," answered Warvold. "I told

him to be there waiting on just this kind of day. If he's not there, I'll be awfully disappointed."

And then, quick as you please, he walked over to the rope, grabbed hold of it, and was gone over the edge with a smile, not another word spoken.

Catherine held up her arms to Armon as soon as Warvold was out of sight. Armon picked her up and placed her on his massive shoulder. He looked down at the two dogs and Odessa.

"Odessa, this could be a little uncomfortable. I apologize." The giant reached down with one arm and grabbed Odessa around the middle, pulling the wolf in close to his side. Then Armon took the two of them to the edge of the cliff, grabbed the rope with his one free hand, and disappeared into the mist, leaving the rest of us standing dumbstruck.

"I don't know about this," said Balmoral, shaking his head. "How can we be sure Roland is down there?"

Murphy shrugged, twitched his tail back and forth several times, and scampered down the rope. Piggott and Scroggs peered over the cliff, the jagged rocks jutting in wild directions, and watched as Murphy slid out of sight.

I looked at Balmoral and he looked at me. We stood on the lonesome cliff with the two dogs and contemplated what to do. I could see in Balmoral's eyes that it wouldn't be long before I was standing at the edge of the cliff alone. He looked back at the lake and the wharf, and I can only imagine the flood of emotions that overtook him.

"These years with Grindall ruling over Castalia have been hard going indeed," he said. "We have to stop him. We're the only ones who know how dangerous things have become. Nobody else will believe us."

He shuffled his feet back and forth in the grass.

"Warvold said it would only take a few days. I'll probably be back in a week." He looked at the two men who had stepped back and were waiting a stone's throw away and yelled to them.

"Tell Mary and Julia I had to go save the world with Thomas Warvold. I'll be back in a week's time." The two men ran off in the direction of the wharf. Balmoral turned and grabbed hold of the rope. He slithered down along the cliff's edge and vanished into the white puffy mist like the others.

I stood on the cliff alone with Piggott and Scroggs. It was oddly quiet as I looked back toward the lake, the sun up and the heat coming on quickly.

"I think this is what they call a leap of faith," said Piggott, and then he motioned to Scroggs and the two of them wandered off in the direction of the City of Dogs. I wondered what would become of them in this new Castalia, what would happen to the rest of the dogs. They'd fought with courage, but how long would the Castalians remember what these sick creatures had done for them? It seemed more likely that the City of Dogs would remain their home.

A leap of faith. All at once I was terribly tired. When would my duty be through? Could I ever hope to sit by a fire and talk with Catherine and Yipes and Warvold? The Land of Elyon was a much bigger and scarier place than I'd thought it would be.

The Lonely Sea is the only way to the Tenth City.

The voice on the wind was the only assurance I needed. I held my Jocasta in the safety of its leather pouch and looked one last time at the fallen Dark Tower. The people were celebrating, free from Grindall and the ogres. It was time to go.

I crawled down, took hold of the rope, and lowered myself slowly into the white fluffy haze.

CHAPTER 25

THE CHASE BEGİNS

It was wet and slippery against the cliff, so my feet kept sliding off, knees and elbows banging against the hard surface. The mist was also wet, covering my hair and face with a soft layer of moisture that felt cool and made my lips taste salty. The mist was so thick I could hardly see the rope in my hands as I descended farther, more aware by the moment that I would never have the strength to turn and go back.

I heard voices from below, muffled by the quiet but constant slapping of water against rocks, the foamy sound of liquid seeping back into the earth. As I continued my slow descent the mist began to clear, and then all at once it was gone entirely. I looked up and saw a thick white layer that seemed to go on forever out into the open sea, a ceiling of misty wet clouds hovering fifty feet off the water. Then I looked down, and to my astonishment there was a vessel, a rather large one, bobbing on the surface of the water. It was impossibly close to the edge of the cliff, so close that it seemed to me it must have crashed against the rocks, water flowing into its belly.

As I approached the deck of the boat I realized that the cliff fell away into an open cave, the boat sitting halfway inside, perfectly safe on the waters of the sea.

Armon bid me to jump with fifteen feet remaining, and how could I resist the chance to jump into a giant's arms?

A man appeared from the front of the boat, a man I'd never seen but knew without hesitation. It was Roland. He looked salty from the sea: tattered clothes, long yellow hair and beard, leathery skin, and piercing cobalt eyes. He wore an odd leather hat on his head, and the sleeves of his shirt were neither short nor long but somewhere in between. His feet and ankles were bare and looked as though they had lacked cover for a very long time, the white curly hairs of his lower legs fidgeting in the wind as he came. He held a platter in his hands with dried fish and bread. He stood among us, and I got the feeling that he was the only crew member left.

"Sorry to hold things up, Thomas," he said. "I had to check the anchors, make sure we weren't going to swerve into the cliffs. She's a good vessel, but the *Warwick Beacon* needs a bit of babying to keep her afloat."

"I completely understand," said Thomas, looking more energetic by the moment.

"Roland has kindly prepared some food for us, and none of us are more excited to get to it than Catherine and me. Shall we eat, then?"

Roland set down the tray in the middle of us. Armon was the first to grab for it. He took bread and fish and presented the food to Thomas and Catherine. I found out later that Roland had been at sea for thirteen years, periodically drifting right near the place we were. For the past

216

year he'd been waiting around the very cliffs that rose above us. In the cave he'd found a fresh spring for water, and he'd always had plenty of fish to eat. The bread was a treat, the flour and oil taken from holdings he'd stored in the boat before departing. There is much to tell of the making of the vessel, the long years at sea, and the adventures Roland enjoyed. But those tales are for another time.

Warvold began to speak and told a great many things, the most important of which I will share with you now.

First he told us something that should come as no surprise: Roland and Warvold were brothers — one the great adventurer by land, the other by sea. There were many secrets between these two. They had managed to send messages to each other by choosing places where Warvold would drop a rope with a bright red flag, meager supplies, and word of what was happening above. Roland also sent messages to his brother, but Warvold mentioned little of these, preferring to keep them a secret.

The very last message Roland had received had come at the bottom of the cliffs at Lathbury, my own hometown. The message instructed Roland to be waiting a year later beneath the cliffs at the farthest western tip of The Land of Elyon, where another red flag would be hanging near the water's edge. The hanging of the flag was a task Armon was sent to accomplish when Warvold left on his journey to rescue Catherine. At the same time Warvold left the letter for me with Yipes, telling him to wait a year before giving it to me. It was Warvold's hope that he could subdue Grindall on his own without help. As it turned out, Warvold was captured and sent to the dungeon, where we eventually found him.

I was, of course, curious as to why he'd been so bold as to attempt this mission on his own without help. To that he replied matter-of-factly, "What are you talking about? I planned for all sorts of help, as you can see by looking around you. Roland, Armon, Murphy, Yipes, Balmoral — and you, Alexa. I hoped I wouldn't need anything more than my own ingenuity, but Grindall proved more clever than I had expected. Still, I was realistic about my chances. I thought I might need help from each of you, but I only wanted to have it when I was absolutely sure I would need it." Once again I was struck by the brilliance of this man. Only he could have planned how each of us would become involved, keeping us out of harm's way until he knew he'd failed in his attempt to save Renny.

Then Warvold told us how he'd managed to fake his own death on the night when he'd walked out to the wall with me. He was aware of Ganesh and his plot to overthrow the walled cities, but Warvold had larger problems to deal with. Catherine had been taken, and he was determined to go to her, to reveal all he knew to the right people at the right time, to free his wife and the Castalians from the hand of Grindall.

And so he'd created an elaborate plan that started when Ganesh attempted to poison him. Warvold recognized the danger and instead took a potion, a potion of his own making that slowed his breathing and his heart to almost a stop. Only Grayson was in on the plot, the trusted librarian and dear old friend. In the days after Warvold's so-called death, Grayson was the one who took care of the body and placed it in the burial box. While everyone else was mourning, the two of them ate toast and strawberry jam and sipped tea in the secret places of the library. When the time came for the funeral, Warvold took the potion again and slept through it all. And finally, when Grayson prepared the body for burial, he replaced Warvold with a long bag of dirt, and sent Warvold on his way.

"I have only a little more to tell you, and then we can put up the sails," Warvold said, that hopeful look on his face, the one that could put human and beast to work on whatever he wished them to do.

"We have struck a great blow to Abaddon on this day, but there is much left to complete. Grindall runs free and we are the only ones who can stop him. He carries with him one of our dearest friends. We are the only ones who can rescue Yipes.

"In the coming days, we will sail the sea beneath the mist and make our plans. We must be as crafty as foxes, for Grindall and the ogres live only to destroy us. The only thing Grindall cares about is the stone and the devastation he can leave as he goes looking for it."

Warvold stopped a moment and measured his next words carefully.

"Nicolas, Grayson, and Pervis — if they read the letter you left for your father, they'll be expecting Grindall and the ogres. And your father, too, Alexa. There is much you still don't know, and I had my reasons for keeping things secret. The fate of The Land of Elyon hangs around your neck, and this burden must be carried with the help of your friends if we are to succeed."

Warvold picked up a loaf of bread and tore a piece out of it, then he said the last of what he needed to say, which was something I already knew.

"With the help of the last stone, we must find the Tenth City."

I felt then that none of us, not even Warvold, knew why we had to go there. Some duty awaited us beyond the Sly Field in this secret place, but we could only guess at what it was.

When Warvold was finished, Roland raised the anchor and Armon got into the water and swam, pushing us away from the cliffs and into the soft wind. The sails went up next, and we were on our way to new adventures, ones I didn't have the strength to even consider until a new day. As the breeze carried us on blue waters I'd only imagined in my past, I curled up on the deck with an old blanket beneath my head. It was cooler under the mist, still warm, but nice. Murphy curled up in a ball at my side and I gently ran my hand across his body.

I whispered words into the wind.

"Don't give up, Yipes. We're coming for you."

And then I was asleep and rocking on the waves, riding the water toward home, enjoying the quiet company of the Lonely Sea.

It would be the last quiet I would know for some time.

To be continued . . .

C·OMİNG S·OON

The Land of Elyon Book 3

The Tenth City

Alexa Daley is lost at sea — drifting perilously close to the cliffs — and a storm is coming that threatens to tear the *Warwick Beacon* to pieces.

Armon, the last of the giants, is tracked relentlessly by the black swarm, whose aim is to turn him against Alexa and thwart her pursuit of the Tenth City.

Yipes is held captive by an evil band of ogres, his fate unknown.

And The Land of Elyon has begun to fail, poisoned by the evil that creeps across the Dark Hills and into Bridewell.

As she moves toward a thrilling conclusion, Alexa must find a way to overcome the Lonely Sea, rescue Yipes from the clutches of Victor Grindall, and unlock the mystery of the Tenth City. But can she find the answers she needs in time to save The Land of Elyon?

ABOUT THE AUTHOR

PATRICK CARMAN maintains that he does not now have, nor has he ever possessed, a Jocasta or any other type of gemstone that offers the power of interspecies communication, telepathic or otherwise. Parties interested in obtaining such a stone are well advised to look elsewhere.

Mr. Carman does, however, speak to young people of his own species, sometimes aloud and sometimes in print. He makes his home in the wilderness of eastern Washington and insists that it is a rather ordinary home and is not, in fact, surrounded by stone walls.

Mr. Carman plays no musical instruments, but he has been known to torture dinner guests with attempts on the harmonica. He divides his time between writing, public speaking, spending time with his wife and two daughters, reading, fly-fishing, paragliding, and snowboarding.

To learn more about
Patrick Carman and The Land of Elyon
visit:

www.scholastic.com/landofelyon

THE TENTH CITY

THE LAND OF ELYON BOOK 3

THE
TENTH CITY

PATRICK CARMAN

SCHOLASTIC INC.

New York Toronto London Auckland Sydney
Mexico City New Delhi Hong Kong Buenos Aires

This book was originally published in hardcover by Orchard Books in 2006.

ISBN-13: 978-0-439-89120-2
ISBN-10: 0-439-89120-5

12 11 10 9 8 7 6 5 4 3   7 8 9 10 11 12/0

Printed in the U.S.A.   40

This edition first printing, October 2007

For Reece

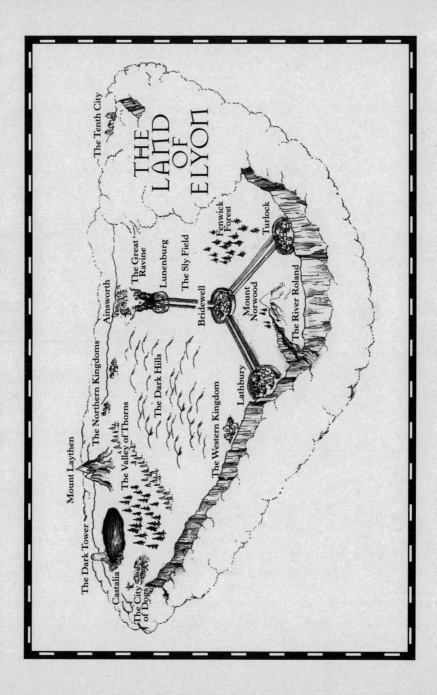

THE LAND OF ELYON

The Tenth City

Mount Laythen

The Dark Tower

Castalia

The City of Dogs

The Northern Kingdoms

The Valley of Thorns

The Dark Hills

The Western Kingdom

Ainsworth

The Great Ravine

Lunenburg

The Sly Field

Bridewell

Lathbury

Mount Norwood

Fenwick Forest

Turlock

The River Roland

Life can only be understood backwards; but it must be lived forwards.

S. A. KIERKEGAARD

AN INTRODUCTION
TO THE TENTH CITY

There are a few notes I would like to offer before getting on with what remains of this story. We've visited many places and met many characters together, and I would hate for readers to find themselves confused by the events to come. Here then are a few reminders to help you keep your wits about you as we make our way to the Tenth City.

The Tenth City begins only hours after *Beyond the Valley of Thorns* comes to a close, with Alexa and most of her friends escaping the Dark Tower. I say *most* because Yipes has been taken by the evil Victor Grindall and his ogres to Bridewell, the last remaining walled city in The Land of Elyon, where he is being held captive with little hope of rescue.

Meanwhile, Alexa is adrift on the Lonely Sea in the *Warwick Beacon*, a boat captained by one Roland Warvold, the brother of Thomas Warvold. Along with Alexa, Roland, and Thomas are Odessa the wolf, Murphy the squirrel, Squire the hawk, Thomas's wife, Catherine Warvold (also known as Renny), Armon the giant, and Balmoral, the leader of the rebellion in Castalia, along for the ride at Thomas Warvold's request.

And what of Alexa's father, Pervis Kotcher, Thomas Warvold's son Nicolas, and the others? We shall see them again before this tale is told.

As our story begins once more, night has fallen on the open sea, and our dear Alexa Daley is about to awaken to a world she's never seen before, a world of water and cliffs.

Come with me now as we travel the Lonely Sea together in search of the Tenth City.

— Patrick Carman
Walla Walla, April 2005

PART I

CHAPTER I

DARKNESS FALLS ON THE LONELY SEA

"We've made good speed today. I can't remember when I've covered so many miles so quickly."

It was a voice in the darkness.

"It would appear that the winds on the Lonely Sea are helping us along. The question is: Who controls these winds, and where are they taking us?"

I was waking from a long slumber on the deck of the *Warwick Beacon* when I heard this voice, and it seemed as though I'd awakened into a world that contained no light. Night had set on the Lonely Sea; not one glimmer from a single star could overcome the thick mist above and around us.

"Do you think she has anything to do with the wind at our back?"

"My guess is she has everything to do with it. She and the last stone are tied to each other in a way I don't understand. She's the one we must protect . . . even at the expense of all the others."

The voices were coming from the front of the ship, about twenty feet away. Listening to their words drift out into the nighttime made me feel as though I were spying on the secret rooms of Renny Lodge, back in Bridewell. I used to love the way the words would drift up the stairs in the lodge, echoing as I tried to make out their meaning.

"We'll be in Lathbury by morning light. That's very fast indeed."

Both Warvold and his brother, Roland, were smoking pipes. I could see the glow from the embers bright near their faces, the distinct outline of their features against the black of the night. Catherine (who I used to call Renny) was sleeping in the cabin below as Odessa and Balmoral watched over her. Armon the giant and Murphy were somewhere on the deck with me, but I couldn't see where. Lying by myself, I was frightened and wished I could see something more than the shadows of the two men with their pipes. I quietly opened the leather pouch around my neck and removed the last Jocasta. The orange glow was so brilliant it seemed to set the air on fire. I'd never known it to be so bright, so fiery in its intensity, piercing every corner of the darkness. I shielded my eyes and looked around as Armon sat upright, staring into the air as the mist above us was lit by the power of the Jocasta.

"Put it back!" yelled Warvold. "Put it back as quickly as you can!"

I fumbled with the pouch around my neck and dropped the glowing Jocasta inside, then drew up the string. The light vanished as quickly as it had come. Night crept back over the deck of the ship as Warvold and Roland strode quickly over to me and knelt down at my side.

"You must never do that again, Alexa," Warvold warned. "Not at night when we're on the Lonely Sea." He put his hand on my shoulder. "With the covering of clouds this place is unnaturally dark at night. The light of the Jocasta can be seen silhouetted from above the mist in The Land of Elyon."

He looked up then, and even though I could barely make out his face in the light of the glowing embers in his pipe, I could tell he was worried.

"You can be sure there are those who are looking for such a light, not the least of which are the bats — the black swarm — and maybe Victor Grindall himself."

Roland struck a match and lit a small lamp that hung by a ragged old rope at the side of the deck.

"A little light is fine," Roland said. "But that thing you've got there — I've never seen anything like it. If anyone was watching from above, they'd surely have seen the mist aglow in orange."

"*Quiet*," whispered Warvold.

He put his hand on his pipe and puffed slowly. At first all I could hear was the creaking sound of the old ship on the sea and the wind billowing steadily through the sails. There was something else, though — something far away but coming closer. A strange sound.

"Put out the light," Warvold said to Roland, "and pocket your pipe."

5

There is a special darkness when you blow out the one lamp in the night, when your eyes still expect light but there is none to be had. It is a total darkness that heightens all the other senses, and on this night I could suddenly hear clearly what Warvold heard.

The sound of a thousand bats shrieking on the wind, their leathery wings beating a mangled drumroll as they came closer.

"Armon!" I screamed. "Where are you? Get below-decks!" I knew he was the one the bats were after.

I could hear the sound of feet scuffling on the deck, but I couldn't see what was happening around me.

"Hold my hand, Alexa." It was Warvold, whispering near my face. I could smell the sweet tobacco in his beard. We listened to the wind as the sound of the black swarm came nearer still. Warvold guided me along the deck until a door was flung open from the floor and faint light escaped into the night.

"Down you go," said Warvold, holding the door upright while he beckoned me inside. I watched as Murphy scampered between Roland's legs and down the stairs.

"Armon first," I said. "We can't risk having him found."

"He won't fit, Alexa," said Warvold. "He's too big. Now get inside — there's no time to waste."

He prodded me down into the belly of the ship until

we were safely below. The door slid down and was locked behind me not a moment too soon.

The black swarm was upon the ship.

The bats were attacking the deck, banging their heads and flapping their wings, clawing everywhere with their tiny black talons. It was a tremendous, horrible noise, and all I could think of was Armon out on the deck, hiding in a corner, trying not to be found. I knew he would put up a valiant fight, but in the end the bats would overtake him and that would be the end of the race of Seraphs, the last of the giants. He would be turned into an ogre, and only ogres would remain.

The clatter on the deck decreased and then stopped altogether, but the bats could still be heard swarming around the ship. Then there was a new sound, a sound of ripping and tearing. Murphy darted across the dimly lit room and landed in my lap, shaking uncontrollably. Balmoral and Odessa instinctively moved to protect Catherine, who had awakened, disoriented and frail.

"They're attacking the sails," said Roland. "It's a good thing the big ones are down. We haven't had need of them with this wind at our back."

The shredding continued for a time, and then the swarm circled the boat again before flying off, the sound of their wings a faint whisper before Warvold spoke.

"It is to our advantage that bats have but a pea for a brain," he said. "They think only of finding Armon, nothing else. Either they've discovered him and have done their terrible work, or they've gone looking elsewhere." Then Warvold fell silent, and we all listened to the creaking of the old ship, the sound of the torn sails flapping in the wind, the last of the bats in the distance.

Murphy jumped from my arms and ran to the top of the steps, scratching on the door in the ceiling to get out. Just then we all heard the same thing, and it stirred a mix of emotions. What we heard was the sound of giant footsteps pounding the deck, walking toward the door. Would it still be Armon, or had the bats found him and transformed him into a beast that would rip the door off its hinges at any moment?

Murphy ran back down the stairs and leaped into my arms. There was a knock at the door in the ceiling, and I yelped at the sound of it.

"Shall I unlock it?" asked Roland.

"I think that would be best," said Warvold. "If he's been turned against us, he'll only knock it in. We don't have much hope if we've got an ogre loose on the ship."

Roland walked up the stairs and pulled away the bolt, then ran back down and stood next to Warvold. Odessa growled, ready to defend us.

The door creaked open, and all we could see was darkness. But one thing was certain — whatever was standing there in the night was dripping something into the room, and my heart skipped with the thought of blood pouring from Armon's broken body.

8

CHAPTER 2

A VOICE ON THE WIND

The silhouette that looked down at us through the doorway was dark against the night sky. It was huge and unmoving, quiet but for the sound of water falling on the stairs leading down into the cabin of the *Warwick Beacon*.

"They've gone," said Armon. "You can stop your worrying."

He was on his knees, sticking his giant head into the opening so we could see him. His hair was wet, dripping salty water on the stairs, but he was smiling and he was still the giant we all remembered.

I ran up the stairs and put my arms around his big, damp neck. He lifted me up through the doorway as he stood, and I was somewhere high in the night air feeling happy and free, the wind flapping Armon's long wet hair against my face.

"You jumped off the ship?" I said.

"I wasn't going to fit into that doorway," he answered. "So I crept overboard in the darkness and slid into the water, then swam out to sea."

"Why didn't I think of that?" I said.

Concerned the bats might return suddenly, I rejoined

the others below. Armon lay down on the deck and poked his head down into the space. Every few seconds he disappeared, swallowed up by the darkness outside, looking and listening for flying intruders. His only companion on the deck was Squire. She'd flown off when the black swarm arrived, but she was back now, flapping here and there on the edges of the ship.

There was a lamp trimmed low sitting between us on the floor. The hour was late, maybe midnight, but everyone was wide awake and listening. The creaking of the old boat on the waves made a constant chatter, but I didn't mind. It was soothing in its own way.

"I'll have to get to those sails sooner than later," said Roland. "We might end up hitting the cliffs if we drift too close in the night."

"The bats are gone," said Armon. "If they come again I can go back into the water and you can get below."

That was assurance enough for Roland. He took Balmoral, Armon, and a lamp with him to mend the sails. The rest of us sat quietly for a moment listening to them at their work, and in the soft light of the cabin I heard a familiar voice stirring in the air. What it said frightened me, and I sat in the cabin wondering if I should share it with the others.

"Warvold?" I said. He only nodded and looked at me while Odessa and Catherine sat silent.

"Did you know that the last Jocasta makes it so you

can hear Elyon's voice?" I looked down at Murphy sitting in my lap, then continued. "Not always, but every now and then. It's the strangest sound, like a whisper on the wind."

"I know of the legend, and I've wondered if it were true," Warvold said. After some hesitation he added, "You must listen carefully for that voice."

I waited a moment more, afraid to say what I thought I'd heard.

"Do you think everything I hear in that voice on the wind is from Elyon, or could it be that Abaddon has found a way to speak to me as well?"

Catherine was still very weak, but she took my hand then and held it, though she said nothing.

"If it's as the legend said it would be, the voice is that of Elyon alone," Warvold answered. He was sitting next to Catherine, and he brushed a bit of hair away from her face. His mind seemed lost in thought.

"Is there something you want to tell me, something you've heard?" he asked me.

I looked at Catherine, so weak and tired, and I wished she would lie down and go back to sleep.

"Yes," I said. "I've heard something just now that I'm afraid to tell."

Before I could explain further, Roland came barreling down the stairs with Balmoral close behind.

"I've taken down the torn sails and raised the larger

one," Roland said. "I know these waters well and can guide us in the darkness. We should be approaching Lathbury just as the sun comes up."

"That's good, Roland — but wait a moment," Warvold replied. "Alexa, have you got something to say to us?"

"I do," I answered; then I squeezed Catherine's hand a little tighter and told them what I'd heard on the wind:

"The voice I heard said we couldn't all stay in Lathbury."

"Why not?" Odessa asked. It was the first thing she'd said in quite a while. Because of the Jocasta, I was the only human who could understand her.

"We can leave Catherine there," I said, "but the rest of us must go on."

Warvold contemplated this bit of news as he relit his pipe, the sight of which seemed to interest Roland and Balmoral. They both sat down on the steps leading down into the cabin and pulled out their own pipes, preparing them as Warvold sat thinking.

I knew from talking with Warvold that there would be a rope waiting for us at Lathbury, running down the length of the cliffs and almost into the water. It had hung there a long time, but Warvold wouldn't tell us who had put it there. As far as we knew, this was our only escape from the Lonely Sea — at least according to Warvold.

"There's more," I said.

"I thought as much," said Warvold. He fiddled with his pipe and blew smoke over his head.

12

Murphy sat nearby, his tail twitching wildly. He spoke quickly and with purpose.

"Does the voice on the wind say anything about finding nuts or treats hidden away on this old boat?"

I smiled and patted him once on the head before continuing.

"We only have five days to bring Grindall the stone or we'll never see Yipes alive again. We must rescue Yipes, and I thought we would leave Catherine in Lathbury and go directly to Bridewell to find him. But it seems that right now we are meant to go somewhere else. There's something Elyon wants us to see, something beyond Turlock, at the point of land farthest away from the Dark Tower."

Roland stopped puffing at his pipe and sat dumbstruck by the news. For an instant he seemed unsure what to say. He was either terribly excited or dreadfully scared — I couldn't tell which by the look on his face.

"Alexa, are you sure about what you heard? Could you have heard it wrong?" he asked me.

I told him I was sure. I knew what I'd heard. It was unmistakable.

"There's something you should know then," he said. He put his pipe back into the corner of his mouth and puffed three quick times. "I have sailed the Lonely Sea for many years, exploring faraway places with secrets and mysteries hard to imagine. But there is one place I have never gone. The place you speak of, beyond Turlock on the far side of The Land of Elyon, is utterly impassable with this ship."

He looked down into the room from the step where he sat and thought a moment before speaking again.

"Fierce winds never die there — they just push everything into the cliffs. No sooner would we round the corner of Turlock and the *Warwick Beacon* would be smashed to bits against the rocks."

Roland kept on, explaining that the place I spoke of was so dangerous he'd never even considered going there. Only once had he tried to approach it, from miles offshore. The winds had been so strong that they nearly capsized the boat before he veered off and ended up all the way near Ainsworth.

"Still," Roland finished, "it would be quite an adventure to try." A smile crept over his face, and his eyes went glassy and distant.

Warvold looked at Catherine, her eyes barely open and her skin a pale white chalk.

"Are you *sure*, Alexa?" he asked.

I nodded, convinced of what I'd heard. I could tell he was troubled by the idea of leaving Catherine's side again.

"We'll need to get Catherine off the boat where she can regain her strength," he decided. "This journey will be too much for her."

He looked at his brother and asked him a question. "Can you stop us at Lathbury, as we'd planned, before we go racing around the corner into the cliffs?"

"I can," Roland answered, and he went along merrily puffing his pipe, the adventurer in him already thinking of the untold dangers that awaited us.

We all sat silent then, wondering what to do. I was worried for Yipes, but I was also scared to go around the corner from Turlock. It seemed that the Lonely Sea was angry in those parts . . . and I didn't see how we could overcome the jagged cliffs that awaited us.

CHAPTER 3

THE STORM

As the sun rose I could see light creeping into the mist above. It made me feel much better as we all milled around the deck waiting for Roland to tell us where we were. Warvold had been particularly quiet all morning, preparing to leave Catherine behind yet again.

As we arrived at the base of Lathbury, Roland pulled the ship closer to the cliffs, but not so close that we were in danger of crashing against the rocks. Roland had a small, two-person boat on deck that he held over the sea on ropes and poles. When the small boat was clear of the *Warwick Beacon*, he let out the ropes until the little vessel bobbed softly on the water. The seas were calm, an ominous silence before the storms that awaited us beyond Turlock.

Warvold sat alone with Catherine, and they whispered to each other things I couldn't hear. I couldn't take my eyes off them, and I was surprised to see them looking my way more than once as they spoke. There was something special about these two, a connection I felt to them that I couldn't quite understand. Seeing them huddled together made me feel sad that they were parting again so soon.

Eventually, the two of them walked slowly over to the rest of us. Catherine gave me a hug, squeezing my little bones tightly in her grasp.

"You be careful now," she said. Then she released me and looked deep into my eyes. "I'll be waiting for you in Lathbury."

I was excited to get back home, to see not only her but my father and mother as well. It had been a long journey, but as I watched Catherine carefully climb down to the small boat I felt certain the most dangerous stretch remained. I wondered if I would ever see her again.

Warvold got into the boat with her and paddled them the short distance to the cliffs where we could all see a red flag hanging from a rope against the rocks. This rope was very thick and even had a seat of leather hanging at its bottom. Whoever put it there was expecting to haul people up the sheer cliffs. I was terribly curious who it might be.

Warvold got Catherine settled in the seat, kissed her, then pulled hard on the rope three times. There was a long pause, and then we all watched as the rope lurched to life and Catherine was carried up the side of the cliff, far into the air, until she disappeared into the mist. When I looked back to Warvold, he was already halfway back to our boat. Squire landed on the front of the little dinghy, keeping him company on the Lonely Sea.

"That can't have been easy," said Murphy, sitting on

my shoulder. "It makes me wonder about Yipes, all alone with those awful ogres. I hope he'll be all right."

I felt awful that we couldn't all go up the rope together and make plans to sneak into Bridewell and rescue him. I was mystified that Elyon was sending us by another way, into a place Roland didn't even think we could survive.

Once Warvold was back on board, Roland lifted the undamaged sails, and the early morning flew by quickly. We approached, then passed around Turlock, the winds not quite as strong as Roland had remembered them.

"Could it be that the winds have finally tired of their constant blowing?" he said.

No sooner had the words left his mouth than the winds became more violent, the waves crashing against the ship and pushing it toward the cliffs. Rain came tumbling out of the sky like no rain I'd ever seen before. It felt as though the sky above us had waited for our arrival and held on to more and more water, month after month, only to drop it all on the *Warwick Beacon*.

There was a sound then, a roaring from the east, and we all turned to see what it was. Through the driving rain we all saw the wind coming straight at us. We could see it off in the distance lifting the water into great waves. The storm didn't creep up on our boat like a cat will sneak up on a mouse. It leaped on top of us all at once without warning, and we began to tumble on the waves toward the cliffs.

We were barely around the corner of Turlock, and

already something was set against us. There was no place for us here, only the rocks and the bottom of the sea. We had ventured into a place we should not have.

"We must turn back!" shouted Roland. "There's still time to swing her around and escape the storm!"

Just then a giant wave rolled over the ship, and we were all left scrambling for a hold. When I could see again, I saw Warvold advancing on me quickly.

"Get below with Murphy and Odessa!" he yelled. "We'll turn her around and try to get out."

I did as I was told and began scrambling across the deck as quickly as I could, holding on to the rail as I went. I looked out into the raging sea just in time to see another wave about to hit the boat, this one bigger than all the rest. I held on as tightly as I could, but it was no use. I flew free with the wave, out into the Lonely Sea.

It was strangely quiet under the water, like holding a pillow over my ears when there were storms back home. It was almost serene compared to the storm raging over-head. The sound of the rain pelting the sea made me feel as if I was under a giant blanket, a thousand tiny pebbles bouncing off the surface.

Don't let them turn back.

In the quiet of the water I heard these five words and I didn't understand them. How could Elyon want for us to be smashed against the rocks or capsized on the Lonely Sea? I felt a blow on my back, and I thought I'd landed in the rocks.

19

To my surprise I was lifted out of the water, into the wrath of the storm, then set down on the deck of the *Warwick Beacon*.

"Are you all right?" Armon yelled, trying to overcome the sound of the howling wind. He had plucked me out of the sea with his giant hands.

"I'm okay!" I shouted back, wiping the water from my eyes and face. "Where's everyone else?"

Armon pointed to the front of the boat where the three men — Warvold, Balmoral, and Roland — were trying to turn the wheel and face the ship back toward Turlock.

I ran across the slippery deck as more waves crashed over the boat.

"Don't do that! Keep going into the storm!" I screamed.

"Have you gone mad?" yelled Roland. "We can't make it, Alexa. If we don't turn back now we'll be thrown into the rocks."

Warvold crawled across the deck on his hands and knees until he met with me, rain running down his face. He took hold of both my shoulders.

"Are you sure, Alexa?"

I looked at him pleadingly and nodded, though I couldn't have expected him to trust me.

"Stay the course!" yelled Warvold. "Point her straight down the side of the cliffs and hang on!"

20

Roland and Balmoral looked stunned, and I wondered if they might throw us belowdecks and turn back anyway. Armon came alongside the men and put to rest any such thoughts they might have had. He took the wheel in his mighty hands and turned it a few times around, heading us perfectly parallel to the cliffs and away from Turlock.

I crawled over to the wheel, and Armon put one of his hands around my waist and lifted me to his side, determined not to let me tumble overboard again. And then we all held on and prayed that the waves wouldn't push us into the cliffs and bring our adventure to an end.

We were a hundred feet from the rocks and closing the gap fast. A short time more and the *Warwick Beacon* would be dashed against the cliffs. I began to think of all the things we'd accomplished, only to find ourselves caught in a storm we couldn't escape. We were utterly helpless against its fury. I looked up at Armon, and he smiled at me, the beads of water running around his eyes and his big nose, and I remembered how I'd felt this very same way when we were pinned down in the Dark Hills, the ogres walking out to find us. Armon had appeared as if out of the very air, and we were saved. Unlikely as it seemed, I had to believe Elyon had some plan we couldn't understand that would protect the *Warwick Beacon* from the cliffs.

The storm seemed to reach its peak, waves and wind

rushing in from all sides, the boat tossed on the Lonely Sea like a feather twisting in a gale. We were spinning around in circles, and I was losing any sense of where we were.

"Something's not right about this!" It was Roland, yelling into the storm. He was frantically turning his head from side to side trying to figure out where the cliffs were in all the rain as the ship continued to spin uncontrollably.

"The storm has changed, and for once I'm excited to say that it's gotten much worse!"

The Lonely Sea must have finally sent poor Roland into a fit of hysteria. He was laughing uncontrollably, throwing back his head as he held the rail of his beloved ship.

"He's gone mad!" said Balmoral.

"No, he hasn't," said Warvold. "He's right. The winds are coming down the cliffs directly at us just as the winds from the sea are pushing us into them. We're at the center of the storm, where two forces push against each other."

We all looked on in awe as the *Warwick Beacon* stopped spinning and righted its course parallel with the cliffs only a hundred feet away. Warvold was right. Wind was billowing both down from the cliffs and in from the Lonely Sea, two forces set against each other, our ship now stuck in the middle of the two.

The storm did not subside. If anything it grew fiercer

as the two sides pushed against each other equally, shooting us down the middle of the eye of the storm.

"Everyone belowdecks!" yelled Roland. And then he looked at Armon. "Everyone but you."

It was the only thing to do. If we stayed out in the storm much longer, one of us was sure to go overboard. Armon set me down on the slippery deck. I huddled together with Balmoral and Warvold, and we slowly made our way back to the door in the floor that led to the cabin. Balmoral flung it open, and it was nearly torn free in the storm as water rushed down into the belly of the ship. Warvold pushed me inside, and I turned one last time. Through the driving rain I saw Armon standing over Roland, the two of them holding the wheel steady. Roland wasn't about to miss the storm of his life.

I stumbled down the stairs, followed by Warvold. Then Balmoral heaved the door shut behind him with a mighty bang, and we were sealed in with Odessa and Murphy.

The *Warwick Beacon* rolled back and forth on the sea, creaking with every crashing wave, and I thought the whole ship would be blown apart. I wondered where Squire had gone off to, if she'd cleared the clouds and was watching the storm from above.

Hours passed as we waited in the damp hull of the ship, hanging on to beams as we rocked back and forth on the waves. I kept thinking the storm would shift and we would crash into the cliffs at any moment. I wondered if our friends were even on the deck any longer, or if they'd been thrown clear into the raging sea.

It was a terrible, long day that seemed to go on forever.

CHAPTER 4

THE CLİFFS

"There are nine cities that I know of in The Land of Elyon." It was Warvold, speaking the words over the sound of the storm outside. It was hard to tell how long we'd been belowdecks, but it was a long time indeed.

I had found a corner to sit in where I wouldn't be thrown from side to side as the boat rocked violently. Murphy sat in my lap, as was his habit. Either he was more frightened than usual — or he was cold, because he wouldn't stop shivering.

"Nine cities that I've seen with my own eyes," Warvold continued, and then he proceeded to whisper each of them too quietly for me to hear, though I knew their names.

Bridewell, Turlock, Lathbury, Lunenburg, Ainsworth, the Western Kingdom, Castalia, and the two Northern Kingdoms.

"But there is one other," Warvold said aloud. "One I thought could never be reached."

He sat silent and steadied himself at the sound of another wave hitting the ship.

"The Tenth City," he told us. "Beyond the Sly Field and through the eternal mist, in a place no one has ever found. I wonder if we might see this place before too long, if this old boat can find its way."

There was very little light to be had belowdecks, only what was cast inside from the cracks where drops of water came in. But I could see the twinkling in Warvold's eyes, as if he'd spoken of a treasure he'd long thought unattainable, now suddenly within reach.

"I wouldn't get your hopes up too high," said Odessa. "Even the animals have searched for such a place, but none have found it. It may be that it's only in our imagination, put there to remind us of who created all this."

I told Warvold what the wolf had said, and we were all met with a long silence from our old friend.

"You may be right, Odessa," he finally answered. "But something tells me if it's a real place, I'm closer to it now than I've ever been. I've traveled the whole of The Land of Elyon and turned over most of the rocks on my way. But the mist beyond the Sly Field is impassable. Somehow it doesn't matter where you go in. The Sly Field always spits you back out again, farther away from where you were trying to go."

I piped in then, interested in what Warvold was saying.

"I read a book once about a man named Cabeza de Vaca. He tried to find the Tenth City, but he got lost, just like you. He finally gave up trying."

"I knew him well," Warvold replied, a slight smile on his face. "Cabeza and I compared notes, but nothing came of it. It's as if whatever lies beyond the field of mist

26

is hidden for some purpose we can't understand. Either that or some riddle keeps us from it."

The sea seemed to calm for a moment, and we rolled up and down on a large, slow wave. Warvold broke the silence as though he hadn't even noticed the storm had turned less violent.

"The Tenth City," he said. "The most secret place, a place untouched by human or beast — and we may yet stumble onto it if we can overcome the storm."

Just as he said it, the door to the cabin flew open, and Roland came bounding down the stairs two at a time. The light from outside was faint, and I understood immediately that we'd passed through the entire day and were approaching late afternoon. A few more hours and night would return.

Roland, dripping wet and breathless, held on to the beam next to the stairs and yelled at us all.

"The storm still rages on, but it's come down a notch. It's the strangest thing. We've been pushed closer to the cliffs, but that unexplainable wind coming off the rock face keeps holding us away from crashing into the rocks. The storm from the sea seems to have worn itself out, and it, too, is less fierce."

"It sounds as though the rains have stopped as well," said Balmoral.

"They have," answered Roland. "Might you take the wheel for a spell if I show you how it's done?"

27

Balmoral was up on his feet immediately and walking for the door.

"Anything would be better than sitting down here any longer," he complained. He was up the stairs and out the door before Roland could change his mind. Warvold and Odessa followed, then Roland disappeared back into what remained of the storm on deck.

For some reason I stayed where I was. Something about what I would see when I went outside scared me.

"Murphy?" I said.

"Yes?"

"Will you promise to stay with me no matter what?"

He leaped out of my hands onto my shoulder, digging his little claws into my wet clothing.

"I promise," he said.

"All right, then. Stay where you are and hold on tight. I have word from Elyon, and I can't do what I'm told without you. I'm too frightened."

Murphy swung his head around and tried to catch my eye. We looked at each other in the dimly lit cabin, and he smiled and chirped.

"I just love being in on all the secret things, don't you?"

I only nodded and patted him on the head. Then I got up, marched over to the stairs, and climbed up into the light of day.

The storm had settled, but winds still billowed on both sides of the boat, holding it steady about a hundred feet off the cliffs. Everyone was gathered around the captain's wheel where Balmoral was keeping the *Warwick Beacon* steadily parallel to the cliffs. I caught Armon's eye and motioned for him to come see me, and he broke away from the group.

He bent down on one knee and lowered his giant head down toward me.

"Armon, there's something you must help me with, but I'm not sure you're going to want to do it," I said.

Armon turned back to look at the group of men standing together with Odessa, then we both looked up and watched as Squire shot through the mist and held steady in the driving wind. A moment later she turned once over the boat and flew back into the mist to places we couldn't see. I wondered then if the storm was happening above the mist as well, or if it was contained below on the Lonely Sea. It was an odd thought to imagine a pristine day above while a storm raged below, but it seemed to me that this might be the way of things. Elyon and Abaddon were fighting each other, the strength of both focused entirely on the *Warwick Beacon* and the treasure it held. It wasn't so hard to believe that things back home might have remained quite ordinary.

Armon turned back to me as if he knew what I was about to ask of him.

"What would you like me to do?" he asked.

Just then Squire shot out of the mist once more between the *Warwick Beacon* and the cliffs, where she hung in the air over the Lonely Sea.

"Can you swim in these waters? Can you make it to the cliffs with me riding on your back?"

"And me!" squeaked Murphy.

Armon stood up and seemed to size up the task.

"I take it only the three of us can go?" he said.

I looked down at the little bag holding the Jocasta and nodded. Without another word spoken, Armon looked once more at the group by the wheel. The only one look-ing our way with some interest was Odessa. The rest were talking among themselves. Armon picked me up and threw me over his back. Murphy held tightly to my clothing with his claws, and I wrapped my arms around Armon's neck. Then the giant leaped into the air so high and so far it was as though we were flying. I looked back and saw Warvold staring at us in wonder, alarmed at this new development.

We hit the water, Armon taking the full blow, and then he was swimming fast for the cliffs. I held on and felt the salty chill of the sea. Murphy was digging in a little too much and caught hold of my skin.

"Murphy, not so tight!"

"So sorry — it's all so exciting, isn't it?" He let go his grip enough for my skin to escape his little claws.

Squire flew out of the mist ahead and down over us,

screeching loudly. Then she circled low over our heads and darted for the cliffs. She landed, and I knew for sure what we were supposed to do.

"Elyon said to follow Squire — that she would lead us where we need to go."

Armon seemed to understand and changed his course slightly. I looked back over my shoulder and saw that Roland was trying to turn the boat and come after us. I waved him off, but it was no use — he kept fighting the storm, trying to right the ship in ways that forces around him would not allow. The winds came up once more, and the storm billowed heavier, pushing the ship out to sea even as Armon pulled us over the last of the big waves toward the cliffs.

Squire was sitting on the rocks screeching over and over as we approached. Armon gave one last stroke, then braced himself as a wave threw us onto the rocks. He held on to the jagged stone, wind roaring down the face of the cliff. Squire was just to our left, and she kept up her screeching until Armon sidestepped over to her and we discovered for the first time that she sat in front of a rather large, dark opening in the rocks. Armon quickly jumped inside the space as Squire flew away. Armon's back was heaving up and down as he tried to catch his breath. The cave we'd found protected us from the wind and allowed us to rest a moment.

"The Lonely Sea just about took all the strength of a

giant," said Murphy. His matted, wet fur made him look scrawny, like a soaked kitten.

"That it did," grunted Armon. He was regaining his strength, but the swim had been more of a challenge than even I'd thought it would be. It had tested the giant's strength, and he'd almost come up short, which worried me as I looked out to the sea. Would he have the strength it would take to get us back to the *Warwick Beacon*?

Squire re-emerged, flying straight at us. I had an uneasy feeling about where she would be flying next. My worries were confirmed when she turned sharply upward the moment she reached us. We peeked our heads out into the storm and watched as she labored against the wind all the way up the side of the cliffs and into the mist, where we could see her no more.

Armon looked over his shoulder at us and found Murphy and me hoping for some reassurance that he could scale the cliffs. He sighed mightily and looked at his own hands in the weak light of the crevice — we all looked at them. I leaned over and put my hand against his, then Murphy ran down my arm and put his paw on the back of my hand — my hand so much bigger than Murphy's paw, Armon's hand that much bigger still than mine.

"If I had hands that big *I* could do it," said Murphy, and for some reason Armon thought this was very funny, and he began to laugh. He stretched out his arms and his back rumbled and cracked against my chest.

"Off we go then," he said. "Before the light starts to fade."

Armon crept out into the wind and took hold of the side of the cliff. Then he began climbing, the two friends on his back shivering with fright at each new step.

CHAPTER 5

TELL ⊙ ONE WHAT YOU'VE SEEN

We were high on the cliff — almost into the mist — when I looked down for the first time. That was a mistake.

Armon had lost his footing and his big leg swung free in the wet air. Looking down made me gasp, but I couldn't stop looking. We were far above the ground, and I could see the waters crashing along the rocks below. I also saw the *Warwick Beacon*, and I hoped Warvold and the others could see us. They had drifted farther out to sea, and I suddenly felt we'd made a terrible mistake. Our companions must have thought we'd lost our minds, but there was nothing they could do to help us or stop us, and it looked as though we might not be able to get back to the boat as it drifted away. A lump caught in my throat, and I began to feel dizzy. I buried my head into Armon's back and promised myself not to look down again.

As Armon lumbered farther up the cliff, struggling for every footing and gasping for air as he went, I tried to take my mind off the fact that the three of us would fall to our deaths if Armon lost his grip on the slippery rock face. I imagined that Warvold and Roland were standing on the boat feeling a little jealous, which actually made quite a bit of sense. The two of them would have wished it were them on the back of a giant, scaling a seemingly unassailable cliff to places no one had ever seen. It put a smile on my face to think that in some ways I'd become their equal, ways I would not have dreamed possible growing up in Lathbury. And then I opened my eyes again and looked up.

The air was thick and moist. We had entered the mist — which meant, I hoped, we were nearing the top of the cliff. We weren't able to see more than a few feet in any direction — an alarming development, since Armon was having enough trouble finding the few places where he could hold on. Now they were even fewer to choose from. But there was one wonderful thing that happened when we entered the clouds that I couldn't quite understand.

The storm was gone.

The higher we rose in the mist, the less wind and rain there was. We could hear the storm below us, but it was strangely peaceful now, as though we had entered another realm entirely. I watched as Armon's arms extended beyond where I could see, his hands crawling from place to place along the cliff, looking for a hold above.

"I'm scared, Armon," I said. "What if we can't get back down?"

He didn't answer me, and it seemed he'd sensed something above that gave him a new strength that only made him move higher and higher at a startling pace. Time passed quickly, and light began to pierce our world of mist. And then, without warning, we were out in a perfectly cloudless afternoon, another fifty feet of cliff above us that was dry to the touch and full of good holds in every direction.

"I have a feeling about this place I can't explain," Armon told me. "Something I haven't felt in a very long time."

Murphy chimed in: "The only feeling I have is that a squirrel shouldn't be climbing so high. This altitude makes my fur feel funny." He held on with three paws and used the fourth to scratch behind his ear like a dog.

Armon wasn't breathing so hard now, and he seemed all the more superhuman to me as he practically leaped from hold to hold on the rock face, taking us higher and higher until we were all the way to the top, and he crawled over the edge and onto The Land of Elyon.

"Stay on my back," he said. He crawled on his hands and knees away from the edge, and I wondered if he was afraid a gust of wind might blow us into the air and down to the jagged rocks below. When he was well clear of the edge, Armon stood up. I looked over his shoulder at the place we'd arrived.

What we saw was both magnificent and frightening in ways I had never experienced before. I had hoped we were being led to a city or a mountain, but what I saw wasn't that at all. Murphy darted back and forth between

Armon's shoulders, trying to see everything in front of him. I only stared in disbelief, my breathing choppy as though the very air around me had gone thin and hard to find.

Armon was walking ever so slowly forward, as though a force beyond his control was drawing him. No one spoke, not even Murphy, and then out of the air came a crystal voice with words I hadn't imagined I'd hear — words I didn't want to hear.

Tell no one what you've seen.

The voice was clearer than before, not on the wind as it had been in the past. I almost expected Armon and Murphy to hear, too — but they didn't. I hoped there would be more for me to tell them, but there was nothing.

Armon continued to walk closer to what lay before us, and then a brutal wind came up and nearly knocked him off his feet. A great cloud of white rushed over the land and began covering everything in front of us. A few minutes later, as we braced against the wind at the edge of the cliffs, what we'd seen was gone.

"Armon, you can't tell anyone about this place," I said. "You, too, Murphy. No one can know."

Neither of them spoke, and it seemed to me that we all understood Elyon had brought us to this very place for his own purpose.

He said something else to me then. Something that, if I followed, would be the start of a plan. I was afraid to share it with anyone when I heard it, but I knew I would have to tell Armon later. I had to think about it first. I had to figure out the exact meaning of Elyon's words.

"We have to go," said Armon. "If I don't leave now, I won't be able to."

Armon turned away from the land before us and craned his neck to look at me where I rested my head on his shoulder. It was clear from the glimmer in his eyes that turning back was very difficult for him. He swung his whole body around and looked out over the mist that covered the Lonely Sea.

"I only hope we can make it back to the *Warwick Beacon*," he said. Then we were over the side heading down, visions of what we'd seen lodged in all our heads as we went.

The descent was much faster than the way up, as Armon moved like a giant spider along the sheer cliff wall, down through the mist, back into the storm below, and finally stood among the rocks at the base. Armon only rested for a few seconds before stepping into the Lonely Sea and swimming for the boat. It was a long way off, but we could see it in the distance, bobbing on the waves. The storm seemed to push us out to sea, so Armon had only to guide us in the right direction. The light of day was almost gone as we approached the *Warwick Beacon*, Warvold and Roland and Balmoral yelling our names and waving us in. In the weakening light, a rope was thrown into the sea, and Armon took hold of it.

When Armon finally climbed over the edge of the

Warwick Beacon, he set down Murphy and me and collapsed on the deck, his huge body sprawled out before us, chest heaving as rain pelted his face.

Murphy was so pitiful-looking with his wet, matted fur. All his bones were showing through and his little face looked exhausted, as though he might fall away sleeping and roll down the deck of the ship.

"Wait till I get back home and tell everyone I went swimming in the ocean and climbed to the top of the cliffs," he said. "They'll never believe me."

Warvold picked me up and hugged me so hard I thought I would burst.

"Please don't ever do anything like that again," he whispered in my ear. Then he turned to his brother and yelled, "Get us out of here! We're nearly around the edge of the cliffs."

He carried me belowdecks and threw a soggy blanket around me.

"Are you all right? Are you hurt? What did you see? What's up there, Alexa?" He was overcome with curiosity and concern, and it nearly broke my heart to sit there shaking my head, unable to tell him what I longed to share.

I sat shivering with Warvold's arms around me as the *Warwick Beacon* carried me away from a place I would never forget and could not understand — a secret place I could tell no one about.

CHAPTER 6

SEPARATED

I remember getting sleepy. I was wet and miserable and dreaming I was in the smoking room at Renny Lodge, curled up on a velvety couch with a good book and a cup of tea, a big fire burning, pipe smoke swirling around the room. And then I don't remember much of anything until I awoke with light peeking through the door that led up the stairs to the deck of the *Warwick Beacon*.

I sat up, awake at the sight of it, thinking the storm would blow in and rouse everyone. Then I realized I was no longer cold and the storm no longer raged outside. There was a warm light pouring down the stairs and a soft morning breeze fluttering around the room. Someone had picked me up in the night and set me in a hammock, where I was warm but still a little moist. I jumped down from the hammock, awake and running for the stairs, excited to see a peaceful day unfolding.

The air outside was right between cool and warm, the crispness of the morning passed but the heat of the day yet to stir. The Lonely Sea was calm but for a few waves drifting lazily on the surface. I looked to my left and saw the cliffs rising into the mist a hundred yards off.

"Ahhh, you've finally woken up." Warvold's kindly voice came from the wheel where he stood with Roland, wind dancing in their hair, ideas of adventure evident on their faces. The two of them had known only risk and danger all their lives, and the reward was the look I saw in their eyes. They were two people full of life to the point of bursting, and I wanted only to be more like them.

"You look as though you've seen a ghost," said Roland as he turned the wheel ever so slightly toward the cliffs.

"She looks well," said Warvold. "Much better than she ought to after the perils of only a day ago."

He walked over to me, and we strode hand in hand to the very front of the *Warwick Beacon*, where we stood looking out into the sea. I turned back to see Armon and Balmoral mending the sails, Murphy sitting on Odessa's back as the great wolf slept at their feet.

"Alexa," said Warvold. "We're nearing Ainsworth, where things will get more complicated. Will you stay with me a moment and let me tell you a few things?"

I was glad to hear we were close to a place where we might regain our footing on land and go after Yipes. We were already starting our third day's journey from Castalia. Only two days remained before Grindall expected me in Bridewell with the last stone.

"Will we be able to reach land, to rescue Yipes?" I asked Warvold.

"That we will. There are a few more surprises I have yet to reveal." He stared out to sea and smiled serenely. "My years in Bridewell may have been lacking in adventure, but they were an important season. I contemplated many things behind the shadows of the walls. I laid many plans." He turned away from the Lonely Sea and looked at me. "Before that — during all those years of my youth, wandering in The Land of Elyon — do you know why I searched, Alexa?" he asked me. It was a question he strained to produce, and he seemed desperate to tell me the answer.

"Because you love adventure, you and Roland both," I answered.

He looked back out to the sea once more, and his voice trembled as he spoke the true answer.

"I was seized by the power of a great affection."

It seemed as though Warvold had given me the key to his entire life in that one statement, and yet I struggled to understand what he meant. I rolled the words over in my head, trying to see in them what had driven him to live such a dangerous life. *I was seized by the power of a great affection.*

"I don't understand what you mean," I admitted.

Warvold looked deep into my eyes, the wind blowing strands of white and gray hair across his worn face.

"Elyon has only one hope for us, Alexa. That we would know he loves us. Do you understand? The one who made you, the one who made everything." He swept his hand across the sea. "He loves you. And more than that, there is nothing you or I need do to earn his reckless affection for us. That love has driven me to fight his enemy, the enemy of us all."

"Abaddon," I whispered.

He stared at me then with such intensity I could hardly hold his gaze.

"No evil can resist the power of love forever." He winked at me and smiled, as if he thought that somehow our band of misfits might yet overcome Grindall and the ogres — even Abaddon himself.

"I have failed, and failed, and failed again," he said. "But no amount of failure can move Elyon's hand of affection away from me. It's inescapable. To live boldly for that kind of love is the least I can do."

I suddenly felt that I, too, was seized by this power of great affection, and I understood why I longed to search and search for adventure. What I'd seen with Armon and Murphy at the edge of the cliffs only gave me more strength to carry on.

"We're nearing the cliffs," he said.

I was surprised to look over and see that we were indeed much closer to the rocks. Everyone on deck seemed to be preparing in one way or another for our departure from the *Warwick Beacon.*

"Find your bag, Alexa. We're soon to leave the Lonely Sea."

I gathered my things quickly and joined Armon near the back of the ship, where he stood with Odessa, Murphy, and Balmoral. Everyone but Armon seemed nervous as they looked at the face of the cliffs, wondering what dangers awaited us as the day unfolded.

"There, to the right," said Balmoral. I strained to see where he was pointing and saw the red flag dangling at the bottom of the rope. Warvold crept up behind us and put his hand on my shoulder.

"Our escape from the sea," he said. "I must say I surprise even myself sometimes."

Roland moved the *Warwick Beacon* closer to the rocks and then told us we'd have to swim the rest of the way.

"She's taken quite a beating already. I'm afraid even a scratch on the bottom might break her to pieces."

Roland was very caring toward the *Warwick Beacon*. It sometimes seemed as though the two of them were married to each other, facing the Lonely Sea together as the days slipped into years.

I took a last bite from the breakfast Roland had given us — dried fish and a crust of bread — and then I asked Warvold who was to go first.

"Why, you, of course," he answered. "Armon can carry you along with the animals. We've already discussed it. He feels quite certain that the rope won't be necessary, though I've warned him he'd better at least tie it around his waist in case he loses his footing."

Armon looked down at us and nodded his approval with a smile. He had a strange contraption made of old sails on his back, and I realized it was there to hold me,

Murphy, and Odessa as he climbed. He bent down low, and Balmoral helped Warvold set Odessa inside the cloth container. She howled and fidgeted, then lay still on one side of Armon's enormous back. I crawled in on the other side and sat down, my legs hanging free in the air. Murphy had it the easiest — he simply jumped onto my lap and scampered along until he sat on Armon's shoulder and dug his claws in for the journey.

"This isn't as exciting as it was the first time," said Murphy. "Without the storm and the uncertainty of Armon's skill, it's almost boring."

Armon smiled and stood up, lifting us high in the air. Then he started over the edge of the boat once more and slipped into the water up to his waist.

"Hang on, everybody," he said. "Off we go."

He began swimming. Odessa whimpered and thrashed as the water came up to our necks.

"Alexa!" cried Warvold. "There's one thing more I need to tell you. It's very important. I'll tell you as soon as we all reach land."

"All right!" I yelled back. It seemed I would never exhaust all the secrets Warvold held.

Before long we were at the cliffs. Armon wrapped the rope around his waist and pulled on it three times. The rope tightened but Armon didn't move. He seemed to be enjoying himself.

"Whoever's up there is probably wondering whether or not they've caught a whale," he said, putting one massive hand around the rope. "If I give it a good pull, do you think they'll come tumbling over the edge?"

We all begged him not to do it, though we knew he was only playing and would never do such a thing.

As he began to climb I had a whirlwind of thoughts running through my head. Could we save Yipes? Who was holding the rope above the mist? When would Elyon speak to me again?

I rolled these thoughts over in my head until we were only a few feet from the mist, and everything started feeling cool and moist. Armon seemed to have mastered climbing the cliffs, moving with great speed and efficiency. The ride was almost serene.

Then something frightening happened. The wind began to blow from the side. At first it was just a steady breeze, but only a few seconds more and it was gusting. Armon held tightly to the wall. The gusts blew harder and harder.

I yelled at Armon, "Why are you waiting? The wind will die off in the mist if you go only a few more steps."

There was a brief silence, followed by a question I hadn't thought of.

"Where's the *Warwick Beacon*, Alexa? I can't turn around to see it."

I swung my head out of the pouch and looked down, hoping to see the boat close by. To my horror it had already moved an alarming distance down the side of the cliff, and it was being pushed farther away with every second. I could barely see Roland and Balmoral fighting with the wheel, trying to right the sails. The wind was ferocious on the water. Warvold stood at the edge of the boat and looked in my direction, hopelessly being carried away on the wind.

"We have to go back, Armon!" I yelled. "They're being blown away!"

Murphy had scampered down my back and lay in my lap out of the wind. Odessa howled as I held Murphy's shivering little body and watched as the *Warwick Beacon* drifted quickly out of sight.

"I can't get down in this driving wind, Alexa." It was Armon, his voice full of distress. "It's getting worse. We'll have to get into the mist if we're going to survive."

Let them go.

It was the voice on the wind saying words I couldn't imagine following. I *needed* Warvold. Without him I was lost.

Armon began climbing cautiously again, taking each footing and handhold with great care. As his first hand disappeared into the mist, a monstrous gust blew in and knocked his feet clear of the cliff.

He lost his grip with one hand, and suddenly we were dangling over the rocks below.

CHAPTER 7

WHAT HAPPENED WHILE WE WERE AWAY

As we swung back and forth in the wind, I looked out into the open water below and found that the *Warwick Beacon* had drifted so far away it was only a speck in the distance. At least Warvold and the rest were spared from having to see us in such peril.

Murphy jumped out of my lap and ran up to Armon's shoulder, digging in deeply with his claws as he went. When he reached his favorite spot he leaned over and, to my astonishment, bit Armon right on the ear.

Armon thrashed his head and screamed, pulling Murphy into the air. But the little squirrel wouldn't let go of Armon's ear. He looked like a large furry earring dangling in the wind.

Armon seemed to come alive though, the pain bringing forth some new rush of energy. He righted his feet under himself, grabbed hold of the cliff with his dangling hand, and quick like a lizard crawled up the rock face. The winds were calm the moment we entered the mist, and things felt under control again.

"Sorry about that," said Murphy. I could see well enough in the mist to find that Armon had taken Murphy by the middle and was holding him out in the air, staring at him. Blood was dripping off the giant's ear, but not as much as I would have thought. Armon's skin was leather thick, and Murphy had only barely broken the surface with his sharp teeth.

"You can set me down now, if you would," said Murphy, his squeaky voice cracking and scared. Armon held him there a little longer.

"That hurt," the giant said. "But it probably saved us."

Armon set Murphy down on his shoulder and turned back to his work at the cliffs.

I was overcome with fear as we went through the mist and into the light of a bright blue day. We were separated from Warvold again, and I felt we'd lost our guide. Then, about twenty feet from the top, I heard a familiar voice that made me feel quite a lot better.

"What in the world is *that* thing?" the voice asked. I looked up and saw Nicolas, Warvold's son, peeking his head over the edge of the cliff. Then another head popped out — to stare down in astonishment. Pervis Kotcher's.

"It's a giant," Pervis said.

"No wonder the rope was so heavy!" said Nicolas. "Is it friendly?"

"Ask him yourself," Pervis offered. I could see from

49

where we hung below that he was fooling with Nicolas. Pervis knew something about giants.

Nicolas leaned out over the cliff and watched as we came closer still, only ten feet from the edge.

"Friend or foe?" asked Nicolas. He was trying to sound brave, but it wasn't working.

"That depends on whether or not you've got any food up there," said Armon, breathing heavy as we neared the end of our climb.

Nicolas smiled down at us, and I began to explain why I was lumbering up the side of a cliff on a giant's back with a wolf and a squirrel as my companions. When we reached the top, Armon stood upright and looked down at Nicolas and Pervis. They both looked up, stunned at the size of this creature. Armon sat down, and I broke free of the pouch and ran to embrace Pervis and Nicolas. It became clear right away that Nicolas was only joking about his concern over Armon; he was aware of giants and ogres just as Pervis was, and though it was a surprise to see Armon, it was one they had hoped for.

"This is a development we hadn't expected," said Nicolas, staring in awe at Armon towering over him. "But it's one we're mighty glad for."

"We'll have to be careful about who sees him in these parts," said Pervis. "He'll have to go the long way 'round."

While they spoke I looked at the place where we stood. It was somewhere on the outskirts of Ainsworth, where large boulders sat scattered all along the cliff's edge. We were hidden for the moment.

"Let's drop the rope and get Warvold up here," said Pervis. "There's no time to lose, and he will have thought of our best course of action to handle a giant in our midst."

"*What?*" I said, surprised. I had been wondering how to tell Pervis and Nicolas that Warvold was alive. Now it seemed that I didn't need to. "How did you know Warvold was still alive?"

Pervis looked back and forth across the faces before him, and then he pointed at Nicolas.

"He told me."

I looked over at Nicolas. He was fidgeting with his hands, a sheepish look on his face. Since Warvold's "death," I'd felt a special closeness to Nicolas. We'd shared letters, and he'd even visited me twice in the past year.

"You knew all along and you didn't tell me?" I said now. It came out more accusingly than I'd wanted it to, but it was hard to hide that my feelings had been hurt.

"I couldn't tell you, Alexa. It would have been too risky with everything at stake." Nicolas walked over to me and knelt down before continuing. The pleading in his eyes made my heart understand, and immediately I was halfway to forgiving him for keeping his secrets.

"I've known all along about both my mother and my father," he explained. "Many times I battled my father to allow me to rescue Mother. And then, after he told me of his plans to go after her, I begged to go along, or at least to go after him, should he fail. But he is a stubborn man, and he has his own ways. My part in this adventure has been to stay home and keep the kingdom safe, to keep things secret. And it was a good thing, too, or many would have perished in Bridewell these past days."

"He's gone," I said, my voice not much more than a whisper.

A shadow passed over Nicolas's features. "What do you mean?"

"Warvold. He's gone. The boat was blown away as we climbed the cliffs. He's not coming back, at least not for a while."

Nicolas looked at the pouch that hid the last Jocasta hanging around my neck. "That's a bit of bad news I hadn't planned for," he mumbled. "Are you certain he hasn't turned back?"

I rolled the pouch over in my hand and recalled the words I'd heard as we hung from the cliff.

Let them go.

"I'm certain."

Nicolas regained his composure and sat on a large stone before recounting all the events that had occurred while I was away. He had told Pervis to be watchful of me, to tell him the moment I vanished from Bridewell. Having heard this news from my father, Pervis raced to

Lunenburg, where Nicolas told him everything he knew (which was a lot more than I'd imagined).

"It was important that we kept things contained to Bridewell to avoid hysteria throughout the kingdom," said Pervis. "I informed my most trusted guards of the danger we might face and sent them far into the Dark Hills to keep watch for anything moving in our direction."

"It's a very good thing we're such a timid people in times such as these," said Nicolas. "The legend of the giants has always been something of a mystery to the people of Bridewell Common. It's talked about more in Ainsworth, where people like such stories. Still, there is a healthy fear of all things outside our kingdom, and a deep longing for the past when my father was still here."

He took a deep breath before continuing. "When we received word from the guards that Grindall and his giants were sleeping in the hills only a day's journey away, I called a meeting in the town square of all the people who remained in Bridewell. Many were already gone. As you know, summer is the time when most are out gathering books for repair. But there were still at least five hundred who remained. We simply had to get them out without alarming the other towns of the approaching danger."

"Ogres," I said. "You called them giants, the beasts that travel with Grindall. Armon is the only giant that remains. The rest are ogres."

Nicolas looked at me strangely, as if I'd made mention

of something of little importance. But it was important to me.

Nicolas went on to tell us that he'd revealed to the townspeople that as Warvold's only son he'd been left with a message from his father. The people, who had once been so enamored of Warvold and who still missed him so much, were very interested in what this message might say.

Now Nicolas pulled a scrap of paper from his vest pocket and read us the note that Warvold had left, the same note he'd read to the people in Bridewell only two days before.

I have given this message to my son, Nicolas, who you can trust. If it is being read to you, then something has happened that requires your immediate action. There is a danger approaching, a danger that is hard to explain and best left unknown. It is a danger that will only last a few days. Then it will pass through and will never be seen or heard from again.

I must ask you to leave Bridewell and go to the neighboring towns in our kingdom until Nicolas summons you back again. Trust me this last time and leave until this danger passes through. Tell no one of this peril, for it will only cause panic throughout the kingdom and bring people where they should not go.

55

Yipes, and I knew we had to rescue him. I had been working on a plan of my own, a plan that meant we'd have to go to Bridewell.

"Warvold and I spoke on the boat, and I know what we must do," I said. Pervis and Nicolas seemed to perk up at this remark. Armon, Murphy, and Odessa remained at my side, quietly listening as things unfolded. It was true I'd spoken to Warvold, so it was only half a lie, but I felt terrible having to tell it.

I continued, "Yipes is held captive by Grindall and the ogres. It would be a tragic mistake to leave him there. The first thing we must do is rescue him."

There was a new look of intensity from the both of them, especially Pervis. I had a plan and our dear friend was imprisoned by our enemy. The motivation they needed had been set in place.

As morning turned to afternoon, we began talking about how we might hide a giant on the road to Bridewell.

CHAPTER 8

RETURN TO
THE TUNNELS

We decided to stay in the Dark Hills while the light of day remained. It was the only way to keep Armon at a safe distance from those who might see him in Ainsworth and Lunenburg. I was very pleased to find that Pervis and Nicolas had brought two horses with them. Murphy and I sat atop one with Pervis in front while Nicolas rode on the other. Armon and Odessa walked. It made for a much easier day of trudging through the Dark Hills. At one point, I walked alongside Odessa alone and we talked of many things — of Sherwin and Darius, the woods and the mountains, and even my secret plans. She was a curious creature, quiet and secretive, not unlike her mate, Darius. I hadn't seen Squire all morning, and I wondered if she'd stayed with Warvold and the others on the *Warwick Beacon*.

Later I talked with Pervis and Nicolas, wondering how they'd known we would arrive as we did at the cliffs. As I might have guessed, my mother had sent word when Renny arrived in Lathbury. Silas Hardy, the mail carrier and friend to my father, had been sent to Bridewell with a message that the *Warwick Beacon* was coming around

"That might not be such a good idea, unless you want them to be stuck out here," I said.

Pervis held the reins and seemed ready to protest before offering a quiet response.

"We're not coming back this way, are we?" he said.

"I'm afraid not," I told him. "We must try to rescue Yipes tonight. After that, we'll be racing for the Sly Field."

Nicolas took both the reins from Pervis in one hand and patted the horses on their noses.

"They know the way home to Lunenburg," Nicolas said. "I'm quite sure they'll find their way by morning." To both horses, he warned, "Stay together now; don't run off in different directions." Then he came around to the side of the larger of the two, and whispered, "She'll follow you." He slapped the horse and off it ran, the smaller one racing behind in the direction of Lunenburg.

As we stood looking into the maze of tunnels that remained in the brush, a thought occurred to me. It was the strangest thing that I hadn't thought of it at all and no one had mentioned it all day.

"Where's my father?" I asked, suddenly concerned for him.

An awkward silence filled the air while Pervis and Nicolas looked at each other as if to decide who would answer my question.

"He was sure you'd return to Bridewell," Pervis finally said. "I tried to make him leave, but he wouldn't."

I pictured ogres climbing over the walls, finding my father alone and helpless.

"You can't have left him there to die?" I pleaded.

Pervis seemed to liven up at my comment.

"You vastly underestimate your father, Alexa. He's not only resourceful, but he knows Bridewell and all its secret places quite well. When we left he was already belowground in the secret tunnels, awaiting your arrival. I told him I'd never bring you back here with those monsters around the place, but he was quite sure you would return whether I liked it or not."

"Did anyone stay with him, or is he all alone?" I asked.

"I'm afraid he's alone, Alexa. He was very persuasive about making sure all my guards were sent away. This was his decision, and he didn't want anyone else put in harm's way."

For the first time I felt regret for my actions. I'd put him in terrible danger.

Nicolas spoke as if he'd read my mind.

"There are some things you have yet to understand, Alexa — things that I think will become clear in the coming days. But you can be sure of one thing: James Daley is doing exactly what he should be doing right now, as are the rest of us, including you."

Murphy jumped into my arms and said to me, "Just think, Alexa. You'll see your father again on this very night!"

Pervis seemed very interested in Murphy, and he walked closer.

"I've been listening to the two of you all day. Is it really true what I've been told? Can you understand what this little creature is saying with all his squeaks and sounds?"

Murphy twitched and jumped and carried on in my arms.

"He says he was digging around in your bag earlier and spied a bag of nuts," I said. "He wants to have some and asks if you might kindly hand them over."

Pervis looked on in astonishment, removed the bag of nuts, and pulled out a nice large one.

"Here you go, little fellow," he said. "That ought to keep you busy for a while." As Murphy chomped away, Pervis shook his head. "Amazing. I thought Nicolas was making a grand joke with me. You really *can* talk to animals, then."

"Let's keep that a secret between just the few of us, shall we?" I said.

Pervis nodded as he crunched on a handful of nuts.

"I can't wait to get to Bridewell," I said, thinking only of my father and Yipes. "Another hour and we can safely move in the dark."

I looked at Armon. His hulking presence cast a shadow big enough for us all to stand in. I knew there was still the black swarm to contend with. I looked into the sky, listening instinctively for the sound of leathery wings on the wind, but there was nothing to be heard.

The hour before dark passed with the making of plans as we sat in a circle eating and drinking, gaining strength for the long night ahead. Nicolas had brought bread and fresh-cooked meat along with a small leather bag full of hard candies — something I hadn't enjoyed in quite a while. It was especially pleasing to watch Murphy eat the candy, his eyes bulging with delight, the sugar sending him into a fit of talking and darting about.

"Is he always like this?" asked Pervis.

We watched as Murphy sniffed and dashed all around us in a fit of activity, then ran up the side of Armon and darted between his shoulders.

"Not always, but most of the time, yes," said Armon, a pleasant air of affection in his voice.

It was decided that Armon was too big to hide or fit into the tunnels as we went about our business in Bridewell. He would travel around in secret and meet us at a place I knew of in the forest. It was somewhere from my past, on the other side of Bridewell — the meadow cast with moonlight where Ander the bear made his home and the forest council met. Armon said he knew how to find it. I only hoped we'd rescue Yipes so he could help me remember how to get there.

I watched Armon as he walked away, sliding back into the darkness from where he'd come to save us only days before. I hadn't realized how comforting his pres-

Only Murphy and I will fit."

63

"I won't allow it," said Pervis, suddenly acting as though I'd tricked him into bringing me to this spot. "I promised your father I wouldn't let you return here, so I'm already in trouble. I can't let you go alone, Alexa. If something happens to you, I'll never forgive myself."

I had expected this response and had planned my answer carefully as we walked through the night. I was about to tell a truly awful lie, one that I thought might be my undoing. But I knew of no other way to rescue Yipes than to sneak back into Bridewell through the tiny opening he and I had used to escape on our way to Castalia.

"Do you know what's inside this pouch?" I asked Pervis, holding the hidden Jocasta out to him.

"Only that what you carry is very important, and that you alone must carry it," he answered.

"This is the very last Jocasta. It's what makes it possible for me to understand what Murphy and Odessa say — and it's also what makes it possible for me to hear another voice as well, a voice on the wind."

"Elyon?" Pervis whispered in disbelief. I nodded, and then I told my lie.

"Elyon has told me to enter the city through a hole Yipes and I used to sneak away. As I said before, it's too small for any of us but Murphy and me. So I *must* leave the rest of you behind."

"What?" whispered Pervis, a bit louder than he should

64

have. We all crouched down in the bushes and watched the tower, but nothing seemed to stir near the flame on the wall.

"I'm sorry, Pervis. I really am — but we have to do this the way I've been told."

He shook his head back and forth and looked to Nicolas for support, but it seemed as though I'd convinced Warvold's son that this was the only way.

"James will be down there waiting for her," said Nicolas. "He'll be angry with you, but Alexa will have him for protection. I'm just glad Grindall knows nothing of the tunnels below the city."

"Couldn't I fit in that hole?" asked Pervis. "I'm not that much bigger than you are, Alexa."

This was something I hadn't thought of, and it got me to wondering.

"I don't think you'll fit, but I can't be completely sure about it."

"I'm going with you. I want to at least try."

I knew by looking at Nicolas that he would never fit, and Odessa was such a large wolf I couldn't imagine her making it inside. But Pervis was a small man, and he was very determined to protect me. It was unlikely, but I had to allow him an attempt.

"You wait here," Pervis ordered Nicolas and Odessa. "If I can't make it in I'll be back in a few minutes. If I fit inside . . ." Pervis paused, thinking. "Well, I suppose you

the room. If he got stuck it would be a long, dark night trying to get him out.

"Oh, dear." It was Pervis, and I had the distinct feeling that he'd gotten himself lodged in the tunnel. I put my arms in and tried to grasp for his hands. I was able to touch his fingers but only barely, so I couldn't pull him into the room. He was indeed trapped.

I turned and sat against the wall, where Murphy jumped on my lap. I couldn't see him — I couldn't see anything. Pervis was stuck in the hole, and I couldn't help him or find my way around. Things weren't going very well, and as I sat there wondering what to do, things managed to get even worse.

From somewhere down a distant tunnel, a light was coming my way, flickering and bobbing back and forth as if whatever carried it were clumsily racing through. Had Grindall known of this place all along and expected my arrival?

It was so dark that I couldn't see Murphy as he dashed from my lap and sniffed the air.

"We'd better hide," he said. "Something smells terrible . . . and it's coming this way."

I felt the goose bumps rising on my scrawny arms. I yelped quietly as Murphy brushed against my legs and scampered back into my lap. We were trapped, and we couldn't even see to hide. All we could make out was the light bouncing miserably on the walls in the distance, coming closer.

CHAPTER 9

·OUT ·OF THE DARKNESS

"Pervis," I whispered, "you've got to get out! You've got to go back."

As the light came closer I was able to see a little of the space around me. The board we'd pushed out into the room lay next to me. Seeing it, I realized there was only one place we could go that might hide us from whatever was coming our way.

"I'm really stuck, Alexa." It was Pervis, whispering from the hole.

"It's all right; just stay quiet. We're coming in with you."

"What?"

There was no time to answer him as I picked up the board and stood it up next to the hole. Murphy jumped in first.

"Come on, Alexa, hurry!" Murphy squeaked.

I got down on my hands and knees with my feet facing the hole. It was awkward, but I was able to back myself inside, feet first. Then, lying there, I picked up the board and pulled it back into place over the hole just as the light reached the room.

Pervis was so close that my feet were right in his face, and I had the feeling that I was probably pushing my heel into his nose. Murphy was doing his best to stay still down near my legs, but sitting still was very hard for him. His twitches tickled the backs of my knees, and I had to struggle not to move my legs in response.

I couldn't see anything in the room with the board back in place, and I began to worry as my grip on the board lessened and I slid forward little by little toward the room. Murphy squeezed up onto my back and made his way up next to my head, where he sniffed.

"No worries," he whispered into my ear. He leaned into the board and pushed it free into the room. I slid halfway out of the hole, staring at the ground in front of me, waiting for an ogre to attack.

Two arms grabbed hold of me by the middle and lifted me out of the hole and into the air. I opened my eyes and stared in disbelief.

It was my father, a big grin on his face. He pulled me into a warm embrace.

"Father!" I said. But that was all I could muster. I simply felt around his large arms and pulled free to look at him once more. It was really him, looking at me with wonder in his eyes, so happy to find that I was safe and unharmed.

"It's so very good to see you, Alexa," he said as he set me down and bent on one knee. "I've been thinking the most terrible thoughts these past days. But you're all right after all."

"At least for the moment I am," I said. I didn't have the heart to tell him I was afraid there was quite a lot more for me to do before I'd consider myself safe again.

"What would be the odds of someone helping me get free?" It was Pervis, still struggling to remove himself from where he was wedged solidly in the hole.

"It's Pervis — he's stuck in there." I pointed to the hole, and my father got up and poked his head inside the dark opening.

"Is that you in there, Pervis? All those extra helpings of potatoes finally got the best of you."

"Very funny," answered Pervis.

"I really ought to leave you in there, since you deliberately disobeyed my order not to bring Alexa back here."

"She made me do it!" he yelled desperately.

My father looked over at me. "It's true she can be very persuasive. Still, I think I'll leave you there awhile. Maybe it will harden your resolve in case you're tempted to disobey me again."

My father was clowning with him. I began to feel sorry for Pervis, all wedged in there as he was.

"Father, Yipes is in Bridewell. He is a prisoner of Grindall, and we've come to save him. That's the only reason we've come back."

This remark seemed to sober my father's playfulness. He immediately put his arms into the hole, took hold of Pervis's hands, and pulled hard.

"*Ooooowww!*" Pervis yelled.

70

My father seemed to take this as a reasonable suggestion, though he remained wary of Murphy and curious about what was going on.

"Fine, then. Have your fun if you want to, but you're not going up there. It's far too dangerous with those ogres around the place. I'll go."

I wasn't sure what I should do. I couldn't let him get anywhere near Victor Grindall. It was far too dangerous.

He'll go by way of the courtyard. You must let him.

It was the voice, once again telling me something I didn't want to hear. How could I send my own father into a place where monsters waited — monsters that had already taken John Christopher from me?

"We'll both go," said Pervis, shifting his eyes between me and my father. "The two of us can do it while Alexa waits down here for us."

My father looked at Pervis in the gloom of the tunnel, and the two of them seemed to agree that it was the only way.

"I came into the tunnels through the guard's entrance hidden in the courtyard," my father told us. "I've been hiding down here since Grindall arrived, so I don't know where they are. We'll go back the way I came in and scout around for where they might be keeping Yipes. My bet is they've put him in one of the prison cells in the basement of Renny Lodge. We should be able to sneak down there at this hour and look around."

"What if there's an ogre guarding the basement?" I asked.

Pervis and my father looked at each other and shrugged.

"We'll have to cross that bridge when we come to it," said my father. "If we can't rescue him at least we'll know where he is. That's a first step."

My father led us through the tunnels and into a room where he'd stored up some provisions and another lamp. He lit the lamp and trimmed it low, then gave me a very firm look.

"You stay here, Alexa. There's nothing you can do but get yourself into trouble if you try to follow us."

I nodded and sat down on his makeshift bed, hopeful that they would find Yipes somewhere within Bridewell without encountering ogres.

Pervis and my father took one of the two lamps, along with swords my father had brought down with him.

As they turned to go, I said, "Father?"

"Yes?" He turned back and looked at me.

"Please be careful. If you even see an ogre, run for your life. They're impossible to stop." I knew the ogres could be defeated, but I wanted Pervis and my father as far away from danger as I could get them. If my father knew that a knife to the top of the head could kill an ogre, he'd waste no time in trying it.

"There's nothing to worry about. I've got Pervis to

velvety couches and the high ceilings. That's where he would be plotting and planning, his awful ogres milling around in the shadows near him, waiting for me to come to him and give him the stone.

But where would he put Yipes?

CHAPTER 10

THE LIBRARY

There had been a long walk through the tunnels, winding this way and that, before we found ourselves at the bottom of the ladder, looking up into the shadows. I took a long, quiet moment to consider the day's events. The questions were coming faster than answers, and my head was swimming with anxiety. Where were Warvold and my other friends? What was my father encountering? Where would this adventure lead? Where was Yipes? Standing there at the bottom of the ladder I soon realized that the only way I would find the answers to any of my questions was to keep on with the journey. Stopping only left me worn out with my own thoughts. And so I climbed.

We reached the top of the ladder. I was about to open the trapdoor that led into the library. Murphy sat happily on my shoulder, wondering what might be waiting for us inside.

"Are you ready to bite some ogres?" I said.

"I can hardly wait." He was a silly little squirrel, but he certainly was brave.

"Here we come, Yipes," I whispered. "Prepare to be rescued by a fur ball and a lanky thirteen-year-old."

I turned the latch, and it clicked ever so quietly. Then the door swung open into the darkness of the tunnel. It no longer squeaked when it opened — Pervis had seen to that last summer when he'd discovered it and forbade me from ever using it again. Though he kept the key and never used the secret door, he couldn't help making the rusty hinges right again.

My favorite chair remained in its usual place, with its back pushed up against the trapdoor, concealing the opening to all my adventures. It smelled a little ogrish inside, but not so much that I thought we might find them sitting around reading books. This was probably the last place they would choose to spend time.

I placed my hands against the back of the chair and braced myself, ready to push it out of the way so we could enter the library.

"Wait," whispered Murphy. He was right next to my ear, so I knew immediately to remain still. Something was near.

A black leather-booted foot hit the old wooden floor of the library, then another. The feet had been propped up on the box where I'd propped up my own feet so often. The boots were not huge, like those of an ogre, and they had silver rings that clanged as they hit the floorboards. A book was placed heavily on the wood box in front of the chair, and whoever it was stood, advanced to the one window in the room, and grumbled. A chain rattled on the floor as he went.

"Where is she? Where is that insolent girl with my stone?"

It was Victor Grindall who'd been sitting in my chair, reading my books, and kicking up his feet on my wooden box. I was very glad then that Pervis had oiled the hinges on the trapdoor! Murphy and I stayed perfectly still, waiting to see what Grindall would do.

I listened as he slumped back down in the chair and picked up his book once more, propping up his feet as he flipped through the pages.

"She must show herself by tomorrow or I'll have to throw you out the window," Grindall threatened, his wicked voice echoing off the walls in the library. "That might not be so bad after all. I'm sick and tired of dragging you around."

"You should throw me out now. She's not coming here. She knows better than to risk it." It was Yipes! He was in the room. It sounded as though he was sitting on the windowsill.

Grindall laughed out loud, a cackle of a laugh that angered me so much I wanted to push away the chair and take him on. The chain rattled on the floor as Grindall played with it in his hand.

"Oh, she'll come. I have little doubt of that. And when she does, I'll kill you both." He laughed again and seemed to settle into the chair. I wished I could see Yipes and know that he was unharmed.

"The two of them must be chained together." It was Murphy, whispering in my ear again. "Why don't I sneak

79

my nostrils filled with that wretched odor of rotting flesh. An ogre was approaching, and he seemed to be in a rush.

When the ogre rounded the corner I could see his huge feet approaching Grindall, trapped in worn leather boots. The feet alone were enough to scare me.

"What is it now?" Grindall asked, annoyed.

The ogre grunted and wheezed, the gurgling sound of his voice a terrible reminder of what would happen to Armon if the black swarm ever found him.

"Interesting," said Grindall. "You're sure you smelled something? Something not quite right?"

The ogre spoke excitedly again as Grindall's feet came crashing off the wooden box onto the floor in front of me.

"She is here then, in the lodge, looking for her little friend," said Grindall. "Well, let's make sure she finds him, shall we?"

Grindall stood, and I heard the chain rattling, a key being inserted into a lock.

"I'm going to look for her, and when I find her I'll bring her here," said Grindall. The ogre seemed to be wrapping the chain around his massive waist. The lock was clamped shut once more.

"Don't eat him! I want her to observe as we put an end to her friend."

Grindall stomped away into the library, and his footsteps were soon lost in the distance. The ogre sniffed the air all around him while I quietly closed the trapdoor, sealing us in. I stepped down the ladder seven or eight rungs and waited, the low-burning lamp at my side.

From where I stood lower in the tunnel I could still hear the ogre smelling the air, searching for something that did not seem quite right. I listened as he grabbed hold of the chair and thrust it forward out of his way. It sounded as though the chair had tipped over and probably lay on its front on the wooden floor of the library. The chains rattled and the ogre grunted, but he seemed to accept that nothing lay behind the chair but a wall. Next he trudged over to the windowsill and took an interest in Yipes. I hoped he wouldn't rip open the cage and make a late dinner out of him.

I climbed back up the ladder and listened at the secret door, not sure what to do. I wondered where Pervis and my father were, if they were safe or if they'd been captured. It was hard to imagine a more perilous feeling than the one I had hanging there from the ladder. I wanted only to be home by the sea, mending books, my world put back together again.

With the chair thrown away from the wall, I couldn't open the door again without being seen. I was at a dead end, my friend locked in a cage and chained to an ogre, an eager squirrel my only help. As I stood listening, it sounded as though the ogre sat down on the floor of the library near the window, grunting and sniffing, his breath labored in what sounded like a wet sponge of lungs.

Yipes began to taunt the beast as he sat against the

"I wouldn't do that if I were you. Grindall won't be happy if you harm me," said Yipes. I could barely hear him through the trapdoor and the stone of the wall. "Besides, with your back turned, someone might *open a trapdoor* and jump out after you!"

What was he thinking? Could he mean for me to open the door for some unthinkable reason? I couldn't understand what Yipes was up to, and I stood on the ladder completely baffled by the unseen events unfolding only a few feet away.

The ogre yanked on the chain — pulling Yipes back into the room — and slammed the cage back down on the sill, shaking it mercilessly.

"Trust me!" Yipes called out.

The ogre was becoming angrier and angrier as I reached my shaking hand out for the latch and took hold of it. I turned it just so and I heard the quiet click of metal against metal.

And then I opened the door.

CHAPTER 11

THE DANGLING CHAIN

As the secret door opened, the air from the library escaped into the tunnel. It was an evil smell, so thick it was like a dark cloud poisoning everything it touched. I saw what I had previously only imagined: The chair was flipped onto its side, pushed into the corner. The ogre stood at the windowsill shaking the cage that held Yipes. The chain was wrapped around the ogre's waist and secured with a lock, the other end attached to the cage where Yipes was bouncing inside.

"You see there," said Yipes, pointing in my direction as he was thrown all around inside the small cage. "I told you there were secret places."

Unbelievable! I began to think Yipes had gone mad, driven crazy by the long days of companionship with Victor Grindall and his ogres.

At first the ogre thought it was a trick and wouldn't look at me, but his curiosity quickly overcame him. The ogre turned and looked at me, my head and shoulders in plain view, and for a moment he seemed not to believe what he was seeing. He shook his head as he'd shook the cage, gobs of thick drool spewing into the room. I was frozen with fear, unable to move, as I watched Murphy dart out between us and onto the sill.

The ogre paid Murphy no attention as he turned his back on Yipes and cackled in my direction. Then he started for me, a grand prize for his master within his reach.

As he turned, the chain followed him like a slithering black snake, winding behind him where it ended at the cage. The window where the ogre had stood was suddenly filled with a great shadow, but it was quickly blocked from my view as the ogre bent over and reached down his awful hand to grab hold of me. I was too afraid to think, too afraid to try to escape. I simply waited for the ogre to pull me into the room and take me to Grindall. A familiar feeling of hopelessness and failure flooded me as the last Jocasta was about to be taken from me and put into the hands of my enemy. I could already hear Victor Grindall's laugh echoing through Renny Lodge.

What happened next was mostly a blur, something I felt even more than I saw. It happened very quickly and without warning. I heard the sound of breaking chains and the cage falling to the floor, which made the ogre turn from me just as he was about to put his hand on my shoulder and drag me into the room. The ogre was pulled back violently toward the window by the chain wrapped around his waist. He made an awful sound when the chain jerked tight and pulled him off his feet, the sickly air and liquid flying from his lungs in a great snorting howl. The ogre was stunned but not destroyed, and as I looked on in astonishment I saw that it was Armon who had come through the large open window. He took hold of the ogre and threw him against the wall, then dragged him to the window and threw him out.

Armon looked back at me for a moment and smiled, then he, too, headed for the window to face the ogre outside. I jumped from my perch on the ladder into the room as Armon disappeared. Advancing to the window, I watched as Armon finished off the ogre and ran for the wall. Then I heard not one but two terrible sounds.

The black swarm was coming from somewhere overhead, and in the night sky I watched as Armon scaled the ivy-covered wall, trying to outrun the furious sound of bat wings in the air. He was so fast it took him only a moment to find his way to the top. He took no time to look back at us as he dropped over the other side and was gone. I listened as the bats came overhead. I watched the stars disappear, the night turned completely black by the mass of dark creatures. They flew over the wall and after Armon. I shuddered with fear for him.

I had little time to worry about this, however, for another noise came almost at the same time as the black swarm. It was Grindall entering the library with ogres in tow, and his voice was filled with rage.

Yipes, sitting in the cage at my feet, hastily said, "Alexa, now might be a good time to make our exit."

"What shall we do? We're trapped!" I said.

"Take hold of the cage and carry me into the tunnel. Quickly now!"

I did as I was told, carrying the heavy cage with the broken end of the chain rattling behind me until I reached the opening. I ran in front of the cage and through the secret door, grabbed hold of the ladder, and yanked on the chain, unsure whether or not I could hold the weight of Yipes dangling from one arm. Murphy, holding on to the outside of the cage with his claws, came right into the tunnel with Yipes.

The cage fell free into the darkness beneath me, and I yelped in pain when its full weight found the end of the falling chain and nearly jerked me clean off the ladder into the air. The chain slipped quickly through my fingers for seven or eight links, then slowed as I tightened my grip, and finally stopped with Yipes dangling back and forth below me.

It took every ounce of strength I had not to let go. Murphy jumped from the cage and held on to the ladder as the chain started slipping slowly through my fingers again. Yipes was dangling high above the ground, and I was close to dropping him.

I watched and listened as things unfolded out of my control all around me. The secret door was still wide open, revealing us to anyone who might look my way. Grindall and the ogres were about to turn the corner, but I couldn't close the door — I held the ladder with one hand and the cage with the other. I was helpless to conceal our escape. At the same moment that Grindall came around the corner, Murphy reached the top of the ladder. He jumped to the trapdoor — which swung free inside the tunnel — then pushed with his tail against the wall. Murphy held on to the back of the little door, and when he pushed with his tail the door swung shut. I watched through the last crack of light as Grindall and the ogres came fuming around the corner.

I tried desperately not to make a sound, but the chain was starting to dig into my hand as it kept sliding slowly through my fingers. I was left with about a foot of chain links yet to go as Yipes hung four or five feet below me. I could hear Grindall and the ogres cursing and yelling in a terrible fury, trying to figure out what had happened. Yipes was gone, and an ogre was dead outside. It gave me some pleasure and renewed strength to think of how angry Grindall must have been as he looked at the scene before him.

"What's happened?" he screamed. "I don't understand!"

He was yelling into the night sky through the window. I'd never heard him so completely outraged.

"It's that girl. It's Alexa," he said, his raging replaced by a malevolent, slow drawl. "But how?"

I couldn't hold the chain any longer. It began to slip through my fingers faster than before, only inches left

88

until it slid out of my hand entirely and Yipes fell with a crash that would surely alert Grindall to the secret door.

"Hold on, Alexa," whispered Murphy. "Only a little longer."

"Search this library!" shouted Grindall. "Tear it all down book by book if you have to. If you can smell them they must be hiding in here somewhere."

I was at once relieved and heartbroken as I heard the shelves start to fall, books flying everywhere, the ogres tearing my wonderful library to pieces. As I finally lost my grip on the chain, I listened to it free-fall through the air, a light clanging in the air around me, and then a great crash as Yipes hit the dirt floor and the chain rattled behind the cage like a dinner bell.

"Stop!" yelled Grindall. I was already moving down the stairs, quietly making my escape with Murphy perched on my shoulder. The sound of ogres walking around above was like a terrible, thundering sky, their weight almost too much for the old wooden floor of the library to hold.

"Stop moving, you fools!" said Grindall. "I heard something."

All was quiet above as I reached the bottom of the ladder and held the lamp over the cage. Yipes was still locked inside, though the cage itself was badly bent on one corner.

"That hurt," whispered Yipes.

"*Shhhhhh*," said Murphy in response, and the three of us sat with only the sound of our breath between us.

"Back to work with you! Keep looking." Grindall had tired of listening, and the ogres were tearing at the shelves once more.

"We'd better get moving," said Murphy.

I set the lamp on top of the cage and took hold of the chain, dragging Yipes on the floor. It was hard work — very slow going — but it wasn't long before the sounds of the library being torn apart were only a whisper somewhere behind us.

"You're heavy for such a little man," I said, huffing as I stopped to rest. Yipes had his fingers through the cage to hold the lamp so it wouldn't topple over. I noticed then that Murphy was doing his best to push the cage from behind.

"Thank you for the help, Murphy," I said. It was unlikely that he was actually doing much good, but I had to commend his effort.

"You saved me," said Yipes, tears welling up in his eyes. He was looking back and forth between the two of us.

"Think nothing of it," said Murphy. "It was quite a good time we had doing it."

I smiled and allowed myself a moment of peace knowing that Yipes — although locked in a cage I couldn't get him out of — was unharmed and in good spirits. My fingers were small enough that I could easily fit them into the cage, and I poked them in. He touched his tiny fingers to mine, and we both knew the gesture was — at least for now — the closest thing to a welcoming embrace we would be allowed.

"We have to get out of here as fast as we can," I said. "I fear Grindall won't stop until he's found this place."

As I took hold of the chain and began pulling again, something occurred to me — even if I could drag Yipes all the way to the ladder that led to the outside, I wouldn't be able to get Yipes up and out of the tunnel. This was beginning to seem like a typical day — Yipes in a cage, the library ripped apart, the fate of Armon, my father, and Pervis unknown . . . and a long, hard journey ahead of me.

CHAPTER 12

ESCAPE FROM
THE TUNNELS

I hadn't been down this particular tunnel in a long time, and I'd forgotten what a difficult walk it was. The first lengthy stretch was not level — it was uphill, and pulling the cage with Yipes in it was backbreaking work. When I'd traveled here before, on my first trip outside the walls, I'd managed the entire walk in about twenty minutes. Tonight it would take hours, and even then I'd be stuck at the bottom of a tall ladder with no way to lift out the cage.

At the top of the ladder would be the wooden door that Yipes had once guided me through. It would be out in the open, but far enough from Bridewell that we wouldn't be seen as long as we reached it before light. From there we would need to travel carefully into the forest and find the place where the forest council was held, the place where Ander the bear made his home. He would be some help to me if only I could make it that far.

I wondered how Armon, Odessa, and Nicolas were faring, but mostly I thought of my father and hoped he and Pervis were safe in Bridewell. My great fear was that they were still within the walls looking for me, thinking

I'd found myself in trouble and putting their lives in danger even as I'd already escaped with Yipes. Still, if they *had* gotten free of Bridewell, it was better that they weren't with me. There were many dangerous paths to come, and I had a terrible feeling that anyone traveling with me was putting his or her life in grave danger.

An hour passed, and then another. Yipes chattered on to keep me company as I stayed quiet, conserving my energy and focusing on the task of getting us at least as far as the ladder. I was spurred on by the thought of ogres tearing their way through the wall that held the secret door and chasing us down the tunnels until we were overtaken and returned to Grindall.

"I think we're getting close," said Murphy. He darted ahead in the dark, and I realized then that the lamp wasn't providing much light. Yipes saw me looking at it.

He shifted his weight in the cage and stared up at the lamp. "I turned it down as far as it would go to save fuel. It's nearly out." As if on cue, the light began to sputter and shrink even more. A moment later it went out entirely, and we were left in complete darkness.

"Is it just me, or does it seem as though things are getting more difficult all the time?" I asked.

"Just don't get turned around and head in the wrong direction," answered Yipes. "If you keep going straight ahead we should be to the end soon."

Murphy scuttled up beside me and brushed my feet, startling me as he always did in the dark.

"Sorry about that," he said. "I really must learn to let you know I'm coming."

"How much farther?" I asked. I was so tired I wasn't sure if I could pull the cage much more.

"It's just up there a little, maybe five minutes if you really put your back into it," Murphy replied.

Five more minutes of dragging the cage in the dirt sounded harder than climbing to the top of Mount Laythen, but I put the chain over my shoulder and started pulling again. Every muscle ached, and my hands stung with blisters from gripping the rough chain for so long. I stumbled into a wall and lost my grip on the chain, picked it up, and kept going in the dark. I felt as if I was sleepwalking, aimlessly trudging along in a nightmare that would never stop.

Thankfully, only a few minutes later my journey came to an end. I dropped the chain and felt the welcome rungs of the ladder and the cool earth of the walls around it. I sat down and rested, and it crossed my mind then that I could have taken the Jocasta out of its hiding place and used it for light.

I decided to pull it out and look at it, something I hadn't done in quite a while.

The moment it was out in the open air, the space we were in grew sharp with orange light. It was like a fire in my hand shooting flames on every wall. The light sped so far down the tunnel it scared me. It was as though the light were made of liquid and would travel like a wave all the way back into the library until Grindall saw it out-lined against the secret door.

"That is quite the Jocasta," said Yipes. "Maybe you should keep it hidden in such a dark place."

I fumbled with the leather pouch and put the Jocasta back inside, but I left the top of the pouch open. The orange glow was contained, and I could point it wherever I chose in a way I'd never imagined. I pointed up the ladder to the door above and stood up.

"I'm going to leave you here and see if I can find help somewhere above," I said. "I hope I've grown enough since the last time I was here to lift that door and get out."

I was drained of so much energy that I had to stop every few rungs and rest, making sure my footing was solid as I went. When I finally reached the top, I took hold of the pouch around my neck and pulled. The leather string tightened around the Jocasta, and darkness returned.

"Okay, Alexa," I said out loud. "You can do this. One big push is all it will take."

Murphy had ridden up with me on my shoulder, and in the darkness I heard him leap from his perch and stand on the top rung of the ladder. I bent down my head and put my shoulder against the big door. Then I pushed with all my might.

It moved — only a little at first. But when I saw faint light creeping into the tunnel, I pushed even harder, until the opening was big enough for me to fit through. Murphy darted into the opening and hopped uncontrollably, yelling for me to keep pushing. I gave one last thrust, and the door jumped off my shoulder a few inches while I leaped for the opening.

I was hoping things wouldn't get any worse, but my strength wasn't enough to carry me all the way through to the outside. The door crashed back down and landed firmly on my back, pinning me between two worlds. I yelped but did not scream, the weight of the door not enough to really hurt me. I squirmed and tried to get free, but I had reached the end of my strength. My legs dangled behind me, and I laid my head on the cool earth, completely exhausted.

"How's it going up there?" It was Yipes yelling from somewhere far below in the tunnel. "I see a bit of light creeping in. Dawn is coming."

His words startled me back to life. I tried to look behind me and see the walls of Bridewell in the distance.

"Murphy, do you see the walls?" I asked.

"I do, and there are ogres at the towers. I don't think they can see this far, but I can't be sure. Stay still."

Murphy ran away into the nearby trees, and I lost sight of him. The best thing I could do was to remain still, so I put my head back down and hoped the light of day wouldn't come on too quickly. I moved my head as close to the opening in the door as I could and tried to talk to Yipes.

"I'm stuck, Yipes, and the sun is coming up. I don't know what to do."

"Oh," replied Yipes. "That's *very* unfortunate. Are you hurt?"

"No, not really, but I can't get free."

There was a long silence from below, and I wondered what Yipes was thinking. I heard rustling in the underbrush near a stand of trees outside, and a moment later Murphy was back . . . and he had someone else with him.

"It really is her! I can't believe it." It was a rabbit, one I'd met before.

"Malcolm, is that you?" I asked.

"Yes, ma'am. It's a pleasure to hear your voice." He hopped back and forth over my back and then came back around and sat in front of me. "*Hmmmm*. This *is* a problem, isn't it? We need someone bigger to help us."

"That's very smart of you, Malcolm. It's getting heavier on my back, and it's starting to really hurt. Can you find someone to help me?"

Malcolm seemed to stew on the thought for a moment. He was a very clever rabbit, but I was worried he would take too long in figuring out a way to get me free.

Finally, his eyes brightened. "Yes! There *is* someone. It won't take but a moment to fetch him. Just wait here, and I'll come back."

Malcolm and Murphy darted off into the trees like two giddy dogs chasing a stick. "Hurry!" I called after them.

When they returned a few minutes later, the sun was coming up fast, and it was almost fully light outside.

There were three of them now. Murphy was the smallest, then Malcolm. My face must have given away my despair at the sight of the third.

"Not big enough for you?" said Malcolm, an air of defeat in his voice. He had found Beaker the raccoon, who stood before me lolling from side to side, assessing the situation. The three of them put together were no match for the door, and it was starting to feel even heavier on my back.

"What's going on up there?" Yipes hollered from below. Malcolm and Beaker scattered into the underbrush until I told them it was only Yipes. This seemed to excite them even more as they talked among themselves about how to free me.

"This is hopeless," I said. I hung in the morning air, my breathing becoming harder and harder as the weight of the door worked against my back. I was getting weaker as the day was getting brighter, and I felt certain we were about to be discovered.

"How long were you planning to hang around up here?"

It was a voice from the ladder behind me, and it startled both me and the animals. Malcolm and Beaker were darting in every direction looking for cover — bumping into each other as they dashed from side to side — but Murphy just stood there and spoke a wonderful word that put a smile on my face.

"Pervis?"

"*What?*" I said, trying to swing my head around to where I could see.

"It's Pervis Kotcher!" cried Murphy.

"Are you hurt, Alexa?" It was indeed Pervis, standing below me on the ladder, pushing my feet and legs aside so that he could get right up close to the door that pinned me firmly on the ground.

"I am *so* glad to see you," I answered. "How did you find us?"

"Never mind about that. I need to know — are you hurt?"

"Only my pride," I answered. "Although this door is quite heavy, and I can't get free of it."

Pervis sighed in relief, then took a moment to decide how he would proceed.

"You said you wouldn't leave the tunnels. See what happens when you disobey?"

There was a silence then, and I thought he was looking below, trying to figure out what we should do.

"But you did rescue Yipes, and I must say I find that completely unbelievable. How do you do these things, Alexa Daley?"

I stammered, trying to think what to say, but he didn't give me a chance to answer. Instead, he pushed ahead with a plan to get me free of the door.

"We're going to have to take a chance and make a run

for the trees. I'll lift the door enough for you to get out, then you run with all your might for the grove. Don't look back until you're safely hidden away."

"What about you and Yipes?" I asked, not wanting to leave them behind in the tunnels.

"I don't have the tools we'll need to get Yipes out of the cage," he answered. "I'll have to lift him out and then carry him to safety."

Pervis paused for a moment as Malcolm and Beaker came bouncing back to the door and skittered around nervously.

"Do you have your spyglass, Alexa?" asked Pervis.

I nodded.

"When you get to the stand of trees, use it to survey the walls of Bridewell. I'll bring up Yipes and hold him here until I see Malcolm come darting out into the open. That will be the signal."

"All right — but you'll need to run as fast as you can with that cage. I don't think you'll have much time to reach the grove."

Pervis nodded and started down the ladder.

"Pervis?" I said.

He stopped and looked up at me. "What?"

"Where's my father?"

It was a question I had been afraid to ask.

"I don't know, Alexa. We split up after we entered Bridewell. He was going for the smoking room and I went around the courtyard. When I heard all the ruckus in the library, I just knew you'd used that secret door. I thought maybe I'd find you down here."

He sighed deeply and touched me on the leg.

"He can take care of himself, Alexa. Right now we have to get you and Yipes out of here."

"Before we go on you have to promise me something," I said.

"What's that?"

"You have to go back and find him."

Pervis seemed to mull over my request before answering.

"All right, I'll do it. As long as I have you safe in the trees and away from Grindall and the ogres, I'll go back for him."

I felt relieved — not only would he go back and find my father, but he would be safe from traveling the dangerous road that lay ahead of me. Pervis inched up a little farther on the ladder and put his shoulder into the door.

"Malcolm — can you see the guard tower?" I asked.

"Oh, yes, indeed I can. I eat many carrots. Carrots are good for eyesight, you know? I can see quite a long ways on a clea —"

"Malcolm! Just tell me if it's clear to go or not," I said.

"Oh, sorry, I didn't mean to get carried away." He peered out along the walls of Bridewell for a long moment, then turned back to me.

"It's clear!" he shouted.

I relayed the message to Pervis, and he wasted no time in pushing up the door enough to let me out. It felt wonderful to have the weight off my back. I quickly darted free, then ran for the trees as fast and as low as I could. Malcolm, Beaker, and Murphy zigzagged in front of me, moving from clump to clump in the underbrush.

When we arrived in the grove of trees, I crouched low and took out my spyglass, aiming it at the walls of Bridewell. There on the closest tower stood an ogre, staring out into the Dark Hills. As I watched, another ogre arrived at the tower and looked toward the grove of trees. I stayed very still until the two ogres began to talk. Then I looked back at the trapdoor I'd been freed of.

Pervis had yet to arrive, so I waited, whispering in the trees.

"Have you seen anyone else out here?" I asked Malcolm and Beaker.

"No," Beaker reported. "But Ander has been keeping us busy on the watch. We all smelled something rotten when those creatures took over Bridewell. And it was very strange how Bridewell emptied out. We keep a close eye on the walled city. It seems to be a place where a great many important things take place."

There was a nervous pause from the animals, and then Malcolm added something more.

"Things aren't as they used to be in the forest, Alexa. Things are . . . well, they're different. You'll see."

I asked him what he meant, but he wouldn't tell me

anything else. My thoughts drifted to Armon, my father, Warvold, Nicolas — everything was coming unraveled. It seemed so many of the people I loved were in grave danger, and I wondered how things could ever be put back together again.

The door tipped open slightly, and I knew that Pervis had arrived with Yipes at the top of the ladder. Peering through my spyglass I saw with some relief that the two ogres were arguing, pointing into the Dark Hills and pushing at each other.

"Go, Malcolm! Now!"

Malcolm was momentarily stunned and darted around in circles in the trees. Then he found his bearings and hopped quickly toward the door where Pervis and Yipes lay hidden.

The door flew open, and the cage was set outside in the open. Then Pervis emerged, and the door disappeared from sight, back into its resting place on the ground. Pervis took hold of the cage and started running across the open toward the trees with Malcolm leading the way. It was a mighty task for a small man like Pervis, but he managed to run quite fast with his arms wrapped around the cage.

I looked into my spyglass again and watched as the ogres continued to look out into the Dark Hills. One of them turned toward the courtyard, and the other crept down the side of the tower back into Bridewell. The remaining ogre turned then, looked directly at me, then scanned the forest to my right.

When I pulled the spyglass down to see where Pervis and Yipes were, I couldn't find them.

"Where are they?" I asked.

"Down here!" answered Murphy. He was scampering down the line of trees to where Pervis had hidden in the low bushes.

"Good work, Alexa," said Pervis. We were all safe in the grove, and we carefully moved farther back into the trees, where we sat in a circle.

"It feels so good to sit down and rest," I said, fully exhausted.

"I can't tell you how much I would like to stand up," said Yipes. "They only let me out of here to go to the bathroom, and I haven't done that in quite a while."

I smiled as Pervis took the cage off into the trees where the two of them would figure out some way for Yipes to relieve himself.

In the morning light, I remembered how much I loved the sound of wind through the trees. I laid back and closed my eyes, and I was comforted by the sound of a million tiny leaves dancing on a summer morning.

As the world spun out of control all around me, I drifted into a deep sleep and dreamed of animals and giants. And I heard the voice of Elyon through the wind.

I am sorry, Alexa. Your father's time has come. He will leave the land of the living before the sun rises twice more.

I woke with a scream and found that things were not as I'd left them.

104

PART 2

CHAPTER 13

THE LESSON IN THE LEAF

Yipes was sitting in the cage, which was next to me, rubbing his head with one hand. When I'd awoken, it had frightened him into leaping up and banging his little head. It took me a moment to shake away the sleepiness and remember where I was.

"That must have been some dream," said Yipes. "I'm not sure I want to hear about it."

"Where has everyone gone?" I asked, startled to find only Yipes there in the grove with me. It was warmer now, but there was a lot of shade thrown from the trees above, and I couldn't be sure how long I'd slept or if I'd slept at all.

"Pervis didn't want to wake you. He's gone to find your father."

"What about the rest?"

"I don't know," said Yipes. "The animals have all scattered — including Murphy — which seems a bit strange. I think they're watching for Grindall, but I can't understand them so I'm not sure. They're around here somewhere."

I stood in the grove of trees and took the Jocasta's leather bag in my hand. I wanted to remove it and bury it deep in the ground so I wouldn't have to listen to it.

"I don't want this terrible Jocasta anymore!" I yelled. "I'm hearing things I don't want to hear, things I hope are not true."

Yipes took his hand away from his head and folded his hands together, rubbing his thumbs back and forth in his lap. He was sitting cross-legged, but it was such a small cage that he still had to turn his head down to fit inside. I stood up and turned away from him. Through the trees and way off in the distance, I could see the walls of Bridewell, cold and alone, empty but for Grindall and his ogres — and maybe my own father, alone and searching for me in vain.

"I used to love Bridewell," I said, the late-morning breeze lifting my hair in little waves. "When my father and I would go there — when I was younger — there was nothing I loved more than the excitement and the mystery of my summers. To explore Renny Lodge and walk down all the cobbled streets pretending I was on special assignment from Warvold himself — some secret task he'd asked me to do — those times were the heartbeat of my childhood. I would imagine that Pervis or Grayson or Ganesh were spies and I'd been sent to uncover them. But there was something special about those times, because while I enjoyed my fun, there was no *real* danger." I paused, frightened by my own words. Somehow saying them made me even more aware that those care-free days were gone, replaced by something almost *too* real, *too* dangerous.

A wayward leaf fell from a tree far above, dangled on the air, then landed at my feet. I picked it up.

"It's summertime, Yipes. Leaves shouldn't fall in summertime. This one's gone old before its time."

I took the leaf over to the cage that held Yipes and poked the stem through so that it stood like a flower.

"Bridewell is taken, and The Land of Elyon is fail-ing," I said. "I feel so lost, Yipes. I want to go home and find things as they used to be. I want to visit Bridewell and explore within the safety of its walls for as long as I please. I want this adventure to be over."

The wind turned up and blew the leaf back and forth against the cage, but it didn't escape the trap I'd put it in.

"You're growing up, Alexa, and I'm afraid there's no turning back the clock," Yipes told me gently. "I remem-ber when I was a boy, all I wanted to do was grow up and get away into the wild. But there came a time when I wished I could be a boy again, that I could turn the world back into a simple place."

He took the stem of the leaf between his finger and thumb and twirled it, looking at it in a way I didn't understand.

"We can't go back, Alexa," he said. "We can't go

109

back once we've started growing up, and the world can't be made simple again."

Yipes let the leaf go, pushing it through a hole in the cage. The wind came up and carried it across the grove, where it skidded on the ground and bounced on the breeze out of sight.

"There is something we *can* do," Yipes continued. "We can reclaim this place for good — we can restore it to what it once was. And then maybe the places of your past will feel something like they used to."

Yipes was right. I knew I couldn't go back, and I knew it was entirely up to me to defeat the terrible evil that had entered our world. But why did my father have to die as part of Elyon's plan? I tried to put the idea out of my mind, but it wouldn't go away.

"A single leaf, fallen before its time," said Yipes. "I wonder what can be learned from a leaf like that, one that will be brown and dead in a day or a week as all its friends stay green and true in the trees above."

"I don't see a lesson there, Yipes. I only see the two of us, lost and alone, with a task beyond our ability before us."

Yipes stared off in the direction where the leaf had blown away. He thought for a moment, then kept on with his prodding.

"You're not looking hard enough."

I thought more of the leaf that had danced away to its death, where it would crumble and decay into the earth, no one to care about it or notice it had gone. I was too

110

tired to think, and all I really wanted to do was go home and sleep for days and days.

"Here's what I think," Yipes said, aware from the look on my face that I was unlikely to offer much in the way of an answer. "That thing, that tiny part of The Land of Elyon, is gone but not entirely forgotten. Elyon had his reason for making it fall into our lap, just as he had his reason for sending you and me on this journey. Sometimes we see something as plain as a dying leaf and our hearts grow sad, but we must always hold true and fight on, Alexa. Whatever happens to us, we will not be forgotten in the end. He *will* remember us."

I couldn't bring myself to tell him what I'd heard just moments ago, that my father wouldn't live much longer, that he would join the leaf before too long. And yet Yipes's words did comfort me a little. Even if this adventure were to take my life and that of my father, we would not be forgotten or left behind. Somehow I began to think better of the leaf. Maybe in death it would find something more than we could imagine.

"What shall we do?" I asked Yipes, thinking I'd had enough of mulling over the questions of this life and the next. "I can't leave you here by yourself, but we really must be getting on. Where on earth has Murphy gone off to?"

"I think we'll have to wait here," Yipes told me, "at least until Murphy shows up again. You look like you haven't slept in days, and this is the safest place I can think of to take some time to regain your strength. That little nap you took won't be enough to get you all the way to the Tenth City."

I protested and argued for a while, but I *was* awfully tired. Sitting there in the grove as the noonday sun hovered overhead, I began to feel sleepy.

"I'll just lie here for a moment," I said, and I reclined right next to the cage, my head resting on my pack. We talked some more in the soft heat of the day. The sound of Yipes's words and the trees swaying overhead began to garble together until I could no longer stay awake. And then I fell into a long, deep sleep.

"Alexa — wake up."

I lurched forward and groaned awake, my body surprisingly sore from the hard ground beneath me. It was still light out, but there was now a coolness in the air around me.

"Now *that* was a nap," said Yipes, smiling from inside his little cage.

I rubbed my eyes and yawned, wondering how much of the day I'd slept away.

"Is it almost evening?" I asked.

"Not quite. It's morning, Alexa. I kept thinking you would wake up, but it remained warm last night and you kept right on sleeping."

"What?" I exclaimed. "I can't have slept all day and night, can I?"

Yipes grinned at me, and I realized I really *had* slept that long. I must have been even more exhausted than I'd thought.

"Yipes, we have to be moving along," I said, gathering my pack and making ready to go. "I know it's just the two of us, but we can't waste any more time here in the trees. I'll have to drag you along until we find our way to the forest council."

"Are you sure there are only the two of us?" asked Yipes.

"What do you mean? Where's Murphy?"

Yipes put his finger to his lips and became very still. Then he whispered, *"Listen."*

All I could hear was the rustling of the leaves in the trees. But Yipes had grown up in these mountains. He could keenly sense people and animals approaching. The first discernable sound that I heard, besides the wind in the trees, was very clear — a shrill, loud noise in the distance. I looked up.

"Squire!" I said. We hadn't seen her in a long while, and I welcomed her presence. She circled high in the air but did not descend, which got me to wondering what she might be seeing from the sky. How I wished I could see with her eyes and know all the secrets of The Land of Elyon so easily.

"Why doesn't she come down to us?" I asked. "I think she would find it quite interesting to see you behind those little bars."

Yipes was listening carefully, his head turned to one side.

"She's here to warn us," he said. "Danger is near."

This was not what I was hoping to hear. Caught alone and defenseless with a very small man trapped in a cage was about as helpless a situation as I could imagine.

"I can't leave you again, Yipes," I said. I looked all around for a place to hide the cage, but the best I could do was drag it between two trees that grew together at the bottom and branched out. We huddled in the grass as I peered through the V at the center of the two trees, keeping my head low so I wouldn't be seen.

We waited and listened until finally I began to hear something new in the distance — something large. Whatever it was, it was moving slowly, lumbering along, breaking twigs underfoot as it went. Could it be an ogre? Or maybe it was Ander, the giant grizzly bear, come to free Yipes from his cage. As I stared out into the grove of trees, I saw something unexpected. It was Murphy, scampering to and fro, yelping at the top of his lungs over the lumbering sound coming from somewhere behind him.

"Alexa? Yipes?" he called. "Where have you gone? Come out if you can hear me!" Malcolm came bounding up behind Murphy, and the two of them circled and sniffed where we had been.

I whispered as loudly as I could, "*Murphy* — we're over here. Where have you been?"

Murphy and Malcolm hopped and darted in our direction. Then Murphy came up the tree to the V where I looked out and sat right in front of my face.

"Oh, I do love surprises, don't you?" he said.

The heavy sound of something approaching grew closer, louder. I thought I saw something in the trees moving toward us.

"Only a moment more," said Murphy, "and I do believe you'll both be very surprised."

I was just about to scold Murphy for leaving us to wonder what might be coming . . . but just at that moment Armon came into view, his giant shoulders so high up in the air, his arms pushing away limbs of trees as though they were toothpicks. I was overjoyed at the sight of him.

"Armon!" I ran from behind the trees into the open space of the grove and stood before him, but instead of embracing me he moved aside, and I saw an even greater surprise. Behind him was Warvold, looking very excited to see me.

I ran to Warvold and threw myself into him. Armon put his giant hand atop my head and scattered my hair from side to side. I couldn't imagine how, but we'd found our way back to one another.

When I looked over my shoulder from my embrace with Warvold, I saw that Armon had gone to the trees I'd hidden behind. He peered into the V, put his whole arm in between, and pulled out the cage with Yipes trapped inside. He then took two giant strides into the grove and set down the cage between us where we all stood staring. Warvold knelt down next to the cage and peered inside.

"I thought I'd never see you again," he said to Yipes. "It looks as though you've gotten yourself into quite a bit of trouble in my absence."

The two of them looked at each other with great joy, old friends finally back together again.

"We might be wise to leave him in the cage," said Armon. "He's easier to look after this way."

Yipes only smiled, overcome with happiness at this reunion.

"Then again, he can be quite useful at times. I suppose we ought to let him out," said Armon.

He reached down and put his fingers into some of the holes in the cage. Then, with no effort at all, he pulled his hands apart and the cage split open like an old burlap sack. Out hopped Yipes.

He kept on with his hopping as he went around our circle, touching a sleeve or receiving an embrace. Then the reason for his strange behavior became apparent as he darted off into the woods looking for a place he could call a bathroom.

"I don't understand, Warvold," I said. "How did you find us?"

Warvold started the story and then had to begin again

when Yipes returned (looking very relieved, I might add). It would seem that Armon had thought the *Warwick Beacon* might make it back around to Lathbury while we were busy rescuing Yipes. And so, after eluding the black swarm, he had spent the night hours running to the cliffs, right to the same place where we had left Renny. Down the rope he'd gone, through the mist, looking out along the water for the *Warwick Beacon* all that next day and night. Finally, a few hours ago, the ship had shown itself on the horizon, the winds having carried it around the far side of The Land of Elyon while I slept. The only stop the ship had made was at Castalia, where Balmoral had gone back to his people.

"It was hard to let him stay, but they need him there, and we couldn't risk losing him in the coming days," Warvold explained. "Castalia must be rebuilt, and Balmoral must lead them. He is where he ought to be, just like the rest of us."

Finishing the story, Warvold told of riding on the back of a giant through the haze of morning, how Armon was tireless in his effort to make it to the forest council, and what a wonderful adventure it had been.

"He is a most amazing creature," said Warvold, looking at Armon with great pleasure. "We came upon you here as we made our way. As we come near to the end, we are back together again, as it should be."

Yipes was free. Armon and Warvold were with me

and Murphy once more. I felt a sudden wave of confidence that we could yet succeed in our task. And then I noticed Murphy looking around the many faces, confused.

"Where is Odessa?" he asked.

CHAPTER 14

FENWICK FOREST

I assured everyone that the most promising place to meet up with Odessa again would be at the forest council. It was here that I had first encountered Odessa with her son, Sherwin, and it was here that we hoped to find help in our quest across the forest and toward the Tenth City.

At the behest of Armon and Warvold, we drew deeper into the wild, away from Bridewell. As we neared the road that led between Turlock and Bridewell, we began finding the stones that used to make up the wall alongside it. Big square blocks sat surrounded by weeds and underbrush. It was a sea of broken wall, scattered through the trees and growing old as though those stones had been there all along. I had a sudden longing to turn and run toward my home in Lathbury, to lie on the bed in the privacy of my own room and sleep the day away alone.

"This road is watched," Warvold warned us. "We must be very careful as we cross into Fenwick Forest. It's hard to say what awaits us in the dark of the wood."

We sent Murphy and Malcolm ahead to scout while the rest of us waited and whispered among the stones and the trees.

I whispered to Armon, "I'm so happy you're safe. How on earth did you escape the bats?"

119

He smiled and leaned down close to me. "A giant is faster of foot than you might imagine," he said. "And I have a few hiding places of my own for times such as these."

The sun rose in the sky, bringing the heat of late morning with it. It frightened me to think of the day drifting away, taking my father with it. I turned back in the direction of Bridewell and saw Warvold crouching in the dirt, looking at me as if he knew I was concerned about something.

"What troubles you, Alexa?"

"Things keep getting more dangerous," I answered. "I fear something terrible will happen soon, and it scares me to think about it."

Warvold nodded, his eyes glazed over as if he were lost in a distant memory.

"I have felt the same as you," he told me. "When we left Balmoral in Castalia, I voiced my fears to him, wondering what he might say. He told me that when you've lived through a generation of troubled times, slaving for an evil man as he has, watching your friends and family fall before you —" Warvold stopped short, overcome with anger and sadness. "When you've lived through a thing like that," he continued, "nothing seems dangerous anymore. It all just seems normal, as though every day brings hardship, and to think it might be otherwise is the way of fools."

"It seems like a dark way to live, never expecting to

see the world rid of things like Grindall and the ogres," I said.

Warvold smiled at me, his anger with the past softening. "Balmoral told me one more thing before he disappeared into the mist at Castalia. He told me the world is full of danger and full of stories. And then he asked me what sort of story we would have to tell if there were nothing for good people to fight for."

Warvold touched my shoulder and looked deep into my eyes. "I think we were meant to fight a good fight, and I think we're better for fighting it."

I hadn't thought of things in quite that way before, but I supposed Balmoral and Warvold were right. If my father had to die in order to free The Land of Elyon from the evils of Abaddon, at least he would die trying to preserve Bridewell and its people. His story would be a good one, remembered and talked about.

"We can cross now." It was Murphy, back from checking the road. He was fidgeting on top of the rock I was hiding behind. As I stood to go, he leaped onto my pack and held on to the leather with his tiny claws.

"Oh, no, you don't," said Warvold. "We need you to stay out front and watch for anything unusual. A rustle in the bushes, a strange smell — if you sense the slightest oddity, you must warn us."

Murphy jumped down immediately and darted back to the road, crossed over, and disappeared into the trees on the other side.

"Off we go then," said Warvold. "Across the road and quickly!"

Armon went first and was across the road in three giant steps before the rest of us could get started. Warvold followed, then Yipes, and finally me. We ran across the road as quickly as we could, down into the thick woods on the other side, Armon clearing a path before us as we went. There was no sign of Squire, gone off again to places I couldn't see.

Something was different about the forest from the way I'd remembered it. Before, when I'd come to visit the forest council, it had seemed wild and untamed but still somehow friendly and inviting. Today I felt afraid of the forest. It was darker than I remembered it, more forbidding. Had something changed this place in my short absence?

"Slow down, Armon," Yipes called. "You'll get us lost."

Armon stopped and looked back, waiting for the group to arrive at his feet. It didn't matter how many times I stood at the foot of this giant — each time I was newly amazed at his grandeur, his overwhelming presence. As I stood beneath him and craned my neck to see his face, my fear of Fenwick Forest began to fade.

"There used to be a trail near here," said Yipes. "It seems that things have grown over. This place is different, wilder than when I last passed through."

Warvold nodded his agreement and whispered, "*Abaddon.*"

"What do you mean?" asked Armon.

Warvold looked around in all directions and squinted up into the trees. He continued, "A long time ago, I traveled through the Sly Field and into Fenwick Forest with a friend of mine. He was a great explorer in his own right, and though we did not find the Tenth City on that day, we both agreed that something else was near these parts. Wherever it is that Abaddon makes his home, it's not too terribly far from the woods."

"Yes, but why the sudden change in the way this place feels, the way it grows wilder?" asked Yipes.

"Abaddon is mustering all his powers to find us," Warvold explained. "I think he knew we would come this way, and so he has made our journey more treacherous. I fear things will change for the worse as we travel deeper into the woods."

The hair rose on my neck, and a cold chill ran through my body.

"Who was the friend, the one who traveled with you?" I asked, though I felt sure I knew the answer before he offered it.

"His name was Cabeza de Vaca — a very interesting man, well traveled and always in search of the Tenth City. He presides over the Western Kingdom now, though I haven't seen him in ages."

Cabeza de Vaca. I'd read his book, used it to judge the distance to the bottom of the tunnel on my first journey outside the walls. It was comforting to hear his name once more.

"In any case, we must travel carefully," said Warvold. "This place is not what it once was, and neither are the creatures that make their home here."

"I think I can find my way to the forest council," said Yipes. "But I wonder now if we ought to go there."

It was a terrible thought. Could it be that Abaddon had somehow turned the forest animals against us? If so, I surely wouldn't want to stand face-to-face with Ander. Even Armon would have a battle on his hands trying to contain a creature so fierce.

"I think we risk it," said Armon. "Abaddon may have turned this wood into a dark place, but we have to hope the animals will be able to help us find our way."

There was silence among the group, as we listened to the wind sweep in around us. Some of the largest of the trees groaned as if the wind might tear them from their roots.

"Yipes, you jump up there on Armon's shoulders," said Warvold. "The two of you can lead the way."

We continued deeper into the forest and found that the farther we went, the more the trees groaned against the pushing of the wind. The trunks became darker, limbs fallen, and our passage was hindered by thorny walls of dead blackberry bushes and thick brown vines along the floor of the wood.

"Warvold," I said, taken aback by what I was seeing, "this place is dying."

He kept walking without answering me, and I felt his sadness at the sight of this once-great forest. A gust of wind blew from somewhere far away, and in the distance we heard a mighty cracking of wood and the sound of a tree falling to the ground. The trees were growing old before our eyes, and looking up I realized that there were no leaves left on them, no leaves flying through the air on the wind. It was summer in The Land of Elyon, but I saw now that the deeper we went into the forest, the more it seemed as if winter had somehow come to this place — a winter without the blistering cold, but a winter none-theless. Everything was dormant or dead.

"We're close," said Yipes, turning toward us from his perch on Armon's shoulders. "Only a little farther and we'll be in the grove."

It was impossible to keep quiet now. With every step Armon took, the forest floor cracked with dead branches. If someone was waiting for us in the grove he would be well aware of our arrival. Armon fought through a final thick casing of thorny bushes with his sword, and there before us was the secret place where I'd first met the for-est council.

The lush grass and towering trees of green and gold

were no longer part of this place. All that remained were the stones the animals had sat upon, surrounded by a sea of death — fallen trees crusted with wrinkled leaves, the lush grass turned to brown stubble. At the far end of the grove sat a large, lonely figure, his head turned down to the ground. It was the only animal, and as we emerged out of the trees and into the open the beast lifted his head and looked at us.

"I had a feeling you might find your way back here." It was Ander, the grizzly bear and keeper of the forest, and he didn't look at all happy to see us.

Other animals crept into view and sat among the fallen trees and ancient stones. Darius and Sherwin were not among them, and many of the faces were not familiar or friendly. As we stood in the gloom of the grove, Ander said something I hadn't expected him to say.

"*Why have you done this to my forest?*" There was anger in his eyes as he rose to his full height and glared in our direction. He began to shake with rage as he looked around the grove. "Answer me!"

I was the only one who understood this booming request. Everyone else heard a monstrous roar of the kind they'd never heard before. I had hoped the forest council would be a place where we could find help from friends. Instead I felt more afraid and unsure than ever.

"What's he saying, Alexa?" Warvold asked. I didn't have a chance to answer him, for at that very moment Ander began charging toward us.

I held my breath and hoped something would stop Ander from his attack. If he wasn't stopped, he would meet with Armon first and the two of them would tear each other to shreds. How could he think that we had done this to his home? Everything seemed to be moving in slow motion as Armon steadied himself, and Ander advanced quickly from the far side of the grove. For the first time that I could remember, I put a direct question to Elyon, hoping for an answer that could stop the charging grizzly bear.

What shall I do, Elyon?

To my surprise, the answer came the moment I'd thought of the question.

Stand between Ander and Armon.

Without further thought, I ran in front of Armon and stood between him and the approaching bear, certain that my short life was about to come to a painful and quick end.

CHAPTER 15

THE GROVE

I remember hearing Warvold's voice, screaming for me to get out of the way. But I stood frozen as Ander came within a few feet of my face, his teeth gleaming in the sun that swept through the branches of the bare trees. I looked into his eyes and he looked into mine, and that final moment seemed to last a lifetime. In his eyes I saw such terrible sadness, a misery he alone could understand as his world was dying all around him. I tried to send a message back in my own eyes: *We didn't do this. We need your help to put it back the way it was.*

Ander came so close and with such force that nothing else existed. Not the wood or my friends or my world — only those desperate, sad eyes. Later I would learn that grizzly bears will often charge an intruder, only to turn at the last second and run off into the trees, as if it were a game to see if the intruder would turn and try to run away. I could not imagine Ander any closer than he was when he turned, his massive shoulder grazing mine as he went by. After he was past me, he stopped faster than I thought possible and reared up on his two back legs, his back to Armon and the rest of us.

Ander made a sound then that I will never forget. It was a sound of anguish and despair, a haunting growl that was caught on the wind and carried through the forest. He was crying.

I sat down in the dead grass of the grove and watched as Ander came back down on his four legs, turned, and stood before us. The many animals who had gathered in the grove were moving closer, acting as though they would all attack us together at any moment. Badgers and mountain lions and wolves — too much for us to overcome.

"Leave them be," Ander said to the animals. "We must take a moment to talk this through before proceeding."

The forest had taken us captive, and there would be no escaping from all the animals of the wood. If they wanted to tear us apart, then we would be torn apart. As Ander retreated to the center of the grove and sat down, I knew we would have to convince him that we were not responsible for what had happened to his home. Either that or we would never see the light of another day.

"Your foolishness may well have saved us," said Warvold. I looked up at him and saw a look of great relief in his eyes. "You will have to talk with him, Alexa. No one else can understand what he's saying."

I started walking slowly toward the center of the grove where the mighty bear sat all alone. Armon came up beside me, sword drawn, and kept my slow pace.

"You'd better stay back with the others, Armon," I cautioned. "He won't trust me if you're towering over us, waiting to do him in."

Armon bent down on one knee and put his hand on my shoulder.

"Are you sure about this?" he asked.

"No, I'm really not sure at all. But I know this bear. Unless Abaddon has somehow possessed him as he has the forest, I think I can talk to him."

Armon sighed deeply, stood, and returned his sword to its sheath. I walked the rest of the way by myself. The crunching of the broken forest lay beneath me as I went, and the air was dirty like the road to Bridewell on a dry day.

Sitting down in front of Ander I felt a terrible loss as I looked at his old claws clumped with dirt. He was an old bear, full of memory, of things I'd only dreamed.

"I'm so sorry, Ander," I began. "But we didn't do this to your forest. It was someone else."

"Was it, Alexa?"

"Yes, it was. Maybe we can put it back the way it was if you'll help us find our way."

Ander put his head down near mine and sniffed the air around me, blowing my hair back as he exhaled. Tiny droplets of water sprayed from his nose and landed on my cheeks. I wiped them away.

"You tried to help us once," he said. "When men built the walls that separated everything, you tried to help us."

I nodded, not knowing what to say.

"But it was men who built the walls to begin with, men who thought nothing of us in all their planning and destroying."

Ander looked across the grove at Warvold, and I turned to see how my friend would react. Warvold couldn't know what Ander was saying, and he was not looking in our direction. Instead, he was standing next to a fallen tree, running his fingers over a broken branch. It looked as though he was feeling very sorry for himself.

"Why must you always make such trouble?" Ander asked.

"I'm only a child," I said, not knowing what else I could offer. "I don't know what to say to you, only that we're sorry the forest is failing and that we want to make it better."

"I wonder how long it would have taken for you to come and cut down all the trees for your houses and your buildings," said Ander. "This forest has been taken by a terrible evil, but in years to come I fear you'd have taken it from us out of your own greed."

"No, Ander! We would never do that," I said. "You have to believe me."

Ander looked at me and for the first time there was kindness in his eyes.

"I do believe you, Alexa Daley. There are some of your kind who want what's best for everything that lives in The Land of Elyon. There are others who want to destroy it." He looked again at Warvold. "Even he wanted only to protect, not to destroy, though he harmed us in the process."

We sat alone in the grove for a long, silent moment.

"What is it that you want from me, Alexa? I fear my time is coming to an end along with the woods."

There was nothing more to do but boldly ask for what we needed.

"Can you help us find the Tenth City, Ander? I don't know what we'll do when we get there, but maybe it will help restore this place if we can find it."

Ander was quiet. He sat thinking, stewing on the problem, trying to decide if a young girl could be trusted with such an immense responsibility.

"What is that you have there around your neck?" he asked me.

I clutched the stone in the small leather pouch before speaking.

"It's the last Jocasta," I answered.

Ander's eyes widened and he moved his head down near mine once more.

"I knew you had a Jocasta but not . . . the last. Let me have a look at it."

I hesitated, then undid the leather pouch and removed the stone, holding it out in front of me. It lit up the grove with orange and gold, and for a moment the place seemed to come alive again.

Ander sighed and looked all around him, remembering what it had once been like.

"I have a secret to tell you, Alexa. One that might help you find what you're looking for."

I put the Jocasta back inside the pouch and waited for Ander to tell me the secret.

"There are things a few of us animals know that elude human understanding. We're born with certain . . . knowledge — knowledge that is only useful at a time such as this." He paused a moment and I listened as a hush came over the grove and all the animals seemed to lean in around us.

"The stone will show you the way," he said. "When you reach the mist of the Sly Field, hold the stone out in front of you. Where others have failed in the Sly Field, you will succeed. Follow where it leads you, and you may yet find the Tenth City."

We both smiled.

"If I find it, if I can defeat Abaddon, I'll do everything I can to restore this place," I said.

"I know you will, Alexa."

Murphy came out of the grove and landed on my knee, looking at me with concern.

"Someone is coming, Alexa. The animals are stirring."

I listened along with Ander and heard the faint sound of something approaching from the woods. A moment later, Odessa came into the clearing. I was happy to see her.

"Odessa!" I said.

Ander sniffed at the air, his big head bouncing back and forth as he stretched his nose out from side to side. As I watched Odessa slowly approach us, I glanced around the grove and noticed something peculiar. All the animals had gone away, leaving bare stones strewn with dirt and leaves. Only Ander remained.

"There is something foul in the air," said Ander. I smelled it as well, the terrible odor of rotting flesh.

Odessa crept forward a few more steps, and then I heard the sound of beings crashing through the trees from every direction, moving fast. I could see their heads bobbing through the trees, their swollen shoulders knocking down limbs as they came, the black cloaks, and the hideous faces.

The ogres were upon us, closing in from all sides.

"Odessa, how could you?" said Ander. He was astounded at the sight of these creatures, and we both knew without hesitation that Odessa had led them to this sacred place, although my understanding might have been deeper than his. I looked back at my companions and saw that they, too, were dumbstruck by this turn of events.

There was nothing we could do as Grindall came into the clearing with a dreadful grin on his face, his menacing laugh echoing through the grove and chilling the air around us.

CHAPTER 16

CAPTURED

The ogres stood all around the grove, their breathing labored and soggy. I stayed where I was, afraid that even the slightest movement might cause one of the ogres to turn angry. They were wild, unpredictable creatures. Everything about them made me nervous and afraid. Only Grindall could control them, his voice like a hypnotic spell from which the ogres could not escape.

Ander backed away from me, moving toward one of the ogres, then turned and ran out of the grove. The ogres did not move. They were focused entirely on keeping me and my companions trapped.

Armon drew his sword, the sound of metal on metal ringing through the trees. He looked fierce enough to take on all of the ten ogres circling the grove, but a few seconds after the sword was drawn everything changed. One of the ogres took hold of Warvold, another Yipes, and a third had his hand on my back, lifting me in the air before I could turn and see him coming.

"Armon the giant." It was Grindall, his slippery voice bringing the ogres to a quick silence. "After all our searching we come upon you unprotected in this rotted forest. How convenient for me."

He looked around the open space and saw that he had

three of his foes trapped, with seven more ogres surrounding Armon. The ogre who'd picked me up knelt down and set me in front of him, but his huge hand remained tightly gripped around my waist. I felt the material on my tunic turning slimy, cold, and slick against my skin. His hand was like a thick, wet mop tied tightly around my waist.

"It appears as though I have gained the upper hand," Grindall gloated. "All of my most hated enemies together in one place, taken unaware by our approach. I would have hoped for a little more of a challenge."

I could tell that Armon was having a difficult time putting down the sword. He wanted desperately to protect his friends, and yet he knew that with one quick squeeze of the ogres' hands three of us would be finished.

"Armon," I said, "put down the sword. There's nothing you can do now. There's nothing any of us can do."

He hesitated, looking all around him, then heaved a great sigh and tossed the sword into the middle of the grove at Grindall's feet. Grindall threw back his head and laughed wickedly. He bent down and tried to pick up the weapon, but it was so big he could barely get it off the ground. Irritated, he called to one of the ogres, "Pick this up, you fool! Get it out of my way."

An ogre took the sword and flung it into the woods. It clanged to a stop beneath a moss-covered tree stump.

"Now then, where were we?" Grindall was enjoying

himself far too much. "Oh, yes, I remember — I was about to have Warvold brought to me so that I might have a word with him."

The ogre that had hold of Warvold quickly stepped toward Grindall. With strong arms he pushed Warvold to his knees and stood breathing heavily a few feet away.

"Get back, you beast!" said Grindall. "I can hardly stand the smell of you so close."

The ogre backed up farther and took his guard with the others encircling Armon.

"Bring me the others," Grindall commanded. "I want them all at my feet while I give them as much regrettable news as I can think of."

The wet hand tightened around my waist and hoisted me into the air. I was dropped on my knees next to Warvold as Yipes was marched over and pushed to the ground with the two of us. I saw Murphy sitting on a stump to my left, free for the moment, and I hoped he wouldn't try anything foolish and get himself in trouble like the rest of us.

"Don't worry, Alexa." It was Warvold, whispering to me.

"Oh, on the contrary, *do* worry, Alexa!" roared Grindall. "You've failed . . . as I knew you would. I have captured everyone with the power to stop me — Warvold and Yipes — and the two most precious of all — Alexa Daley and Armon the giant. In all the far reaches of the land, you four are the greatest enemies of Abaddon. How pleased he must be with me."

He stifled a laugh and looked at Armon, surrounded by ogres. Then he returned his gaze to the four of us at his feet. Odessa strode up next to him and sat down. Grindall ran his long fingers over her coat.

"Wolves. They simply cannot be trusted," he said. "Unless of course you're me. Then they can be very useful."

Grindall stared at Warvold with a peculiar smile on his face.

"Look what's become of your beloved Land of Elyon. Thistles and thorns covering a dead forest. It would seem the powers that rule are not the ones you claim."

"Get on with it, Victor. What do you aim to do with us? Where will you take us?" asked Warvold.

"More to the point, where will *you* take *me*?" answered Grindall. He looked at the leather bag hanging around my neck.

"It will only help us find what you seek if you leave it around my neck," I said, sure of what he was thinking. Victor Grindall had searched for the last Jocasta for a very long time, and now he wanted only to possess it.

"I see," said Grindall. He took the leather pouch in his hand and toyed with it. "All the same, I would feel so much better if I could keep it myself."

He pulled up on the pouch and yanked the leather necklace over my head, releasing the Jocasta from my control. Then he opened the pouch and pulled out the stone, which shone brightly in his hand. There was a collective gasp in the grove from the ogres as they looked at the treasure before them. They seemed afraid of it, as though it might destroy them if they were to touch it.

I had finally lost control of the last Jocasta. I felt sure that the quest had also been lost, that I was near the end of my journey, and that it would end badly.

"Now then," said Grindall, placing the Jocasta back in its pouch, "how am I to find the Tenth City so I can return this treasure to its rightful owner?" His laughter spread over the grove uncontained, then he became quiet before shouting a question at me.

"How do I find the Tenth City?"

I was defeated, my friends were taken, Armon was hours from an encounter with the black swarm. There was nothing left to do but tell Grindall what he wanted to know and hope that somehow Elyon would save us, that somehow he had a way to keep the ogres from defiling the Tenth City and driving him away forever. I pleaded once more with Grindall, just to be sure he couldn't be persuaded.

"If you take these ogres to the Tenth City, they will ruin it. They will drive Elyon away from this place, and Abaddon will rule completely. Are you sure this is what you want? Are you so sure you will remain powerful once he is set free to rule entirely?"

Grindall answered without hesitation.

"I'm quite sure of my place, Alexa. You can stop your worrying about how high and how mighty I will be when this day comes to a close. There is but one way to rid the world of Elyon, and that is to bring evil into his precious Tenth City. It's my *duty* to drive him away. When I do, I'll have power to burn."

He looked at me with such malice I knew then for sure that he was lost forever.

"Go to the Sly Field," I said. "When you get there, take out the Jocasta and follow where it leads you. There you will find the Tenth City."

I'd said it. The secret was out in the open air. There was one last chance, but I couldn't let it show in my voice. Grindall looked down at Warvold, reared back, and kicked him with all his might. I gasped as Warvold went down, watching the blood spill from the side of his head.

"That's for leading me around in circles all these years," said Grindall. Then he looked at his ogres and commanded them: "Gather these prisoners and hold them tight. I'm certain they will want to come along and see their precious Tenth City come to an end."

The ogres all laughed grotesquely, spitting and coughing as they did, until Grindall raised his hand and all was quiet once more.

"Armon!" he yelled. "If you try to break free of our group or make mischief, you'll bring a swift death to your friends here. If you so much as veer a foot away from your leash, Alexa will be the first to go." The ogre that held my waist squeezed his mighty, wet hand tighter. I yelped in pain.

Armon was shaking with anger. Unable to contain himself, he yelled into the air as Grindall laughed and laughed. The forest groaned and swayed at the sound of so much anguish in Armon's voice.

"Now, here's how this is going to work," Grindall continued. "Armon, you'll be tethered to one of my ogres, and that ogre will be tied with a rope to another. If you try anything foolish, Alexa will go first, then Yipes. Take care, last giant. Their fate rests in your hands." Grindall paused, then added a final item, saying it as though it were an afterthought. "Oh, and one more thing, Armon. You'll need to carry old Warvold there, since he appears to be unable to move. We could leave him here to die, but I think I'd rather he woke up at just the right time so he can finally see the Tenth City for himself. And watch me destroy it!"

As Grindall began walking from the grove, I looked at Warvold lying beside me. He wasn't moving, and for a frightening moment I thought he was dead. Armon carefully picked him up and cradled him in his huge arms. Warvold stirred, but only a little. Armon looked at Warvold with great love and compassion, and as an ogre began tying a thick rope around Armon's neck, I was surprised by the expression on Armon's face. He looked at the ogre not with hate but with compassion and sorrow.

Early afternoon was upon the broken forest. We began walking toward the Sly Field in a long line, to places I'd never been and had little hope of ever returning from.

CHAPTER 17

THROUGH THE SLY FIELD

I'd forgotten how swiftly Armon and the ogres could travel. Their strides were so long, like three or four of a grown man's. When they ran, it was amazing how fast they could get from one place to another. It was clear that Grindall wanted to find the Tenth City quickly, before anything else could go wrong. He had fashioned something of a chair that rested on two poles between two ogres. He sat there like a king, high above the rest of us, Odessa at his feet. It looked like a rocky ride, and Grindall often yelled at the ogres to stop being so clumsy. All the while he held the leather pouch around his neck with one hand and ran his other hand along Odessa's thick mane.

Besides Grindall's haste, there was another reason we were moving so fast, a reason I hadn't expected. The grove in the forest was nearer to the Sly Field than I'd imagined it was, and after we managed to make our way beyond the trees and thicket, the Sly Field appeared as if out of thin air. The forest came quickly to an end, and we were all surprised at what we saw.

This was a mythical place, a place where almost no

one ever went, and so my expectations were set rather high. I thought there would be fantastic creatures or strange formations shooting out of the ground high into the air. I thought there might be sounds I'd never heard, smells I'd never smelled, and all sorts of wonders I'd never imagined before.

But there were none of these things. An ogre had me held tight to his smelly, moist side, and when he stopped at the edge of the Sly Field I turned my head up and looked out to see —

Nothing. It was as much nothing as I'd ever seen in my entire life. It was flat and brown and barren. And it went on forever. It looked like an endless, dreary desert of hard earth, not a hill or a bump as far as the eye could see. And it was quiet, so quiet that even the ogres held their breath, listening.

Somewhere far in the distance, on the horizon, it was white. But it was so very far away I couldn't be sure what was there, or if there was anything there at all.

As you might imagine, there wasn't any reason to go slowly when there was nothing to trip on or duck under. Armon and the ogres could have run with their eyes shut and managed the terrain. I must admit I was a bit let down by the place. It was nice that it wasn't as dangerous as I thought it would be, but did it have to be so boring and lifeless? I felt about as hopeless as I'd ever felt, dangling at the side of a stinking ogre with my guts being bounced out of me, watching the dead earth race past.

144

An hour into our journey, I craned my head to see how Yipes, Armon, and Warvold were doing. They were all in front of me, Yipes in the grip of another ogre and Warvold still looking lifeless as Armon carried him across the Sly Field. I heard a sound overhead and craned further still, twisting my body to see what it was. To my great surprise and excitement I saw Squire circling overhead. I hadn't seen her since we'd left the stand of trees near Bridewell, and it was wonderful to see and hear her now. Could it really have only been that morning that I had stood on the other side of the road to Turlock? Things were moving so fast. It felt to me as if all the unseen powers around us were racing to the end of time itself, wanting to get things over with.

I heard Squire screeching in the air once more. Unfortunately, I was not the only one.

"It's that wretched bird," said Grindall. "Stop!"

The whole lot of us came to a halt in the middle of the Sly Field. I looked around in every direction. It was amazing how barren it was, but the white at the distant end was closer now, and I began to think it looked like clouds.

Grindall pulled a bow from beside his chair and set it with an arrow.

"Come on down a little lower, you mangy bucket of feathers," he said, aiming into the air with one eye closed. I looked again at the chair he was seated in. There was a leather compartment that was used to hold the bow and another that held a sword. A third, long and round, held ten or twelve arrows. As I looked at this one, something strange happened.

The arrows began to move around, only a little, but enough that I could tell something was inside the leather container. A moment later, Murphy's head popped out, and he looked right at me. I gasped without thinking . . . causing Grindall to point his arrow down at me.

"What is it, afraid I'm going to pick your friend out of the sky?" He laughed and let the tension off the bow. "Not today, I'm afraid. She's too high, which is where she'd better stay if she doesn't want to be eaten for dinner."

Squire screeched from the safety of the air as Grindall put away the bow and the arrow. I looked back to find Murphy, but he was gone, hiding. I felt sure he was thinking up things he probably shouldn't do.

"What are you waiting for?" barked Grindall. "It's hot, and I want a breeze. Move!"

Armon and the ogres began running again, and I watched as Grindall petted Odessa. It was a miserable sight to see him sitting up there treating my one-time friend like a trusted pet.

As we continued on, I thought about the few hours that remained of the day. If Elyon had told me the truth, my father would be dead in four or five more hours. I could hardly help but feel overcome with grief.

A half hour passed with only the sound of giant feet

against dry earth. I hadn't looked up in all that time, and was beginning to fade into a half sleep when Grindall suddenly spoke.

"Stop, you fools!"

When we lurched to a halt, I looked up and saw why Grindall had given his order.

The white in the distance, the white we had all seen, had changed. It had come alive.

My breath caught in my throat as I watched the white mass coming toward us like a flood of water on the land. It looked like a wall of white waves, and I was certain then that the end really had come. There would be no way to outrun the approaching fury before us, and I realized why very few people had entered the Sly Field and lived to tell about it.

"Don't worry about a thing — it's not what it appears to be," came a crackling whisper. At first I thought it was the voice of Elyon, but how could it be with Grindall carrying the last Jocasta? I looked toward the voice and saw Warvold, his head hanging back from Armon's arm, facing me. He'd awoken. I looked at him and smiled, very happy to see that he was still alive. I was afraid if I spoke to him the others might hear, and Grindall might become enraged at our conversation. Warvold continued to stare at me as the white waves grew nearer, coming even faster now.

"What's happening?" yelled Grindall. The ogres were agitated, and they began to stir and back up. I thought they might start to run away, back toward the forest, which would have been a pointless effort.

"Stay where you are!" Grindall commanded. "There's no escaping this thing, whatever it is. If it means to have us, then have us it will."

I kept looking at Warvold, watching him, hoping he wouldn't slip back into his dreams. Even though I trusted him, I was terrified of the white waves bearing down on us.

"Have you tricked me one last time, Warvold?" said Grindall. "Would you really take us all to our deaths just to see me destroyed?"

Grindall turned to the oncoming wrath of waves and laughed, raising his arms as if mocking the power that had come against him.

"There's something I must tell you, Alexa," whispered Warvold, his voice like a thin wisp of air. There was something about his voice that made me pause. With something so big and terrible approaching us, how could I hear such a small voice? It struck me then that the white mass of waves was as quiet as the Sly Field itself — it made no noise at all. It approached as quietly as a snake slithering on the earth, closer and closer. As Warvold shut his eyes and slipped back into unconsciousness, the waves passed over us.

If you can imagine what it feels like to wake from a dream and open your eyes only to see that the world has disappeared, then you can imagine something of what it felt like the moment we were overtaken. Imagine looking at your hand and only being able to see it if you place it a few inches from your face. The world had gone white, with a mist so thick it took my breath away.

"How curious," said Grindall. I could hear his voice, the way he was concerned but happy he hadn't been drowned. Still, the touch of happiness in his voice was gone a moment later as he commanded those around him.

"Armon! If you're thinking of using this development to your advantage, I don't recommend it. Alexa and Yipes are still in the hands of my ogres, and I'd hate to think what would happen to your friends if you attempted something."

"I'm only standing here, the same as everyone else," Armon answered. "I'm wondering what you intend to do, now that we're lost in the Sly Field."

The next minute was silent but for the grunting and shuffling feet of the ogres. During this long silence, something happened that greatly comforted me, something wonderful in the middle of a terrible situation. In the secrecy of the mist I felt something grab hold of my foot, then crawl slowly along my leg until it reached the place around my waist where the ogre had hold of me. There was a tiny flit of a noise, then whatever it was landed on my exposed shoulder, holding tightly with its claws so as not to fall. It was Murphy, come to be close to me once he knew he could not be seen. It made me wonder how he could have found his way in the white that was everywhere. Maybe he had used his sense of smell or could simply see a little better than I could in this strange place. I could see my own hand if I held it in front of my face, and now, as Murphy burrowed in between my arm and my chest, I saw his face and I was happy. He whispered in my ear, but with the Jocasta gone I couldn't understand him. All I heard were the pleasing sounds a squirrel makes.

"Alexa, are you all right?" It was Yipes, risking a question in the mist.

"Quiet! All of you stop your talking. I'm trying to think." It was Grindall, shouting down at us from his unseen chair.

The stone will show you the way.

I thought again about what I'd seen on the cliffs at the sea with Armon and Murphy two days before. The storm had been raging on the water far below, pushing the *Warwick Beacon* out to sea, and we'd witnessed what Elyon had sent us there for. As I hung there on the side of the ogre and reflected on these things, I didn't know what I should do. I'd brought things this far . . . but now they felt out of my hands.

As it turned out, it didn't matter what I thought or what I said. As I was busy with the ideas in my head, the mist began to glow with a brilliant orange light . . . and in that light I saw the wicked face of Grindall staring right at me.

"*Ahhhhhhh,*" he said, "how perfectly marvelous!" He crowed as he held out the Jocasta, then moved it in a circle in the mist around him. The orange light died a quick death in every direction — every direction but one. As Grindall held the Jocasta in a certain place, the orange light flew out of the stone and illuminated a thin pathway of light ten feet in front of us.

"Go that way! Slowly!" Grindall yelled to the ogres beneath him. They obeyed, and as they went, the pathway of light continued ten feet in front of them. When he moved the light and held it in any other direction, the pathway disappeared and we were lost once more. How I wished I could have the Jocasta back and be rid of this dreadful man and his ogres!

"To the Tenth City, and quickly!" Grindall said, the back of his head a silhouette surrounded by fiery light. We were on the move again, slower now, following a pathway that only showed itself in bits and pieces.

I could only imagine where the path would lead.

CHAPTER 18

THE PATHWAY

Grindall and the ogres had a memory of what the Sly Field looked like before the mist overtook them, and Grindall used this memory to encourage the ogres to continue moving quickly. True, they could only see a few feet in front of them, but there was nothing but flat land in all directions. Going slowly would only bring on the night sooner, and who knew if the Jocasta could provide light through mist and darkness working together against us?

Grindall seemed more agitated the farther we went, barking orders without ceasing, holding the Jocasta out in front of him as far as he could, aiming it just so.

The warmth of the sun had been blotted out, and a moist coolness filled the mist. Murphy shivered in my arms and bore his nose up into my neck as we trudged on. I wondered what he might be thinking. In the past, his little mind was most dangerous at perilous times such as these.

"We're close — I can *feel* it," said Grindall. He commanded his ogres to stop and turned in our direction, holding the Jocasta near his face so we could all see him. He was strange-looking in the mix of light and haze, like an evil spirit come to haunt the Sly Field and live in our nightmares. He held the stone beneath his chin. Shards of light shot up over his face.

"Armon?" he called out.

There was a pause, and for a moment I thought Armon had escaped with Warvold and was hiding somewhere off in the distance. But then he spoke, and I had to admit I was glad to hear him so near to me.

"I am here," said Armon.

"Hand over Warvold to the ogre you're tied to — I have something for you to do." It was a command made with unnerving pleasure. Whatever Grindall was up to, he was acting as though he was about to enjoy something wicked.

"Get one of your own monsters to do your bidding. I'm not letting him go," answered Armon.

The thin light on Grindall's face revealed his changed expression — he was toying with Armon, and he knew who was in control.

"Ogres, give Alexa and Yipes a squeeze, won't you?"

I felt a gigantic arm tighten around my waist and heard the sloshing of the ogre's insides against my head as he laughed. I felt infected by this creature, as though I'd been next to him so long I would never get the smell or the feeling away. Neither Yipes nor I made a sound for a few seconds, trying our best to hold out, but when I felt my ribs about to crack in two I let out a scream that filled the air.

"All right! I'll give him up and do as you say," Armon cried. "Stop what you're doing to them!"

I felt the ogre loosen his hold on me. I could breathe again, but I felt sick. As I gasped for air the smell — the awful wet smell — finally got the better of me, and I threw up. I couldn't really see what I'd done, but now the ogre was laughing as whatever had come out of my mouth ran down his leg and only added to the aroma of death all around me.

"Whichever one of you ogres is tied to Armon, take Warvold from him," said Grindall. I listened as the ogre grunted and laughed.

"You may hold him," said Armon, speaking to the ogre in the thick of the mist. "But if you harm him in any way, you'll have me to answer to." The ogre became quiet, knowing full well that Armon was but a hair away from taking matters into his own hands.

"Have you got him? Have you got Warvold?" asked Grindall.

The ogre grumbled and moaned something, and then Grindall said something that broke my heart.

"Take him over your head and throw him as far as you can. He's dead weight, and he serves no purpose. I don't want him seeing the place he's searched for his whole life, even as I destroy it. Throw him!"

"NO!" Armon, Yipes, and I all cried at the same time. I could tell that Armon was swinging out his arms, trying to grab hold of the ogre. The pressure on my waist tightened again, and I gasped and screamed. I squeezed Murphy tighter than I ought to have and he squirmed free, darting off into the Sly Field to places I could not see.

"Alexa!"

Time stood still in the Sly Field as I heard Warvold's voice call to me, loud and authoritative.

"There's something you must know —"

At that very moment I heard the ogre howl, and though I couldn't see it, I knew that Warvold was flying through the air. I listened and heard the thud as he hit the ground somewhere far away in the white of the Sly Field. I cried out for him, screaming and clawing to be let go from the ogre so I could run into the unknown and find Warvold. My captor laughed while I swung my arms and legs trying to get free, until finally I hung there, sobbing and broken. Would I ever hear what Warvold wanted to tell me, or had his voice been forever silenced?

"So good to have the trash thrown out, don't you think?" said Grindall. I couldn't look up at his hideous face surrounded in burning light and a sea of mist. He was the most awful man I could have imagined, and I only wished that he would go away and leave me and my friends alone.

Armon and Yipes were silent, so silent that I wondered if they were still alive. Maybe Armon's heart had finally been broken entirely, and he'd had enough of our world — and Yipes, he was so small, maybe the ogre that held him had squeezed a little too hard and snapped his insides into pieces. The only thing I did hear that made me realize I wasn't dead myself was the ever-present voice of Victor Grindall.

"Ogres, we are very close to the Tenth City. I can *feel* it. Can you feel it, Armon? You should know. It's your home, isn't it? Don't you wish you could go back there again and get away from all this garbage around you?"

There was no response from Armon, only the heavy breathing of the ogres.

"Answer me!" yelled Grindall. "Don't you want to go home, Armon?"

"The Tenth City is yours, Victor Grindall. You've got what you wanted. Just leave Yipes and Alexa with me and finish what you came here to do." From his voice, it was clear that Armon's spirit had been broken at the thought of having let poor Warvold out of his care.

Grindall laughed and laughed. He laughed so hard I thought he might fall out of his chair.

"To see you falling apart like this is a pleasure I did not expect to enjoy. But what a joy it is!" Grindall proudly summoned his minions. "Onward, ogres! Onward to the Tenth City where we can do some real damage."

And then we were moving again, every stride of the ogre wrenching my swollen side. Until then I hadn't realized how sore I was. It was as if I had a deep bruise through my entire middle from the pounding, and it was all I could do not to hang there crying.

The next thing I must tell is so very frightening that I hesitate to finish what I've started. I knew when I began this story I would eventually find myself here, in the Sly Field, with my memories of this place so fresh and real. These things happened quickly, without warning, and one on top of the other in such a way that the details are blurred in my mind.

What I remember most is that it started with the sound of bats.

CHAPTER 19

NEARING THE END

"I know that sound, that lovely sound," said Grindall.

We all heard it coming from somewhere beyond the Jocasta-lit pathway. It was the sound of the black swarm, the sea of a thousand bats, and it was directly in front of us.

"They've found it! The bats, they've found the Tenth City! How perfect for me!" Grindall exclaimed. "Now I can add one more to my host of ogres on the way in. Armon, I'm afraid this day is about to go from bad to terrible for you."

"Armon, run! You *must* run away!" I yelled. "Don't let them take you. It's not worth it."

At that very moment I heard a strange sound, a snapping sound, wet and soft.

"Armon? Where are you?" asked Grindall, holding the Jocasta out in front of him to try to see farther. It was a useless effort, as even the sharp light of the Jocasta only lit the ten feet in front of him. We could see Grindall, but he could not see any of us, which gave us certain advantages he hadn't thought of.

I heard the soft, wet snap again — it was a very strange sound — this time followed by a thud on the earth.

"Ogres, I've had enough of this nonsense! Squeeze

the life out of Yipes and the girl. The bats will take care of Armon." The black-winged creatures were swarming closer now, not far from Grindall at the front of our group. The ogre that held me laughed hideously and began to squeeze tighter and tighter until I went from feeling pain to feeling nothing at all. And then I heard the sound again. *Snap, squish,* and this time a groan above me. The ogre released his grip around my waist and tumbled to the ground.

I lay breathing next to him, trying to figure out what had happened. I held my arms around my own waist, rocking back and forth, waiting for whatever trouble would find its way to me next. There was a giant hand on my shoulder, and then Armon's face was suddenly so close I could see his eyes.

"Stay very still," he whispered.

"Where's Yipes?" I whispered back. Armon only had time for two words, but what wonderful words they were.

"He's free."

I shivered as the three snaps I'd heard made sense to me now. Armon had waited just long enough to take the lives of three ogres. First, he'd torn free of the rope that held him and snapped the neck of the ogre he had been tied to. That task complete, he'd managed the same assault on the ogres holding Yipes and me in the mist. Thinking back on it now, I realized that Armon had hours in the Sly Field to observe the ogres and where they were placed in the group, how they lined up. Even when the mist overtook us, the ogres remained in much the same positions as we traveled along. Armon used this knowledge to do what he'd done. I was again stunned at his power.

"Run, ogres! Run into the Tenth City — take it and defile it!" Grindall screamed, knowing things were spinning out of his control. "Follow the sound of the bats and run with all your might!"

Go, I thought. *Run.*

I had to trust in Elyon. I had to believe this was what was meant to happen.

Grindall held the Jocasta out in front of him, and I strained to see what would happen. As I had suspected, Murphy had plans of his own, and he was darting up Grindall's arm toward the last stone. I couldn't see what happened next, but I could guess from Grindall's shattered voice that Murphy was attacking his hand, the hand that held the stone. It flew free in the mist as the ogres charged on, and then I lost sight of it. A moment later there was only the mist all around me, a faint orange glow somewhere at the edge of my sight, and nothing but the sound of bats and ogres and Victor Grindall shouting as they charged into the Tenth City.

Only it wasn't the Tenth City at all.

On they ran and ran, Victor Grindall held high above the rest, the bats leading the way, until all we could hear were their screams as they fell over the edge to the place they all belonged — the home of Abaddon — the great pit at the edge of the sea.

I'd tricked them.

The screams seemed to last forever as we listened to them falling deeper and deeper into the depths. The bats struggled to fly out, but a force greater than their wings was pulling them down, back to their dark source. Their shrieking was the first to fall to nothing. Then the ogres' cries vanished. Finally, even Victor Grindall's terrible voice could be heard no more.

The silence lasted only a moment before the broken world came alive in ways that my memory will never let go of. The land shook violently, and a great, anguished roar charged up from the pit. It echoed through the Sly Field, the force of the voice carried on a thunderous wind that blew out of the darkest places in The Land of Elyon.

Abaddon.

His messengers had been returned to him. He no longer had a hold on our world. His isolation was now complete.

Elyon had won.

A hot wind rushed over me and threw me onto my back, dust sticking in my eyes and pouring over my clothes. I pried open my eyes and saw that the searing wind had blown the mist clear from the land and water, and I was stunned to find we were quite near to the edge of the cliffs. The terrible voice from the pit ceased, and the burning wind accompanying it subsided. At that one moment in time I saw things I'd only imagined — I saw The Land of Elyon for what it really was.

The clouds that had always hung over the water at the edge of the far cliffs had risen. They were no longer covering everything below. They had risen high into the sky, where they rested in soft clumps. I looked in the far distance and saw bright blue water, vast and beautiful, free of its loneliness at last. The water, no longer hidden from us, seemed almost to dance and sing. But this was only the beginning of what I saw. The rest was even more surprising.

We had arrived at the very edge of the great pit that held Abaddon. It was wide and curved like a snake. Where the pit wall rose up it created a twenty- or thirty-foot ledge before meeting up with the far cliffs that dropped off into the sea. It was on this ledge that Armon and I had stood after swimming to shore from the *Warwick Beacon*. It was the great pit that we had seen, that Armon was drawn to in some terrible way as Abaddon called to him. We'd not seen the Tenth City then, we'd only seen this terrible place, and in seeing it we knew that we would have to find a way to get Grindall to come here. It had been our plan all along to lead Grindall and the ogres to this place and to hope that we could find a way to trick them into thinking it was the Tenth City, to trick them into falling into the great pit.

There was yet more to see, and this last part was the

best of all. In that moment, looking at the scene before me, I finally understood how much Elyon loved me — how much he loved all of us. For you see, just beyond the farthest edge of the great pit lay the Tenth City. It was the one place where the mist did not rise completely — it only rose a little, enough for us to see bright lights of every color shooting into the sky and the edges of tall, golden structures. I wish that you could have seen what I saw that day. The Tenth City was positioned at the very edge of the great pit, between its awful darkness and the rest of The Land of Elyon. All this time, as I'd wondered if Elyon had left us or never existed at all, he'd been standing between us and Abaddon, holding the darkest evil back from coming out and flowing over everything.

It was hard to imagine why Elyon had chosen to use me — a lanky girl of twelve when everything began — to finally bring an end to Abaddon, Grindall, and the ogres. He had used the smallest man I'd ever known, a squirrel, and the last of the giants to help him accomplish his plan. I was at once overcome with gratitude that he had chosen to do such a remarkable, dangerous thing. That he would make me feel so important was beyond my understanding.

After the clouds rose into the sky and the mist cleared away, the rumbling of the earth began once more, even fiercer than it had been before. The great pit that sat against the cliffs seemed to stretch itself out. The edge of the cliff that held the great pit to The Land of Elyon crumbled and shook, and then it began to slide down toward the sea. I remember Armon kneeling next to me, holding my shoulder with his huge hand, as we watched the cliff slide all the way down into the water, taking the great pit with it. All of the powers of evil had been contained in that one place — the fallen Seraph Abaddon, Victor Grindall, the last of the ogres, and the black swarm — they were all captured and put to rest.

The water boiled and danced, turning black and frothy, taking with it the great pit and all who were in it. The waves crashed over the stones, and a new cliff was born, this one at the edge of the Tenth City, which stood glowing and perfect before the vast sea.

CHAPTER 20

THE TENTH CITY

It was as though nothing else existed but the sight of the world changing before our eyes. To watch a cliff slide into the sea and witness the Tenth City sitting at the edge of everything was a miracle. I never felt so safe as I did in that moment, when I knew that Elyon would always be there to protect me.

I don't know how much time passed, but finally something happened that seemed to shake the group of us back to life. The hot winds disappeared, and the mist moved back to surround the Tenth City. My first thoughts were of Warvold. He was lying lifeless, alone somewhere behind us, and we were given a clue where when Squire screeched from the air. I looked up and saw that she was flying low, circling in the distance. Her cries were like a funeral song echoing over the Sly Field.

"I'll go back and get him," Armon said. "It will only take me a moment, but I think it's best that I go while the rest of you wait here."

As Armon walked away from us into the Sly Field, I took the Jocasta in my hand, unsure if it still contained the power it once did. It had been in the hands of Victor Grindall — had almost fallen into the great pit — and

I feared my time of speaking with the animals was behind me.

For once Murphy was not only speechless, but also as still as a statue as we looked at Odessa standing before us.

"What shall we do to her?" said Yipes, looking at Odessa. "She betrayed us."

I looked in the direction Armon had gone and saw him in the distance, still walking away from us. He and I both knew a secret the rest did not.

"That's not exactly true," I said. "Things are not quite what they seem."

"This sounds interesting," said Yipes, a hopeful look on his face. "Do tell."

"Armon and I knew about the great pit," I explained. "Elyon asked me to bring Grindall and the ogres here, though I didn't know why at the time." I paused, looking toward Armon once more. "It had to be completely believable. If we'd told anyone else, there was a chance Grindall would know we were tricking him. Murphy was with us when we saw the pit, but we didn't even tell him of our plans with Odessa."

"What are you saying?" Yipes was practically hopping out of his pants with anticipation.

"Yipes," I said, "Odessa did not betray us. I asked her to lead Grindall and the ogres to us, to bring them out. If anyone is a hero in all of this, it's her."

Murphy jumped to life, squeaking and carrying on, and then he leaped onto Odessa's back, where he sat

166

proudly. If not for my anxiety over Warvold I might have smiled just then, because I understood what Murphy said. I understood his relief. The power of the Jocasta remained.

I put out my arms, and Odessa walked forward. I hugged her wonderful neck, her fur like a soft pillow against my face.

"Thank you, Odessa. Without you we would have failed."

I pulled back and looked at her full in the face, and she spoke to me with the tilt of her head and a low growl.

"If I had known Grindall would treat me like his pet dog I might not have agreed," she said. "I came very close to biting his hand more than once today. I'm just glad I was able to hold myself back until the very end."

We sat together in the Sly Field, the four of us, and no one spoke. Me, Yipes, Murphy, and Odessa — we were all wondering when Armon would return with Warvold. I wondered if we could have saved him. Everything had happened so fast, but thinking of it now, I felt sure that if Armon had tried to fight Warvold's death, Yipes would have also been killed — and probably me, too.

"There's nothing you or anyone else could have done," said Odessa. "If Armon had fought Grindall, then our loss would have been far greater, and it is very likely that Grindall and the ogres would not have ended up where they did."

Yipes nodded his agreement, and I looked back over

my shoulder toward the Tenth City. It was completely covered with white again, and the mist had spread to the very edge of the cliff where it hung like great gobs of cotton on the wind. I turned the last Jocasta in my hand and watched it beat brighter, then softer, back and forth as though it were alive.

My thoughts turned to Pervis and my father. I hoped they were all right, but I had no way of knowing.

The minutes passed until finally we could all see Armon coming back, a body draped across his arms. From a distance it looked like a father carrying a small, sleeping child off to bed, to a place where the child could dream happy dreams. But the closer he got the more Armon looked like the giant he was, and the body he carried looked more lifeless than asleep.

We went toward him then, unable to wait any longer. Squire had lit upon Armon's shoulder, where she seemed to be resting after a long day of flying with no place to land. When we all met at last, Armon knelt down before us and held Warvold where we could see him, and then I saw something I hadn't seen before and I never saw again after. I saw a tear fall from a giant's eye and a bitter sadness so big it nearly broke my heart in two.

"This time there's no tricking death for our old friend," said Armon. "His journey has finally come to an end here in the Sly Field."

I touched Warvold's face and ran my hand along the cloth that covered his arm.

Bring him to me.

It was the voice on the wind, the voice of Elyon.

Bring Warvold home where he belongs.

I held the Jocasta in front of me and realized that it might yet lead us to the Tenth City as Ander had said it would.

"We have one last thing to do," I said. "We must find the Tenth City."

This one statement seemed to shake everyone back to life, determined to bring Warvold to the place he'd sought all his life.

We were up and moving right away, walking the Sly Field toward where we'd seen the edges of the Tenth City in the clouds and the mist.

"Let's not tell anyone about how Warvold came back from the dead and we found him in Castalia," I said, thinking already of all the questions waiting for me back home. "There are those who will say they saw him, but I won't say that. It will be as though his ghost joined us one last time. It will make his life and his death that much more of a mystery, which is just as he would have wanted it."

"That's the thing of legend, Alexa," Yipes said. "And there's no one who ever deserved such a thing more than Thomas Warvold."

It wasn't long before we reached the edge of the mist once more. I held out the Jocasta and stepped inside. Everyone else followed close behind. As I had hoped, the Jocasta lit a trail in front of me, and I followed it into the depths of this secret place. We were closer than anyone had ever been to the Tenth City, and the earth beneath my feet felt somehow more sacred than that of any of the places I'd walked before.

The mist was darker than it had been, and I realized with a shock why this was. Night was coming in The Land of Elyon. Was it really true that my father would not live through the day? Had I been able to change that? Once the thought had come to me, I couldn't put it out of my mind. I continued leading the way through the mist with slumped shoulders and a downcast spirit. To my great surprise, in the very next step I took, the lighted pathway before me disappeared entirely. Worse still, the light from the Jocasta had gone out completely, and we stood in the darkening mist as lost as we'd ever been.

Throw the stone, Alexa. You can't keep it. It's time for you to give it back to me.

I tried to look back and see my friends in the mist, but I couldn't make out any of them. The deafening silence had come on again, the sound of nothing at all, and everyone seemed to be holding their breath, waiting for me to do as I was told.

"I heard the voice that time, Alexa." It was Murphy, his little voice breaking the cold silence.

"I heard it, too," said Yipes. "And better yet, I heard Murphy just now. How are you, my little friend?"

"Who are you calling 'little'?" said Murphy. "I'm taller than you from where I'm sitting on Odessa."

170

"Quiet," said Armon. "This is no place for that kind of silly talk."

Armon was not angry — he was awestruck. This was the place of his birth, a place he never thought he'd see again. It was a place he'd longed for all his life, hoping against all hope that he might find a way back in.

"This may be the last time we speak," I said. I knew that everyone would understand I was talking only to Murphy and Odessa. "I'll miss you both very much. You've been the best sort of friends a girl could hope for."

Odessa crept up next to me, Murphy on her back, and rubbed her big head against my side. Everything that was left to say between us was said in the way the two of them looked at me as only animals can.

"Throw the stone, Alexa," said Murphy. "It's time."

I squeezed the last Jocasta in my hand and felt along its slick surface with my thumb. Then I held it up and threw it into the mist as hard as I could. All of the mist in front of us was blown away, and I saw something that made me very happy.

The Tenth City is not a place that's easy to describe, probably because it's not of this world and there are no words to make it real. The best I can do is try, and hope you understand at least one thing — the Tenth City is where I want to go when I leave The Land of Elyon.

Imagine the most perfect pathway with trees and flowers all along its edge and not a dead thing anywhere. No crusted leaves, no withered branches — even the pathway

171

itself seemed alive with colors. Think of the most beautiful place you've ever seen, and then imagine nothing dead or dying there. Imagine everything in your sight becoming not more dead with time but more alive. The trees, the hills, the fields — all so bright and alive and getting more so right before your very eyes. As I said, it's hard to describe, and I've done a poor job of it. And yet there were things I saw and things that were said that might help you understand a little bit more.

This pathway I've described wound all through the fields of green and gold, bordered by the tall trees swaying in the breeze. Walking up this pathway was John Christopher, looking as happy as I'd ever seen him. As he came closer, I saw that there was no longer a C branded on his forehead, that he was stronger-looking than I'd ever imagined he could be. He was holding the last Jocasta in his hand. Coming to a stop before us, he spoke. His voice was just as I remembered it.

"What a pleasure to see you!" he said. "I only wish I could come out and embrace you all, but I'm afraid this is as far as I can go."

He held out the Jocasta in front of him, and it began to glow once more.

"Thank you for bringing this home," he said. "One day you'll all find your way here as I have, and you will have adventures that make the ones you've had so far seem very small indeed."

I smiled at this thought. It was a wonderful comfort

to know that when my life in The Land of Elyon came to an end I wouldn't be lost or destroyed or forgotten — I would begin the *real* adventure.

Armon.

The voice of Elyon came clear.

"Yes?" Armon answered, his voice only a whisper. I turned back and saw that his head was turned down, his face to the ground, holding the crumpled body of Warvold.

You've found your way home.

Armon slowly looked up, and I realized something that made me both sad and happy at the same time. Armon had not only found his lost home, he was *going home*. He was the last of the Seraphs that had become giants through Abaddon's trickery. I imagined that Elyon smiled to think that Armon would provide the companionship he'd hoped for so long ago. Armon was a different sort of creation than I was. He filled some deep need Elyon had for a being more closely like himself.

Armon hesitated, looking down at Warvold in his arms. He was thinking the same thing I was — wouldn't it be wonderful if Armon could carry Warvold's body into the Tenth City? When Armon looked back up again, he let his eyes rest on me, holding my gaze, as if something were about to happen that he wasn't sure how to explain. And then Elyon said something that took my breath away.

Bring Alexa's father with you.

Thinking back on it now, I remember my whole life

passing in front of me, the details of my short life streaming through my mind in a haze of thoughts. I thought of
all the times I'd sat with Warvold, feeling things for him
that I couldn't understand, strong feelings that were
more than just friendship. I thought of how alike the two
of us were, how he had always treated me like a daughter
when I came to Bridewell, how he seemed to have missed
me more than he ought to have.

I also thought of Renny — my mother — and of the
mother I thought was my own, Laura. These were the same
two sisters who had escaped Castalia and hidden in the
clock tower where they'd found Armon. And Nicolas —
he was my brother, my older brother by a good deal.
That explained a lot about my feelings for him. I had
always thought him handsome and wonderful, but I'd
never felt a girlish crush on him as I thought I should. It
was all very hard to imagine, and yet somehow it was as
though I'd known all along that Warvold was my father,
and there had been a thin veil hanging in my mind
between what I thought was true and what I could see. I
didn't feel betrayed, which surprised me. I felt something
altogether different — I felt complete, whole, and right
in a way I'd never experienced before. I felt as though I
could finally admit that somehow I was never the person
I thought I was, but now that I knew the truth about
myself, it was as if I was breathing new air that filled me
in all the right ways.

What would I do when I got home? How would I talk with my mother — my two mothers — and the man I thought was my father, not dead after all? It was all very confusing, and yet I was overcome with a feeling of rightness and boldness I'd never known before.

"Don't be angry, Alexa," said Armon. "Your mother and father had to protect you, and this was the only way. Without you The Land of Elyon would have failed."

He looked so perfect, holding Warvold in his arms, his face full of sorrow and uncertainty. He knelt down in front of me, and I walked the three steps that put me close enough to touch my father. Even in death he had a thin smile on his face. I touched his face, tears rolling down my cheeks, and then I hugged him, knowing it would be the only time I would ever see him and know him for who he really was.

"He loved you, Alexa," said Yipes. I looked back at him, hoping he hadn't been aware of this secret, and in his face I saw that he was as shocked and surprised as I was. All of this had been kept from him as well, and I felt good to know that he hadn't hidden it from me all this time.

Yipes went on, "He never tired of talking about you. Thinking of it now, it seems I should have figured this out on my own long ago."

"I know what you mean," I said. And then I turned to Armon. "I'm not angry, Armon. I'm sad to see you go, and I'm confused, but I'm not angry. Everything is all right."

Armon rested Warvold in his lap, reached over with his one free hand, and pulled me close to him.

"It's time for me to go," he whispered. "My time here has been —" He broke off, overcome with emotion. He looked over my shoulder at Yipes, Odessa, and Murphy, then back at me. "You've been the friends I'd only hoped to find. Thank you for what you've done."

He took hold of Warvold, rose up to his full height, and began walking toward the Tenth City. Yipes, Odessa, and Murphy came alongside me and we huddled together, watching Armon carry Warvold home, to places we couldn't go just yet. Armon passed into the Tenth City and stood beside John Christopher, and when Armon turned around, Warvold was alive once more, his eyes sparkling, looking right at me. Armon set him on his feet, and the three of them — Warvold, John Christopher, and Armon — all smiled the most wonderful smiles. They were home in a place we would all be one day, and I knew then that we would see one another again. I knew then that we would have more, bigger adventures together when it was our time to leave The Land of Elyon.

The mist rolled back over the Tenth City, slowly at first, and then all of a sudden it was gone, and all we could see was white before us.

Abaddon is defeated. It's time for you to go home, Alexa Daley.

The mist stopped short of us, and we stood in the Sly Field as the last of what Elyon had to say to us was said. I

176

knew without trying that my time of talking with Murphy and Odessa and all the other animals was over, and that the voice of Elyon would no longer be audible to me.

"I suppose it's just the four of us now," said Yipes, and Murphy danced around on Odessa's back, squeaking and carrying on. Squire screeched from the sky above, and I understood what she'd meant to say.

"Make that five," I said to Yipes.

He looked up into the clear blue sky and then back at me. "Let's go home," he said, and the four of us began the long walk across the Sly Field.

CHAPTER 21

TOWARD HOME

We stopped in the night and laid out what little we had of food and comfort, which was a very little indeed. We stared up at the starry night, talking about all the adventures we'd had. The next morning we reached the edge of Fenwick Forest and were relieved to find that it was not as dead as it had been when we'd last seen it. Things were growing — flowers and leaves on the trees. The forest was finding its way back to the way it had once been.

We made our way to the grove and found all the animals I'd met so long ago waiting for us: Beaker the raccoon and Henry the badger; Picardy, the beautiful black bear, who stood with her mate who had returned since the walls had come down; Boone the bobcat, Raymond the fox, Vesper the woodchuck, Malcolm the rabbit — they were all here to greet us one last time.

Odessa ran forward when she saw her mate, Darius, and her son, Sherwin. It was marvelous to see them together again. Murphy stayed on her back and had some sort of words with Darius, words I was sure Darius could not understand, and then Murphy ran over to my feet and I picked him up.

"Will I ever see you again?" I said. "I think maybe I

won't, but that's okay. We've had a good adventure together."

I set him back down, and he looked up at me, his two front feet craning into the air.

"I'll miss you, too," I said, sure of what he'd tried to say to me.

Finally, I looked straight up the grove and saw Ander. Yipes and I walked toward him until we stood only a few feet away. He looked happy to see us, and that was more than any of his words could have given me.

Yipes and I walked on, some of the animals following for a while, until we were alone at the edge of the wood. Home was still a long walk down a dusty road, but we didn't mind. The two of us talked the morning away, enjoying our memories of Warvold and the places we'd been together.

An hour into our walk, we heard horses coming up behind us from a long way off. Looking back toward Bridewell, we saw someone coming toward us at a fast clip. Not long after that, we saw that the cart was driven by James Daley, the man I had thought was my father all my life. Nicolas sat beside him and Pervis Kotcher behind, the three of them looking very excited to see us on the road to Lathbury.

The moment the cart met up with us, James Daley halted the horses and jumped down onto the ground, running to greet me. He bent down on one knee and took me in his arms, and it felt like it always had. He was still my father in many ways, and I still loved him very much.

"You gave us quite a scare, Alexa," he said. "We've been trying to find you ever since Grindall and the ogres left Bridewell."

"We've got quite a story to tell you," I said. "But for now you should know that Warvold is gone, I mean really gone this time." I paused a moment, letting that sink in. Pervis and Nicolas had heard me say it, and they stayed back, quietly contemplating the news.

"Did he say anything to you — anything you might not have expected — before the end?" Father asked.

I took a moment to think this question over, wondering how I should respond. This man had acted as my father when I needed a protector. My true father had always favored this man, and I favored him, too. I didn't want to hurt him now, not after all that he'd already been through.

"I know the secret," I said, and then I whispered, "Does Nicolas know?"

I didn't get a response — just a pained look.

"*Father*," I said, and he smiled a little, his eyes lighting up. "You're still my father. You always will be."

It was truly how I felt. Warvold had not abandoned me. Instead he had put me in the care of this wonderful man while he stayed close by and made sure I was safe. Warvold was my father, but so was James Daley.

"He knows," Father said. "Nicolas knows."

180

I walked over to the cart and stared up at Nicolas.

"Why didn't you tell me?" I asked. "All these years you never let on. It makes me feel as though maybe Thomas Warvold favored you over me."

Nicolas stepped down off the cart and put his arm on my shoulder.

"Nothing could be further from the truth," he said. "You were always on his mind. You're all he talked about when it was just he and I. He knew he'd done the right thing. If Victor Grindall had known about you, I'm afraid you'd have been gone a long time ago. And The Land of Elyon would be in much worse shape than it is right now."

We smiled at each other, and I was suddenly very happy to have an older brother. There was a lot to talk about, but now wasn't the time. I felt an overwhelming desire to see Catherine and Laura. With the cart, we could be home quickly.

I sat by my father with Yipes next to me while Pervis and Nicolas took the back end of the cart. There were many questions and much discussion on that ride home to Lathbury, and the hour-long trip passed very quickly. It was odd in a way, this trip home. I was on the same road where it had all begun, only this time there were no walls but the ones around Bridewell and we were going in the opposite direction. As the conversation wound down, I turned to my father and made a request.

"Father?"

"Yes, Alexa."

"Tell me about when the walls were built, won't you?"

"That old legend? You've heard that a million times already."

But he was a storyteller, and this was one of his favorites, so he told it once more, and I loved hearing it more than I ever had before. We arrived in Lathbury just as he was finishing, and I felt a sudden sadness as I realized my adventure was over as well. My heart ached for Murphy, Odessa, John Christopher, Armon, and Warvold, and I wondered if I would ever stop missing them.

We drove through the town and stopped right in front of my little house. I stayed on the cart for a long time while everyone else got off and stood waiting for me. Then the door to my house opened up, and two women stepped out. One was my birth mother, the other the mother who'd raised me. They both looked at me as though they weren't sure how I felt about them. These two sisters, who had held on to the secret for so long in order to make me safe; now they were worried that I might not love them anymore. Sometimes adults can be silly that way.

I came down from the cart and ran to them, embraced them, cried with them until there were no more tears left for anyone. Even Pervis and Yipes were blubbering, which eventually got us all laughing a little and began the process of healing our broken hearts. I had to tell them both that Warvold was gone, and that Armon was gone, too. But I also got to share what I'd seen of the Tenth

City, how we'd all be going there someday, and how we would meet up with them again.

I stayed in Lathbury for a while after that, and Yipes stayed with me. We took time to rest and eat lots and lots of food. We mended books just for fun. I took long walks along the cliffs with Catherine and Laura, sometimes the three of us together, other times just with one of them, and we talked about things that are secrets between mothers and daughters. It was breathtaking to look out over the bright blue of the Lonely Sea where once there were only clouds.

Balmoral came to Lathbury a week after our arrival. We had the joy and the sorrow of telling him everything that had happened. He talked of progress in Castalia, and he brought with him the body of John Christopher. When we buried him near the cliffs it helped me to start looking forward rather than back, which was something I needed to begin doing. As exciting, difficult, and memorable as our pasts can be, there comes a time when we have to get on with living.

Almost a year went by, and Yipes never left to go back to his home in the mountains. I think that somehow he and I needed each other more than ever; to be apart would have been too hard. And then one day the two of us looked at each other in a way that we both understood.

"There's adventure to be had out there," said Yipes.

"I know," I replied.

"What would you think of wandering off to Mount Laythen for a spell? You're old enough, you know. They'll let you go. I've heard tales of a strange man who lives in those parts, inventing strange things."

I looked at Yipes for a long time without answering, and then I said something that had been haunting me since we'd returned home.

"I wonder where Roland and the *Warwick Beacon* have gone off to."

It wasn't too long after I said these words that I saw the *Warwick Beacon* on the horizon through my mother's spyglass. It came to a stop at the bottom of the cliffs, and Roland climbed up the rope that hung there (a rope, by the way, that was hidden well enough and had been put there by James Daley. He had fashioned it with a crank that was surrounded by tall rocks, a crank that Laura had used to hoist up Catherine out of the Lonely Sea when she'd first come home).

The whole town greeted Roland, and Catherine was especially happy to see that he was safe. He was Thomas Warvold's brother, and I think he knew before we told him that Thomas was gone.

"We'll see him again," he said, but he was still very sad to learn of the news. He seemed to age before my eyes at the thought of his brother forever gone from The Land of Elyon.

"Where have you been all this time?" I asked.

Roland just looked out over the sea with a half smile on his face, the wind at the cliff's edge dancing in his hair.

"Home," he said. "Where I was meant to be."

Thomas and Roland Warvold, the two greatest adventurers of our time. One by land and one by sea — and the one by sea was still busy at his adventures.

Roland stayed on for a time, and then Yipes and I began pestering him about his plans. The three of us sat by the cliffs above the *Warwick Beacon* and talked about our future. Then one day Roland decided it was time to go. The town gave him enough provisions to last a very long time and threw him a big farewell party. The farewell party wasn't just for him — it was for Yipes and me, too. After long discussions with Catherine, Laura, and James, I was able to convince them this was what I was meant to do. I'd been home long enough.

And this is where the story I've been telling you finally catches up to where I am now, sitting on the deck of the *Warwick Beacon*, writing down everything so I won't forget it. Yipes and Roland are my companions, and we are on the water somewhere far away from The Land of Elyon. The crisp sea air is salty on my lips and thick in my hair. As I look out in every direction I see nothing but blue water everywhere, and I wonder if there's anything out here to find. I ask Roland the same question I've asked him a hundred times already.

"Roland, is there much out here to discover? Out here on the Lonely Sea?"

Roland is at the wheel, looking very much like the captain he is, and he gives me the same answer he always does.

"More than you can imagine."

I do wonder where this story will lead, if there will be more adventure in this life and what it will be like when I return to the Tenth City someday in the distant future. For now I am content — as you should be — to sit on the deck of a ship at sea with Yipes at my side, not knowing where the story will lead me next.

ABOUT THE AUTHOR

PATRICK CARMAN maintains that he does not now have, nor has he ever possessed, a Jocasta or any other type of gemstone that offers the power of interspecies communication, telepathic or otherwise. Parties interested in obtaining such a stone are well advised to look elsewhere.

Mr. Carman does, however, speak to young people of his own species, sometimes aloud and sometimes in print. He makes his home in the wilderness of eastern Washington and insists that it is a rather ordinary home and is not, in fact, surrounded by stone walls.

Mr. Carman plays no musical instruments, but he has been known to torture dinner guests with attempts on the harmonica. He divides his time between writing, public speaking, spending time with his wife and two daughters, reading, fly-fishing, paragliding, and snowboarding.

To learn more about
Patrick Carman and The Land of Elyon
visit:

www.landofelyon.com

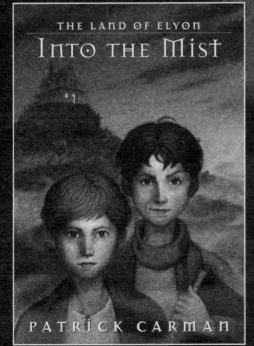